TRANSCENDENCE

Shay Savage

Cover Design: Mayhem Cover Creations

Interior Formatting: Mayhem Cover Creations

Editing : Chaya & Tamara

DEDICATION

For all those who didn't want a story about a man who *acted* like a caveman, but a story about an *actual* caveman! Hoh!

Special thanks to the fabulous team of people who helped pull this together: Chaya, Tamara, Heather, Adam, Ellie, Holly, Jada, Jamie, and everyone on my street team for the constant encouragement and support!

IMPORTANT AUTHOR'S NOTE

Located in the left hemisphere,Broca's Area is the part of the brain associated with the comprehension of both verbal and non-verbal language. It's what allows you to understand English, learn to speak Chinese, use sign language to communicate across the room, or even to play Pictionary.

Yeah, Pictionary.

Reading the words on this page also uses Broca's area to take symbols and transform them into words your mind recognizes and comprehends. This part of the brain is completely responsible for how Homo sapiens communicate.

So what if someone has no Broca's Area in their brain?

Meet Ehd, the caveman. Ehd is a completely fictitious form of a human-like primate (we'll call him Homo savage, m'kay?), who is pretty much exactly like modern humans except he lacks Broca's Area in his brain.

What does that mean?

What it means is Ehd CAN'T learn to speak. He just doesn't have the ability. He's still highly intelligent and capable of learning; he'll just never associate the sounds someone makes with any objects or actions. He might learn to associate a sound with a desired behavior - that is, he can figure out that if he makes a certain sound he can influence the reactions of others, but he'll never truly associate the sound with the action like your two-year-old will.

It is very much like your dog that might learn a whole bunch of commands, but s/he doesn't actually *know* the word "walk." That doesn't mean the dog isn't smart; it will still pick up the leash and carry it to the front door. It just means it doesn't have the capacity for language.

So, no matter what, Ehd's never going to speak English or French or COBOL. It's just not within his capabilities. He's still a bright boy, though - he'll come around in many ways.

If this doesn't make sense, or you happen to be a neurologist, and you're mumbling "BS" under your breath, just remember, while you're muttering that, I'm muttering "artistic license." ;)

Enjoy!

TABLE OF CONTENTS

CHAPTER ONE

I awake to cold and near darkness like I do every morning.

Around me is the chilled stone of the rocky cavern where I live. There is warmth from the animal furs that surround me, and it's difficult to push myself away from them to crawl across the dirt and rock and add a log on top of the glowing coals in my fire pit. Within moments, flames lick around the edge of the wood, and I wrap my fur around me a little tighter to ward off the cool air until the fire can further warm the small cave.

The faintest glow can be seen coming from outside the crack that leads to the outside, but I can't quite bring myself to venture out just yet. My body is weakened, and there is little inside my mind that wants to push on—to survive.

It's been so long since I've eaten.

As I watch the flames grow higher, the need to relieve my bladder becomes urgent. With a deep breath, I force my muscles to push myself onto my feet and move to the ledge just outside my cave. The air is even colder on the outside, but the springtime sun holds the promise of a warmer day.

I listen to the morning birds sing for a while and wonder how long it will be before there are eggs to collect from their nests. I hope not long, though I know if I wait until that time it will be too late.

I need to eat.

Not for the first time, I consider just going back into my cave, lying down, and letting the hunger take me. I'm tired, cold, and alone. I'm not sure there is any reason for me to continue to work so hard just to keep myself alive.

With a long sigh, I decide not to give up just yet.

I look at the long, straight stick propped up against the edge of the cave's opening and reach over to grasp it. It's sharp at the end, but I'm not sure if it's sharp enough to pierce the hide of a large animal. I know I can't fail again, or it will mean my death, so I bring the stick inside and reach for a piece of sharp flint from my collection of simple tools.

With the end of the stick lodged underneath my arm, I begin to run the piece of flint over the end of the stick, further sharpening the point. I go slowly, being careful not to push too hard or work too fast—I've already broken two other spears with impatience, and I can't afford to break another.

The effort takes most of the morning, and I am further delayed as I start to leave the cave because I see movement across the field of brown grasses. I position myself at the entrance to my cave and watch closely as a pack of canines trot into the valley.

They are enormous, the largest male nearly the length of two of me with his long tail. They have huge heads, long snouts, and short, stocky necks. The pack of predators moves swiftly across the field with their snouts moving from side to side as they track the scent of some other animal.

Hyaenodons.

The first memory I have of hyaenodons was when I was a boy, and they came into my tribe's area in the forest. My mother had grabbed me and two of my siblings and fled the area as soon as she saw them, and we didn't come back until nearly nightfall. When we returned, the pack had destroyed much of the food we had stored for the winter, the meat from our recent hunt, and had killed two of the men who tried to keep them away from the rest of the tribe.

The animals are vicious predators and attack anything they encounter. Once, they discovered my small cave when the fire was low and not enough to scare them off. I had to leave my kill behind and hide in the forest until they left, but they ate all the meat from my kill, destroyed the hide, and scattered the bones.

I hold my breath, hoping they won't notice me or my cave. Though the smell of fire usually keeps them at bay, their own hunger could drive them to ignore the odor like they had before. I grip the shaft of the spear and feel sweat from the palm of my hand collect there. The hyaenodons continue across the open area and then disappear into the trees on the far side. I let out a breath of relief to see them moving north, away from the steppes where I hope to hunt. I still wait a while longer before venturing out, wanting to be sure they will not backtrack and smell me.

Once I'm sure they are gone, I start the journey to my pit trap. The climb to the top of the plateau is rugged and difficult, but doesn't take too long. The wind whips around me as I reach the top, and my fingers clench around the end of the pointed branch as I see the antelope herd at the far edge of the open space. I only hope the spear will be strong enough to pierce the hide of one of the antelopes coming over the horizon. Of course, they will first have to fall into the pit I spent three days digging. My mind flashes back to a time when there were others, and the hunt was much easier.

It feels like such a long, long time ago.

I am alone now.

Crouching down, I move slowly and carefully, trying to hide myself behind the rocks and stay downwind from the animals. My heart begins to beat faster in my chest when I see how close the herd is moving to my pit trap. I move into position and hunker down behind the protective boulders.

Before long, I can hear the scratching sounds of the herd as they approach. I duck a little lower behind the boulder where I hide, tense and anxious. My stomach has long since stopped growling, but the hunger is still there, reflected in the weakness of my body. In the back of my head, I know that failure this time means death—it has been too long since I have eaten. I am quickly losing my strength, and once that is gone, I will not survive much longer.

The dry air whistles around me and blows the grasses of the steppes back and forth. I tense as the herd passes me slowly, trying to hold in my breath so as not to alert them to my presence. If they are frightened too soon, they may not run in the right direction.

I time myself as perfectly as I can, and jumping out from behind the rock, I run. My throat aches as I scream and wave my arms at the beasts. Startled, they all begin to flee from the sound of my screams. I chase after them, taking in air quickly so I can yell at them again as I circle around the back end of the herd and try to force them a little closer to the cliffs. Their hooves pound the dry grass as they run, many of them swerving away from the hole I have dug even though I have covered it with long, thin twigs and leaves to hide it.

I cry out but in frustration this time. I race around to the right, hoping to at least push one or two toward my goal. They aren't going in the right direction, and I feel a sob of desperation lodge in my throat. Just when it seems I will spend another night hungry, one of them tears away from the rest of its herd and scampers toward the hole.

A second later, it disappears with a bleat.

I breathe a sigh of relief and almost drop to my knees. Nauseated and dizzy from the exertion, I half stumble, half jog to the side of the pit. The tips of the animal's antlers are visible as it screeches and tries to jump to freedom, but I have dug the hole too deep; it has injured its leg in the fall, and it cannot escape. Cautiously, I move to the edge of the pit, take careful aim at the animal's throat, and thrust my spear as hard as I can.

The antelope screams again and kicks at the walls of the pit, causing a shower of dust to fall on top of it and then lies still.

As tired as I am, I can't allow myself to rest. As the animal bleeds, its scent will attract other predators—those that are larger than I am. I have no time to waste. I jump down into the pit and carefully extract my spear from the neck of the antelope. I am pleasantly surprised the weapon is not broken, and I may even be able to use it again. I toss it up and out of the hole and then heave the carcass up and over my shoulder. My knees try to buckle under me, and another wave of dizziness hits. I try to ignore it as I shove the body out of the hole and then climb out myself.

Once I am on flat ground again, it is easier to grasp the animal's legs and toss the whole thing over my back and shoulders, and I'm glad the harsh winter didn't completely deplete my strength. Once I get the carcass properly positioned, I start back toward the cliffs and begin the descent to the valley below. It's difficult to keep my footing holding the animal, but I'm driven by my hunger. Once I reach the bottom, there is only the short trail up to the opening in the rock left to overcome. I pause for a moment as my thighs and arms burn with pain and then push on. As I reach the crack between the boulders, I realize I can't walk into the cave while carrying the beast. I have to shove the antelope through the rock first and then follow.

Just inside, the coals from my fire burn brightly though there is no longer any flame. I quickly rebuild the fire—it should keep any competition away from my kill—and sit back on my heels for a moment to breathe. My rest is short-lived, and I quickly start working on my dinner. I roll the carcass over, slice it open from throat to belly with a chip of flint, and waste no time cutting off a few strips of meat to lie across the spit over the fire. I have to force myself not to eat it raw though my stomach implores me to do so. I will only be left feeling sick if I do; I've been in this position far too many times not to understand the benefits of patience.

After the first few pieces are set up to cook, I immediately skin the beast and lay the hide over two large rocks on one side of my cave. I will clean and cure it another time when I have more strength. I need something to help hold the rest of the carcass up off the floor, and I look around for my spear, knowing it will be the perfect tool for the task. I do not see it, and I realize I have left it next to the pit trap.

I place my head in my hands and push against my eyes. There is so much pressure in my head that it causes my temples to pound. I can't believe I have been so careless as to leave my weapon behind. At the same time, I'm too exhausted to even consider going back for it. I rub at the hair on my face and neck and shake my head at my stupidity.

This is the kind of mistake that has nearly cost me my life many times since I have been alone.

Wetness falls from my lashes as I lean back and wrap my arms around my legs. I stare at the fire and let the tears fall, trying to convince myself that I will feel better and think more clearly once I have eaten the meat cooking on the spit.

Memories flood my mind.

It is early morning, and I sit wrapped in furs and my mother's embrace as one of my older sisters grinds grain against a rock. My mother's arms are warm and comforting, but I push away from her, anxious to join the other boys and men as they practice with spears and hammer-stones.

I reach up with my hand to wipe away the tears. I have no idea how long it has been since I felt the comfort of another person's presence, only that many cold seasons have passed since then. Though I had already become a man before I was left alone, the memories of the woman who birthed and cared for me are the hardest to keep at bay.

A pop from the fire pit draws my attention, and I go to check the cooking meat. Some of the thinner pieces seem warm enough, and I devour them quickly before adding more strips of meat to the spit. I drink out of a water flask made from the stomach of an antelope I killed the previous summer and eat a few more strips of meat.

With slightly renewed energy, I rise to my feet and head back down the path toward the steppes to retrieve my spear. With the thought of more cooked meat waiting for me, I run lightly toward the pit trap but stop abruptly before I reach the edge.

There is an odd sound coming from the hole—high pitched and terrifying. I freeze as I try to understand it. At first I think it is another antelope—a straggler who fell after I left—but the noise is not that of a beast. It is like nothing I have ever heard before. I move a little closer, and the sound becomes louder and somewhat frightening. I take a step back away from the hole, intending to turn and flee, when something about the sound triggers another memory.

Flames are all around us, the heat licking my skin and the smell of burning hair in my nose. There is a young girl—I recall her from a neighboring tribe—trapped between the wall of flame and her terrified mother. Before the mother can try to reach for the child, flames encompass them both. The forest is too dry from the drought, and the flames are spreading too quickly. The mother cries out in fear and hopelessness. A moment later, there is only the sound of the crackling fire as it covers the trees.

I shake my head to make the images go away, and I hear the sound again. I'm sure it is not an animal, and my heart beats faster as I take a few steps closer to verify my suspicions. There is movement inside the hole, a flash of pale skin and what looks to be slender fingers poking out of the hole and then disappearing again.

I peer over the side, and I see it.

Not it—her.

I see *her*.

At the bottom of the pit, there is a young woman not far from my own age, with shining brown hair that flows over her shoulders and down her back. She sits on the ground and leans back on her hands, staring up with wide eyes that go even wider as they meet mine. I feel a tightening in my groin at the very sight of her, and my tongue darts out over my lips.

Though I recognize her femininity immediately, the strange coverings on her body do not show her to be female. In fact, they are the strangest furs I have ever seen. I can't determine what kind of leather might have been used to make them, and the color of the clothing around her torso is like that of the setting sun—deep purple and bright pink. On her legs is even stranger stuff—dark blue and wrapped so closely around her, I can see the outlines of her thigh muscles and calves. She wears coverings on her feet as well, and there are cords wrapped around holes in the material. Like the rest of her coverings, I can't figure out what it is either.

My eyes move back to hers, and I tilt my head to one side to get a better look at her.

She opens her mouth and screams.

I have to take a step back from the shrill sound. It hurts my ears. I narrow my eyes and grunt sharply, but she doesn't stop. If anything, she gets even louder. I can't allow her to continue, or she is going to attract attention—possibly from predatory animals. Deciding to ignore her strange appearance, I step to the edge of the pit and jump down.

Her cries grow more piercing, and the sound is starting to hurt my head. I move toward her, and she propels herself backwards on her feet and hands until she hits the dirt side, sending dust all over her. She yells out again, stands, and tries to claw her way to the top of the hole. She's too small to be successful, and her fingers only barely reach the edge.

Her shoulders rise and fall as her hands slide down the dirt walls. Her sounds stop, and nothing but her breath can be heard as she turns slowly and her wide eyes travel over me. I move closer and look down at her.

I feel the corner of my mouth turn up. Though clearly an

adult, not a child, she is a tiny thing. Her head barely comes to my chest. It's her hair that intrigues me though—it's very straight, and it shines in the sunlight. I reach my hand up to my shoulder and grab at my own hair, which is rough, tangled, and full of dust and leaves. I had cut it down with a flint knife at the end of the last summer, but it was now near my shoulders again. I take a step closer and reach out with my other hand to touch the smooth locks around her head to see how different it feels.

Again, she begins to cry out, and I am tired of the noisy sounds. It's dangerous to be making so much noise, and it really does make the sides of my head hurt. I close the gap between our bodies quickly and cover her mouth with my hand to silence her.

I'm surprised when she doesn't acquiesce but begins to frantically struggle against me instead. She grasps at my arm, and her nails dig into my flesh as she tries to pull my hand away. She kicks at me, and the strange coverings on her feet scrape at the skin of my leg. She is still screaming, but the sound is muffled underneath my hand.

I still can't properly feel the texture of her hair, so I further restrain her by pushing my body against hers, holding her up against the wall. With the increased leverage, she can't move as much, and I slowly drag my hand down the length of her hair.

It's so, so soft!

I have never felt anything like it. It runs all the way from her head to her waist in long, straight strands that do not bunch up together like mine do, but lie next to each other in beautiful lines. The color isn't unusual—just a shiny, light brown—but the feel of it on my palm is glorious.

I look to her face, and her eyes are closed tightly. Oddly enough, her eyelids are blue, and there is pink and brown coloring running up to her eyebrows. There is also a dark blue, almost black line right around her eyes—both above and below.

I move my hand up and gently touch her eyelid with the tip of my finger. The bright blue color comes off of her skin and onto mine. I look at my finger a moment before trying to wipe the color back onto the skin between her eyebrow and eyelid.

She bites my hand, and I jump back, surprised at the sudden pain and not the least bit pleased. My eyes narrow into a glare, and I push my body harder against hers, roaring into her face as I grab onto her arm to show my dominance. Her eyes meet mine, and I can see and feel the fear in her. I am quickly contrite, not truly meaning to frighten her, though I do not want her to bite me again. I take her chin between my fingers and grip it as I growl softly in warning.

She goes motionless, and I know I have won her over. I turn her head gently to the side with a firm grip on her jaw and use the other hand to touch her hair again. I am fascinated by its texture. As I touch it, l look down the rest of her body, still confused by her strange, colorful clothing. My fingers run over the fabric at her shoulder, and I hear her sharp intake of breath. When I look back to her, her eyes are downcast, and her lips are drawn into her mouth around her teeth. I pull at the skin below her lip to stop her from hurting herself, and a shudder runs through her body.

The heat from her body warms me, and I think about how she is the only person I have seen since I have been on my own. She's small but looks to be healthy. She has strong teeth, judging by the bite-marks on my hand. Even though her clothing is strange, she could make something more suited to a female from the furs I have in my cave, and I decide I'm going to bring her back with me.

Glancing up at the top of the hole, I know I will have to get her out of it though part of me wants to keep her right here, knowing she cannot move away from me. I look her over and feel myself smile again. Even out of this space, she will not be able to escape me. She is small and obviously weak. Though I am not as strong as I will be later in the summer when I have had more food, I am still much more powerful than she.

Thinking of the meat cooking over the fire causes my stomach to twist again, and I decide I need to get us both back to my cave quickly. The day is getting late, and the sky will soon turn the colors of her strange tunic.

Kneeling, I wrap my arms around her legs. She lets out a squeal, but thankfully, it only lasts a moment. I rise up and toss her out of the top of the hole, quickly following by pulling myself up with my arms. By the time I have tossed a leg over the side, she is on her feet and looking in all directions.

There's little to see—the dry grass of the steppes and the jagged cliffs to one side. Off in the distance, the edge of a row of evergreens can be found, but the other trees are nothing but bare trunks now. There is a small creek and a lake beyond, but they are too far to be seen from here.

I take her wrist in my grasp and start walking toward the cliff walls and my home. As she had in the pit, she begins to struggle and grab at my hand and arm. She tries to back away from me, her arm extended as she turns and tries to escape through the use of brute force.

It's…cute.

I yank her toward me, and she stumbles a bit before her body crashes into mine. Her mouth moves, and a lot more sounds come out. She's not screaming any longer, and the odd, varying tones are not like anything I have heard before. I don't like them—not at all. They are a little quieter than the yelling, but they are still loud enough to attract attention. I place my free hand firmly over her mouth again but only for a moment. I don't want to be bitten.

Her eyes narrow, and the next sounds almost resemble the snarl of a great cat. Well, the young of a great cat, maybe. The thought makes me laugh, and she cringes away from me again though I do not release her wrist.

She is so beautiful—her smooth hair and her deep eyes and her creamy, pale skin. I don't like the noises she makes, but she looks to be able enough, even if she is small. I briefly wonder if she is fertile and if she would bear a child who looks like me.

I like this idea.

A lot.

Finally, after all this time alone, I have a mate.

CHAPTER TWO

I bend over to grab the forgotten spear in my other hand. Though the woman must understand that her resistance isn't working, she continues to pull at my fingers as I drag her toward the cliffs and the cave. I don't know why she does so—it's not working, and the sun is low in the sky. Before long it will be dark, and she has to understand how dangerous it will be for her if she is left out in the open at night. Many nighttime predators were going to be waking up soon and starting their nightly prowls. We need the safety of the cave.

Apparently, she doesn't care because she continues to screech and make those awful noises all the way back to the rock. I sigh and trudge on, hoping once she is inside and knows she is safe from the elements, she will stop with the noises.

Thankfully, there is still some light outside when we reach the slight incline to the opening in the rock and my cave. I stop just outside and push her in front of me, pointing toward the dark crack in the rock. She looks at it and then to me, her eyes narrowed. Sliding my hand up to the top of her arm, I urged her forward and closer to the crack between the large rocks with another push. She resists, and I shove her harder, my patience waning. Her hand flies out in front of her as she stumbles over her own feet, and I wonder if the strange foot coverings are somehow hindering her movement.

She manages to catch herself on the edge of the rock near the opening, but she makes no move to go inside. Instead, she turns back to me, and her mouth opens again. More sounds come out— louder this time. She yanks her arm from my grip, and her hands ball into fists that she shakes at me as she makes more sounds. With my head tilted to one side, I listen for a moment, but it is just noise, and I tire of it quickly. I'm hungry and I want her inside where we will be safe before the sun sets.

I growl low at her and step forward, pressing her against the rock next to the cave's opening. My hand goes over her mouth again, but this time my fingers slip around her jaw to hold it closed so she cannot bite. She looks over my shoulder, but there is nothing to be seen for miles around us. Capturing her attention, I look straight into her eyes for a moment before I step back and push her toward the cave entrance again.

This time, she complies, and I take a deep breath. At least she is coming to her senses and doing what I want. She doesn't have to turn sideways for her shoulders to fit through the opening as I do, but her steps are still slow and cautious. Again I consider her strange footwear and think they might be the cause of her hesitation.

The narrow crack in the rocks is only a few feet long and quickly opens up into the small, single area that is my home. As we enter, we both pause while our eyes adjust to the firelight. There is still some sunlight since the cave entrance faces the sunset, but it is darker than being out in the open.

I have been here since the autumn after the forest fire destroyed my home and tribe. I have always thought it was a good, comfortable cave, but now that I have brought my new mate here, I wonder what she thinks of it. I grasp her hand and show her what I have, which takes very little time. It's not a large cave at all, just a single room with a depression in the back where I could store containers of food if I had any to store. Along the back is a small ledge which is good for keeping items off the ground. The ledge holds my flint and stone tools as well as the stomachs of two antelope which are filled with water. A little embarrassed by the lack of food, I show her the stone-lined fire pit in the front of the cave with the meat cooking on the spit. I point to the position of the fire, which allows the smoke to go out the entrance without making it difficult to breathe inside, even in the winter.

I glance at her, feeling nervous as I release her hand. She clasps her hands together in front of her, and her head moves slowly from one side to the other as she examines her surroundings.

Does she think it is good enough? What if she thinks it is too small? After so much time alone, I hadn't considered that I might find a mate and hadn't collected the things she would want and need to start her life with me. Now that I am thinking about it, I realize I have very little to offer a mate, not even much in the way of food.

With that thought, I remember my cooking and kneel down by the spit on the fire, my sudden and ravenous hunger overshadowing my thoughts surrounding my mate's first impression of my home. I tear off a strip of the meat and chew on the end of it. It is warm from the fire and nicely fat from the animal's winter stores. I gnaw on it until I have devoured the first piece, grab for another, and then another after that.

When I look up, I see her watching me. As I chew, I wonder if she is also hungry and groan at myself. Here I am hoping to impress my new mate with the cave, and I haven't even fed her! Choosing what looks to be the best piece, I jump quickly to my feet. She startles and steps away from me as I approach, holding out a strip of the antelope's tender flesh for her.

Her eyes are wide again, and her hands tremble. Her head jerks from one side to the other as she continues to back away from me. I hold the meat out to her in offering again, but she starts making those sounds just before she bolts off to one side, heading back to the entrance of the cave.

Instinctively I dart after her, grabbing her around the waist before she can get more than an arm outside. It will be dark very soon; the sun has almost completely disappeared over the horizon. She would never survive the night alone and out in the open. I pull her back against my chest and drag her toward the fire.

My ears start to ring with the sounds coming from her mouth. She alternates between screams that sound as though she is in agony and the strange, more fluid sounds that come from the back of her throat. They are unusual, rhythmic, and I still don't like them.

Her fingers claw at my arms as I wrap them both around her torso and sit down on a torn grass mat next to the fire with my mate in my lap. I hold her tight against me as I look around the cave and wonder what she does not like. She is obviously very upset about something, and she continues to twist and turn in my grasp as I try to determine what could be considered so lacking.

It occurs to me that it might be the whole place. It is small— perfectly fine for me but not large enough for her and her children. I only have one grass mat, and it's not very well made, but she could make more of those over the winter. She has certainly noticed I don't have any food left over from the winter and is probably worried I won't be able to provide enough for us both. Except for my recent kill, I don't have any food at all. She might even think I don't have enough wood to keep us warm, but I have more in another crevice in the rock up above the cave. It is too dark outside now to show it to her, but I could reassure her in the morning.

I let her struggle against me until her movements slow down and eventually stop. I am pleased that I was right about my strength compared to hers. She would at least know I was strong enough to protect her.

I feel myself smile again, and I wonder if she will eat now.

Before I can offer her the meat once more, my mate's body shudders from her head to her feet as she begins to shake in my arms. I quickly flip her around so I can see her face, and I notice the tears staining her cheeks as the moisture is caught in the light from the fire. I examine her quickly—as much as I can see, anyway. With her strange clothes, it's hard to see if her legs might be injured, but I don't think she has been hurt. She is crying, but I don't understand why. Was I already a bad mate for her? Was my cave really that inadequate? I would find her another one—there had to be more around in the rocks. If not, I could search for a new place, one that was bigger and better and perfect for her.

I *will* provide for her. I *will* protect her. I will give her anything she wants.

Another memory rolls around in my brain, images from when I was young, and my father held my mother tightly in his arms after one of my baby sisters died. She had also cried like this, and my father held my mother close to him, making quiet sounds in her ear until she stopped.

I whimper softly and pull my mate close to my chest, cradling her against me. At first, her hands push on my body as she tries to free herself from my grasp, but she is already exhausted from fighting me earlier and quickly gives up. Her head slumps down to my shoulder, and I bring my hand up to run down her hair. The feeling of the strands through my fingers is just as intriguing as it was before though I can't enjoy it as I might since she is shaking in my arms.

My mate continues to sob.

I hold her for a long time, rocking her back and forth, my arms gently wrapped around her. I don't know what else to do. The strange painted-on coloring around her eyes makes dark circles all the way down to her cheekbones. It smears further across her face as she wipes at her eyes.

When I try to offer her more food, she begins to sob again, so I

guess she isn't hungry.   The sun completes its descent, and the
cave darkens. She finally stills, but tears still run down her face.
Only the light from the fire shows me that my mate's eyes are still
open and staring blankly off to one side. I feel my own fatigue
setting in as the night covers the grasslands outside.

I have to move—my legs are numb from inactivity and having
her sitting on me. I lift her and place her on the ground next to me
and stretch, trying to ignore how she has startled again. I stand but
only take a minute to get my legs working again before I rebuild
the fire, bank it for the night, and turn back to my mate.

She is watching me with red, swollen eyes. I have to swallow
hard because of the strange feeling in my throat when I look at her.
She pulls her knees up to her chest and places her chin on them,
and her eyes move to the flickering flames. I drop down to my
hands and knees and approach her again, moving slowly this time
so she doesn't startle. Her look is wary as I get closer, but she
doesn't try to get away.

I reach out and run the tips of my fingers over her leg, feeling
the strange, almost rough texture of the material. There is no fur
on it, but it doesn't feel like any leather I have ever felt. I move
my other hand to my waist where my fur is tied around me to have
some comparison. My clothing is much softer than what she is
wearing. She cringes a bit, and all of her muscles become tense as
I touch her. I shift a little closer, trying to figure out just what she
is thinking as I look into her bright blue eyes, but I have no idea.

Moving to her side, I reach out and run my hand over her hair
again. She doesn't try to push me away this time though another
shudder runs through her body. I stroke the soft strands just a few
times before I realize there are tears falling from her eyes again.

I look at her more closely, but I still don't know why she cries.
Taking a deep breath, I realize I'm too tired to figure it out now
and decide to go to sleep. I get up on the balls of my feet first,
then reach one arm underneath my mate's knees and wrap the other
arm behind her back as I stand. She lets out a little yelp as I lift her

but then goes silent. I turn and carry her to the back of the cave where I sleep.

At least my bed is something she can appreciate. I had dug out a long, shallow trench and filled it with dry grass from the steppes. Covering the grass are several of the furs I have made over the many seasons I have been here. The bed is deep and soft; the furs are warm and comfortable, and I will hold her and keep her safe throughout the night. The corner of my mouth turns up as I carry her to the spot where we will sleep, and I kneel down to lay her on the furs. It is very dark here in the back of the cave, and I can only barely see her trying to look around me to where the light from the fire can still be seen.

She makes no effort to remove her strange clothes for sleeping, and I'm not sure exactly how they come off. I decide to let her leave them on if she wants but quickly remove the fur wrapped around my body and toss it off to the side.

My mate's eyes go wide, and I hope she can see my strength. I smile at her slowly and then kneel down beside her to get into the furs. I place one hand near her shoulder and toss my leg across her waist.

My mate's eyes fill with tears again as she screams and begins her barrage of indecipherable noises. Her hands come up to cover her face as she shakes her head back and forth when I crouch above her. I don't understand what has upset her so much, and I quickly look around to make sure the bed is as I left it.

It seems fine, and I remain confused as I crawl the rest of the way over her body and place my back near the wall. As I reach out and grab for her, I am met with her struggling resistance and more shouting. She turns so her back is toward me and tries to get out of the bed. I hold tight as she wriggles against me, and my grip on her body doesn't falter as she continues to cry and scream.

I take in and let out a long breath, wondering what I should be doing to calm her, but I am at a loss. Without knowing what else to do, I pull her back tightly against my chest and wrap my arms around her waist. From the firelight, I can easily see the entrance to the cave and further protect her from anything that might seek to harm her in the night.

Remembering the hyaenodons from earlier in the day, I hope they have moved far enough away not to hear her. If they can hear her, I hope the smell of the fire will keep them away from us. She is fighting me so much, I can't let go of her to cover her mouth. Her fingers pull at my arms, but I don't release her. She wrestles with me but doesn't win. I am resolute in my desire to keep her safe even if she seems determined to do something to hurt herself. It doesn't require much strength to hold her, and I think she is probably already exhausted from her previous tirade. Before long, she begins to slow her movements, and shortly after that, she drops to the furs.

Glad she's finally decided to let me protect her, I relax my grip a little and pull my arm out from underneath her. I place my hand on the side of my head to prop myself up and look down at the woman who will now share my bed.

Even in the dim glow of the firelight, I can see how stunningly beautiful she is. Maybe it's because it has been so long since I've seen another person, but I don't think so. I wish I could see more of her body, but her strange coverings obscure most of her skin; only her hands and face are visible.

I inhale deeply through my nose, and her scent is unique. She smells sweet, like overripe fruit, and I realize the scent comes from her hair, but not her skin. I lean a little closer and sniff at the base of her neck.

Everything about her is unusual; her clothing, her hair, the color around her eyes, which is now mostly smudged away. I find it enticing and exciting.

She turns over to look up at me, and her eyes are red-rimmed from crying. My chest clenches to know she has been so sad, and I again wonder what I can do to make her feel safe. She stares at me with apprehension, and I decide to try to comfort her the way my father had comforted my mother in the past.

With my arm still around her waist, I slowly move my hand up and down her side. I hope the sensation of touch will calm her, but her body tenses instead. She wraps her arms around herself, and I think she might be cold; her clothing doesn't seem thick enough to keep her warm. I reach down and pull one of the furs up around her, but she still doesn't relax.

I have no idea what she needs, and I wonder what might have happened to her to make her so sad.

I suddenly realize that she must have lost her tribe just as I have. Though I don't know how she got where she is, I do know there are no people anywhere near here except for me. I haven't seen another person since the fire drove me from the forest. Though I had looked for many days through the blackened tree stumps for signs of other survivors, I had found nothing but the bones of my people.

Now that I comprehend, my heart aches for her. I know what it is like to feel alone though I have grown so used to it, I try not to think about it now. I wonder if she has been alone for a long time and decide she must not have been. If she had, she would have been more receptive to me as her mate. She is frightened of me, and though I have tried to show her I will keep her safe and provide her with a home, she is still scared.

She must miss her family and tribe terribly. Maybe she even had a mate in her tribe, and she misses him, too. There had been no females my age in my small tribe, and I had been waiting for one of the girls to begin her womanhood before I took her. I had been several seasons older than the one closest to me in age, and there were no other tribes nearby to trade mates. If an older woman's mate had died, I might have mated her instead.

But they all died at once, and I had no one.

I remembered how frightened I had been in the beginning. The fire had destroyed the berry bushes in the forest and the homes of the rabbits I liked to hunt. I was a man but had only killed larger animals twice and then with the help of the other men. I nearly starved before finding the freshwater lake among the pine groves and figuring out how to catch the fish at the edge of the water.

Looking down at my mate, my fingers reach out and brush strands of her beautiful long hair away from her forehead. The softness distracts me from her sorrow, and I pinch a few of the strands between my fingers to hold them out and look more closely. The firelight brings out the slight tinges of red in a few of the strands, but it is the texture that intrigues me the most.

As I look back at her face, I can see she is still frightened. Releasing her hair, I reach up and let the tips of my fingers touch the tear stains on her cheeks. I feel like crying for her—lost and alone out on the steppes. I touch slowly her cheek and jaw before my hand finds her shoulder and the incredibly smooth tunic covering her. Like her hair, I find it fascinating. I have never felt anything as smooth and soft. It's lightweight, too—as if it were made from strands of a spider's web.

I stroke her hair again to feel the difference between its softness and the texture of the clothing and find myself again fascinated by how soft and beautiful it is. I know I am very lucky to have found such an attractive mate though I am really just thrilled to have another person with me. As I take a deep breath, I inhale the scent of her hair, and the combination of sweet fruit and possibly some kind of flower confuses me—it is still too early in the season for buds to be blooming. Pulling her close to me, I run my nose from her hairline to her temple.

Definitely fruit.

She tenses again, and I'm reminded that she is sad and frightened about the loss of her people. I look into her eyes and tilt my head to the side, wanting her to know I understand. I touch my nose to her temple again—gently bumping her skin in a show of companionship.

Her tongue darts over her lips, and she makes her rhythmic

sounds again. She is not as loud this time, but the noise is strange and unfamiliar to me. I continue to watch her closely until she stops making the sounds and lets out a long breath. She sniffs and turns away from me again but seems to have settled down somewhat.

I lay my head next to hers and strengthen my grip around her body. I keep my eyes open and watch the entrance to the cave until I hear her breathing slowly and regularly with sleep. Only when I'm sure she is no longer awake do I allow myself to do the same.

⟶ ••◦●◦•• ⟵

I wake during the night.

At first, I'm confused by the presence of the body next to me. Though in the tribe we shared communal sleeping areas, I have slept alone for so long I forgot how warm and comfortable it is to have someone share a sleeping area. I smile to myself and nuzzle into her hair for a moment before I remember my duty to protect her.

I rise up on my elbow and look around the cave. I survey the normal, darkened shapes in each corner and verify there is nothing out of the ordinary. The fire is down to coals but still brightly burning without any danger of going out. I let my fire extinguish my first season alone, and that had nearly caused my death. I certainly won't let it happen now that I am responsible for a mate.

Deciding not to take the slightest chance, I slip out from under the furs, add two pieces of wood to the fire, and peek outside the cave's opening to make sure all is as it should be. The moon is round and bright in the cool night sky, and the grasslands surrounding the cave seem quiet and peaceful. After relieving myself over the edge of the rocks, I shiver and return to the furs.

Thankfully, my mate does not wake up as I crawl back into the furs beside her. I know she needs to rest. I take a moment to look at her in the flickering firelight. Her eyes are closed, but the blotchy remnants of her sorrow are still evident on her cheeks.

I want to touch her skin, but I don't want to wake her. Unable to control the urge completely, I touch the skin of her face carefully. I reach down to her strange clothing again, and my fingers brush from her shoulder, over her breast, and down to her waist as I enjoy the feel of the cloth compared to the rough skin of my hand.

She stirs slightly, so I still my movements, deciding to be satisfied with leaving one arm wrapped around her. I stretch out next to her and pull the furs up to make sure she is warm enough. Her mouth opens slightly, and she makes more strange noises in her sleep. The sounds are very soft and deep in tone. Her face scrunches up a bit, and her breathing becomes more rapid. I hold her closer to me until she relaxes back into deeper sleep.

I know I must be right, and she has recently lost her people. I wonder what happened to them and if I will ever know for sure. It doesn't matter now, anyway—I will be her mate, and I will take care of her from now on. I just need to figure out a way to stop her from being frightened of me. There are so many things I will need from her as well: she will need to gather food for the winter, cook the meat I bring back for her, and accept me into her body so I can give her children.

The thought of that brings another smile to my face and a tingling feeling between my legs.

However, she seems so frightened of me now, I don't think she would readily position herself on her hands and knees so I can fill her. Still, I am much stronger, and if I want inside of her, I can just hold her while I enter her body. Joining with her in such a way would still feel very good, I imagine, but I don't like it when she yells and cries, and I think she would probably do that if I have to hold her down to mate with her.

These thoughts are making my penis lengthen and become stiff. I consider stroking myself, but I am afraid it will wake her. I sigh as I look down on her sleeping face and wonder how long it will be before I can properly mate with her. I touch her cheek softly again, and I know when I decide to lie with her, I want her to enjoy it. So how do I get that to happen?

Finally, after thinking about it a long time, I decide I need to make her like me.

CHAPTER THREE

The second time I wake in the night, my mate is crying out in her sleep again. At first I think she has woken up as well, possibly disoriented to find herself in a different home and without her tribe. However, her eyes are closed while her mouth makes those sounds, and her muscles tighten in distress. Again, I hold her to me, hoping to offer her comfort even if I can't fix whatever is wrong with her. After a minute she calms, turns toward me, and lies in my arms.

As I begin to fall back into slumber myself, it occurs to me that my mate is going to need a lot of care. If I want her to like me, I'm going to have to show her that I can take the place of her tribe. I'm sure I can be enough for her if I make sure she has shelter, provide enough meat for her to cook, and of course, put a baby in her. A list of things to show her starts forming in my mind and continues into my dreams.

The next time my eyes open, there is faint light coming through the opening of the cave. I raise myself up on one arm and look down at my mate as she continues to sleep, wrapped up in my furs. Her eyes are closed, and she looks so peaceful as she lies there that I don't wake her even though it's getting late in the morning, and there are many things I needed to point out to her.

For a while, I also stay in the furs and just watch her sleep, memorizing the shape of her jaw and the shade of pink that covers her lips. As sunlight peers through the rocks, her hair shines around her face, and I can't help but touch it and revel in its softness again. First, I push it off of her forehead, and then I smooth it over her shoulders. It seems to have tangled somewhat in the night, but it's still just as soft as before. I tuck it gently behind her ears, and her eyes finally open.

My mate blinks a few times as her eyes focus on me. I smile just a little—careful not to show my teeth—but her eyes still get wide as they dart around the small cave. I can see the tears start to well up again, and I know I will have to show her everything as quickly as possible. She is obviously not impressed with what I have, and I can't blame her. I have only barely provided for myself over the seasons and haven't even thought about acquiring the things I would need to support a mate.

I am going to change that now.

I whimper low and brush at the corner of her eye, wiping the tears away. As gently as I can, I lean in close to her and touch my nose to hers. She startles a little, but at least she stops crying. I pull my legs underneath me and jump over her to the edge of the sleeping furs and hold my hand out.

She only looks at it, and her eyes widen again. She looks away from me quickly, takes a few deep breaths, and then glances back to my eyes. I reach forward and touch her hand with mine. When she does not pull back, I intertwine our fingers and tug at them until she sits up. I can't help but feel some excitement as she responds to me. She has not yet screamed or made any other strange sounds, and she doesn't seem as frightened as she was yesterday. Maybe she will accept my cave after all.

Once she stands up and takes a step away from the furs, I release her hand and grab my fur to wrap it around myself. My mate makes another sound as I dress, and I look to her for a moment. She glances away again and clasps her hands in front of her stomach, and I think about how she will look with a large, round belly. The thought makes me smile.

Crossing the short width of the cave, I head over to get one of my water bags. I hold it out to her, but she only looks at it, her eyes narrowed. She makes some noises with her mouth, but they are still fairly quiet and don't hurt my head this time.

I tilt my head and hold the water bag out to her again, but she still doesn't take it. I look down at it to try to determine if it is somehow unappetizing, but it looks fine to me. It is a simple water bag made from the stomach of an antelope I killed in the spring. It had been a large buck, and I managed to make a few things from its body. Between this one and the other water bag, I usually have to make the trek to the fresh water lake only every few days.

I wonder if her people carried water in a different way, and maybe she doesn't know about carrying water the way I was taught. I bring the water bag back close to my body, unwind the sinew holding the top closed, and take a short drink myself before offering it to her again.

This time, though tentative, she reaches out and takes it from my hands. I watch her expectantly, and she slowly brings it up to her nose and sniffs. Her face crinkles up for a moment as she turns away but then sniffs again. She takes a small sip before quickly handing it back to me.

I'm elated. She took the water from me, so she knows I can at least provide that much. All I need to do now is show her what else I can offer her as her mate, and then she will like me. Reaching out, I take her by the hand and lead her to the entrance of the cave. She steps out into the sunlight of the new day with me and looks over the grass steppes. The day is warm already, and the sun shines and sparkles on the dew. It is a beautiful sight.

I look over to my mate with a smile, and she bursts into tears.

When I reach out to comfort her as I did last night, she places her hands against my chest and shoves. As she pushes me, she makes a high-pitched, screeching sound.

Startled by the noise and her physical attack, I jump backwards and crouch a few feet away from my mate as she sits with her back against the outside wall of the cave and shakes with her cries. Her hands are over her face, and her hair falls around her head like a fur blanket. I want to touch it again, to try and comfort her like I know I should, but when I try to get close to her, she screams and snarls at me.

I don't know what to do.

So I stay where I am, sometimes reaching out to her with my hand but never quite touching her. I don't think she notices because her eyes are covered. As the sun slowly climbs in the sky, my stomach growls as if my body knows there is food nearby. My mate must be hungry as well since she would not eat anything last night. I want to go inside and get some of the meat, but I don't dare leave her alone.

I'm a little confused as to why I have such a strong desire to keep her in my sights. I'm afraid she won't be here when I come back out, and I will have to track her down so she doesn't get hurt. I'm also afraid she'll be scared if she uncovers her eyes and I'm not there to protect her, and I want her to know I won't abandon her. I don't want her to be even more afraid than she is already.

My legs get tired, so I sit on the ground a few feet from her and just wait instead. I can go a while longer without food, even if the smell of cooked flesh so close to me is very tempting. It makes my mouth water, but I also know I have to take care of my mate first.

The sun's rays creep closer to the bottom edge of the rocks, and its warmth will soon be upon us. My mate finally takes one long, shuddering breath and raises her head again. She looks at me with red eyes and a quivering lower lip. Her expression tears at me; I want to go to her, but I'm not sure if she wants me close.

For a long moment, we just look at each other. When she doesn't make any of those loud noises again, I shuffle forward, little by little, until I am close enough to touch her. I slowly reach out with my hand, and when she doesn't flinch back, I wipe some of the tears from her cheeks. My mate takes another deep breath and closes her eyes for a moment. Her shoulders slump, and her head drops forward, but she doesn't start crying again. I wonder if she has run out of tears.

I move a little closer and kneel down in front of her. I don't reach out to her again because she still seems a little hesitant. I sit there with my hands on my thighs, unmoving as she watches me. Eventually, her mouth opens and many sounds come out again, but they are the softer rhythmic noises she made before falling asleep, not the loud ones. She looks out over the steppes as she makes the noises, then pauses, looks to me, and makes more clatter.

I tilt my head and watch her lips move, wondering why she does this so much. After some time, the pitch of her sounds suddenly rises and becomes louder. I flinch at the abrupt change, and she goes quiet as she stares out over the land behind me. Her shoulders rise and fall with several deep breaths, and then her head swings around and she stares straight into my eyes.

She makes another noise. It's not the loud noises from before, nor is it the long rhythmic noises I had just endured. When she makes this noise, she taps her chest with her finger. She's silent for a moment while we look at each other, and then she repeats both the sound and the motion.

"Elizabeth."

I feel my smile on my face as I understand what she is doing. Though it's a strange one, she has a name-sound just like I do, and she's telling me what it is. I try to make the same sounds.

"Ehh..beh." I frown. Why is her name-sound so difficult and so long?

She frowns right back at me and says it again.

"Elizabeth."

"Beh-tah-babaa."

She sighs and her forehead wrinkles.

"Elizabeth. Eeee-lizzz-ahh-beth."

"Laahh…baaay."

She shakes her head back and forth, and I wonder if she has an itch. She repeats the sounds a few more times, sometimes combining it with a lot of other sounds. I am starting to get a headache again as she gets a little louder. She taps her chest again.

"Beth!"

The sound is shorter but still very odd.

"Beh-bet."

"Beth," she repeats.

I've had enough. I reach out and touch her shoulder.

"Beh."

"Beth."

I tap her a little harder and growl.

"Beh," I repeat. I tap her again. "BEH!"

Her eyes widen a bit, and she inhales sharply. A moment later, her shoulders drop and she sighs.

"Beh," she says quietly.

I smile as I watch her hand reach out, and a single finger touches the center of my chest. More sounds from her mouth, but I know what she wants. She wants to know if I have a name-sound too.

"Ehd!" I say proudly.

After so much time on my own, I am lucky I even remember my name-sound.

"Ehd?"

"Ehd!"

"Ehd," she says as a small smile finally comes over her face. It is a beautiful sight, and my body almost tingles with excitement. She has given me her name-sound and asked for mine, which must mean she has accepted me. If she hadn't, she wouldn't have given me such valuable information. Now she will take me as her mate willingly, and we will form a new tribe with our children.

I jump up and grab her arm to help her to her feet. She stands and brushes dust from her coverings before I take both of her hands in mine. For a moment, I look at her eyes, which are still red with her sadness. I hope now that she has accepted that I am her mate, she will be happy. I lean forward slowly and run the tip of my nose over hers again, starting at the tip and moving all the way up to the place between her eyes. I look at her again, and though I can still see her wariness in her eyes, she does not pull away from me.

Then I begin to show my mate her new home.

Since we were already outside the cave, I start by showing her my impressive collection of wood. There's a large crevice outside the entrance to my cave that isn't big enough for someone to live in but keeps the wood nice and dry when it rains, and it's very easy to retrieve more wood when the supply inside is running low.

Beh looks at the wood and then back to me, but she doesn't seem impressed. I show her again, but her reaction is still one of disinterest. She looks out over the field away from the cave and up the cliff to the steppes but not at the wood. I'm disappointed that she doesn't seem to like it because it really is the best I have to show her, but I push on, determined to impress her somehow.

The rest of the day doesn't go any better.

I do not understand my mate.

I show Beh everything I think will impress her, but she does not react the way I think she will—not at all. I am trying, but she is just…odd. After she won't look at any of my furs or the smooth rocks around the fire pit, she sits down near the entrance to the cave and cries half the day. Then she begins these strange little movements of twisting and turning her body around. I can tell she needs to relieve herself, but she doesn't do it! She just keeps looking around the outside of the cave, then back at me, and then around again. I finally get tired of her doing that, grab her wrist, and drag her over to the place where I usually empty my bladder and bowels. I relieve myself to show her the best place to go and then stand there and wait a while, but Beh won't do anything! She just starts making lot of noises again! Eventually she pushes my arm until I am standing on the other side of the scrub brush and looking away from her. Then she finally relieves herself and stops fidgeting.

So strange!

Afterwards, we go back into the cave, and Beh is finally willing to eat something. I give her the best pieces from the antelope, but she doesn't seem to like it at all. I want to show her the last fur I made—it is the softest and covered us the night before, and I hope she will use it to make herself more suitable clothing—but when I try to take her to the back of the cave, she pulls away from me. Once I give up on that, we go outside and I show her the edge of the wooded area where there is a lot of good wood to refill the cache near the cave, but she doesn't seem impressed by that either.

At this point, I'm frustrated, to say the least.

I don't know how well our mating is going to work when each thing she does makes less sense than the last, and everything I do appears to leave no impression on her at all. Earlier in the morning, I had thought getting her to like me would be fairly simple, but now that I have shown her everything I have, she seems bored, and I do not feel like a very good mate.

Beh obviously agrees.

Since nothing I have around the cave demonstrates my worth, I decide to show her the nearby lake. It doesn't take long to get there, and maybe she likes water and will appreciate how close it is. I think the area is beautiful, and I hope she will enjoy it as well. I reach out my hand and gesture toward the evergreen forest on the horizon. The lake is just on the other side of the stand of trees.

For a moment, she just looks at my hand, and I can feel my heart sink in my chest. She has not made any more noises for a while, nor has she cried since this morning, but I know there is still something wrong. I just don't know what it is.

"Beh?"

Her eyes move up to mine slowly before she looks down to

my outstretched fingers. She silently places her hand in mine and stands. Her eyes stay focused on the ground, and I reach out to touch the tip of my finger to her chin, tilting her head up so she is looking at me. I watch her throat bob as she swallows, and then more sounds come from her mouth though they are hushed. I hear my name-sound word in with the other sounds she makes.

I wish I knew what she needs from me. I have given her shelter, water, and food. Maybe I will try to give her a baby tonight, and that will make her happy. I have no idea what else she may need from me. It has been so long since I watched my parents and the other couples from my tribe; I don't remember if there is something else I am supposed to do.

Beh's eyes close for a moment, and she lets out a long deep breath. She's done that many times since this morning, and I think it must be to soothe herself.

Even in the act of comforting her, I seem to be lacking.

Something in her look changes as her eyes open and her fingers clench slightly in mine. I return the grasp as I lead her out of the cave and down the trail. The air between us feels peculiarly charged to me, and I am very aware of her presence even when my eyes are on the horizon, watching for danger. I turn and look back at her as we reach the open grasslands, and she looks back at me with a small smile. The clouds choose to move out of the way then, and when the sun hits me, the warmth penetrates my skin. I smile back at Beh and run my thumb over the edge of her hand as we walk together across the steppes.

Maybe I have misunderstood her, and she does appreciate the few things I have. At least now she is receptive to me, and she offers no resistance as I guide her over the lands I've learned very well. I look from left to right many times, not allowing myself to be lost in thought or memories like I might have on another day. I have a mate to protect now, and I'm not going to be surprised by any hidden dangers.

Thankfully, the trek is uneventful. Beh looks around the forest as we pass through, and I am glad of it. I hope she spots some plants she can start gathering for food stores. I don't know what plants can be eaten except for the few I recognize. Once I found a bush with berries that I thought would be all right to eat, but they made me sick instead. Since then, I had stayed away from any plants unfamiliar to me, and that left only the few that I know. There are sometimes raspberries and pine nuts, which I have collected in the past, but it is still too soon in the spring. I also know the grains that grow on the top of the grasses can be eaten, but it takes forever just to collect a handful of them! When I cook them, they are chewy and not at all tasty like my mother had made for me when I was young.

I look at Beh as she looks closely at everything we pass, and I am glad I have a woman to collect food for me again. Maybe this winter I won't be so hungry all of the time. I will bring her meat and protect her, and she can do the other things we need, like gathering food and cooking. She can also use woven reeds to make the same kind of dishes my mother always made. I've tried, but I can't seem to make them tight enough, and they always leak.

I'm sure my mate will be able to do it though.

I squeeze her hand gently as we head up the slight incline, through the rushes, and down the hill on the other side. The lake comes into view as we come around a clump of trees, and I can tell by my mate's expression she is surprised.

It's a large lake with lots of different fish. A stream to the north feeds it, and I have found trout swimming near its large rocks. The shoreline is covered in round stones that lead to the rushes near the woods.

Releasing her hand, I walk to the water's edge where I can stand on the rocks and wait for fish to come close enough to catch. Sometimes I have stabbed them with a spear, but it's not too hard to catch them with my hand once I figured out how. There is a small group of fish near the bank, and it is not long before I have caught one.

I turn and hold it up for my mate, and I feel my heart begin to pound faster in my chest as she breaks out in the first, genuine smile I have seen from her. I have no choice but to return the grin because I have finally, *finally* done something right, and her expression confirms it. Though it has taken me most of the day to find some way to impress her, the look on her face is definitely worth whatever effort it takes in the future to see that smile as often as possible.

She is so, so beautiful to me, and I know now that Beh will be happy with me.

I catch two more fish for my mate and lay them out on the rocks for us to take back to the cave. The sun is warm in the sky, and the light sparkles on the water as I head to the edge to wash off. I still have blood on me from killing the antelope, and I don't like the smell.

I remove the leather straps around my shoulders that hold my two water skins and lay them on top of a rock along with the fur covering around my shoulders. I remove the fur wrap from my waist as well, leaving it on top of everything to keep it dry.

Beh makes a strange sound, and when I look over at her, she has turned around to face away from me. I look off into the distance to see if there is something out there that has alarmed her, but I see nothing. I move a little closer to her, but she won't turn around. Even as I move around her, she keeps spinning away from me. She doesn't seem upset but simply won't look at me.

I don't understand her.

I dip my hands in the water. The sun hasn't yet warmed the water much this early in the spring, and it's very cold. I don't like the cold, so I only use a bit of water to wipe some of the blood off of my arms before I shake them to remove drops of water.

Glancing at Beh, I see she is still sitting on the rocks and not looking at me. She has the end of her tunic wrapped around one of her fingers, and she seems to be using it to rub her teeth though I don't know why she would do that.

"Beh!"

She glances at me, pulls her clothing back to her middle, and quickly ducks her head and looks away again as I walk away from the lake toward her. As I get close, she looks over to me with wide eyes, gasps, and then quickly ducks her head into her hands. I come up behind her and reach out to touch her shoulder.

She jumps up off the rock and takes a few steps forward, her hands still over her eyes. I don't understand what she is doing *at all*. Why is she hiding her face and eyes? I look around again, wondering if there is something frightening or dangerous that I had not noticed, but there is nothing there.

I do see her arm and hands also have blood on them from where she fell in the trap. She probably wants to get it off of her before it starts to smell too bad. Deciding there is no way I'm going to figure out what is wrong with her now, I grab onto her arm and pull her toward the water line. She comes with me though her hands stay over her face, which causes her to trip over her strange foot coverings again. Tired of the things harming her, I crouch down in front of her and try to figure out how to get them off.

There are little ties laced through them, and when I examine the knot, I realize it isn't a complicated one and determine how to untie it fairly quickly. Whatever the ties are made of, they are much easier to unknot than leather or sinew. Beh starts making sounds again, but I don't pay any attention until I hear my name-sound.

"Ehd!"

I look up at her and see she has at least uncovered her face and is looking down at me. She takes a step back, making more sounds with her mouth as she does. I glance up at the sky, knowing it is starting to get late, and we will need to leave the lake soon. Whatever is wrong with her, we don't have time for it. As her mate, I must take care of her, which includes making sure the blood is off her skin. I also need to keep her warm, so I have to get the strange clothing off of her so it will stay dry. Next time we come to the lake, we will bring extra clothing so we can wash the ones we're wearing.

I examine the unusual clothes on my mate, trying to find the ties that hold them together, but I can't determine how to take them off. The leggings have strange loops all around her waist, but I don't think they will help get the clothing off of her. The loops would be useful if she tied carrying pouches to them, and I wonder if that is their purpose. There is also a round bit in the center near her stomach right above where the odd cloth folds over itself, but I don't know what to make of it. When I press my finger against it, it's cold and hard like a stone but doesn't feel like any stones I have encountered before.

Beh pushes my hand away, so I look to the other garment around the top half of her body.

The tunic seems to be all one piece and not even wrapped around her with a tie at all. While Beh makes more noise, I walk slowly around her and try to understand how to get it off. I finally decide it just has to go up and over her head, which I do not like at all. To remove it or put it on, her eyes would be covered, leaving her blind for a second. That is definitely not safe for my mate.

She will have to use some of the furs in the cave to make herself some proper clothing.

I reach out and wrap my fingers around the edge of the tunic at her waist. Beh makes another sound and pushes my hand away. I wait for her to remove it herself, but when she doesn't, I grab at it again, and again she pushes my hand away and makes a lot more noise. I growl at her and grab the material tighter as I try to pull it up over her torso.

Now she is really yelling and not only pushes me away but takes a few steps backwards and shakes her finger at me. More sounds come from her mouth, and there is no doubt she is angry, but I am becoming angry as well. One thing I notice with her sounds now is the inclusion of my name-sound amongst the noise.

I reach out, growling, and grab at her arm, pulling her toward me. She shrieks and hits me in the chest.

I try to grab onto her arms, but she is very, very wiggly! I only want to take care of her, help her clean off the blood from the antelope, and show her I can be a good mate for her, but she won't let me!

I growl again and manage to catch her wrists in my hands. I hold them down at her sides until she stops struggling and glares at me. Her chest rises and falls as she slowly relaxes her muscles. When she eventually seems to calm down, I release her and start to pull at her strange clothing again, but she yells at me.

"Ehd, NO!" Beh raises her hand and smacks me on the nose.

I step back in shock.

Finally, after a moment's hesitation, I realize how wrong I have been about her.

CHAPTER FOUR

My nose hurts.

I blink my eyes a few times while I try to figure out what just happened. One minute I was going to help my mate into the lake to get clean, and the next thing I know, she's yelling and...and...

Did she just...just...*hit* me?

In the *nose*?

A hundred different thoughts and emotions go through my head all at once. At first, I am angry, and I want to lash out at her —even hit her back. Then I remember that she is my mate, and I am supposed to protect her. How could I keep her safe if I hit her? I am much bigger than she, and I could hurt her if I struck out at her in anger. She will also be afraid of me if I hurt her, and I don't want that. Then I become frustrated because I have no idea why she would hit my nose when I am only trying to take care of her.

Slowly, I begin to comprehend, and pain rips through my chest.

I think back to her reaction the first time I touched her shining hair, the way she did not want to take meat from my hand, and how she cried when I brought her to my furs. I remember how she didn't want to relieve herself near my cave or come with me to the lake. Once we got here, she didn't even want to look at me.

She doesn't like me.

I thought when she gave me her name-sound that she would take me as her mate, but she hit me on the nose, so I must have been wrong. She does not want me—not at all.

Beh doesn't want me for a mate.

I take a short step back, and my eyes drop to the stony shore of the lake. It feels like my entire body is trying to melt right into the rocks below my feet. Closing my eyes for a moment, I recall the first few hours after I realized my tribe was gone, and I was the only survivor. After searching for more people almost an entire cycle of seasons, I remember finding the cave I live in now and resigned myself to being alone.

I will still be alone.

I'm not prepared to give her what she needs, and she does not want to share my cave. I don't have enough to offer her, and she hit me in the nose to let me know she does not find me acceptable.

"Ehd?"

I take a quick step back, realizing I have just been standing there staring at the ground for a long time. I glance up into Beh's face for a moment, but knowing now that she doesn't want me, I don't want to look at her and see how beautiful she is. I don't want to see what I can't have.

My eyes land on the fish I caught earlier, and there is an ache in the center of my chest. For a moment, I want to hurl them out to the center of the lake out of spite, but I don't seriously consider wasting food. I caught them for Beh, and they are still hers.

I walk slowly over to where the fish are drying out on a rock near my clothes. I grab the first of my fur wraps and tie it around my waist. I had intended to tie the fish to the leather strap that holds my water skins to carry them back to the cave, but now I don't think that is going to happen. Instead, I take my outer fur and place the fish in the center of it, wrapping the edges around so they don't fall out. I stand up and walk back to her, drop down to the ground in front of her, and hold out the wrapped fish.

At least she will have something to eat tonight.

"Ehd-"

I don't look up even though I recognize my name-sound in the sounds she is making. I wish she would let me take care of her, but I also understand. Why would she want me as a mate? I have nothing to offer her, not even a decent mat to sit on in the cave.

If I had known, if I had realized she was coming, I would have done it all differently. As it is, I would do anything for another chance to win her. I wish there were something as simple as another male to fight for her. At least then I would know exactly why I lost.

She takes a step forward, and I close my eyes to wait for her to take the wrapped fish from my hands. I don't want to watch her turn and walk away from me. Maybe I had been wrong all this time, and she has a tribe nearby. Maybe she had just wandered a little too far and fallen into my trap. I don't know, and though the idea of a tribe of people close to me would have thrilled me a few days ago, now the thought turns my stomach. If she is from a tribe close to me, she probably already has a mate. I would not want to be somewhere where I had to watch Beh be with another mate.

I feel the fur-wrapped fish leave my hands, and a little noise escapes my throat. I will not open my eyes though—I refuse to watch her go away. I hold my breath and wait for her footsteps to be out of my range of hearing, but I hear no steps at all.

There is a soft, light touch of fingertips on the edge of my jaw.

"Ehd," she whispers. Her finger trails over the tip of my nose, and my entire body shudders as I finally look at her. She makes more soft sounds as she crouches down in front of me and balances on the balls of her feet. I still feel like I'm melting, but this time I am melting into her—into her face, her eyes, her touch. We look at each other in silence for a moment before she huffs out a long breath. Her fingers run over my cheek and across my jaw again, and more soft noises come from her mouth.

I still don't like the noise too much, but at least the sounds aren't loud. I am more confused now than I was before though. Why isn't she leaving? She obviously doesn't want me, so why hasn't she left? She must have other people nearby because it would be too dangerous for her to be alone.

Alone.

I whimper as she makes more sounds, and she keeps touching my face. I don't ever want her to stop. The feel of her fingers moving through the short hairs of my beard is indescribable but also makes me wonder: Does she think I am not old enough to be her mate? My beard is not thick like an older man's would be.

Her thumb runs over my nose again, and her lower lip disappears behind her teeth. She utters more quiet sounds, and my name-sound is among them again. Her eyes are as soft as the sounds she makes, and I start to doubt.

I doubt everything. Everything I have thought since I first laid eyes on her at the bottom of the pit I dug to hunt antelope is uncertain now, and I have to try to figure it out.

Did she not mean it when she hit my nose?

Will she still be my mate?

Do I not have to be alone?

"Beh?"

I have to know for sure. Does she accept me as her mate or not? Did she react too quickly because of whatever I did to upset her but didn't really mean what she did? Is that what she is telling me now?

I have to know.

Her hand doesn't leave the side of my face as I rise up on my knees and reach out to touch her face as well. I am a little surprised when she doesn't pull away from me, and with trembling fingers, I place my other hand on the other side of her face. I lean forward slowly until the tip of my nose touches hers. Her eyes close, and I can feel the stiffness in her arms, her nervousness coming through in her posture and muscle tension, but she doesn't move away.

Very, very slowly, I run the tip of my nose all the way up to her forehead and then back again. I can feel the warmth of her breath against my mouth as I stop and pull back a bit, looking into her clear blue eyes and hoping against all hope that this means she is going to accept me after all.

I'm not going to guess what she might be thinking—not anymore. I will not risk making another mistake and angering her. I want her; I know I do. It is far beyond not wanting to be alone anymore. I want her—only her.

I will do anything to make Beh mine.

I take a deep breath and let it out again. Beh smiles at me as she lets go of my face and places her hands over mine. She pulls me away from her and we slowly stand together with her hands holding mine. She looks out to the lake and sighs heavily.

I move closer and lean down so I can touch her nose with mine again. Beh's eyes close as I do, and I can see the corners of her mouth turn up a little at the same time. I reach back up and place my hand on the side of her face before I run my nose up one side of hers and then down the other.

This time when my skin meets hers, her shoulders are more relaxed, and she does not seem as nervous. I lay my head on her shoulder, tilting my face toward her neck so I can run my nose along her throat, too. I inhale slowly, taking in the scent of her. It's different than it was the previous day; the scent of fruit is muted now, nearly gone. As I turn toward her hairline, the fragrance is more noticeable but still much weaker than before.

I feel her hand on the back of my head but only for a moment before she takes a step back and brings her hands up to my wrist to break my hold on her. I watch intently as Beh takes my hand, turns me so I am facing the tree line away from the lake, and then makes more sounds. Her finger points toward the trees, but I don't see anything there when I look. I turn my head back toward her, but she takes my head in her hands and turns it back to the forest again.

She does this again before I realize she doesn't want me to look at her.

What does she think I will see?

She makes no sense at all.

I glance at her eyes and can see the frustration in them. It is the same look she gave me this morning when she needed to relieve herself, and she wouldn't do it until I had turned my back to her. Does she not want me to see her body? Why not? Is there something wrong with it, and she is embarrassed?

I remember a girl in my tribe who was missing part of her arm. She had not been attacked by an animal but had just been born with part of it not there. There were tiny nubs that looked like they were supposed to be fingers, but they were right at the end of her elbow. She always kept it covered up so no one could see that it was different.

Did Beh also have some kind of deformity? Is that why she wears such strange clothing over her legs, to hide a flaw? Maybe she's afraid I won't want her if I know there is something wrong with her. The girl in my tribe was usually alone; no one wanted to be with someone who looked different. Maybe Beh has been shunned by her tribe because she has something wrong with her, and that's why she is alone.

The skin around my neck feels hot as I consider that she might have been mistreated. I don't care if there is something wrong with her! If her legs look strange, or there is something else wrong with her body, I don't care! She's my mate, and I'm going to take care of her. She won't ever have to be alone again.

I reach my hand out and touch the top of her leg as I look up at her.

"Beh," I say softly as my fingers creep up her leg. I wonder if whatever is wrong is something I can feel from the outside of her clothes.

Her hand comes down and grabs at mine, moving it away

from her and holding it next to my side before she lets go and points toward the trees again. I want her to know that it doesn't matter—whatever is wrong with her, it doesn't matter to me, and I will still provide for her. I try to touch her again, but she takes my hand and moves it away, making more sounds and eventually covering my eyes with her hands for a moment. She looks like she is going to start crying again, so I give up for now, drop down, sit on one of the larger rocks nearby, and turn my back to the lake.

As soon as she walks out of my field of vision, I don't like it, not at all.

Beh seems pleased at what I've done, but she is now behind me where I can't see her. How am I supposed to protect her? What if something in the lake tries to hurt her? I listen intently to the sounds behind me, closing my eyes and concentrating hard. I can hear the sound of her feet on the rocks and then the slight splash of water.

My breathing increases with my nervousness for my mate's safety. I'm glad I can hear the water moving, but not being able to see her makes me feel anxious. My mind keeps coming back to the night of the fire and how I hadn't been close enough to see it start or to get anyone away from the area before it all went up in flames.

Finally, I can't stand it anymore, and I glance over my shoulder quickly to make sure she is all right.

Beh stands in the lake with the water coming up to her knees. She is bent over and rinsing her arms in the cool water with her long hair lying in strands across her back. Some of it falls over her shoulders, and the tips touch the water.

I swallow hard, and I have no idea why she didn't want me to see her before. There is nothing wrong with her, nothing at all. In fact, everything is *right* with her. Her legs are long, and I can clearly see the firmness of the muscles in her thighs. Above them her hips curve out sensually before her waist draws my eyes back in again. Her spine is straight, and she is absolutely, positively glorious.

When I first saw her, I thought I had never seen a more beautiful woman, and that was when she was wearing those weird clothes. Now that she is standing there with her back to me, leaning over...

I have to swallow again. I'm suddenly very hard and very much want to try to put a baby inside of my mate. It's far more intense than the physical feeling I know I will have when I am inside of her. I want to see her stomach get round and know the child inside of her is one I put there. I want her to give birth to a baby that looks like her and me.

I don't just want it. I *need* it.

As much as I need water and food and shelter, I need to be inside of her—I *need* to give her a baby. My hands shake with the very thought of it, and my legs coil under me, ready to stand and go to her, to take her right now.

Then she turns, and our eyes meet.

I know immediately that she is not happy.

Not in the least.

I turn away quickly, cover my face with my hands, and close my eyes tightly at the same time. I can hear her loud sounds behind me though she doesn't sound as angry as she was before. I hear more splashing, more sounds from her mouth—including my name-sound—and the rustle of her strange clothing, but I do not turn around to look.

I will have to save my other thoughts and ideas for later when we are in our furs. For one reason, my erection completely disappeared when she looked at me like that; for another, I don't think she would be very receptive right now anyway.

Beh is angry, and I don't want her to be angry with me.

I hear the crunching sound of her feet on the rocks, followed by her hand on my shoulder.

"Ehd?"

I look up at her tentatively, and I'm glad to see her looking down at me without anger. There actually appears to be just the hint of a smile on her lips. I smile back—just a little—and slowly get to my feet. Beh shakes her head back and forth slowly as she makes more sounds.

I reach out with one hand, and she makes no move to stop me as I place it against her cheek. Her hair is wet now, and drops of cold water cascade down my arm. I move toward her, and her eyes drop to the ground as I gently brush my nose on her cheek. I don't want to push my luck, though, since I did not do what she wanted, and I know she is still not happy with me, so I drop my hand and step back.

Beh sits by the edge of the water while I pick up the fur-covered fish, unwrap them, and attach them with sinew, tied to the leather straps that hold my water skins. I quickly rinse out my fur wrap in the lake. The weather is not too cold, and I don't want to wear the fur again now that it is wet, so I tie it at my hip instead. With fish hanging on one hip and my fur on the other, I check the sky to see how late it is and go to Beh.

She is sitting on a rock with a small stick in her hand, slowly pulling snarls out of her hair. She's looking out over the lake, and I'm not even sure she realizes I am ready to leave now. I start toward her with the intent of leading her back to the cave, but the motion of her fingers, the stick, and her hair captivate me.

I have never seen anyone use a stick in such a way, and I instantly touch my own thick and matted hair. I recall women in my tribe using their fingers to sometimes pull out knots, but never a stick.

Beh lifts her hand to the top of her head, and she inserts the stick between two strands. She pulls down slowly, pausing a few times as the little branch gets stuck. I stare at her, mesmerized by the movement of her arms, fingers, and the flowing strands of her hair. She repeats the act over and over again, and the rhythm is strangely soothing.

Strange—like everything about her.

My mate.

My Beh.

She turns her head turns toward me, and I see a smile on her lips as they open, and more sounds come out. I take the last few steps that will bring me to her side and crouch down next to her, watching her movements closely. By the time her hair has dried, it is smooth and tangle free again. I reach up and touch the ends slowly and then brush my fingers through them, watching her face to make sure she doesn't mind me touching her.

"Ehd?" Beh tilts her head toward one shoulder and makes more sounds. She reaches out and touches the side of my head. She gestures with her fingers and then puts her hand on my arm, pulling me toward her and turning me slightly.

Then she places the stick between strands of my hair and moves it down.

"Ah!"

I jump up and grab at my head.

That hurt!

Beh covers her mouth with her hand, but I can see humor in her eyes. I glare at her, and she bites down on her lip as she drops her hand. She motions me back toward her, but I take a step away. More noises come from her mouth, and I still don't like them.

Beh sighs and then she takes the end of her hair and holds it out. I watch as she runs her hand down it, and I can almost feel my own fingers start to strain toward the strands, wanting to touch them myself. She holds her hair out again and beckons me.

I hesitate only a moment.

She keeps motioning, and I slowly move back to her side. Once I'm close enough, I reach out and touch her hair, reveling in it. I let her move me back down to a sitting position where I can reach her hair and she can reach mine. She goes slowly, and now that I am a little more prepared for the feeling, it doesn't really hurt that much—just a tugging sensation and the occasional, sharper pull.

When that happens, I yelp again, and Beh uses her hand to rub the spot. The action makes it feel better, but I also like that my mate is touching me. The whole time she is running the stick through my tangles, she lets me stroke her hair.

After Beh uses the stick to untangle my hair, she takes me back to the water's edge and coaxes me to tilt my head toward the cold water. She rinses my hair and then she combs through it again. Once she is done, she sets the stick down on the rock, looks me over, and smiles. I can't help but smile back at her—just the look on her face warms me more than the sun.

When she is done with my hair, she looks all around my face for a few moments. She rises up to her knees and cups my face in her hands. My heart beats a little faster as I feel the warmth of her body close to mine, but I am soon confused as she takes her thumb and pushes against the corner of my mouth.

I slowly open my mouth for her, and she looks inside. This I understand—she is checking to see how many teeth I have. At least with this, I am most impressive. I'm young and still have all of my teeth. Her eyes narrow a bit, and her nose wrinkles as she looks me over, and I feel a little nervous as she continues to examine me.

Her eyes settle on mine for a moment, and then she reaches down and takes from my hip the fur I washed earlier. She turns it around so the smoother leather part is showing and then wraps it around one of her fingers like she had done with her own clothing earlier.

Then she reaches in my mouth and rubs the edge of my front tooth.

I lean back to break the contact, confused, but Beh is insistent and eventually has her fingers in my mouth again, rubbing each of my teeth with the edge of the leather. When she finishes, she hands me one of the water skins, so I take a drink.

I run my tongue around in my mouth, and my teeth feel quite strange. They seem smoother than they were before. As I consider the difference, Beh wets another corner of my wrap from the water skin and uses it to rub at my forehead and cheek a little. She dips the edge in the water and rubs a little more—this time at my chin, neck, and jaw. I try to sit still as she cleans me off, and I can't help but remember again how my mother would do the same at the stream near our forest home, starting first with my father and then the children from oldest to youngest.

I never liked it, and I still don't, but I let her do it.

Beh finishes and then leans back a little, focusing on me from a different angle. Her eyes widen for just a moment, her lashes flutter, and she coughs a little before she looks away. Her cheeks become pink as she rinses out the fur and hands it back to me quickly.

I reach out and touch her cheek, but she ducks away from me and stands up with her arms wrapped around herself. I stand, too, confused, but I don't have much time to think about it. We have been at the lake far too long, and I need to get my mate back to the cave before dark. We won't have time to gather anything in the forest today, but I don't have any baskets for carrying such things anyway.

Thankfully, I now have a mate to make such things.

As I lead Beh from the lake's edge through the reeds, I grab several of the long, thin plants and hand them to her. Beh reaches out and gives me a quizzical look as she takes the reeds in her hands. I select more, hoping there will be enough for her to make a basket. I only have time to collect a few, but we can always get more later.

I'm glad to see Beh looking around the forest floor for food, especially when she stops and makes a loud sound with her mouth. I look at the plant she has found, and it looks familiar to me though I can't remember what it is until she places a little piece of it first in her mouth and then in mine.

Mint. It has a strong smell and a fresh, biting taste that leaves a cool feeling against my tongue. It's a plant my tribe would sometimes rub on meat to make it taste better when it wasn't as fresh any longer.

I chew the little leaf as Beh collects several more. When she's done, I hold my hand out and feel warm when Beh accepts my grip. She allows me to take her back through the forest, across the steppes, and to the rocks where my cave is.

Our cave.

I'm surprised that the sun is nearly setting as we approach the crack in the rock. Even though I certainly do not like some of the things that happened at the lake, this day is the best day I have had in a very, very long time. It goes by so quickly! I have my mate now, and being with her is much better than being alone. Feeling grateful for her presence, I cook the fish for her on rocks near the fire inside the cave.

Beh is silent as she sits on the single mat and takes the flat pelvic bone of a wild pig that serves as a plate but only picks at the food. I am ravenous after such a quick and busy day and devour two of the fish right from the hot rock next to the fire where they cook.

After I have my fill, I bring the water skin to Beh and hold it out to her. She accepts it from my hands with less hesitation than she did this morning and takes a drink. I quench my own thirst and then settle back down next to Beh and the fire. As she continues to pick at the fish's flesh, I reach up and scratch the top of my head and pause.

My hair is…is *soft*!

Like hers!

All the tangles are gone, and it hangs well past my shoulders in fairly straight strands. I run my fingers through it, hold it out away from my head, and try to turn in such a way that I can see. The strands escape my fingers, so I grab on to them again, tilting my head up and looking out of the corner of my eye to try to get a better view.

Beh laughs, and all my attention goes to her.

I haven't heard that sound in so long; I have almost forgotten what it sounds like.

The firelight glitters in her eyes as they crinkle up in the corners, and she tosses her head back as the sounds come out of her mouth. She wraps her arms around her stomach, and her whole body shakes with her laughter.

I give her a big smile, trying to contain whatever it is bubbling in my chest. As I smile at her, she stops laughing, and the pink tinge covers her cheeks again. This time when I reach out to touch the warm spot on her cheek, she doesn't pull away from me. I run my thumb over her cheekbone, and the color deepens.

Beh makes soft sounds as her eyes stay locked with mine. Leaning toward her, I watch closely to see if she will move away from me. When she does not, I touch the tip of my nose to her cheek and run it along the bone there. I inhale slowly, memorizing and savoring the scent of my mate.

Her hand covers mine where it still lies on her other cheek. She pulls it away from her skin, and I try not to feel too disappointed as she pushes me gently away with the palm of her hand on my chest. She still holds my hand between hers, laying it on her lap as she laces her fingers together with mine.

My mate is scared. I'm pretty sure it's not me she fears, but still, she is afraid of something.

I move closer to her, shifting myself to one side so our thighs are touching, and we are both facing the fire. One arm is crossed over my body, my hand still grasped in between hers. I wrap my other arm around her shoulders and pull her close to me. Beh lets out a long, shuddering sigh as she places her head on my shoulder.

I'm going to have to be very gentle with her.

Beh rests her head on my shoulder as the fire slowly turns to coals. I'm a little chilled without the wrap around my shoulders, and I realize my mate may also be getting cold. I turn to look at her and notice her eyes are closed. She has fallen asleep sitting up, leaning against me.

I wriggle my hand out of her grasp and try to move slowly as I turn toward her, slip my arm under her knees, and lift her up. I carry her to the back of the cave and lay her down in the middle of the furs. Once I verify she's sleeping soundly, I rebuild the fire and check around outside for any danger before I join her.

As soon as I lie down, she rolls to her side and tucks her head against my chest. I start to smile, but I see a single tear on her cheek as I wrap my arm around her, and my smile disappears. I pull the fur around us both, making sure it is tucked around her tightly before I lay my head down and close my eyes.

When I open them again, I'm met with my mate's gaze. Though I'm disoriented for a moment, the warmth of her body in the furs is welcoming in the cool morning air. One of my arms is still around her middle, and I pull her a little closer to me as I touch the top of her shoulder with my nose. She smiles, and my morning is perfect.

Beh only eats a small amount of the dried antelope meat and drinks a sip of water for her breakfast. I'm worried that she does not eat enough food to give her strength and wonder if she is already concerned that we will not have enough for the winter. I decide she must begin collecting food, so I bring her the reeds so she can start making collecting baskets. As I approach her, she tilts her head to one side and looks from me to the reeds.

She doesn't start weaving. Instead, she gets some of the mint leaves she gathered the day before and rubs them against her teeth, much like she had with the end of her clothing back at the lake. When she's done, she chews up another leaf and then goes just outside the cave to rinse her mouth with water from the water skin.

I follow her to keep her safe.

When she's done, she hands me some of the mint leaves. Unlike Beh, I did eat enough for breakfast, and I'm no longer hungry. When I don't do anything with the leaves, Beh sighs and takes them from me. Then she makes me open my mouth and rubs my teeth like she did with hers. Afterwards, my mouth tastes cool,

54

and my teeth are smooth again.

I look to my mate and blink a few times, licking my teeth and lips with my tongue. Beh chuckles and reaches up to wipe a bit of mint from my mouth. She hands me the water skin, and I rinse my mouth with the water like she did before we go back into the cave.

Beh goes to the edge of the fire and calls out my name-sound. I sit down next to her and look over the reeds I gathered. I hope she's ready to start weaving, but she isn't. Instead, she pokes her finger into the dirt and swirls it around. She uses my name-sound, points at the swirls in the dirt, and then points at other things. Considering how insistent she was about bathing, I'm surprised she wants to play in the dirt.

After a while, I grow tired of it all. I have no idea what she's doing, and I see no reason for it. Trying to direct her toward something useful, I pick up the reeds again and present them to Beh as she sits on the floor. She doesn't do anything, so I reach out and push the reeds at her a little more. Beh continues to just look at me in confusion, and I wish I had a basket to show her so she would know it is baskets we need, not mats or something else. I'm not even sure what else could be made out of reeds, but Beh should know.

Despite my prompting, Beh does not weave any baskets. In fact, once I sit down and try to tie a few of them together—just to show her what I want—she does start to intertwine the leaves, but she does *not* make baskets. She just ties them up in knots, which I take from her and untie. I try to hold the reeds in such a way that they look like a basket, but when Beh tries, she is no better at it than I am!

In fact, she's worse!

Frustrated, I toss the reeds to the floor of the cave and stomp out through the crack. I huff through my nose and try to figure out just what I should do next. We have already wasted a lot of time we should be using to gather food, and we still don't have any baskets. Beh needs to make baskets, and I need to hunt. That's how it works.

Apparently, Beh doesn't know this.

I don't know what to do. The bright sun reminds me that spring will provide us with much of the food we will need to survive the winter. Though the cold is never too bad inside of the cave, we will need food if we are both to survive. Meat will still be available though not plentiful. I realize Beh will need furs for clothing as well, or she won't be warm enough. I will need to hunt more and kill larger animals to give her what she needs.

Though summer has yet to come, my mind conjures up images of what could happen to Beh if she isn't warm enough or doesn't have enough food during the winter. She's so small, she won't fare well.

I must keep her warm.

I have to make sure she has enough food, too. Beh is my mate, and I have to provide for her, even if she doesn't make a basket to collect food.

I march back into the cave, take her by the hand, and head out to the steppes. Beh watches as I follow the line of trees on the other side to a grassy field where the grains stand on long, green stalks. They wave in the cool breeze as I walk into the center of them, look around and sigh. I have nothing else to carry them in, so I will have use my fur.

I take the wrap from around my shoulders and lay it on the ground, shivering a little in the wind. I grab the first stalk and try to pull the grains off the top one at a time. After collecting a few in my hand, I get frustrated and try to pull them all off at once. The grains scatter in the wet earth.

This is usually the point when I go back to the cave, pull out my spear and start hunting, but I can't do that now. I have to have food for Beh. If she won't make baskets and collect it for us, I will have to do it.

I take a breath and try to relax myself a little. As I start to pick up the dropped grains, Beh kneels beside me and starts picking them up as well. She places them on the center of my fur and then moves to one of the other stalks of grain. Within minutes, she's gathering much faster than I, but I don't stop. Actually, I try to catch up with her. It quickly becomes a game: who can get the grains off the stalks the fastest without spilling any on the ground.

Beh even laughs when I drop a whole handful, and the sound is lovely.

We are at it all day, and we collect much of the grain in the field.

With the fur tied up in a bundle to keep the grain from falling out, I toss the sack over my shoulder and take Beh's hand as we head back. Once we are inside again, I gather up one of the furs from the bedding and lay it across the low rock shelf on one side of the cave. Then Beh helps me pour the grains from one fur to the other so I can warm up.

It's quite cold as the sun begins to set, and I'm shivering by the time we're finished. Beh starts make a lot of noises with her mouth again. She hadn't really done that all day except when she laughed, and it was kind of nice. She grabs another fur from the bed and wraps it around me as she practically pushes me into the fire. She makes more, louder sounds as I take a deep breath and stare up at her. She sighs as her eyes meet mine, and though she still makes those sounds, she is much quieter now. She places some of the antelope meat on the cooking rock near the fire and sits back while it warms. After a few minutes, she pulls out the stick she had used before and starts to work on her hair.

I warm up slowly as I watch her intently. This time when she looks back at me, she smiles and moves closer. She reaches up, and she starts to pull the stick through my hair again. The slow, steady movements lull me as I watch the fire burn. As I feel my eyes drooping, I shift and lay my head down in her lap. Abandoning the stick, I feel her fingers take their place on my scalp as the warmth from the fire, the fur, and her touch soak into my skin.

Finally, after so much time despairing, I know contentment.

CHAPTER FIVE

Beh still sleeps though I have been awake since before light started to shine through the crack in the cave's entrance. I have already been up to stoke the fire and warm the small enclosure. As I lay next to her, I can't stop touching the hair on my own head.

It's never felt like this before.

It doesn't feel quite as good as Beh's does, but it still feels good.

I touch hers for a while, too, but soon she turns slightly in her sleep, rolling away from me. It's still chilly this morning, and Beh seems to realize this even though she doesn't wake up. She pushes her back up against my chest, her body seeking the warmth I am all too happy to provide.

I drop my hand from my hair and wrap it around her waist, pulling her closer as I tug the fur up to her shoulders. She sighs and settles back down against the fur she has tucked under her head. I don't know why she likes it like that, but she rolls up a few scraps of fur into a small ball and places it under her head when she sleeps.

My mate is strange.

But she is mine, and she can shove a fur under her head if she likes. I will keep the other ones over the top of her so she will stay warm.

I watch her face. She is peaceful and quiet in her sleep. As I look at her, I get a feeling in my stomach that I don't understand. It doesn't take long before the strange feeling moves lower, and I realize what it is. My tongue runs quickly over my lips as my mind begins to think of what it will be like to mate Beh.

She is *my mate. I can mate with her whenever I want. At least, I* should *be able to...*

I feel the fingers of my hand twitch automatically across her stomach. I brush against the smooth, soft material of her clothing as I move my hand down until it reaches the edge. I can feel a thin sliver of skin between the top part of her clothes and the odd, rough fabric of the lower part.

My heart begins to beat a little faster, and my neck and face warm with the flow of blood. I swallow once, and my gaze shifts along the length of her body. With my mouth open, I inhale her scent, and I feel myself grow hard. Instinctively, I rock my hips slightly against her back.

It feels really good.

I push against her a little harder, angling downward along her body. I reach inside her clothes, and I press the palm of my hand on her bare stomach. I pull her against me at the same time my hips push the opposite way.

There have been times when I have wrapped my hand around my shaft and moved it up and down until my seed has erupted. It always felt good to use my hand, but not like this—this is much better.

I rub against her again.

"Ehd?"

I didn't hear her wake up, but I'm glad that she did. I touch my nose against the side of her cheek and rock against her again.

"Beh," I sigh into her hair. It still smells good though the scent of fruit seems to be gone.

"Ehd!" Beh grabs at my hand, pushes it away from her skin,

and scurries out of the pile of furs, away from me. She hauls the top fur toward her and wraps it quickly around the top part of her body. Many sounds come out of her mouth—loud, fast, and harsh.

I look over to her, confused. I don't understand what she is doing.

Beh turns away and looks toward the fire, still making a lot of sounds. She is angry. That much is obvious, but what I've done wrong is a mystery. I start to move closer to her, but she cries out, stands, and wraps the fur more tightly around her shoulders. More loud sounds come from her mouth as she backs away from me and goes to the cave's entrance.

I stand as well, following her outside. She is crying, and I don't want her to be sad. Yesterday she was happy; I know she was. We had to work hard, but she was happy. Now she's upset with me, and I don't know why.

When I get close to Beh, she turns and narrows her eyes at me. I stop short as she holds her hand out and points at me with her finger.

"Ehd, no!"

Every muscle in my body halts.

I remember the sound from before, when I tried to help her undress at the lake. I take a quick step back, cowering slightly. Is she going to hit my nose again? I whimper and watch her closely as she pulls her hand back to her chest. She stands in the dim morning light and stares at me a moment. I can see hurt in her eyes.

I want to go to her, to hold her until she feels better, but I'm certain she won't allow it.

"Beh?" I say softly.

Beh groans as her hands come up and cover her face. She rubs her fingers into her eyes so hard I'm afraid she will hurt herself, but when she takes them away, her expression is softer. She looks from me to the ground and back to me again before making more sounds with her mouth.

They are soft noises again, though, so I listen carefully. I don't want her to say that *no* sound again. She doesn't, and after a while, she sighs and takes a step toward me. I flinch a bit, and she holds out her hand to me slowly.

Tentative, I reach out my own hand. When our fingers touch, Beh comes closer and takes my hand in hers. She whispers more sounds as her thumb runs over the back of my hand. Her eyes meet mine, and they are expectant. She looks out toward the steppes, makes more sounds, and looks back to me again. Her eyes are questioning, but I don't know what she needs.

I never know what she needs from me.

Unexpectedly, Beh takes a step forward and places her mouth on the side of my face.

Her lips are warm and soft, and I have no idea why she would do such a thing. I look at her out of the corner of my eye as I take a slight step backwards. I lift my hand to my cheek and touch the spot, rubbing at it a little.

Beh's lips smash together, and she seems to be holding in a laugh. I don't understand why, but I'm glad she doesn't seem to be sad now. Maybe whatever I did wrong was fixed when she put her mouth on my face. It would not surprise me.

My mate really is rather strange.

And beautiful.

Twisting my fingers around hers, I bring Beh back into our cave and get her a drink and eat some of the dried antelope meat. When we're done eating, Beh uses more mint leaves to rub her teeth and mine before heading out to find more food to store for winter. Though I have not tried for some time, I decide to make some traps in the pine forest to see if I can catch rabbits. Beh's strange foot coverings don't seem like they would keep her warm at all, and rabbit fur would be good for her hands and feet if it gets too cold in the winter months.

I think back to the previous spring and wonder how I managed to even keep myself alive. Before I had Beh, I didn't think about winter until the temperature changed from hot to cool again. Now I have to think about everything much sooner, even before the weather turns hot. I'm glad I'm alive—glad I didn't give up—because now I can take care of Beh. If I hadn't survived, she wouldn't have anyone to take care of her now.

I set three traps before we go back to the field and collect more grain. This time, I think to bring an extra hide with me so I don't have to use the one I am wearing. We work quickly, but when a rumble of thunder crosses the sky, we must head back to the cave with all we have gathered.

We are barely through the crack and into the cave before the rain starts to fall. I'm pleased I brought more of the firewood from the hidden space above the cave into the living area the day before, so I don't have to go out in the wet to get more. I build up a roaring blaze and drag one of the older furs from the bottom part of the sleeping area for Beh to sit on. It seems better than the grass mat I tried to weave last year, which is already falling apart.

I take my mate by the hand and lead her to the fur to sit. I drop down on the mat and tug at the edges of it to try to fix it up a bit, but it is no use, so I give up. I decide to finish working the antelope hide instead, hoping it will serve as some proper clothing for my mate.

Beh spends a moment staring intently at the mat I made, and then she looks over to the pile of reeds we brought back the day before. As the rain continues to pour down outside, Beh reaches over and pulls a pile of the reeds closer to her. She picks up two strands and twists them together just as pointlessly as she had before. She looks back at my mat and lays a few of the reeds side by side.

After a few minutes of staring at the reeds and the mat, she makes a short sound with her mouth, picks up the reeds, and starts weaving them in and out. I watch her intently while I work and for some time as she weaves many reeds together. Often she gets them tied up in knots, growls at herself, tears the whole thing apart, and then starts over again.

The second time she doesn't fare much better.

By the time the rainstorm finally subsides, she has managed to weave a decent-sized mat out of the reeds. The strands are woven tightly, and appear to hold together pretty well. I tilt my head to one side as she smiles broadly and lays the thing out on the ground.

Then she sits on it.

I narrow my eyes, watching her face.

It is not long before she squirms, whines, and then gets up again. She takes the mat in her hands and looks it over, feeling the surface of it and then looking at her fingers. She finally glances over to me, shakes the thing, and makes more growling sounds.

I guess she thought it would be comfortable.

Beh obviously isn't happy with the results, but I think it looks pretty good—just not something you would want to sit on. That is why my sitting mat is made of grass. I shift and hold it up to her, but she scowls at me. I move a little closer and reach out to take the reed mat from her. I look it over, bend it in the center, and use two pieces of sinew to tie the edges together, making it loop at the bottom. I tie a couple more pieces going down the side until it looks like it would at least hold the dried meat or berries. Grain would fall out, but it could certainly be used for something.

I hold it up and smile at Beh.

She smiles back, takes a long breath, and moves closer to me. I give her the grass mat to sit on as I go back to the antelope hide. As I scrape and work on the hide, Beh starts trying to make something else with the remaining reeds as the rain begins to fall hard again.

I remember other rainy days under the thick canopy of trees where I worked alongside others in such a way. It feels good to work beside someone again, especially when that someone is Beh. She may be strange; she may not know how to make baskets, and she may be very noisy, but she is my mate, and I'm thrilled she is here.

I focus on the hide, hoping to make it perfect for her. I don't know how long we work in silence next to each other, but suddenly Beh lets out a cry, and I look over to her.

Her face lights up with her smile, and she holds high a somewhat rounded object made out of reeds. It's entirely possible it could hold something if it absolutely had to. Beh laughs and turns it around, obviously proud of her accomplishment.

My heart beats faster, and my body tingles in her presence.

———————— ••◐◑◐•• ————————

Warm, soft furs and the scent of my mate's hair.

This is how I wake up, just as I have for the last several mornings. While I sleep, my mind creates images of Beh on her hands and knees in our furs as I enter her body, and now that I am awake, my body wants to continue along the same path.

I don't understand why, but Beh doesn't like this. When I rub up against her, she uses that *no* sound, and sometimes she gets angry, too. She does not mind when I touch her with my nose though, so I pull her body closer to mine and run my nose across her neck, inhaling her scent as I go along. I try not to push my hips into her back at the same time though it is still very, very tempting.

I hope if I am patient, she will let me put a baby inside of her soon.

A flash at the cave's entrance signifies yet another day of thunderstorms. I will have to go out today and check the traps I set —rain or not. At least I don't have to go all the way to the lake for more fresh water. The rain has filled my water skins from a trickle just outside of the cave.

Beh wakes slowly to my gentle touches on her neck, shoulder, and ear. For a moment, she rolls over and tucks her head into my chest. She pulls the fur up around her head and hides underneath it.

My mate does not like waking up in the morning, and it makes me smile when she does this. I don't really think much about how

I spent my mornings before Beh, but now that she is here, I can't imagine waking up any other way.

Even though I know she is sometimes sad and scared, and I think she still misses her tribe—wherever they are—I can't help but feel happy about her being here. She is extremely confusing, and I never seem to know just what she will do next, but I'm still glad she's here with me.

I didn't understand how lonely I had been until I had her.

She is most strange when it comes to her body, and I don't understand why. She doesn't seem to realize that going out to relieve herself alone isn't safe and gets angry with me when I follow her—especially if she has to relieve her bowels. I don't watch but stand and look the other way. Even that worries me somewhat, and I fear I will turn around to find her gone.

By the time Beh's eyes open completely, the rain has tapered off a bit. I bank the fire for the day, and we both head toward the pine forest. I have caught two young rabbits in my traps, but when I hold them up for Beh to see, she covers her eyes and shakes her head.

Strange.

I tie them at my waist and decide to head to the lake after all. The rain has slowed to a misting, and the clouds are beginning to thin out and blow away. I go to the far edge of the water where there is a small pile of flint, thinking it would be useful for Beh to have her own knife. I'm not good at flint knapping, but I should be able to make her something useful.

Beh sits down next to me as I pick up the flint as well as a nice, round stone to use to break off pieces. After a while, she stands and walks a few feet away near the small stream that feeds the lake. I can still see her out of the corner of my eye, so I don't worry. I continue working the flint until I have a knife that should be suitable for Beh to use on the antelope hide to make some new clothing.

I brush bits of flint off my legs as I stand and look over to my mate. She has her back to me and she is bent over. I can't tell what she is doing with her hands until I move closer. I come up behind her and look over her shoulder.

My mate is really, really weird.

She is also absolutely covered in brown, mushy clay.

She laughs and holds a large lump up to show it to me. Her mouth moves, and she makes enough noise to scare away a group of birds near the shore.

She is so, so strange.

I look at her out of the corner of my eye and wonder if there really is something wrong with her. She continues to make a lot of noise as she begins to smoosh her hands into the clay by the side of the bank. She comes up with two more handfuls and shows them to me. I just keep looking at her, wondering why she's playing in the mud.

She shakes her head and makes more sounds, gesturing wildly and pointlessly in the process. I reach down and try to pull her up by her elbow, but she bats my hand away. I growl under my breath and check the sky. It doesn't look like it's going to start raining again, and it's still early in the day. I suppose if she really wants to poke around in the clay, I will let her.

I sit on the rock next to her and watch as she squeezes and smooths the clay into a rough ball and then starts poking her thumbs into the center of it, making a hole. She continuously makes sounds as she pokes and prods at the stuff. For the most part, I ignore her—choosing to work on another flint knife instead. I sit close to her and occasionally glance at her out of the corner of my eye as I work. She seems to be very intent on whatever she is doing with the sticky clay.

At one point, she starts digging more of the clay out of the side of the inlet with her fingers and a small, round rock. I watch for a moment and then look around the shore for a better, flatter digging rock. I find one that is perfect and come back to her side.

I have no idea what she is doing or why, but I help her

anyway. With the flat rock, I sweep over the bank of clay and bring a large slice of it closer to her. Beh claps her hands together and makes more noise. She's smiling, so I think they must be good noises. She seems pleased, so I watch her go back to whatever she is doing with the clay while I finish my knife. By the end of the day, I have two good ones along with several chips that will be serviceable during the winter as well.

It is time to go back, and when I reach over to tap Beh, I see she has formed the clay into shapes. There are two round, hollowed out cups and two flat, round shapes. She is still smiling and seems proud of herself—much like she was with the basket she made that now holds the dried antelope meat.

After she goes to the water and washes all the clay off her arms and hands, Beh gives the cups to me and picks up the flatter pieces. Huffing out a breath, I carry the squishy cups. They're too floppy to be useful for anything, but Beh seems so excited about them and obviously wants to take them with us. I have no idea what she plans to do with them—drinking out of clay would just make water taste like mud—but I like how happy she seems about them.

By the time we arrive back at the cave, the sun is beginning to set. I lay the fish over the drying spit, and Beh fiddles around with the clay objects she made. She puts them near the fire and sits back with another big smile. She looks at me, makes some more sounds, and then helps me place the fish over the cooking rocks.

When the fish is cooked, and we have eaten, the cave is dark, and it is time to sleep. Beh continues to make soft noises with her mouth as we lay down in the furs. The sounds are almost constant, and I wonder how I will ever fall asleep if she keeps it up. I watch her mouth move for a moment and then look up into her eyes. They shine in the firelight.

She lies on her side as she continues with her sounds. One of her hands waves back and forth in time with the noises she makes. After a while, I can't take it anymore, and I reach over to cover her mouth with my hand. She quiets immediately, and I'm grateful. I pull her body close to mine and wrap the furs around us for warmth. Once we are settled, I look over to the fire to make sure it's banked and also give the cave a quick once-over to be certain all is well.

It seems to be. The cave is secure and my mate is safe and happy, so it must have been a good day.

Beh opens her mouth and starts making more racket, but I quickly cover her mouth with my hand again. I look down at her and lean close. I draw the tip of my nose over her cheekbone and down her jaw. Beh sighs and sinks into the furs. I lift my hand to touch her hair, and I tangle my fingers in it to feel the softness.

Beh reaches up and brushes the side of my face. She smiles slightly as her fingers run over my cheek and down to my shoulder. Her fingers trace the line of the muscles of my arm. She whispers something, and her cheeks tinge with the blood running underneath the skin. Her finger keeps tracing my bicep.

I flex, showing her my strength.

My mate's eyes dance over to mine and then back to my arm. More whispered sounds escape her as she smiles more broadly. I tighten my muscles again—flexing my arm, shoulder, and chest as well—and she seems pleased. She must realize I am strong enough to be able to protect her if she needs it as well as able to hunt for her and her children.

I want to give her those children.

I feel the tightening in my groin again, that same feeling I often have when I look at her. Her fingers glide over my arm and down to my wrist, leaving my skin with a tickling, tingling sensation. I move my hand from its usual place on her hip around to her stomach and then up to her shoulder. My fingers brush over her breast as they travel upward, and Beh stiffens.

I watch her lower lip disappear into her mouth, and I wonder if she might be hungry again. I stroke the side of her neck with my fingers, and Beh shivers in the firelight. I lean close to her again, running my nose along hers. I stop at the space between her eyes and inhale her scent.

The images from my nightly dreams rush through my head, and I feel my body react to my thoughts and the closeness of my mate's body. I watch her eyes as they stare into mine, her expression soft but uncertain. I don't want her to worry about anything. I want to take care of her in each and every way I can.

And I want her to care for me, too.

I don't care if she ever makes a basket that can hold grain, but I want her to be here with me. I want her to be close to me as I work or fish, and I want her to lie next to me in the furs at night. In my mind, she is with me always and forever.

Finally, it's clear to me that I want her for more than children.

CHAPTER SIX

The next day, Beh takes my hand as soon as we have eaten and leads me out of the cave. She points across the field to the pine forest and lake. I'm not sure why she wants to go back there again already, but I am willing to do whatever I can to please her.

Beh collects more mint leaves along the way, making me stop long enough to use one of the leaves to clean my teeth. Beh seems to think it is something we should both do in the morning and sometimes even at night, before we sleep.

Once we arrive at the lake, Beh goes immediately to the clay near the stream and starts poking around in it again. I watch the edge of the lake long enough to catch a fish to eat and then return to the flint near where she sits. She makes a few more objects with the mushy clay and sets them on the rocks before she approaches the lake to wash off her hands.

"Ehd!"

I look up from my flint and see Beh standing near the water. She makes more noise, and I stand to go to her. I smile as she takes my hand in hers but then frown as she pulls me toward the water.

I've already fished, and it's far too cold to get in the lake, so I stop and pull my hand from her grasp. Beh looks at me with her head cocked to one side, makes more noises, and points at the water.

I take a step back.

Beh's sounds become louder as she places her hands on her hips and raises her eyebrow to look at me. I narrow my eyes and look back at her, unsure exactly what she wants, but quite sure I don't like it. With a sharp noise and an equally sharply exhaled breath, Beh leans down and fills her cupped hands with water. Drops fly from her skin as she walks back to me and dumps the water on my arm.

My head fills with memories of my mother taking me to a stream in the summertime and making me stand in the water as she washed me off. I growl and step back, pushing the water off my skin. It's far too cold for washing, and my furs might get wet if she dumps water on me again.

It becomes apparent washing is exactly what Beh wants me to do as she tries to pull me closer to the edge of the lake. My mate might like to wash herself and clean off her teeth all the time, but I don't like the cold, and I'm not about to get in the frigid water.

I pull my arm away from her with a grunt and turn my back to her. I don't know why she seems to think getting in the water is a good idea, but I remember losing my balance while fishing early one spring, and I was chilled the rest of the day.

When Beh tries to take my arm again, I yank it away from her, pick up the fish I caught, and start toward the edge of the forest. I turn to look at Beh, and she is watching me. I stand still until she picks up the clay objects she's made and silently follows me home. I don't want my mate to be angry with me, but there is no way I am going to get in that cold water.

I cook the fish on the fire back at the cave, and before we are done eating it, Beh is making continuous noises again. I try to ignore the sounds, but it's not easy when she rarely stops. I hush her with my hand over her mouth, and it works for a while. Instead of making more noise, she brings mint leaves to me.

Since I refused to get in the cold water, I think I should probably rub my teeth with mint. Beh likes it when I do that, and I hope it will appease her. She does the same with her own mint sprig, and we soon crawl to the back of the cave and the warmth of the furs.

I get into the furs first, and Beh climbs in after. She lies on her back and looks up at me as I prop myself up on my elbow and watch her closely.

I can smell the mint on her breath, and I lick my teeth to feel how smooth they are. I wonder if her teeth are smooth as well, and I think they probably are. As I ponder, Beh's tongue darts out over her lips and captures my attention.

The curve of her mouth as she smiles up at me is enticing, and I can feel my desire to give her a baby growing as I stare at her. Beh's cheeks darken, and I tilt my head down to run my nose along her cheekbone as my arm wraps around her.

"Beh," I whisper her name-sound against her ear. My body is tightening inside of me, and in return, I tighten around my mate. We are close enough that I am sure she feels my want of her against her leg. I try not to press against her, but it's difficult.

Everything inside of me screams to roll her over, pull her hips up to meet mine, and take her.

She's my mate.

I see her throat bob as she swallows, and her palm presses lightly against my chest. Her fingers trace the line of muscle above my pounding heart. She makes a few soft sounds as her eyes dart between mine, and her fingers stroke softly against my skin. It feels so good, and I want more.

I bring my nose to the side of her face and stroke her skin gently before I move down her jaw to her chin. I cup her face with my hand as I look into her eyes again, touch the tip of her nose with mine, and hope she understands I only want to give her a baby. I don't want her to be afraid anymore. I want her to know I will care for her always. If I give her a baby, she'll know I will hunt for them and protect them with my life.

I run the tips of my fingers along the top of the unusual tunic she wears. The material is so soft, but not as soft as her skin just above it. I bring my fingers up the side of her neck until they rest on her cheek. I touch the edge of her mouth with my thumb, and the corners twitch into a smile.

Her eyes meet mine, dark and burning with the reflection from the firelight. I feel my chest rise and fall with my breaths as her hand mimics the motions of mine. It tickles a little as she rakes the tips of her nails through the scruffy hair on my face. I feel her take a deep breath before she closes her eyes. Her hand drops back down to my chest, and then Beh tilts her chin up, and her lips touch mine.

Before I have a chance to wonder just what she is doing, the smooth, soft touch of her lips have pressed against mine and rapidly departed. I blink a few times, looking from her lips to her eyes and considering.

Considering what?

I'm not quite sure.

Beh's eyes drop down from my face to her hand where it rests against my chest. Her lower lip is again attacked by her teeth. I place my thumb against her chin and tug at the skin until her lip is free and she looking at me. I wrap my finger up and over her chin and then run it slowly over her lips—back and forth. As I release her chin completely, her tongue moistens her lips.

Does she like that, having her lips touched?

Does she like having her mouth touch mine?

Do I?

Yes.

Yes, I do.

I grunt softly and tap her lips with my finger, my eyes imploring her to show me how to do that again. I was caught off guard the first time, but now I want her to do it more. I place my hand on the side of her face and tuck my fingers under her jaw.

With gentle pressure, I move her face a little closer to mine.

Beh leans into my hand as she moves nearer, and our lips touch again. Her arm comes around and cradles the back of my head as her fingers weave in and around my hair. It feels good, like it does when she pulls out the tangles. Our lips stay pressed together as her other hand moves from my chest and up to my shoulder.

She pulls back, breaking her lips away from mine to catch her faltering breath. I can feel my throbbing need of her intently as her hand runs down my arm. I don't want her to stop touching me. Actually, I want her to touch more of me.

"Beh," I murmur softly against her cheek. Beh's eyes stay on mine as I reach down and grasp at the tie holding my wrap around my waist. It slips out of its knot easily, and I push it away from my hips, exposing my hard organ to her, hoping she is impressed. As her hand runs down my arm again, I capture it with my fingers and bring it lower, pressing her palm to my length as I angle my hips toward her.

As soon as she touches my flesh, I hear her gasp, and she quickly pulls her hand away from me.

"Ehd…no."

I immediately stop my movements and look up at her warily, but she doesn't seem angry. She reaches down and wraps her hand around the edge of my fur wrap and covers me. She makes more sounds, and she runs her hand along the line of my jaw. She moves her head and touches her mouth to mine again.

With the touch of her lips on mine, I am once again captivated. Though my need for her remains apparent to me, even if she has covered it, this is a nice, distracting alternative. My fingertips ghost over her lips. Beh smiles and places her hand over mine. She makes more sounds, ending with a sound that reminds me of a snake.

She makes the same noise again.

"Kiss." She leans close and makes our mouths come together,

then repeats the sound. "Kiss."

I tilt my head to one side and brush my hand across her mouth. I watch her lips and tongue as she makes the strange hissing noise again. I lick my own lips, and I can almost taste her on them.

"Kiss."

There is a tickling feeling in the back of my head—something in my mind that feels strange. I narrow my eyes a little, and I feel like I am standing on the edge of a cliff, looking over the brink and feeling the wind in my face.

"Kiss, Ehd."

"Beh." I make her name-sound reflexively as I hear my own, and the sensation in the back of my head increases. I focus on her mouth as she brings us together again. I close my eyes this time, just as she does, and I feel her lips part slightly as her tongue touches my lips.

My mate is definitely strange.

And I like it.

I open my mouth and taste her and feel her tongue against mine and confirm that her teeth are indeed smooth like mine. It is a bizarrely automatic action. I never would have considered doing such a thing, but now that I feel her lips against mine and her tongue reaching into my mouth, it seems as natural as breathing. I'm captivated by the feeling—warmth and moisture, softness and pressure all at once. I feel my body shiver against hers, and my need for her grows more urgent.

I moan into her mouth.

Beh pulls back, panting, and her face is flushed. I watch her intently as her hands move to my shoulders and she tilts her chin down, still breathing hard. I keep my hand against her face and run my thumb over her cheekbone first and then her lips.

I definitely like it—lips and mouths and tongues together. When my tongue runs over my own lips, I can taste her there, and it's as if she's laid claim to me. I feel myself smile, and Beh returns the gesture through her blush. She makes more soft sounds, and this time I cover her mouth with my lips instead of my hand, which is very effective.

I *definitely* like this.

By the time she breaks away from me again, my lips feel tired from the abnormal exertion. I pull my mate tightly against my chest and try to ignore the continuing throbbing underneath my fur wrap and what it means when she will not touch me there.

She doesn't really want me for a mate, not completely. She is willing to stay with me and work beside me, but she doesn't want to mate. She doesn't want me to put a baby in her.

I place my forehead to her shoulder and let out a long breath, trying to hide my sadness.

⊷•••◦❨◗◦•••⊷

The light rain stops completely during the night, and the sun is shining brightly by the time my mate's eyes open. I have been watching her for some time now, and I have come to the conclusion that I must do more if I am going to win her over. Even though she is here with me, and she is obviously my mate now, I want her to want it, too. I want her to open herself to me…give herself to me. After the previous night, feeling how wonderful just her mouth on mine felt, I have been plagued with thoughts of how good it would feel to have my penis inside of her.

So now I am going to do everything I can to make her happy and convince her to mate with me.

I start with breakfast.

As soon as her eyes open, I kneel beside her with fresh pieces of rabbit meat in my hand. I cooked them very slowly over the coals, and I've blown on them to cool them off a little because I want the temperature to be just right for her—not too cool or too hot. I stare into her eyes as she rolls over and pulls the furs up under her arms. She props herself up on one elbow and smiles up at me through blurry eyes.

Her mouth makes sounds, and I silence her with a piece of the meat. She gnaws at it slowly and seems to like it as she swallows and accepts another one from my fingers. I give her a drink of water, careful not to spill any on her, and then offer her more of the tender flesh.

Once she has eaten her fill, I hold her hand and take her outside of the cave to relieve herself. As soon as we reach the area, I let go of her hand, turn, and cover my eyes with my fingers so she knows I am not watching her. When she places her hand on my arm, I know she is done, and I smile down at her. She gives me a half smile back, but her brow is furrowed.

I wonder if I have done something wrong.

Determined, I take her back to the cave to gather up what we need for another trek to the lake. I want to check the rabbit traps I reset as well as give Beh a chance to wash, which she seems to like to do. Every time we go there, she spends some time washing herself in the water, which is beginning to warm nicely now that summer is upon us. When she goes into the water, I try not to look at her body, but it's difficult.

I startle as Beh makes a squeaking sound when we get into the cave. I rush around her, holding my arm out to protect her from whatever has frightened her, but there is nothing there. When I look at her face, she is smiling and pointing toward the fire. I follow her finger to the little cups and plates she made from the clay and then look back up at her, confused.

Beh makes more sounds, kneels next to the fire, and holds up the little brown cup. I take it in my hand, and I am surprised at how hard it is! It's no longer mushy and soft but feels more like a rock. The edges are rough and scratch the tips of my fingers. I turn it over and over again in my hand. Even the inside of it is dry and rigid. I look back to Beh, amazed at what she has handed to me.

She holds up one of the plates as well, which is also dry and unyielding. I give her the cup back and examine the plate a little more closely. I try to bend it with my fingers, but it doesn't bend at all. It doesn't even feel like clay anymore, and I wonder just how strong it is.

I knock it against one of the cooking rocks, and it shatters with a horrendous sound. The noise is loud and echoes through the cave. I jump up and back away, bringing Beh with me. She is yelling now, and I wrap my arms around her to shield her from the thing.

After a moment, I realize it is just sitting there in pieces, and I let my struggling mate free. She stares at the plate, now broken into three pieces, and her eyes go wide. Beh drops down to her knees and reaches for the fragments as a strangled cry comes from her mouth. She covers up her lips with her hand, but I can still hear her repeating the same set of sounds over and over again while I stand behind her, unsure and ashamed.

"Ohmygod...ohmygod..."

I know immediately that I haven't just destroyed the clay plate she made, but I've also ruined any chance at all I had of making her want me to put a baby inside of her. I didn't know the plate would break—it seemed so sturdy in my hands! Though it felt like a hard stone, it is apparently more like the flint I use for tools, easily broken if not handled correctly.

"Ohmygod...ohmygod..." Beh rocks back and forth on her heels, and I want to go to her and hold her against my chest, but I'm afraid. She is so upset, and I'm the reason for it. I have definitely made a huge mess of this, and I watch helplessly as she picks up a couple of the pieces and holds them in her hands.

I hear her mumbled sounds turn to sobs, and she holds the pieces against her chest, and I cannot stand it anymore. I move up behind her, reaching out and touching her shoulder with my hand. She turns quickly and screams horrible sounds at me. The pieces fall from her hands as she stands up and continues yelling. As she does, her hands reach down to the strange wraps that cover her legs. In the center of it—right below her navel, there is a small round thing. She grips it, shaking the little object as she screams, and I cower from the sound.

With another sob, Beh drops down to the ground again and grabs into her hands the pieces of the plate I have broken. When my mate turns her head to look at me, I can't meet her eyes. I drop down into a crouch and lower my head. My hair falls over my forehead, effectively hiding me from her. I wish she couldn't see me at all, but I can still feel her eyes on me.

Though I still feel the urge to hide, I have to follow when Beh rushes out of the cave with the pieces of clay in her hands. Even if she does not want me at all, I have to keep her safe. I follow her at a distance as she runs off across the grasslands with the clay pieces still clutched in her fingers. I have to jog at a good pace to keep up with her and run faster as she approaches the pine forest and the cover of trees. Beh runs all the way to the lake, goes right up to the side, and flings the broken pieces far off into the water.

I come to a quick halt on the rocks behind her and tense, waiting to see what she will do next. A moment later, Beh drops to her knees and lets out a long moan. Risking further wrath, I go to her and wrap my arms around her from behind.

I don't understand. I never understand, but I hold her as tightly as I can until her struggles subside, and she turns toward me. Her arms go up and around my neck, and she tucks her head against my chest. My mate alternates between crying, screaming, and smacking her palm against my chest or shoulder as she makes her strange noises. All I can do is hold her and wait until she collapses in exhaustion and closes her eyes. I feel her relax against me as her breathing becomes metered and quiet.

I look down into her tear-stained, sleeping face and sigh. Pulling my legs underneath me, I slip one arm under her legs and the other behind her shoulders. I brace my legs underneath me and stand up with her in my arms. I'm grateful she's small and not too heavy to lift this way. Her head flops against my chest as I turn from the water and carry her up the bank, through the woods, across the steppes, and into our cave.

Looking around the cave, I decide not to lay her down in our furs. Instead, I lower myself slowly in front of the fire and continue to hold her close to me. I use one hand to add more wood from the pile but manage to let her sleep at the same time.

It is late in the day when she wakes, and her bloodshot eyes look up at me. I feel the shiver run through her body as she stares at me, looks around the cave, and then closes her eyes again for a moment. When she opens them again, she pushes herself from my lap and goes to the small rock shelf where the water skins sit. She picks one of them up and brings it back to us.

I watch through my hair warily as she picks up one of the small round cups she made and pours water into it. She holds the cup out to me and then pours a second cup when I take the first from her hand. I look at the water for a moment and then quickly drink it down. I run my tongue over the edge of the cup, and it tastes like mud in my mouth. It is not like the cups my mother created out of broad leaves laced tightly together, but it certainly still holds the liquid securely. Though the sides of the cup have a muddy taste on my tongue, it doesn't make the water taste like dirt.

Beh is looking at me as she drinks from her own cup, and I try to smile at her with my head bowed down—still hiding. She looks down to the ground, but there is now the hint of a smile on her lips. She reaches over toward the fire, and I can hear a slight scraping sound. I glance up through my hair and see her gathering up tiny broken shards still on the ground. I know I should probably do it myself—it is my fault the plate is broken—but I'm afraid to move. I only want to do things that made her happy today, and I am failing miserably.

Beh stands with the broken bits in her hands and heads toward the entrance to the cave. I crawl behind her, still unwilling to let her go out alone but also not wanting to show myself in my shame. Once we are both outside, she takes the remaining broken pieces and tosses them off the cliff and into a shallow ravine before she turns back to me. I'm standing right by the cave entrance, pushing myself against the rock wall, hoping she won't yell that *no* sound at me again.

Beh walks up to me and stands very close. I let my eyes meet hers, and she takes a long, deep breath. She lifts her hands away from her sides and takes my fingers in her grasp. With a small tug, she brings herself against my chest and tips her forehead on my shoulder. My arms go around her, and I feel her relax into me.

"Beh?"

She turns her head to look up at me and smiles, but her eyes remain dull. My thumb strokes her cheek softly as she makes muted sounds with her mouth. I want to put my lips on hers to make her quiet again, but I'm not sure how well that would be received at the moment. I still feel lost and confused. Without knowing what else to do, I pick her up and carry her back into the cave as the rain begins again. She makes a little squeaking sound as I lift her into my arms but doesn't protest as I lay her back on the furs and bring her the remaining rabbit meat from earlier.

I feed her a little piece at a time from my fingers, followed by sips of water from the cups she made. My mate is quiet as she eats, and I alternate between feeding her and slowly stroking her arm with my fingers.

After the meat is gone, Beh's eyes meet mine. She watches me carefully as she reaches up and runs her hand over my cheek. With her fingertips, she slowly pushes the hair from my forehead. I lean against the warmth of her palm, and when she smiles this time, the firelight hits her eyes and makes them sparkle. She leans forward, and her lips brush softly over mine.

Finally, I am forgiven.

CHAPTER SEVEN

The spring rains have finally ended. Though the sun is high in the sky, Beh still hasn't moved from our bed. Eventually, I climb back into the furs with her and nuzzle against her neck with my nose until she is roused. She still seems tired, and when I take her outside to relieve herself, she gasps loud enough for me to turn around to make sure she isn't harmed. There is nothing around her to pose any threat, but she is squatting near the ravine and looking down at her hand. There is blood on it, but I don't think from her expression she is injured—just worried.

Her eyes widen, and she glances up at me as I approach to find out what is wrong. Her strange leggings are around her ankles, and she starts to stand to pull them up her legs—she still doesn't want me to see her body—but then stops and looks to her hand again.

She is bleeding. Her eyes well up with tears, and at first I think she might actually be hurt. As soon as I am close enough, I know from the smell of the blood that it is different from a wound, and I know why. It is her bleeding time. What I do not understand is why that makes her cry. She is too old for this to be the first time her blood has come.

I bend down and pick her up with her leggings still down around her lower legs. Even though she pushes at me, gets all wriggly, and makes loud sounds, I don't stop or put her down. I remember the other women of my tribe—especially my mother and sisters—and what they did during their bleeding time. I carry Beh back to our cave and hold her still until I can dig one of the older furs out from the bottom on the depression where we sleep. I spread it out on the floor and sit Beh on top of it.

I know she doesn't like things to be messy.

She bursts into tears again as she pulls at her leggings but stops before she gets them all the way on.

I don't have any of the things like my mother used to give my sisters when they were bleeding, but I think I can figure something out. I quickly cut strips of antelope hide—one to tie around her waist, and two to go between her legs and catch the blood. I don't have any wool or anything to put between them to help absorb, but I know some dry grass can be used until we find something better, and fold some in between the two straps of leather.

I start with the strap of leather around her waist and pull her up so she is standing. She pushes at me, but I grab her hand. Since she is using her other hand to hold her lower garment part way up her legs, she can't push me anymore. I kick at her ankle until she spreads her legs and lets me maneuver the other pieces between her thighs. Then I wrap the ends around the strap around her middle. It seems to fit reasonably well once I get the whole contraption on her. Beh alternates between laughing and crying as she shifts around, adjusts the straps, and then hugs me.

My mate is weird.

She is also very tired and keeps crying off and on throughout the rest of the day. Thinking she might want to untangle her hair, I bring her a stick from one of the trees outside, and she cries again. I bring her a drink of water, and she cries again. I bring her some meat from the fire, and she cries again.

I give up and plop down a few feet away from her.

She looks over at me, her chin begins to quiver, and she starts crying again.

I move closer, and she wraps her arms around me. We stay inside the cave where I keep the fire going and feed her pieces of dried meat as she lays on the old fur and rubs her stomach. When the piece of leather strap and grass are filled with blood, Beh replaces it with another one. I go to the ravine to throw the dry grass away and wash the leather even though the water there has a foul odor and isn't really any good for cleaning or drinking. I will have to go to the lake for that, but I don't want to go too far away from Beh.

I place the somewhat washed leather up high in a tree with the hope that no predators will be attracted to the scent and steal it. I make her several more from an old hide, and she cries when I give them to her.

Thankfully, Beh feels better the second day, and she follows me to the lake to wash out the leather pieces in the clean water. After a few days, Beh stops bleeding and crying, and my head stops hurting.

⋙ ⟫•●◑◆◐●•⟪ ⋘

There is nothing—nothing in my entire existence—that compares to waking up with my mate curled tightly against my chest. Though I had not realized it at the time, the loneliness had weighed heavily on me during my time of isolation, and now I'm beginning to wonder if I would have survived much longer on my own. I could hunt and protect myself, but the lack of companionship had been slowly destroying my will to live.

Before Beh, I hadn't thought about the loneliness in such a way. Maybe I just ignored how I felt when I would lie awake and look out into the darkness of my cave, listening to nothing except the crackling of the fire and the wind outside. I only remember feeling empty inside.

Now that Beh is beside me, like she has been for the first part of the spring season, I feel warm and full.

Tensing my muscles, I pull her closer to me and nuzzle my

nose against the top of her head. Beh sighs in her sleep but does not move as I hold her close, watch the burning coals, and doze off again with my mate's body pressed close against mine.

The next day, we head out toward the lake again. I bring along the antelope fur so I can wash it and finish it for Beh. Along the way, I collect three rabbits, which means Beh will have good fur for mittens and foot coverings for winter, too. She still doesn't seem impressed by the rabbits, I notice, and like the last time, she won't even look at them when I try to show them to her.

Once we reach the lake, Beh goes immediately to the place where she found the clay before. I swallow hard, wondering if she is still upset with me, but she doesn't appear to be angry. She seems excited to find the clay again. Before I start on the fur, I follow her to the little stream and find a nice, flat digging rock. I pull the clay together in a pile and then watch her form some of it into smooth balls. I make a couple of them for her, and she smiles at me with sparkling eyes as I work. When I'm done, Beh smiles and places her lips against my cheek. My heart begins to beat a little faster as I wait and hope she will bring her lips to my mouth as well.

She doesn't, and after a moment, I frown and grunt to get her attention. Beh looks over at me with questioning eyes, and I reach out and place my fingers on her lips. After a moment, I remove them and press them over my own mouth.

Beh's lips press together as she holds back a grin. I lean forward a little, still hopeful, and she narrows the distance between us until her mouth is on mine. I close my eyes and revel in the warmth of the sun, her lips, and her presence. Her fingers creep up around my neck and dig into the back of my head, holding me closer as her mouth opens to mine and our tongues touch.

If I weren't already on my knees, I would have fallen to them.

I reach my arms around her shoulders and bring her body closer to me. There's a rock digging into my knee, and I don't care. I can feel myself getting hard, and I don't care about that either. Just this—just her lips against mine—*that* is a wondrous thing to me.

Beh pulls away from me, breathing hard and leaning her forehead against mine. I lock eyes with her, silently pleading for more when Beh makes that sound again—the one that sounds like a snake.

"Kiss."

I tilt my head looking first to her mouth and then back to her eyes.

"Kiss, Ehd."

"Beh…" My fingers stroke up her arm and down again as my eyes focus on her mouth.

She moves forward and presses her lips firmly against mine, then backs off again.

"Kiss."

I wish she would stop making noises and just keep our mouths together, but she keeps doing the same thing over and over again. She touches my mouth with hers, makes that snake sound, then does it again. I don't understand what she is doing, and it is frustrating.

I growl low and dig my fingers into her hips. I tug her closer to me and place my lips tightly on her mouth to silence her. I reach into her mouth with my tongue, and she moans against me. All other thoughts inside my head depart until nothing is left but her scent and her taste.

When we finally stop, Beh's cheeks flame red, and she looks down to the muddy handprints I have left on her clothing. Her eyes dart back to mine, and she raises an eyebrow at me. I watch her carefully, wondering if the mess has made her angry and what she might do if it has. She doesn't seem vexed though and uses her own clay-covered hand to brush some of it away. This makes it worse, and she snickers and shakes her head from side to side.

I decide she must not care very much if the strange clothing gets dirty. She must know I am preparing the new fur for her to replace the odd things wrapped around her body now.

They look so uncomfortable.

Toward the end of the day, Beh has a stack of clay dishes sitting in the sun on the rocks, and she is in the lake washing off. I've found a small group of wild onions, which I've pulled out of the soft ground near the edge of the pine forest and washed off in the lake. I wonder if Beh knows how to cook them. I've eaten them often because they are one of the few plants I know I can eat without becoming sick to my stomach, but when I try to cook them, they burn in the fire. I know my mother used to cook them, but I can't remember how.

When Beh comes out of the water, I hide my eyes. She dresses quickly and comes over to me, making sounds with her mouth through her smile. I watch her approach, and I am thrilled when she leans over and covers my mouth with her lips again. She drops down beside me, and I hold up the onions.

Beh takes a bunch of them in her hand and turns them around and around. She brushes a bit of dirt I have missed off of one bulb and makes more noise. I'm about to reach out and cover her mouth when she jumps up and cries out. I am immediately at her side, wrapping my arm around her and holding her against me, looking all around for whatever alerted her.

My mate giggles and covers her mouth with her hand until she has contained herself. I narrow my eyes, and she brushes her fingers over the edge of my jaw before darting away toward the edge of the lake again. Near the water are several tall plants with long, brown tops—cattails—which I recognize. Beh continues with her noises as she reaches down to the bottom of the plant and pulls one up—root and all.

As soon as she pulls it out, I recognize it. This is a root my mother would cook for us, but I had no idea it came from the bottom of a cattail. I only remember using the long stalks to entertain my brothers. They liked to pull them apart and send the seeds flying in the wind.

We work together to dig up more of the roots, and soon we have too much to carry back in one trip. Beh prattles on the entire time, and I'm starting to feel another ache in my head from it. Leaving her clay bowls and plates behind, we gather up the onions, cattail roots, and rabbits in my fur before heading back to the cave. Beh wants to use the new fur I've made to wrap up the food, but I pull it away from her hands and wrap it around her shoulders instead. I don't want it to get dirty because it's for her.

We head back to our home after a wonderful day of work. Beh seems as confused as I am about cooking the cattail roots and the onions, and eventually we just let them sit close to the fire until they are at least warm enough to eat. Afterwards, we sit and watch the coals, and I wrap my arm around Beh's shoulders. She leans against me, and I inhale the fresh scent of her hair.

⫸ •••◉❰◉•••• ⫷

Beh and I fall into a routine through the summer.

I can't help but think of my tribe as Beh and I work side by side, gathering grains in the fields and plants in the forest. She knows some other plants we can eat aside from the cattails, and we store what we don't eat in the clay pots Beh has made. She has even fashioned covers for some of the pots to keep the moisture out. As the back of the cave becomes full of such things, my worry about keeping my mate healthy through the winter diminishes.

Beh leaves most of the clay dishes to dry in the sunshine for a day before she sets them near the fire for a long time. Only when she indicates they are ready does she let either of us put anything inside of them. With one particular pot she makes, she spends even more time keeping it close to the fire. She never seems completely happy with it in the morning and lets it set again. Eventually, she takes one of the clay plates and sets it inside the coals and then places the pot on top of it.

I have no idea what she is trying to do, but like I have thought many times before, my mate is strange, and it doesn't matter to me that she is.

When I look at her, my chest feels larger. Sometimes my heart pounds, and often my penis grows hard and thick, wanting to put a baby in her. In the night, she places her lips on mine and lets my hands touch her face, arms, back, and legs—but never her breasts or the warm spot between her legs. She will run her hands over my chest and arms but never below my waist.

It's driving me insane with desire.

There is also a mystery around her—a very, very strange mystery. Specifically, it's around the top half of her body. It's another piece of clothing wrapped around her back, over her shoulders, and around her breasts. I can feel it when I put my hand on her back, though when I try to feel it in the front, Beh pushes my hand away. I have no idea what the thing is, only that it is pale pink—like the beginning of a sunset on the clouds—and that she only takes it off when she is bathing.

As I relieve myself into the ravine, the morning air is decidedly cooler than it has been in recent days. I wonder how long it will be before the leaves on the trees begin to fall and there is snow on the ground. I should try to hunt another large animal before then. We have a decent amount of dried meat and fish in Beh's clay containers, but winters can be unpredictable. Having more would be better. It would also provide a larger piece of leather for carrying the last of the grains in the field or arrowroot plants back to the cave.

Beh's pots are good for storage inside the cave but too heavy to carry around. Since the antelope is for Beh's winter furs, I did not scrape the fur off to make more supple leather that could be used as a carrying pouch, and Beh's baskets aren't much better than they were in the beginning. Beh hasn't made any clothing for herself out of the fur though she does wrap it around herself when she is cold.

Maybe I will go out onto the steppes and look for a nearby herd of antelope or horses. It will take a long time to dig another pit trap, but it will still be helpful. Beh can gather more of the field grains while I dig.

I return to the cave with this thought in my head, and find Beh hovering over the pot she has been warming in the fire for many days. She has filled it with water and placed it close to the fire. She sticks her finger in the water every few minutes, and I wonder if the water is getting hot in the clay pot. Eventually she seems satisfied and adds some of the arrowroot and wild onions to it, as well as a little of the pheasant meat from the bird I caught and roasted yesterday.

A sudden, long forgotten memory comes into my head. It is the image of my mother hovering over pots of tightly woven leaves. She would place rocks in the fire until they were hot and then place them in the woven basket to heat the water inside. Beh's way seems to take less time.

I watch in silence, and when Beh is done, the stew she has made is pretty tasty. It is undoubtedly the best thing I have eaten in a very, very long time. As I tip up a clay bowl and pour the contents into my mouth, I groan with appreciation and then pull Beh into my lap to hug her to my chest.

She giggles and wraps her arms around my neck. When she tilts her head up, I capture her lips with mine. I'm too happy to wait for her to instigate the action like I usually do. Beh hums against my lips, and I hold her tightly to my chest.

When we part, Beh narrows her eyes a little as she looks up at me. It is a look I have seen on her face before, usually right before she tries to do something I have never seen her try before. It is a look of resolve and determination.

"Beh," she says as she points to her chest. Then she places her hand on my shoulder. "Ehd."

I tilt my head to the side and hug her gently.

"Beh," I repeat.

She smiles, leans closer, and places her lips against mine briefly.

"Kiss."

I frown. I hope she isn't going to start making that snake noise over and over again. Reaching up, she touches the tips of two fingers to my lips and then to her own before she repeats the sound again. I watch her eyes dance around my face. She sighs and then points to herself and then me, saying our name-sounds again.

Strange mate. I smile at her so she knows I accept her oddities.

Beh sighs, this time in frustration.

"Kissssss," she says again, touching our lips with her fingers before she leans in and gives my mouth a quick peck. "Kiss!"

I tilt my head the other way so I can see around her and wonder if there is more of the stew to eat.

"Kiss!" Beh wraps her arms around my neck and comes very close. I can feel her breasts touching my chest. She touches her lips to mine... "Kiss," ... again ... "Kiss," ... and again ... "Kiss."

She leans back and I whimper, trying to move closer to her face so I can repeat the motion. I want to taste her to see if she now tastes like the stew we had for breakfast, but she places her hand on my chest and pushes me back. I frown again.

Beh presses her fingers to her lips, makes that sound, and then touches my mouth again. I lean in a little—hoping she'll put her mouth on mine. This time I'm going to be quick enough to taste her.

But she doesn't.

Instead, she takes my hand and places my fingers on her lips, then makes the sound again.

"Kiss."

Then she places my fingers over my own mouth. My eyes narrow. I don't understand this game she is playing.

"Kiss," she whispers softly. With my palm on her mouth, she makes the sound over and over again. She touches her chest, says her name-sound, does the same to me, then goes back to the snake sound.

I watch her lips as she makes the sound and notice how her lips spread wide, her teeth nearly come together, and I can see her tongue touching the back of her teeth through the little space between them. My mate has very nice, straight teeth. I run my own tongue over the back of my teeth and hiss like a snake.

"Sssss…"

Beh's eyes widen and she smiles broadly. Then she cries out, startling me. She wraps her arms back around my head and attacks my mouth with hers. Her tongue runs over mine with more gentility than her original motion would imply, and I am glad to find out she does taste like the stew.

She breaks away, and we smile at each other. My muscles tense up in anticipation of her doing it again, but she sits motionless, just watching me. When I lean forward, she leans back and makes the sound.

"Kiss."

Again, I am a little distracted by her tongue on the back of her teeth and the way she sounds like a snake. Well, almost, but not quite. The first sound is harsher, and her tongue flicks the top of her mouth when that part of the sound comes out. I try to move my mouth and tongue the same way.

"Kzzhh."

Beh squeals with joy and plants her mouth on mine again. When she breaks away, the sparkle in her eyes is beautiful. She makes a lot more sounds but still ends with the same noise.

"Kiss."

"Kzzzzzz."

I am rewarded with her lips and tongue and her hands wrapping into my hair.

<hr />

"Khzz!"

The warmth of my mate's mouth covers mine, and it sends

tingles of sensation through the rest of my body as her tongue traces over my lower lip. The game that annoyed me in the beginning is now my favorite thing to do. Every time I make the sound, she touches her lips to mine, and I make that sound as often as possible.

At night, I make it over and over again.

Beh pushes my shoulders lightly with her fingers as she breaks away from me with a laugh. She makes more sounds, but none of them are the hissing sound, so I sigh and go back to my work. The spear I used to kill the antelope is still in good shape, but I'm fixing it up anyway. I use a long sliver of flint to slowly shave off flakes of wood to make the point sharper.

Beh sits beside me on a rock near the water, running a stick through her wet hair. The lake water is almost too cold for bathing, but Beh does it anyway. Now she smooths out her hair, and as much as I would like to distract her with placing our mouths together, I love how her hair feels when she's done. I also hope she will do the same with mine as well. Earlier, I dunked my head under the water and shook out my hair, but it was too cold for me to get in.

Throughout the summer, Beh continues to push me into the lake to wash off, but it isn't so bad when the water was warm. She uses soaproot to help get the dirt off of my body and out of my hair, though she still never lets me help her. She doesn't want me to see her without her strange clothing in place, even when the sun beats down and it is hot in the cave.

Now the weather is beginning to cool again, and summer is departing quickly.

I glance at Beh as she continues to work through the snarls in her hair, and I work the flint against the wood. Her arms are raised up above her head, and I like the curve of them, and I think about touching them. Thinking about her arms leads my eyes to look to her shoulders and back and finally to the curve of her backside.

I swallow hard when she drops her stick and has to bend

forward to retrieve it. My heart beats faster, and my tongue pops out to moisten my lips.

My hand hurts, and I realize I've nearly cut myself open with the flint. Luckily, I haven't—it's just scratched. I've managed to dig a gash in the upper part of the spear, though. It's fixable, but it looks strange. The little chunk that came off is an odd shape— almost like two tiny fingers next to each other, but held slightly apart.

Looking up at Beh, I see her running her fingers through her hair, and I wonder if the little piece of wood was bigger, would she be able to use it to untangle her hair?

"Khzz?" I know I am pushing my luck—she just put her mouth on mine when she started on her hair, and she isn't even done yet. She looks at me sideways and narrows her eyes before she leans over and presses her lips quickly to the side of my mouth. I frown. It's nice but not what I want.

Beh giggles and makes more mouth sounds.

Once she is done with her own hair, I discard the spear and flint and kneel close to her. I bow my head toward her, and she uses the stick to smooth out my own hair, which just touches my shoulders now. Once she is done, we collect her most recent clay pieces—a fairly large bowl and a lid to go on top of it—and head back home.

Beh holds her bowl in her arms as we walk across the field, and I walk beside her. As we get close to the edge of the woods, I stop and pull up a clump of yellow nutgrass I noticed on our way to the lake. Beh ends up a little ahead of me, and I watch her from behind as she walks.

I like the way her hips move, and my mind wanders, thinking about what they might look like bare. More importantly, what would it look like if she were bare with my hands wrapped around her hips, pulling her back against me.

Is she going to let me do that any time soon?

Trying to force the thought from my mind, I sigh and move to catch up. As I get close, I notice there is a tiny hole in her clothing up by her shoulder. I can see the little strap of pink underneath it. Without actually thinking about it, I reach out to poke at it.

Beh glances over her shoulder at me, and I give her a little smile. She smiles back and turns her eyes back down the meandering path. I poke at the little hole again—my finger fits just inside of it, and Beh looks over fast enough to see my finger inside the little hole at her shoulder.

Her face immediately contorts into an expression of sorrow, and she lets out a long moan followed by a lot more sounds. The bowl is still in both hands, but she seems to be trying to both hold it up and touch the hole I have found. She stops abruptly and turns, shoving the bowl into my arms as she continues to make noise and closely examine the little tear.

My mate is upset, but I hope now she'll make something out of the antelope fur I gave her. I would even give her my own fur wrap if she preferred, but it wouldn't fit her very well. It would probably fall right off of her.

That idea didn't sound all that bad.

Finally, looking to her face, I see her tears.

CHAPTER EIGHT

That night, I hold Beh tighter than usual and make sure she is sound asleep before I let myself doze. She didn't cry as hard as she did before, but there were many times during the evening when she had tears in her eyes. I know how frustrating it is to have to make new clothing, but I don't understand why it upsets her so much.

I don't like it when my mate is sad, and I don't know what I am supposed to do to make her happy again. I consider my previous plan of doing everything I can for her all the next day, but I also remember how that turned out the first time I did it. I need something better.

A gift.

When people in my tribe were mated, they gave each other gifts. Men would bring their best furs and women would bring their nicest collection baskets to show they would be able to help sustain each other. I'd given Beh all the furs I had made recently —the large antelope hide, the smaller pieces of rabbit fur—and had even tried to give her my own fur, but she hadn't worn it, nor had she made anything from the other furs. I showed her all the flint knives I have that could have been used to shape the fur into wraps, but she never used them.

Beh has to know winter is coming, and she will need warm clothing. I often put the antelope fur over her shoulders when she is shaking from the chilled air. The strange clothing she has is not thick enough—even the especially weird material of her leggings. Though it feels thick and sturdy, it has no fur and doesn't seem to be warm.

I shift a little in our bed, pulling Beh's head into a different position on my shoulder. She sighs in her sleep and snuggles against me. Her hand lies on my chest near my shoulder, and her fingers twitch against my skin.

What could I give to Beh?

I fall asleep with this thought in my head, and while I sleep, my mind continues to consider it. I dream of Beh.

She is sitting by the edge of the lake and pulling tangles from her hair. As she sits, the part of her clothing that covers her arm suddenly rips and falls to the ground. She wipes at her eyes and continues with her hair. She looks out over the water and sniffs. I know she is still sad, but she is trying to forget her torn clothing as gooseflesh appears on her now bare arm. A moment later, the other arm loses its covering. She stands, dropping the stick she had been using, and the leggings she wears also shred and fall to the ground at her feet, which are suddenly bare.

Beh covers her face with her hands and lets out a sob. I want to go to her, but I am not what she wants, and I know it. With shaking fingers, she bends over to retrieve the stick, sits back on the rock, and continues to run the stick through her hair.

My eyes open, and I check the darkened cave. The fire is low, so I wriggle out from Beh's embrace and add wood to it. I check outside, and the night is clear, quiet, and cold. There is still some time before dawn. Before I crawl back to the warmth of furs and my mate, I add several more logs to the fire so we will have good cooking coals when we wake.

I run my nose over Beh's temple and use my hand to brush hairs from her forehead. I think of my dream and wonder if Beh is sad because her clothing is falling apart, and it reminds her of her life before I found her. No clothing lasts forever, and hers seems particularly flimsy.

I hold her closer and wish I knew what to do. We can try to look for her old home, but I don't even know where to start. If it would make her happy, though, I would try to find it for her. I also know that if we find it, her tribe may not accept me. I recall the one and only time I ran across other people since my tribe was wiped out from the fire.

There were many of them, and they all walked in a line across the steppes. I had only just found my cave the season before, and I was out hunting with my spear. Working alone, I could never get close enough to the animals to use the weapon. When the people came into view, I cautiously approached them, but as soon as they saw me, four of the men in the front ran at me. They screamed and shook their spears, so I ran away.

What would I do if we did find Beh's tribe and they chased me away but kept Beh? I look down at her face, which glows red in the firelight. What if I had to come back here again, alone?

A quiet whimper escapes from my throat at the thought. I do not want to lose Beh. I want her with me. There is no way I am going to let her go looking for her tribe if there is even a possibility they won't accept me with her!

I remember my dream again and the sad look on her face. It makes my chest and stomach ache to think of it. I don't want her to go away and back to her own tribe and leave me alone again. It's not even about being alone anymore—I know I don't want to be without Beh. Having her here to warm the furs with me at night and gather food with me during the day is the most important thing in the world.

For me.

A cold shiver runs through me as I realize there is something more important. I want Beh to be happy. If she would only be happy with her own people again, I would have to let her go back to them—even if they would not let me join her.

There is nothing more important than Beh, and if making her happy means my own sorrow, I will have to accept that.

I don't sleep the rest of the night.

⟡

The afternoon sun is warm even though the air is getting colder each day. Nights are longer, and it won't be many more days until it is cold enough for snow. The steppes are fairly dry though, and there usually isn't too much precipitation during the winter, but winter nights can get very cold, even without snow.

In my hand, I hold a wooden object made from the knot of a tree. I close one eye as I look at it closely. I've been working on the shape for many, many days—since the day I thought of it while watching Beh run her fingers through her hair. My other hand holds the edge of a flint blade to the wood, and I carve off another tiny slice.

I used to dread the coming of winter for many reasons. I was never very prepared for it and rarely had enough food stored up to keep healthy. My bones would ache around the joints, and one year at the very end of winter, strange spots appeared on my legs, and I was so tired I could barely move. Once spring came and I found other things to eat, the spots went away, and I felt better.

I also dreaded the long winter nights when I would lie alone, cold and empty inside, just waiting for the sun to rise again. My mind would go through winters when I was a child, and everyone in the tribe would gather together in the longhouse. It was the tribe's common shelter, made of the large bones of animals, covered in hides, mud and thatch. There was a hole in the very center of the top, where the smoke from a large fire would escape. When we were all together, the center fire and our body heat kept us warm.

This winter is going to be different though. I smile to myself as I think of Beh in our sleeping furs last night, sticking her cold nose against my bare chest underneath the fur blanket. It made me shiver, and not just from the cold.

I'm almost looking forward to the long nights this winter because Beh will be here for me to protect and care for as the days grow short. I also hope by then she will let me mate with her because spending the winter trying to give her a baby is something I really want to do.

"Ehd?"

I turn away quickly, shoving my hands underneath the extra piece of hide I brought with me just in case she tries to see what I am doing.

Beh makes some more mouth sounds and places her hands on her hips. I look up at her but keep my hands hidden and my body tense, not sure what she is going to do. She moves her head from side to side as she looks down at me a moment but then sighs and smiles. She tries to walk around to the front where I sit, but I twist my body, hands, and the fur around so she still can't see underneath the furs in my lap. She tries to sit next to me to see what I have in my hands, but I won't let her.

"Kiss?"

My eyes fly over to hers, and I know exactly what she is trying to do. It is likely to work, too, if I think about it for too long. Instead of giving in, I pull one hand out from under the fur, wrap the fingers of my other hand tightly around the object hidden beneath, and grunt sharply. My arm coils around the outside of the fur, and I lean over the whole bundle with my eyes closed. If I can't see her, I won't give in to her suggestions and show her what I have.

She makes more sounds, followed by her hand grabbing at the fur and trying to pull it back. I hold tightly to it and wrench it away from her, growling low. I don't want her to see it; it's not done yet! Beh make more noises, her sounds sharp and succinct, and then she rights herself and takes a step away from me.

I sigh heavily as she huffs through her nose and walks back

toward the cave entrance. As soon as she slips through the crack in the rock, I turn back to the fur and slowly remove the little object, holding it up in the sunlight again. I have been working on it for many days, trying to get it just right.

It looks a little like a hand but with only three fingers. There is a round part made from the knot of a fallen tree I found near the edge of the forest, which will be the part she can hold onto. Protruding from the knot are three finger-shaped extensions carved from the wood, and I am making it for Beh to help her untangle her hair.

It will be my gift to her.

Taking a closer look at the edges, I come to the conclusion that I am mostly done with what can be accomplished with my flint carving knife. I just need to find the right kind of rock to smooth it out. Once it is smooth, Beh will be able to use it to pull the snarls from her hair after she washes it. Her hair will be shiny and soft, and when I run my hands through the strands, it will feel so good between my fingers. I think it will help her hair stay soft as well when she won't be able to go to the lake to wash.

Sighing a little to myself, I hope she might also use it on my hair.

I decide it's as good as I can do with the flint. Wrapping the little wooden claw in the hide, I stand up to brush wood shaving from my legs. Right as the dust and flint chips fall from my furs, I hear Beh's scream.

Over the past several months, I have heard Beh yell when she is angry and when she is upset. I have heard her cries that come with tears. The sound that comes from far off to the side of the cave—right at the line of trees where Beh usually goes to relieve herself—is definitely Beh, but it is not a sound I have heard from her before. It makes my entire body go cold.

I know Beh is in trouble.

Dropping Beh's gift, I hold the sliver of flint tightly in my hand as I race toward the sound. She is still calling out, and this time I can make out my name-sound in between the other sounds as well.

"Ehd! EHD!"

"Beh!" I yell back. I move my head from side to side fluidly, focusing on which direction the sounds originate and about how far away. With my mouth open, I inhale deeply to try to find the scent of both my mate and anything that might be threatening her. I twist and turn through the small grove of trees that line the ravine, and when I speed around one large cedar, I encounter a terrifying sight.

Beh stands with her back against the bottom of a cliff. Her mouth is open, and a continual string of sounds emanates from it as she leans her palms against the sheer cliff and kicks out with her slender legs. On one side of her is the little ravine with a trickle of foul water running far below, and in front of her is a huge, large-tusked boar.

He is one of the biggest ones I have ever seen with coarse black hair sticking out from his body. His hooves are sharp and covered in mud. I can see a hole off to one side where he has obviously been digging right near where Beh usually relieves herself. The creature ducks its head low to the ground and squeals out a warning before it starts to charge.

I'm too far away. I can't get to her in time.

My eyes never leave the scene as I run with my feet pounding on the ground and my heart pounding in my chest, knowing there is no way I can get there fast enough to stop what is happening. Beh tries to kick out at the beast, but she doesn't make contact with him. He butts toward her foot, and his tusk catches on the bottom of the long, strange leggings near where they encase her calves.

With a terrible sound, the material rips all the way up the side of her leg to her hip. Beh begins to scream again as the boar takes a step back, shakes his head free of a piece of cloth caught on his tusk, and paws at the ground as I finally get close enough to distract the beast.

Without putting any thought into how dangerous it is, I run forward—yelling as loudly as I can at the creature—and throw my body at his. As soon as my chest hits his hard, muscled body, the wind is knocked out of me, and I am momentarily stunned. I have to take a second to force air into my lungs again. Though the boar is short-legged, his massive, thick body is long.

The great boar squeals and bucks, trying to dislodge me, but I grab one of his tusks and hold on tight, knowing that if he tosses me away, he will go after Beh again. I throw one of my legs over his back and tighten up around him. I have to make sure my thighs are as anchored to his sides as they can be. He bucks again, but I manage to get one arm under his snout without letting go of the massive tusk and try to pull his head to the side.

My other hand still holds on to the slim piece of flint I had been using to make Beh's gift. It's nothing like I would usually use to attack and kill so large a beast. It's not even strong enough to cut through his thick hide had he been dead, but it's all I have. With the blunt part of the flint against my palm, I shove the tip as hard as I can into the thick skin of his neck.

The boar shrieks and bucks. I can feel warm blood as it covers my hand and wrist, but it's not much—I've barely cut into his skin. I have to find the thick vessel at his throat if I have any hope of killing him.

I have to save Beh.

The boar twists and turns his head—trying to gouge me with his long, sharp tusks. He alternates between attempting to stab me and kicking his feet out behind him, trying to dislodge me from his back. My legs tighten around his flanks and my heels dig into his sides. As I adjust myself to hold on, he whips his head around, and I feel a sharp sting in my forearm as one of his tusks connects with my skin.

The pain is awful, but a flash of the creature going after Beh runs through my mind, and I refuse to let go even though I can feel the blood running down my arm. Beh is screaming, but I can't look at her and hold on at the same time.

I dig the flint into the animal's neck again, making several small cuts and generally angering the boar but not doing any real damage to him. I can't get a deep enough cut across his throat where I need it to be while he continues to flip and twist his head around, trying to slash me with his overgrown teeth.

Out of the corner of my eye, I see my mate moving toward us, crying out for me. In her hand is a long, but very thin, branch from a tree. I make a sound that is somewhere between a growl and a whimper. Not only will that sized branch not come close to diverting the boar, it will likely direct his attention toward another target.

He will go after her again.

I have to do something before she gets too close.

With a roar, I pull my arm up from around the creature's neck where I am trying to cut him, ball my hand into a fist, and slam my knuckles against the creature's forehead, right between his eyes.

Momentarily stunned, he stops the thrashing of his head long enough for me to get the flint in the right position to open his carotid artery. I can feel the difference immediately as warm blood gushes instead of trickles over my hand and arm, and the boar staggers to one side. I only have to hold on to him for a moment before his legs buckle and he collapses. I'm stunned, lying partially under the beast, but he is finally dead.

My breaths come in pants as I shove the corpse away, push myself to my feet, and stagger backwards. With wild eyes and clenched fists, I stare at the body, daring it to rise again and threaten my mate. The little sliver of flint is sticking out of the boar's neck, coated in thick, red fluid.

I feel Beh's small hand against my arm, and I turn swiftly toward her. I take a single step to get her within my reach, bend slightly at the waist, grab her tightly around her hips, and throw her over my shoulder.

I will never let her out of my sight again.

Beh makes that squeaking sound as I settle her against one shoulder, then bend down carefully to grab hold of the boar's hind leg so I can drag it behind me while keeping Beh safe. Hoisting her up more firmly in my grip, I move as quickly as I can without risking dropping her

She's squirmy—not as much as the boar was, but right now, I don't care. I feel my stomach churn, and I'm desperate to get her back in the cave and safe with me. She is making a lot of loud sounds, and I hear that *no* sound a few times as her hands slap painlessly against my back. In response, I smack her backside a couple of times with the hand that holds her, just to quiet her a little. If the boar has a mate, I don't want her coming after us. Even in my frantic state, I'm careful not to hit hard; I would never hurt my Beh.

By the time I reach the path right outside the cave, she has stopped wiggling and is still. I let go of the boar outside the crack, knowing that I can't leave it there long, or it will attract other animals. I rapidly turn us sideways to fit both Beh and myself through the entrance to the cave. Before she can protest, I pull Beh from my shoulder and toss her into the furs at the back of the small cavern. I fall in after her, covering her completely with my body, wrapping her up in my arms, and trying to stop my heart from beating so hard.

In my mind, I see the boar slashing at her over and over again.

My arms tighten around my mate. I register her hands wrapping around my head and holding me as I hold her, and I am slightly calmed. I breathe in short, sharp pants against her shoulder, and I squeeze my eyes shut to try to stop the burn behind them.

She's my mate.

I was almost too late.

She could have died.

I cry out and bury my face in her neck as the horrific thoughts and images of what could have been overwhelm me. I try to stop the thoughts, but they keep coming. Even when I hold her as tightly as I can, all that comes to mind are thoughts of her being hurt. What if she is injured and I haven't seen it? It could have happened before I arrived. Swallowing hard, I lean back and look down at her shocked and tear-stained face. The cut on my arm throbs, and I quickly look over Beh to see if she is wounded anywhere.

I should have done that before, and I'm angry with myself for not considering it earlier. I remember the boar going after her leg and causing the rip in her strange leggings. What if her leg is cut? My hand reaches down and rapidly examines the skin of her leg—now clearly visible with the odd material of her strange clothing torn all the way up one side. It hangs in tatters from her hip.

I still can't see around it, and unlike a fur wrap, how to open and close the strange leggings is impossible to determine, but I have to know if she's hurt or not. Frustrated, and with my muscles still tense from the fright, I grab at the edge of the garment and tear it the rest of the way off. The whole top part of the clothing rips and pulls away in my hand, leaving a section of it still wrapped around her other leg. The little, hard, round piece near her stomach pops off and flies into the air before it drops to the dirt and rolls toward the edge of the fire pit.

I am immediately distracted by something extraordinary.

Underneath her leggings is another garment I have never seen before. It's wrapped just around her hips, crossing low on her waist, down between her legs, and presumably covering her buttocks. I brush my fingers over the edge of it to feel the extremely thin material. It's rough and bumpy, feeling a little bit like the underside of a thickly veined leaf. It has lines and patterns in it, too, and it is the same pale pink as the mysterious wrap around her breasts and back.

At first, I think it might be her bleeding time, but there is no wool or absorbent leather between her legs, just this little covering. It is so thin, I can see the short hairs underneath it.

The bit of cloth is so... so *tiny*.

And pink.

Beh's whimper draws my attention back to her face, the streaks of tears over her cheeks, and her teeth nearly embedded in her lower lip. I feel my chest clench, and the pressure behind my eyes starts again as I quickly look the rest of her over. I don't see any wounds on her, but what if the boar had gotten her leg instead of the cloth? I could have lost her, and I haven't even given her a baby yet. As I realize this, a sense of panic paralyzes me.

My mind is completely consumed by the thought.

What if there is another boar in the area? What if she falls, gets hurt, and dies? What if there isn't enough food to hold both of us until spring? What if I get sick and I still haven't given her a baby? What if a hyaenodon finds our cave in the night, and I can't fight him off?

We have to mate now before it's too late.

I have to put a baby in her.

Every fiber of my being screams at me—I have to put a baby inside of her before something happens to one of us. The longer I wait, the more likely a tragic event could occur. There is nothing more important for me than to give my mate a baby. I have to give her one quickly before anything else can happen.

Desperately, I move back from Beh, grab her by her waist, and quickly flip her over to her stomach. I can hear her mouth sounds, but I can't concentrate on them—I am already far too focused on what I know must be done. I breathe faster as I think of how we will come together. I grasp her hips with both hands to bring her up into position with my legs between hers. I kneel behind her, and though the tiny little scrap of material was interesting before, I need it out of my way now. I pull it down her legs to her knees, but it gets in the way of holding her thighs apart. With a frustrated growl, I lift her legs off the ground and pull the cloth to her ankles. I meet further resistance from her foot-coverings, but manage to pull the bit of cloth around them. I turn my gaze back to her body, and she is fully exposed to me for the first time.

The scent of her sex is intoxicating.

Dropping her legs back to the furs, I push them apart with my knees. I lean forward and run one hand down the course of Beh's back as the other hand pulls away the fur at my waist. Taking a deep breath, I wrap my fingers around my hard shaft. Her heat and scent encompass my senses as I place the tip of my hard flesh against her opening, completely giving in to the instincts that drive my very being.

Finally, my ears pick up the sound of her *no* word.

CHAPTER NINE

She doesn't shout the sound. In fact, it's hardly more than a whisper, but the intense emotion and fear behind it is enough to halt my movements completely. I have to hold my muscles still, force myself not to move, not to thrust into her. I can feel myself right there, right at her opening, closer than I have ever been to a woman.

The urge is nearly unbearable.

Nearly.

The soft little cry of *no* from Beh, however—*that* is unbearable.

I uncoil my fingers from my rigid flesh, and my arms go around her body. I pull us both over to our sides and hold her to my chest as I try to calm myself. I can feel my own heart beating against her back as a shudder runs through her body, and the vibrations from her shaking ripple through my arms.

She shifts her position, and her hand reaches down to grasp the little piece of material from the furs beside her, and she pulls it up her legs to slide it back into place. I can hear her crying, and again, I don't know what to do, so I don't do anything. I just keep my arms around her body and hold her tightly against my chest until her cries slowly ebb.

Does she never want me to mate with her?

If she doesn't, why would she hold on to me?

What did I do wrong?

She starts to move again, and I am terrified she is going to try to get away from me, so I grip her a little tighter. Instead of trying to escape me, Beh just rolls over within my grasp until she is facing me. She wraps her arms around my neck and tucks her head into my chest like she often does at night. I stroke her hair, and I listen to her quiet sounds as she struggles through her tears.

Beh tilts her head back to look at me, and her hand cups my cheek. Her fingers run through my beard as she makes more sounds, shakes her head back and forth, and looks into my eyes like she is searching for something.

My chest tightens again as I look at her face, and I wipe her tears away. As I do, she wraps her fingers around my wrist, and I tense again, waiting to see if she will push me away. She doesn't, but turns my hand over instead and exposes the long cut down my arm where the boar gouged me. It is not deep and isn't bleeding any longer, but it is dark red and angry looking. Beh lightly touches around the outside of the wound, and I flinch a little.

Instantly, she looks at me, her eyes full of sadness as tears spill from them again. Her hand covers my cheek and jaw again as she makes more soft sounds before leaning in closer and placing her mouth against my lips. They feel warm and soft against me, and I moan as I pull her flush against my skin. I can feel her bare legs against mine, which is different from what I am used to feeling. They feel so very soft—nearly as soft as her lips. I almost want to break our embrace to get a better look at them.

Almost.

I grip her hip as her fingers tug at the hair on the back of my head. It seems like it should hurt, but it doesn't—it feels wonderful. Wondering if she would like it, too, I wind her long hair once around my wrist and pull back.

When I pull, her mouth parts from mine, and she gasps as her neck bends back. Not wanting to end the activity, I follow her head with my own. I work my lips against hers, and this time she moans at me, and I pull her hips toward mine.

My penis is still hard, and when I pull her against me, it rubs up against her pubic bone. I try to hold in the whimper that wants to escape from my mouth at the feeling and have to restrain myself from pushing it harder against her.

It feels so good there.

So *right*.

I really want to put it inside of her.

Why doesn't she want me?

Her mouth opens, and I feel her tongue touch mine.

It seems like she wants me when she lets me do this with her. When her fingers run through my hair, or when she holds my hand as we walk to the lake, it feels like she wants to be my mate, but she doesn't want me to give her a baby, and I don't understand why not.

Is there something wrong with me? Does she see something about me that she thinks will be bad for her children? Is that why she doesn't mate with me? I wonder if it's because I'm alone. Could she believe my former tribe abandoned me because there is something wrong with me?

There is no way for her to know what really happened since she wasn't there, so this could be what she thinks of me. She might think I am not good enough to be a part of a tribe, and she is only here with me now because there is no other tribe for her. That would explain why she stays with me—because she has no one else. It also explains why she doesn't want me to give her a baby —because she thinks there is something wrong with me.

Maybe that is why she cried again when she saw my arm. Does she think I won't be as strong now?

I break away from her and rise up on my knees, determined to show her I can still care for her and her children. Her eyes open wide as I reach down and pull her from the furs, pick her up, and then bring her back out into the sunlight. Beh shades her eyes from the brightness as I set her down gently, and I let go of her hand long enough to grab the boar and raise his body up over my head.

It makes the muscles in my arms and shoulders ache, and it's also a little cold outside without any furs covering me, but I don't care.

Beh looks at me with one eyebrow raised and then quickly looks away with crimson cheeks. She does not appear impressed, only confused. I put the boar down and run back into the cave. I select my sharpest flint knife and bring it back outside. I quickly and efficiently remove the boar's hide to show her how well I can provide animal skins for her. I tuck the edges of the hide into the rocks above the cave so it can dry, and I quickly remove the best pieces of meat from the boar to roast over the fire. Taking her hand again, I bring her back into the cave and next to the fire. I quickly wedge the meat onto the spit and lay it across the burning coals.

Looking up into her eyes, I see they are sparkling in... amusement? I narrow my eyes at her, and Beh bites into her lip as she offers me a smile. I find myself focusing on her mouth again and wondering if I could bite her lip a bit as well.

Would she like that?

"Khhzz?" I whisper.

Beh smiles again, and a bright red tinge covers her cheeks. I take the answer to be affirmative, and I shuffle a step on my knees to get closer to her.

A sharp pain in my left knee stops me, and when I reach down to see what has caused the pain, I find a tiny round...thing. When I pick it up, it feels cold in my hand, and I realize it is the little bit that flew off of Beh's leggings. I hold it up near the firelight to try to get a better look at it. I put it in my mouth and bite down, but it only hurts my teeth.

Beh laughs and reaches out, taking the little round thing from me. She holds it in her palm and looks at it, suddenly growing quiet. She makes more sounds—soft and subdued as she flips the thing over. On the opposite side, there are raised shapes in the circle. Beh runs the very tip of her finger around it and sighs softly.

Her eyes look to me, then back to the thing in her hand. A single tear tries to make its way down her cheek, but she captures it with the back of her hand before it has the chance to get far. Beh closes her hand over the little round thing, capturing it in her fist. She squeezes tightly, then turns her hand palm down and releases it back to the ground.

Beh moves forward quickly, and I'm pushed backwards a little as she throws her arms around my neck and firmly plants her lips on my mouth. She tightens her grip on my head as her bare legs straddle my naked waist. I reach around and grasp her backside—supporting her body as she plunges her tongue into my mouth.

As our mouths move together, I realize Beh wants to be with me, but she doesn't want to have my baby inside of her. Women are supposed to want a baby in them, aren't they? But my mate doesn't. Is there a reason to have a mate who doesn't want to make a baby?

Yes, there is.

I want her here with me. I don't care if my mate is unusual and doesn't want me to put a baby in her. I'm still going to keep her.

With Beh's hands in my hair and her mouth firmly attached to mine, I wonder what just changed. Obviously, she has made some kind of decision in her head though there is no way for me to know why she has had a change of heart. I can feel my body relax as I feel her relax, and her mouth is soft against my lips while she presses her body hard against me.

I support her with one arm as the other slides up her back and over the thin material of her tight-fitting tunic. My fingers brush over the unusual strap across her back, and I am reminded of the tiny bit of clothing that separates my hardened male flesh from her sex, and I groan into her mouth.

Beh breaks from me for a moment, and she looks into my eyes. For a while, we just look at each other, and then she releases the back of my head and trails her hands around to my cheeks. She leans forward and touches her lips to the side of my mouth before her hands let go of my face entirely.

I set her back on her feet, and Beh looks at me for a long moment. Suddenly, she reaches to the hem of her tunic and quickly pulls it up and over her head, giving me my first good look at that strange thing that wraps around her breasts.

When I had a tribe, I'd seen plenty of women's breasts, from my mother and my sisters to those of the other women of my tribe. Summers can be hot, and most people wore very little clothing during the warm months. I never really thought too much about them. As I became a man, I would think more about a female's backside because that is what I thought of holding as I mated with her. Breasts were just too…commonplace.

But that little scrap of triangular cloth, and the way it holds, lifts, and *hides* her female curves from my eyes, has suddenly made her breasts far more interesting than they ever had been before. My eyes dance to Beh's, and there is a hint of a smile on her face. I look back to the round, hidden flesh and find myself leaning a little closer, my eyes slowly taking in what can be seen and wondering exactly what they look like underneath. I wonder if Beh will choose to show them to me.

I would really like to see them.

I grip her hips as I look back to her eyes and lean in to run my nose over her jaw. I reach her ear, inhale, and sigh against her skin. She shivers, and I hope she is not too cold. I look back to her eyes, but she doesn't appear to be uncomfortable. Her breathing is faster, and she tightens her grip on my shoulders.

My nose runs down the side of her neck and to her shoulder. When I reach the thin strap of cloth there, I sniff at it, curious about its purpose. I follow the edge of it down to her collarbone, then change my course and run my nose across the top of her chest. When I reach the strap on the other side, I move back to her shoulder, up her neck, and over her chin. My lips brush hers softly before I touch the tip of her nose with mine, and we both stare at each other.

Beh's hand drops from my shoulder and covers my fingers at her waist. My chest tightens as she pulls my hand away from her skin; I am afraid she has changed her mind again, and she won't let me touch her there. Instead, she brings my hand up her side, around to the front, and covers her right breast with it.

"Hoh!" I hear myself make a strange, grunting, breathy gasp. It's not a sound I recall making before, but it seems to fit both my state of shock and awe. Beh smiles as my thumb traces the top edge of the triangular shape, and the rest of my fingers flex and grip gently.

I glance at my mate, and she is smiling at me with humor. I smile back, unable to help myself. Cautiously, I raise my other hand to cover her other breast—still over the top of the funny fabric. Beh does not appear to object, and my hands mimic each other's movements as they explore the softness of her skin where I can touch it and the heavy feeling of her breasts in my hands as I lift them.

She lets me touch her in this way for some time before she takes my face back in her hands, places her lips against mine softly, and then pulls away from me again. For a moment, I am confused and hurt. Did I do something wrong again? Why is she leaving? But my concern doesn't last long, and I watch Beh extend her arm and take my hand in hers. We stand together, and she begins to lead me away from the fire.

With my hand in hers, Beh leads me to the rock shelf at one side of the small cave. She lifts both of the water skins and swiftly empties them into one of the larger pots she has made before she hands the skins to me. She takes a few steps toward the crack to the outside, then halts and looks down at her bare legs and then to my naked body. She shakes her head slowly and then walks back to the furs.

She picks up my wrap and hands it to me as her cheeks turn red again. I quickly wrap it around my waist and then watch as she picks up one of the sleeping furs and tries to do the same. It is not going to work. It isn't cut right for wearing, but my mate doesn't seem to know that.

I wonder how her tribe can make such strange and complicated clothing but not even know how to wear a simple wrap! I take the sleeping fur from her and drop it back into the pile before I get the antelope hide I had prepared for her days ago. It still isn't cut for her shape, but it will do. She takes it in her hands and tries to put it on, but it's not right at all. Finally, I take it back and put it around her myself.

She is my mate, and if she doesn't know how to dress herself, then I'll do it for her.

I cut two long straps of leather from an old skin and tie them around her waist to hold the wrap together. When I'm done, I take a step back to get a better look at her.

She's beautiful.

Well, except for those strange things that are still on her feet, but the rest is lovely.

She picks up the water skins and takes my hand again, this time leading me outside and down the trail toward the pine forest and the lake. When we get there, she takes me to the water's edge and points at it. I look into the water to see if there is a fish she wants me to catch, but I don't see any. My eyes turn back to hers, confused.

Beh sighs heavily, reaches down into the water and brings a handful of it out, which she then dumps on my arm. I jump back; the water is cold! Beh starts making more sounds and pointing at the water some more, and I don't like it. I growl a little and back away.

She approaches me and takes my hand again, turning it over so the underside is pointing up. Her finger runs along the edge of the cut from the boar's tusk—close but not quite touching it. She makes a lot more noises and points at the water again.

My mate is strange.

She tries to pull me back toward the lake, but I won't go. I usually want to follow her anywhere—but that doesn't include going into cold water! We struggle a little before she tosses her hand in the air and goes back to the water's edge alone. I watch intently as she fills the water skins and brings them back to me. When she tries to pour the water on me from the skins, I back away again.

She fills the skins again and then just drops them beside her as she removes the fur she is wearing and begins to unwind the strange little ties that hold her foot coverings. She glances back over to me, and I quickly look away. She doesn't like it when I watch, so I always pretend not to. Instead, I look over at the tree line for a while and then glance quickly back at my mate—just to make sure she is all right. She has the fur wrapped around her shoulders, and I can see the funny little pink things in her hands as she scrubs at them in the water with a pile of crushed soaproot plants.

I realize that if she's washing them, she's not wearing them.

My heart starts to beat a little faster, and I lean over to one side to see if I can get a better look. Beh turns her head and almost catches me, but I'm fast enough to look away before I meet her eyes. When I look back again, her shoulders are shaking a little, and I wonder if she is sad or cold. I move a little closer just to be sure she doesn't need me, and her eyes meet mine.

They sparkle.

She's beautiful.

She stands and wraps the fur around her a little tighter, tilts her head to the side, and peers at me.

"Kiss?"

I feel my body tense and shift toward her automatically before I can stop myself. She glances up at me, smiles coyly, and lays the little pink scraps of material on a large rock to dry. She leans forward a little, and the edge of the fur drops from her shoulder. Before she can pull it around herself again, I can see just a hint of the slightly darker pink of one of her nipples.

It's the same color as the little bits of fabric.

I take a step forward, and Beh licks her lips as she adjusts the wrap and sits back down at the water's edge. I move slowly to her side, still cautious, and sit down next to her. She covers herself completely with the fur as she leans forward and brushes her lips against mine but only for the briefest moment. She backs away immediately afterwards and points at the water again and makes a lot more noise.

I narrow my eyes, understanding now what she is trying to do. She wants me to bathe in the water and doesn't seem to care that it's too cold. I growl low, shifting back away from her a little but not much.

Beh changes position, angling herself toward me and reaching out with her hand. As she does, the edge of the fur falls from her shoulder again, and I can see a quick glimpse of one of her bare breasts underneath. Heat covers my groin as my eyes widen, and Beh takes my hand in hers to pull me forward. I feel my breathing increase along with my heartbeat as she brings my fingers yet closer to her breast. Just as my fingers twitch in anticipation of feeling her smooth skin, Beh turns my hand away from her body and plunges it into the icy water.

My mate is quite serious about this bathing thing.

I don't like it.

Not at all.

But I do let her wash my arm because every step of the way, she places her mouth on mine, and I like that. She pays a lot of attention to the scrape on my arm as she cleans away all of the dirt and blood from my skin. When it becomes clear she's trying to get me to submerge myself in the water completely, I back away, but she slowly coaxes me forward, pulls away my wrap, and I shiver and shake as she washes my back in the cold water.

I didn't mind so much in the summer.

Beh grabs my hand and holds it against my thigh. She rubs back and forth, urging me to wash my legs while she cleans my back, and I comply reluctantly. Looking at her over my shoulder, I see her stern look and go back to washing. I don't understand why I'm doing this in the freezing cold, but apparently I will do anything to make my mate happy, even follow her into cold water.

Once she decides my body is clean enough, I get out of the water and sit on a rock with my arms wrapped tightly around my knees. I feel her come up behind me, and she places the antelope hide over my shoulders and touches her lips to my cheek. My eyes dance over her body, now clothed in nothing except for the little scraps of pink cloth. I wish I could react to it, but I'm just too cold. Instead, I watch her, trying to understand if she is angry with me or not.

I turn my head and sniff at the fur around my shoulders. It already smells a little bit like Beh though she hasn't worn it very long yet. I like it. It smells like her side of the furs where she sleeps. When she comes back from the side of the lake, I stand so we can go back to the warmth of the cave. I wish I could bring some fire with us so we could stay warm near the water, but I don't have anything that will hold a hot coal.

I wrap the antelope hide around Beh, and she watches me closely as I do. She narrows her eyes a little as I tie the leather strap around her waist but looks up at me with a smile when I'm done. I touch the side of her face and feel how cold she is, just like me. I need to get my mate back to our cave to warm her.

I place my arm over her shoulder and pull her close to me as we start to walk back, and I notice immediately that Beh's smell is different. I turn my head into her neck and sniff. She smells more like the lake now than she smells like herself.

She snickers as my nose tickles the side of her face, and I smile at her. She makes noises with her mouth, so I silence her with my lips. I like the way she tastes, and my stomach growls. Beh laughs aloud this time, and we make our way back to the cave.

The boar meat is nearly cooked through when we return, and Beh takes the pot of water and puts it on the coals. It heats quickly, and she adds wild onions and nutgrass to it while I go outside of the cave to finish with the boar's skin and meat.

I sit right in front of the cave's exit just to make sure Beh doesn't leave without me noticing.

The boar's skin is perfect for Beh—it is soft and supple as I work with it, and once it is finished she will be able to make clothes out of it. I narrow my eyes a little and consider since she didn't know how to wear clothes, she must not know how to make them either. The boar's hide will have to dry first, and Beh really needs something now.

I enter the cave and gather up the antelope hide I have already prepared. I decide to go ahead and cut clothing for Beh myself— she will need something under fur skins to keep her warm since the winter months are close. It doesn't take long to cut out pieces for her top and bottom, and I use a strip of leather to tie it all together on one side.

Once the clothing is done and the rest of the boar meat is ready, I take it inside to hang near the fire. The boar was large, and it will give us a lot of good meat. I look around at what we have gathered over the past few days as well, and I know we are going to be okay.

Beh makes a lot of sounds at me as I tilt my head and look at her, kneeling by the fire and stirring around with a smooth piece of driftwood whatever she has put into the stew. I hold up the clothes I have made for her, and after a few tries, she manages to figure out how to put them all on. She leaves the little pink things on as well, but that's okay. They may be a little strange, but I kind of like them.

We eat heartily, and there is still enough left over for later as well. I remember how many times I had gone without food for days and realize it was not so much because there was no food to be had; I just didn't have a good enough reason to search for it.

Now I do.

I reach out with one finger and slowly draw it across the skin of Beh's forearm. She covers the pot with a clay lid and turns to looks at me. Her eyes are intense, and they make me feel strange. I look down to the smooth rock floor of the cave and try to stop breathing so hard. When I glance back up, Beh's eyes are staring at the fire, and I quickly shift so I am a bit closer to her before she can look back and notice.

Beh runs her hand through her hair and bites down on her lip as she glances over at me. I can see the color of her cheeks and neck deepen as she looks to her hands.

I scoot a little closer.

Looking at her sideways, I reach out and touch her arm with my hand again.

"Khhiss?" The sound I make is soft...pleading.

The corner of Beh's mouth turns up as she pushes her lips together. She leans in, and I lick my lips in anticipation. A moment later, her warm mouth is on mine, and I feel her hand slide up my arm, over my shoulder, and into my hair. I sigh at the sensation and feel Beh's tongue as it enters my mouth.

I can taste stew, the boar meat, and *her* all on my tongue at once. It is strange and wonderful, and my entire body seems to hum as she raises herself up onto her knees and wraps both arms around my head. From that position, she is angled slightly above me, and as we separate, I look up into her face.

So pretty.

I reach up and run my fingers over the edge of her cheekbone and down her jaw. My hand touches the edge of the boar skin wrap at her shoulder, and I feel very pleased with myself. Not only did I provide her with meat for her dinner and clothing for her body, but I made her something I know how to remove.

I pull at the leather strap, and it falls away from her shoulder. I can see the little pink straps around her shoulders, and I brush the edge of one of them with my nose. They smell different now—just like Beh and I do. The scent of the freshwater lake and soaproot are the most predominant scents of our skin and her clothing. I remember the scent in her hair when I first found her and wonder if she had rubbed fruit on the strands before I met her.

As I look back up to her face, Beh's fingertips mimic my own. She runs her hands around my cheeks, my jaw, and my forehead— even over my eyelids as I close them. When I open them again, her breathing has changed, and I can see her chest rise and fall as rapidly as my own.

She releases me long enough to push the rest of the boar's skin from her body. When she straddles me again, she is wearing only the little pink bits of cloth around her breasts and sex. I grasp around her middle, and her smooth skin feels warm even though she shivers at my touch. Sounds come from her mouth, and I hear both my name-sound and the hissing sound, which I try to repeat.

"Beh...khhz..."

Her mouth turns into a smile, but it does not make her eyes sparkle like they usually do.

Something has made her feel sad, but I don't know what it is.

I don't even know if it is something I can fix.

I do know I will do anything within my power to make her happy.

Finally, after looking into her eyes for a long time, I take her to our furs.

CHAPTER TEN

I kneel down slowly and place Beh in the center of the furs. I stay on my knees beside her, just looking down at her as she lies comfortably in the middle of the fur-lined depression. The air between us is different—charged. I can feel it in my skin and hear it in her breathing. Something is different, and for some reason, it's scaring me.

I can feel the heat in my groin and the hardness of my flesh under my furs, and I know my body is straining to put a baby inside of her as soon as possible. Before long, the weather will be cold, and Beh will have to have a baby in her soon so it will be big enough to survive the next winter.

I also just...*want*.

I want to feel her body underneath mine. I want to know what it feels like to be inside of her. I only know what it feels like to touch myself with my own hand—I have never had someone to mate with before. When the urge to mate with her came over me earlier, it was more instinctual rather than rational, but now I'm thinking about it; I'm thinking about it in great detail.

I want to give Beh a baby, but there's more.

I also want to see her, to touch her, and to feel myself inside of her body. I want to inhale the scent of her back as I take her, and I want to watch the rhythmic motions of her shoulders as we move together.

I want her to smile against the furs as we come together.

I want to see her eyes light up.

"Ehd?"

I realize I've been kneeling in the same spot for quite some time.

Beh's fingers tentatively touch the edge of my leg. Her teeth capture her full bottom lip as she looks up to me and then back down to her fingers as they trace through the fur of my wrap where it lies across my thigh.

In the way.

I hesitate, wondering if I should remove it now or wait a while. I'm confused, knowing what I want to do but not completely sure how I will be received. The last time we were in this spot together, I had been so worried; I hadn't known what else to do. I'm still worried, but the worry is of a different sort. I still want her to have my baby inside of her, but she doesn't react the way I expect a woman to react. She is so strange, and she doesn't appear to want a baby at all.

Or maybe just not one that looks like me.

My chest tightens as I crawl over her to my place on the far side of the sleeping furs, wondering if I shouldn't just hold her and keep her safe in her sleep. I know how to do that, and she doesn't seem to mind when I do. She rolls toward me like she usually does, and I'm not sure how to approach her. She never gets on her knees or turns her back to me like I remember my mother doing with my father.

The complexity of what rushes through me is still overwhelming, and my mind races through all the possible scenarios. I want to reach out and touch her—run my hands over her skin, inhale her scent, hold onto her hips as I move in and out of her—but I'm frightened as well, and I don't understand why.

Her hand touches the side of my face, and I feel myself melt into the sensation. My eyes close and my body relaxes. When I open them again, I can see her slight smile in the dim light of the fire though her face is somewhat shadowed by the darkened cave. I reach out with my finger and trace the edge of the shadow around her cheek.

I lick my lips, my eyes darting to her mouth. Before I can utter the "kiss" sound, Beh's lips are against mine.

Her warm mouth is soft, and I wrap one arm around her waist and pull her against my body as her tongue touches my lips. Her fingers wind into my hair, pulling me tight against her mouth as her tongue massages mine. I feel myself harden further, and I can't help but push against her leg a little. It feels so good when I do, especially when I pull at her hip at the same time.

Beh grips my shoulder and then runs her hand down my arm. Her fingers twine together with mine at her hip, and she moves my hand up until it cups her breast through the thin, rough fabric. I moan into her mouth as I squeeze at the soft flesh. I can feel her nipple under my palm as it hardens and pokes back at me. I pull back from her mouth to look down at my hand, but instead, I end up watching hers.

Beh releases my hand and moves slowly up my forearm. When she reaches my elbow, she drops her hand to my waist, then around to my stomach. Her fingers tickle the little hairs there that form a line just below my navel. With one finger, she follows the line down until she reaches the top of the fur wrap around my hips.

She grabs at the knot, releases it, and pushes the wrap away.

I stiffen and groan audibly as I feel her fingers come into contact with my penis, and then another quiet whimper escapes from the back of my throat as she keeps going. Her eyes meet mine for a moment, and they are wide and clear; her pupils are large in the firelight. I stare back at her for a moment before we both look back down. She strokes slowly up from the base to the tip, then wraps her little hand around me and runs all the way back down, then up again.

My stomach tightens, my breath hitches in my throat, and my heart pounds with new vigor. Involuntarily, my hips thrust forward, pushing myself into her hand as she moves up and down again. Only a moment later, my hips find a rhythm I can't control, and I'm thrusting into the palm of her hand.

The buildup of pressure is swift and powerful.

It doesn't even occur to me to try to hold back.

My entire body shudders even though the feeling is concentrated much closer to her hand. I cry out as I release, feeling my semen spurt against her hand and my stomach. Beh's fingers grip gently, stroking me several more times before she lets go of my shaft.

I look upon her with amazement.

It has never felt like that when I used my own hand. Not even close. Beh's eyes sparkle with her own excitement as she smiles right back at me. I try to take a deep breath to calm down my heart as I look into her eyes. There is a plethora of emotions coursing through me, and the combination is something I've never felt before.

I don't even know what to think of most of it.

So I don't.

One thing I recognize—there is a feeling of *contentment* that I have not felt since I had been with my tribe. I can't seem to do anything but lie in the furs and stare at my mate in utter amazement as my heartbeat slows down and my breathing returns to its regular rhythm.

Beh is here with me, and she has made me feel complete. I look at her with an unhindered smile before I close my eyes and tuck my head into the place between her neck and shoulder. I inhale the scent of my mate...

...and fall asleep.

⟫•••●❁●•••⟪

For the first time I can remember, I sleep long enough for the light of the sun to be brighter than the firelight when I wake. When I open my eyes, I immediately notice Beh's absence from our furs, and panic sets in. I bolt upright and call out.

"Beh!"

From the other side of the fire, I hear her soft noises, along with my name-sound. My heart is still racing, but it slows as my body relaxes. I rub at my eyes and look over to where she sits. There is the pot of stew she made last night, and I can see she has also placed more of the boar meat on the spit for cooking.

My mate made me breakfast.

I can't stop smiling as I crawl out of the furs and think of the night before. My whole body tingles with the memory, and I bounce out of the depression in the back of the cave and over to my mate. She sits by the fire, and I drop down to my hands and knees next to her to look at her beautiful face.

Beh turns to me, and her cheeks turn red. She's so pretty–vibrant and healthy-looking—when that happens. She looks down to the ground, and her lips squish together. She seems to be holding in a smile. I lean in a little closer and brush the tip of my nose across her cheekbone. Beh makes soft sounds as she looks up at me, but I don't find them at all annoying this time. My nose follows the line of her hair up to her temple, where I inhale deeply at her scent before I jump back up and run outside the cave to relieve myself.

It's a beautiful day, sunny and bright though the breeze is chilly on my naked flesh. I don't care; I feel too good to be concerned with the cold. I watch my stream of water arc out into the ravine and think about Beh's hand coiling around my penis.

I wonder if she'll do that again.

I mean—if she touched me there, then surely she'll let me put a baby in her now, right?

It takes just three running steps to get back to the cave entrance, and I feel like I weigh nothing. I'm still smiling, too; I can't seem to stop. My eyes fall on the little pile of boar remains, which happens to be next to the little piece of antelope fur left over from making Beh's clothes. I walk over to it, checking over my shoulder to make sure Beh isn't peeking out of the cave, and pick up the little bundle. In the middle of it is the piece of wood I have been carving for Beh.

I glance toward the cave again before I wrap the wood in the hide and tuck it under my arm. I will have to hide it until we go to the lake again, where I can use small rocks or sand to smooth it all out before I give it to her.

Looking around, I decide to hide it up with the extra wood. I take down several pieces of wood, which I will use to replenish the stack inside the cave, and tuck the little bundle inside. I look at it closely and scrunch up my face, not liking how alone it looks. I decide I don't want to leave it there and bring it back out again.

I'll have to sneak it inside and put it in one of the little folded pouches inside my fur wrap. That way it will be with me all the time, and I'll know it's safely where Beh won't find it. Maybe we will go to the lake today, and I can finish the gift while Beh makes pots or gathers cattails. We definitely need to do a little more gathering to make sure there is plenty of food for the colder months. I have been very hungry the past two winters, and I can't let that happen to Beh, especially if she is going to have a baby in her.

One that looks like me.

I smile again, bounce on my toes, and head back inside the cave.

Beh doesn't look up as I walk back in and look over at her. I quickly race over to the sleeping furs and tuck Beh's gift inside so it can't be seen. When I look back, Beh is leaning over and seems very intent on whatever she is doing. I don't want to disturb her work, so I move over to her quietly and crouch down, watching.

She has one of my flint knives, and she's cutting up the dark blue, thick material she used to wear over her legs. She has cut many pieces into squares the size of both of my hands, and I watch her stack them neatly next to the fire. I reach out to touch one, but she makes the *no* sound, and I cringe.

I look at her warily as she moves the pile out of my reach and then makes a lot more sounds. I listen closely, but I don't hear the *no* sound or the *kiss* sound, so I sit back and wait. Once she has cut all of the material into pieces, she uses two of them to lift one of her pots out of the coals and sits it in front of me. Then she lifts the lid and puts it off to the side.

I peer in, and the pot appears to be filled with just water. Beh dunks one of the little squares into the water, wrings it out, and then holds her hand out toward me.

I look at her palm and then back to her face. Beh makes some noise, and I consider making the *kiss* sound at her or maybe just putting my mouth on hers. As I consider that, my mind flashes to the previous night, and I look at her hand in a different way, remembering what it felt like when she wrapped her fingers around my penis and moved back and forth.

I'm getting hard, and when she reaches out again, I realize she must want to do that again. My heart pounds in my chest as I bring myself up onto my knees and reach out to her, take her face in my hands, and cover her mouth with mine. I feel her hand on my chest, but she doesn't move it down again. Instead, she is pushing at me a little.

Our lips part quickly, and she pushes me back on my heels again. I narrow my eyes in confusion as she takes my hand and turns it palm up. She brings the cloth out again and runs it over the scrape on my arm.

"Ahh!"

I jump and cry out, quickly moving away from her and the hot cloth in her hand. Beh makes more noises and reaches out for me again. Her noises get louder as she shakes her hand toward me and points to my arm. She starts moving toward me, and I scramble back a bit before she latches onto my arm.

"Ehd…"

Her sounds become softer, and I find myself straining to hear them. As I lean forward to listen, Beh swipes at my arm with the cloth again. I flinch, but I'm more prepared for it this time. The heat from the water actually feels...nice. I relax and move back close to her as she wipes down my arm gently, rinses the cloth in the pot, and then runs it over my face.

It feels good when I'm expecting it.

Definitely better than the cold water at the lake.

I reach out and touch Beh's thigh with the end of my finger, and she takes my hand and wraps it up in hers. Our eyes meet, and she gives me a small smile. I return it broadly, and even though I know I should not try to put a baby in her now—we need to go out and gather food, and I need to find some sand at the lake to finish Beh's carving—I am sure she will want to when we return to the warmth of our furs when the sun sets.

That's when I'll give her my gift.

Beh finishes washing me and herself in the warm water from the pot, and we collect what we will need for the day's work. The sun has made the day fairly warm, and we make good progress, collecting the rest of the grain from the field and the nutgrass from the edge of the forest. As we walk through the pine forest toward the lake, there are many pinecones filled with pine nuts that are ready to be gathered. Beh places several of them in the funny shaped reed basket she made when she first became my mate. I added a leather strap to the top of the basket so she can wear it around her neck to carry things.

The green pinecones are still in the trees, and Beh reaches up into the branches to pick them. I watch as she tries to jump and grab some that are out of her reach, but she can't get to them. I come up behind her, delighted at her playful squeal as I grab her waist and lift her up high to gather the rest.

When she has picked enough to fill her basket, I slowly lower her down to the ground again. She turns to face me, but I keep my hands at her hips. She smiles up and me, and I look into her bright blue eyes, wondering what makes them sparkle even though we are in the deep shade of the forest where the sun doesn't reach. I run my nose over her temple, up into her hair, and then down over the bridge of her nose.

Beh closes her eyes and sighs as she tightens her grip around my shoulders and lays her head against my chest. We are close enough that I can feel her heart beating through my furs. I lay my head on top of hers and just hold her for a moment.

Again, the sense of contentedness and completeness encompasses me.

She wraps her hand around mine as we continue our way to the lake. When we get there, she digs up more cattail roots and bulrushes. She still can't weave anything that looks like a basket, but she keeps trying. We can still eat the roots and the end of the bulrush stems anyway.

While she does that, I sneak over near a sandy part of the lakeshore and turn my back to her. I pull out the little piece of fur that contains the wood carving with the three prongs I hope Beh will be able to use to get the tangles out of her hair. I pick up a handful of sand and rub it into the edge of the wood with the pads of my fingers. I glance at Beh frequently, not wanting her to be out of my sight for very long, but still work diligently on my task.

I want it to be done so I can give it to her as soon as possible. I never gave her a mating gift, and I want to give her this today so I can put a baby in her tonight.

Just the thought of it is enough to make me hard and leave me wanting to give Beh a baby even when I'm not looking over at her as she kneels next to the shore to pull out roots. When I look at her and see her backside raised in the air as she reaches out to pull up another handful of bulrushes, it takes every bit of control I have to stop myself from just rushing over to her and taking her now.

I'm pretty sure she wouldn't like that.

The thought brings a lump to my throat and leaves me soft.

I rub vigorously at the carving, pleased at how smooth it is becoming. The rounded part where Beh can hold onto it is nice and soft to the touch, and the long parts don't have any more rough spots around them to catch on her hair.

I look back over my shoulder to check on her, and she is standing up, brushing dust from the fur wrap around her legs. She looks so beautiful in normal clothing, and I love the way it hangs from her hips. She still has those strange foot coverings on, but I don't mind them so much. My eyes move up from the fur around her waist to the antelope hide around her shoulders. Her long, dark hair lies on her back in contrast to the light tan hide.

I feel my heartbeat in my chest, and I hope she will like her gift. I look it over again, turning it around and around in my hands as I check for any additional rough spots. I don't find any, so I decide it is as good as it is going to get. I tuck it back inside the fold of my wrap and go over to where Beh sits. The day is getting late, and we should be heading back to our cave.

Our cave.

I smile to myself and wonder how I survived without her.

Between the cattails, bulrushes, pinecones, and grains, we have quite a load to carry back with us, so I can't hold her hand as we go. It has been a very successful day for gathering though, and Beh makes noises with her mouth all the way back to the cave, occasionally looking up at me and smiling.

I wish she weren't so noisy, but I'm willing to endure the noise to have her with me.

When we return, most of what we have gathered goes to the back of the cave where it is the driest. Beh selects some of the food and adds it to a pot of water near the fire. I follow closely behind her, sit as close as I can next to her, and bend forward so I can look her in the face as she leans over the pot.

Beh looks at me sideways and pushes her lips together to curb her smile. I'm not sure why she tries to stop it, but she looks pretty when she does that, and I want to put my mouth on hers again. Instead, I reach inside my wrap and grab hold of the wood carving.

I take a long, deep breath and look into Beh's eyes.

Finally, with a slight shiver, I give Beh her mating gift.

CHAPTER ELEVEN

Watching Beh's face, I pull the wood carving out slowly, unwrap it from the scrap of fur, and then carefully place it in front of her before I shuffle back a little to sit away from her. I can feel the tightness in my muscles as I wait to see how she will react.

Beh sits back from the clay pot on the coals and looks down to the little object in front of her while my heart pounds. Her graceful fingers cover it and lift it closer to her eyes, and her brow furrows as she turns it around in her hands. Her mouth moves and sounds come out as she tilts her head to look at me. My eyes dart from her face to the carving, trying to figure out if she likes it or not. She seems to just be confused.

Then I realize she may not know its purpose, so I reach out tentatively and place my palm against the hand holding the carving. I gently maneuver her hand to the side of her face, make sure her palm wraps around the carving in the right place, and push the prongs between strands of her hair. I pull down slightly, just until the prongs of the hair carving come into contact with a snarl.

I sit back again and watch Beh's face. Her expression is unreadable as she pulls the hair carving the rest of the way through her hair. She brings her hand back around in front of her again to look more closely at the gift. Her eyes widen as she glances from the carving, to me, and back again.

My hands start to sweat, and I rub them against my legs.

Beh brings her other hand up and cradles the hair carving for a moment, turning it around again and running her fingers over the whole thing. Again, her eyes move to mine. Her brow is furrowed as she makes hushed sounds, ending with her pitch increasing slightly as her breath seems to get stuck in her throat.

In the light of the fire, I can see a tear in the corner of her eye. *She doesn't like it.*

My body feels like it is collapsing inside of itself, and I drop my eyes to the floor of the cave. How was it wrong? Did it pull too hard and hurt her?

I made her cry.

I only want her to smile and be happy and not have to look for a new stick that is the right strength to smooth out her hair. I don't mean to make her cry. I want her to like it. Why doesn't she like it?

Does she just not want a gift from me?

I glance quickly up at Beh again and notice her eyes are back on the hair carving. She makes more sounds, and I hear my name-sound at the end of them just as she looks back up. I can see tears in both of her eyes now, and my heart drops further in my chest. I look away, wondering again if she really doesn't want to be my mate, and suddenly I feel a terrific force against my chest.

Beh's arms tighten around my neck, making it almost impossible for me to breathe and nearly knocking me over in the process. Her legs circle my waist, and she holds on tight and mutters the same noises over and over again. When she pulls back, she is in my lap and looking down at me, her eyes still wet with tears, but sparkling along with her bright smile as well. Her hand lies against my rough cheek as she looks into my eyes for a moment, her smile never faltering, then leans in close to me and touches the tip of her nose to mine.

My chest relaxes, and I can breathe again.

She has never done that to me before. She has accepted my nose-touches but never touched me back—not like that. She will put her mouth on mine, even if I don't make the kiss sound, but she has never touched my nose with hers before.

Her fingers scrape gently through my beard, scratching at my cheek in the process. It feels good, but I am distracted by the feeling of her nose running up the center of mine, stopping between my eyes. Her lips replace the tip of her nose, and she presses them against the spot in the center of my forehead for a moment before she looks back into my eyes.

"Ehd..." She whispers my name-sound before she places her lips to mine briefly. More sounds, but I barely notice them. I am captivated by her eyes as she looks at me. I reach up with my finger and brush away the wetness that is still in the corner, and Beh's cheeks are tinged with her blush as she closes her eyes for a moment.

She's so beautiful.

A sharp hissing sound brings our attention from each other and back toward the pot on the fire. The water is spurting out of the edge of the pot and falling into the coals. Beh laughs softly as she disengages from my arms and picks up the scraps of cloth to remove the hot pot from the fire. As soon as it has been moved, she picks up her hair carving again, turns it around in her hands, and then tries it out.

It moves easily through her hair, and I can tell right away that it works better than the jagged sticks she has used. She makes very quick work of the tangles—much faster than usual—and then reaches out to grab my hand. She brings me to her side and twists me around so I am facing away from her. She gets up on her knees and starts pulling the hair carving through my hair as well.

I can't believe how good it feels.

As she works the knots out of my hair, her free hand wraps around my shoulder, massaging the muscles there and around the front of my chest. I relax against her, leaning back a little and looking up and over my shoulder into her face. She pauses in her actions for a moment to move her hand up to my chin and place her mouth on mine.

When she is done with me, she brings over one of her bowls full of warm water and washes the scratch on my arm and also both of our hands. Using one of the clay cups, she scoops the stew into a bowl and then moves to carefully straddle my lap with the bowl still in her hand. She raises her eyebrows a bit as she looks at me with her lips turned into the hint of a smile. She blows gently on the stew to cool it and then holds up a flat piece of driftwood about the size of two long fingers. She uses it to scoop up food from the bowl, looks to my face, and holds the driftwood out toward my mouth.

The smell of the cooked food is delicious—the hint of nutgrass and grains mixed with the boar meat is making my mouth water. My mouth opens automatically, and Beh places the driftwood between my lips. As my mouth closes around the food, she slides the driftwood back out again, leaving the stew in my mouth.

I chew and smile up at her, then watch with wide eyes as she takes another scoop of the stew and places it in her own mouth. Her lips wrap around it slowly, and she twists the little piece of wood over. I can see her lick across the edge of it as the food coats her tongue. The strange grunt escapes from my mouth again.

"Hoh!"

I have no idea why, but just watching her place the food on the driftwood and then into her mouth has made my penis stiffen underneath her. As she continues to alternate back and forth—first offering me a bite and then taking one herself, I find myself more aroused than I have ever been before.

We eat the entire meal this way—Beh serving me first and then herself, one bite at a time.

By the time the bowl is empty, I can hardly move. My muscles and my mind seem locked and awaiting whatever Beh will do next. I have this feeling that if I move, there is only one thing I will be able to do—haul her off to our furs and take her.

She places the bowl down beside her and runs her fingertips up my arms. Wanting to feel her hands on my skin, I quickly shrug off the warm fur around my shoulders and let it drop behind me. There is only a little sunlight still shining through the crack in the rock, but it's enough to see her cheeks darken as she looks down at my chest. Her hands descend, and I wonder why her touch makes me shiver even when her hands are warm.

The pads of her fingers brush over my flat nipples and cause me to suck in my breath. I look at her face and see her lower lip caught between her teeth. She watches her hands intently as they flow evenly over the skin of my chest and stomach. She brings them slowly back to my shoulders, and a shudder runs through my entire body. I wrap my fingers around her hips and pull her down against me as I revel in the warmth of her body against my hard flesh.

Her mouth is on mine again, and I'm not even sure who initiates the act. It is as if we both move together this time. The touch of her lips against mine and the taste of her tongue in my mouth is almost enough to make me ignore the burning between my legs and the overwhelming desire to flip her over.

She pulls away, breaking the contact with our lips but continuing to look into my eyes. I still my hands though it isn't easy. I want to pull her down against me. I want to push up against her. I want to bury my length in the warm channel I know is just a little piece of fabric away.

Her fingers run through the hair on my face as she makes more sounds. I watch her eyes carefully—they are so intense as she continues. Beh shakes her head from side to side, makes more sounds, and then lets out a long sigh. She leans in and rests her forehead against mine.

I can't help myself; I push up against her.

The friction feels so good.

Beh's eyes close, and her hands drop to my shoulders. When she opens them again, she looks sad.

"Oh, Ehd…"

"Beh…khhhz?"

Her lips brush over mine before she climbs out of my lap, but it is not near enough. She turns around, and for a moment my heart begins to pound as she leans over a little. I rise up on my knees, but just as I think she wants me to give her a baby now, she moves to adjust the position of the pot near the fire and stands back up.

She turns to face the entrance to the cave with her hands running up through her hair and pulling at the roots a bit. She is frustrated—I can tell—but I am frustrated, too. I knew I wanted to mate with her the first day I saw her and brought her back, but Beh doesn't seem to know if she wants a baby or not. Sometimes she seems like she does, but other times I don't know what to think.

I stand as well, and Beh looks over her shoulder at me. I see her eyes run from my face down to my feet and back again. I quickly remove the wrap around my waist and let it fall, leaving me bare before her. Her eyes widen, and she takes me in with her eyes again.

"Beh." I take a step closer to her. She does not move away, but doesn't move toward me either. My eyes are locked with hers, and I take another step. My heart pounds and I am panting like I have just run all the way back from the lake, but all I can see is Beh. In my mind, all I can feel are her lips against mine and the warmth of her bare skin as her hands roam over me.

I can smell the scent of her, mixed with the smoke from the fire. It is her hair and skin combined with my own smell on her, but as I inhale deeply—trying to calm myself—I can smell more. My nose tingles with the scent of her sex.

"Beh."

Another step and she turns to face me. Her feet shuffle backwards, but only slightly.

"Ehd..." Her sounds are so soft, I can barely hear them. It does not matter anyway.

I want her.

I reach out and grab her by her wrist, bringing her close to my side before the fingers of my other hand tangle in her hair. I bring her face close to me and look down into her wide, expressive eyes.

She took the mating gift I gave her and she likes it. I know she does. If she accepted the gift, she is allowing me to provide for her. She gathers with me, cooks my food, and is living in this cave with me. She *is* my mate.

If she is my mate, I'm going to give her a baby.

It's what I'm supposed to do.

I decide I am not waiting any longer, and I press my lips firmly to hers as I bring our bodies together. I can feel my length pressed against her belly, and I reach my hand around her back to hold her tightly against me. Beh's hands move to my chest, but she does not push me away. Using my body as leverage, I maneuver her over to our furs.

My hand drops to the edge of the fur around her waist, and I pull it from her body and drop it to the ground. I know the little scrap of material still covers where I want to be, but it won't be there for long. Beh moans into my mouth, and her hands push against my chest just as the edge of my foot hits the edge of the furs.

I drop to my knees, pulling her along with me, not breaking apart from her lips. My hand remains firmly against the back of her head as I push her over backwards, laying her against the furs and covering her with my body. Against the flesh of my leg, I feel the edge of Beh's foot covering. I feel additional pressure on my chest as she presses her palms against my skin and turns her head to the side, breaking our connection.

"Ehd..." Her eyes stare into mine as she turns her head back. Her breathing is labored—just like mine. I can see fear in her eyes, but at the same time, she reaches up and strokes my cheek with her fingers. I don't know what frightens her.

Images come to my mind—the couples in my tribe as they were newly mated. Living within the close community did not allow for much privacy, and I remember how the females would sometime cry out if their new mate was not gentle with them.

After the boar had attacked her, I had been afraid she would not survive. The need to give her a baby had overwhelmed me, and I had been rough with her. I realize that I probably scared her before, and that is why she is frightened of me now.

Looking down at my mate, I slowly run the tip of my nose along hers. I barely touch her skin as my nose skims across her brow and down her jaw. When my lips cross hers, I lightly press against their warmth.

I want her to know I will be gentle with her.

I won't hurt her.

I will never, ever hurt my Beh.

Touching her nose with mine once more, I use my fingers to trace over her cheek and neck, down to her shoulder, and over the smooth fabric of her odd tunic. I trace my fingers slowly along her arm to the very edge of the sleeve, and I tug at it as I look into her eyes.

Soft sounds pour from her mouth, her whispered breath covering my lips. She raises her head, and I feel her tongue touch mine. For a moment I am lost in her taste again. She runs her hands along my shoulders and arms as her neck arches her head back into the furs. The foot she has placed against my calf shifts, scraping at my skin with the rough bottom of her foot covering.

It hurts a little, but I don't care.

Raising myself up on one hand, I look down at Beh for a moment before I run my other hand from her shoulder, across her breast, and down to her waist. I move back and onto my knees as I wrap my arm around Beh's back and pull her up with me. I tighten my grip around the material at her waist and start to pull it up, but Beh covers my hand with hers, stopping me.

My brow furrows as I look back to her, but I breathe in relief when she reaches to the hem and pulls the whole thing over her head herself. The lovely pink from her strange breast-wrapper looks pretty against her skin, and I find myself peering over the top to see more.

The thought causes the muscles in my stomach and thighs to flex involuntarily, and the head of my hardened penis taps against Beh's leg. Her eyes drop down and glaze over. I can see her throat bob as she takes a deep breath and reaches both of her hands around her back at the same time. A moment later, the most amazing thing happens.

The strange material that has always wrapped around Beh's breasts suddenly pops right off of her!

"Hoh!" My eyes widen as my breath escapes from my throat. Beh's lips squish together, and her eyes sparkle as she watches me look at her. My eyes jump from her face to the perfectly round, dark pink circles in the center of her perfectly round, lighter pink breasts.

I move my hands slowly, reaching out for them.

I stop with my fingers almost, but not quite, touching them.

Beh wraps her fingers around the backs of my hands, and she pulls forward until I'm touching them both.

They're so soft!

My chest rises and falls as my breathing increases, and my hands slowly push against the supple flesh. I gently touch their centers with my thumbs, and Beh lets out a gasp. Her hands grip my upper arms, and when I look at her, I can see her eyes are focused on my hands, and the colorful parts of them are shielded by their dilated, black centers. One of her hands releases mine and trails down my chest, leaving a ticklish trail that makes my abdomen clench.

Then she wraps her hand firmly around my erection.

Slowly, Beh's hand strokes over me, and I feel as though I will lose my balance and fall back into the furs. It is a good thing I'm holding onto her breasts, or I might. Beh's eyes remain cast down as she touches me. The combination of watching her face, having her breasts in my hands, and her hand on my penis all at once is more than enough to cause the tightening in my stomach that is usually followed by the release of semen.

My eyes close and my head tilts upwards as my muscles clench. I try to hold back—because I'm not ready yet. I need to be inside of her first, or I can't give her a baby. But it feels so good...

I groan and drop my head to her shoulder. Beh's other hand moves up my back and into my hair, and then she tugs me toward her and our lips meet again. She feels so warm, and when my thumbs run over her nipples again, they harden and Beh moans into my mouth.

Her hand strokes me again, and the tips of her fingers roll around the head. She breaks away from my mouth and looks down again, and I follow her gaze. She uses her fingers to trace over the skin around the tip, and when her hand strokes back toward the base, the head is revealed.

Beh makes another quiet sound, but I barely hear it. The sight of her hand on me is too much, and the pressure collects in my knees and abdomen before it rushes to meet in my groin. My lower body tightens, and I cry out with her next forward stroke, spilling my semen to the furs below us.

As I try to control my panting, Beh runs her fingers over my softening member. When our eyes meet, hers still dance with firelight, and there is a slight smile on her lips. I am torn, for the feelings she has induced are beyond compare, but I am disappointed I was not inside her body when the feelings overtook me.

I'm also exhausted.

I drop down to the furs, trying to pull Beh with me at the same time. She makes a bunch of sounds—some of them kind of loud—then grabs the soiled top fur from the rest of the bedding and tosses it toward the back of the cave before joining me. My arms go around her, and I snuggle against her shoulder for a moment before I hear that *no* sound again, and I flinch.

I look quickly to her eyes, cringing from her and wondering what I have done wrong. She had been smiling, but is she angry I did not give her a baby yet? When I focus on her, I am further confused. She made that sound, but she does not appear to be upset. Her lips are pursed together like she does when she is trying not to laugh out loud.

Her head moves slowly from side to side, and she reaches out her hand to take mine from her waist. She brings it back to her breast, and I am again enamored by the soft feel of her flesh there. Examining her nipple a little closer, I watch the skin around it further tighten, and I run my finger around the hard nub in the center, and Beh hums.

I look to her face, and she is smiling now, her eyes hooded. Does she like this? I do it again, and her back arches a little, pushing her breast harder against my palm. I try doing the same with her other breast, and Beh rolls her shoulders to place herself flat on her back, which gives me better access to both breasts at once. The other nipple also hardens when I touch it, and Beh moans.

I watch her face as her teeth bite into her lip, and her hooded eyes close for a moment before she looks back to me. Her hand slides down my arm, over the top of the hand that covers her breast, and then down her own stomach.

My eyes widen as her fingers disappear inside of the little pink fabric covering her sex. When I look back to her face, there is a grin on her lips, and she makes more sounds at me. I look back to her hand, and I can see her fingers underneath the fabric as they move in a little circle.

Beh moans softly, and when I look back at her face again, her eyes are closed and her lips are slightly parted. She breathes deeply, but quickly, too; I can hear the panting sounds between her moans. My eyes quickly shift from her face to her hand as I watch, fascinated, until Beh's hand retreats as a soft sigh comes from her mouth.

"Ehd…" she whispers as her hand touches mine. Her fingers are wet. I can see them glistening in the firelight. They wrap around my hand and guide it down over her smooth stomach and to the edge of the little pink thing at her waist.

I swallow hard as understanding comes over me.

She had been touching herself, and I cannot help but think of times I had stroked my penis with my own hand the way she did with her hand wrapped around me. Even though I didn't have a mate to give a baby to when I had touched myself, I had still done it just because of the feeling it produced.

Does Beh get that feeling, too?

Does she want me to make her feel like that, the same way she did for me when she touched my penis and brought about the climax of feelings that made my body shudder?

Can I make her feel like that?

If I touch her the same way she was just touching herself, would she make that same noise? Would her face contort with pleasure the way it just did, and would it be because of something *I* did to her?

If it's possible, I definitely I want to try.

Beh's hand pushes the pink fabric down her legs as she guides my fingers toward her sex. My fingers touch short, coarse hair along their journey, which causes me to gasp. Beh hums again, and then shifts her legs, using her toes to push off her foot coverings and the little tubes of cloth that encircle her feet beneath the thicker coverings. The pink scrap also falls to the side.

Beh's eyes meet mine, and she offers me a quick smile as she pushes my hand further down. With her fingers atop mine, she slides them across her outer folds and then back up before settling at a spot right at the top.

As she rolls the tips of my first two fingers in a circle, I can feel a small bump hidden just below the line of hair. This is the spot where Beh seems to focus my touch, and she guides my hand and fingers with hers on top of them. With a little more pressure on my knuckles, she leads me lower, and I feel the end of my finger touch her opening.

"Mmm...Ehd..."

"Hoh!"

Her moan, combined with my name-sound, creates a stirring that starts in my stomach but quickly spreads. It warms my skin and makes my heart beat faster. Though her hand had brought my essence from me only a few minutes ago, I can feel my penis begin to stiffen again.

I rise up on one hand so I can see our hands better, and I watch as she brings my fingers back up to the top of her folds, circles them around, and then leads them back to the opening just below though she does not push my finger farther inside of her than just the first knuckle.

As she sets a steady rhythm for me to follow, she stops placing pressure on my hand and eventually lets go, allowing me to touch her without assistance. I circle the nub hidden at the top, move down to touch her opening, then back up again several times as Beh shifts and moans against the furs.

She is glorious.

With her hand, she reaches out and wraps around my neck, and she pulls my lips to hers. Beh bends her knee and brings her foot up close to her buttocks and lifts her hips to push against my hand. I continue the same rhythm until she puts her hand back over mine and pushes the heel of my hand against the top of her mound to add more pressure.

She arches her back a bit and groans out my name-sound again.

I clench my fingers and move them against her faster as she holds my hand against her flesh and tilts her hips. Her face and breasts are flushed and beautiful, and her eyes—nearly closed—

look down at our joined hands. I have pushed the tips of two of my fingers just inside of her—a little farther than they were before —and they move in and out of her.

Again, she arches her back, but this time she also lifts her hips to press my hand harder against her sensitive flesh. I don't slow my movements, but I look back up to her face and see her eyes closed and her head tilted back into her furs. Her hips jerk once more, and I watch her mouth drop open as she cries out.

The sounds she makes are both fluid—like those she makes often—and guttural. I recognize my name-sound amongst them, and it makes me smile as she collapses against the warm furs of our bed. Her hand covers the center of her chest as her panting breaths begin to slow, and I recognize that she has experienced the same feeling I get when she has her hand on me.

I made her feel like that.

Me.

Well, she did help somewhat, but it was still my fingers on her.

As her eyes open partway, and she looks up at me, I become very aware of my own desire for her between my legs. My fingers stroke over her once more before I bring them back. As I do, I inhale, and the scent of her covers me.

A groan escapes my lips as the scent enters my nostrils and fills my brain. I stare down at my hand and see the wetness from her sex, glistening in the light from the flames of our fire. I bring my fingers closer to my nose, inhale deeply, and then reach out with my tongue to taste her fluids.

Another low groan comes from deep inside my chest. It is almost a growl. I am throbbing with the need for her, and as my groin muscles tighten and shake, every instinct within my head tells me it is time.

I must give her a baby.

Now.

I toss one leg over her thighs and firmly grip her hips. I hear my name-sound and look to her flushed face and wide eyes. I can see her hesitation in the deep blue of her irises, but everything inside of me tells me she is ready—that this must be done without hesitation.

I lift her hips and roll her over in one quick movement, keeping her hips up higher than the rest of her. Beh's shoulders and chest lay against the soft furs, and her elbows bend to position her hands just beside her head. I wrap my hand around the base of my shaft as I close the distance between my hips and hers. With my knees, I push her thighs farther apart and hear her gasp.

The head of my penis slides between her folds, instantly coating me in the same wetness that covers my fingers. My breath rushes from my lungs at the completely indescribable feeling. When I had touched her here like this before, there had been warmth, but no moisture. I move my hips slightly—just enough to run the head over that little spot at the top of her sex, and I hear Beh whimper beneath me.

Her hands grip the edge of the fur beneath her.

The sight of her below me—the curve of her backside as it flows and dips to her waist, the arch of her spine as my fingers run up the edge of it, and her soft, flowing hair as it hangs around her neck and shoulders—is far more than I can resist.

I glide my hand up and pull back on the foreskin, exposing the thick head at the end of my shaft. It sparkles in the firelight with the moisture from her body combined with my own pre-ejaculate. I slide through her folds once more as Beh's shoulders move with her rapid breaths. Her hips move slightly, enough to push back against me.

It is then I position myself at her opening and slowly begin to push.

CHAPTER TWELVE

So, so warm.

And wet.

Even right at the very entrance to my mate's body.

When my hips first tilt forward, nothing happens. The end of my member doesn't fit inside of her narrow opening, and a lump rises into my throat as a terrible thought enters into my head.

What if I don't fit inside her?

After all this time of waiting for her to want me, what will I do if I am unable to mate with Beh?

I take a calming breath and assure myself I will fit inside of her. Women are supposed to stretch there so babies can be put inside and come back out when they're ready. If something the size of a baby can come out, surely my penis can go in.

It's big, but it's not *that* big!

Deciding I just need to try again, I grip myself a little harder with my fingers up closer to the tip and push again. I feel slight pressure around the head of my penis as it stretches her opening before her body suddenly gives way, and I slide partway inside of her. I hear Beh's muffled cry against the furs, and I pause.

I run my hand up the center of her back until I reach her neck. I can feel the sweat collecting there, and the motion of her hurried breaths is more evident under my palm. She makes whispered sounds through her sharp breaths, and I cringe as I wait to hear her *no* sound.

She doesn't make that horrid noise, and as I feel the tight muscles of her back and shoulders begin to relax around me, I also feel her push back with her hips again. With my eyes locked on the place where we are joined together, I sink further into her with a groan.

I feel tears come to my eyes as I realize I'm finally there, finally inside of her, if only partway. We are joined together as if we are one person now instead of two, and nothing I have ever felt compares to being connected to her.

Rising higher up on my knees, I run my hands over the warm skin of her back, sides, and waist. I grip her firmly and use her hips as leverage as I pull back and thrust forward. A long moan tears from my chest as I feel myself push totally into her, and my length is entirely encompassed by my mate's tight channel.

For a moment, I can't move. I'm too overwhelmed by the physical feeling of being inside of her. I have never felt such a feeling before, and it is nothing like it had felt with either my own hand or hers.

Warm.

Wet.

Snug.

Though tight, the sensation is strangely comfortable, and the urge to move is not quite as powerful as it was before. I could stay right where I am without moving for days upon days, possibly seasons. The feeling is brief, and a moment later, the urge to thrust returns with more fervor, and I can't help but move. The instinct to drive into her is too dominant to be ignored. I pull away from her heat and then push us back together slowly. I do it again—pulling out no more than halfway before sliding back home, my penis nestled deeply within her body.

Beh cries out each time I thrust forward, and the sound

distracts me somewhat from the feeling of her muscles tightening around my penis as I push inside of her, retract, and push again. One of her hands grips into a tight fist, capturing part of the fur beneath her, and the other flails out beside her as she reaches back toward where we are connected.

Remembering what she did before, I run my hand around from her hip and cover her fingers as she touches the spot right above where my body enters hers. I don't try to guide her motions as she had mine, but just lay my first two fingers over the top of hers. When her fingers flex, mine move in tandem, adding to the pressure against her sensitive spot and trying to memorize exactly what she does.

I want to do it to her again later.

As she sets her own rhythm, I match it with gentle thrusts inside of her—slowly pulling back and pushing forward until my body is flush with hers. She rocks back on her knees, meeting my movements as we grind slowly together.

The sight of my long, hard shaft being engulfed by her body is magnificent. Just watching it move in and out of her makes my whole body tense with anticipation of coming inside of her. Having her hand bring about my climax was amazing but nothing like the feeling of moving in and out of her.

Starting with a low moan, Beh's breaths speed up along with her fingers. Trying to match her desire, I thrust deeper, harder, and faster into her. The increased friction of the faster movement, coupled with Beh's cry of my name-sound, bring me to the brink of what little control I have over my body's response to her. My eyes close as the tension begins to build in my abdomen and thighs, and my hand abandons hers to again grip her hip. With both hands, I pull her against me as I shove forward, grunting with the effort of every stroke.

My mate's cries diminish as she nearly collapses into the furs, and I hold her tighter to keep her from falling away from me as my pace increases again. I can feel her slick internal walls clenching my shaft as it further opens her body to receive the seed I will give her.

The seed to start a child growing inside of her.

As memories of violent storms rush through my head, I can almost hear the crash of thunder and feel the charge from the lightning as the sensations from the pit of my stomach and groin converge, join, and explode outward. The sound from my throat is nothing less than a shout of triumph as my head tilts back to the ceiling of the cave, and my semen rushes out of my body and into my mate's womb—the potential for a new life actualized.

The short, panting breaths from my mouth and the crackle of the fire join with the echoes of my scream and reverberate throughout the cave. With my fluids coating her insides, I slide easily back and forth a few more times before I push deep inside again. As I lean forward to bring my chest against her back, I feel the few remaining throbs from my shaft inject her fully; making sure everything I have given her finds its place inside her body.

Holding myself inside of her as deeply as I can, my arms wrap around her and clutch her tightly against my chest. I breathe heavily through my nose as I press my forehead against her shoulder. I can hear Beh breathing hard, too, and I feel her legs shaking against mine.

I pull back a little and roll us both to our sides, still holding her body against mine. I try to keep the correct angle to stay inside of her, but my softened penis slips out anyway. My warm breath covers her bare shoulder as I lay the side of my face on the back of her neck. I try to breathe deeply, but it takes some time before I can calm myself.

Her scent is slightly different now than it was before I mated with her. It is muskier, darker, and stronger than before. It makes me feel slightly dizzy to inhale the smell, and I wish I wasn't so worn out. The scent makes me want her again, but I can barely move.

A sense of extreme satisfaction comes over me, both

physically and mentally. I have completed mating with Beh, and now I will give her a baby.

Beh's hands grip my forearm around her middle, and she pushes her back closer to my chest. One arm rises and wraps around my neck as she turns her head toward me. Her cheek is reddened, and I think it may be from the furs rubbing against her face as I thrust into her. I touch the red spot gently with my thumb, and Beh closes her eyes. I lay my forehead against her shoulder and close my eyes as well. With a deep breath, I feel my body relax with hers.

"Ehd?"

My eyes open only a moment later to find Beh staring at me over her shoulder. There is a strange smile on her face as her hand strokes over my jaw. Her sounds are hushed as she utters them, her eyes intent on mine as she does. She repeats the same sounds, and though there is wetness in the corners of her eyes again, she does not appear upset.

"Khzz, Beh?"

Her smile widens and she leans in to press her lips to mine. It is only a soft touch and brief, but her eyes stay on mine as we part, and the same sounds come from her mouth again, and I tilt my head to the side, listening to the three short sounds she utters in a row. She reaches up to the space between my eyes and rubs against the spot between my brows. My eyes close a little as she runs her fingertip over my temple and across my jaw.

My mate starts to move, and at first I dig my fingers into her hip to hold her in place, but Beh wriggles and rolls around in my arms until she is facing me. I loosen my grip just long enough to let her reposition herself before I hold her against my chest again.

Beh's hand moves down from my cheek to my chest, and I can feel my pulse against her slim fingers. She presses the flat of her hand directly over my heart and looks back to my eyes. In the darkness of the cave, there is a light inside her eyes that makes my heart beat faster. I know the emotions I see there are also reflected in my own gaze though I have never felt this way before. Beh softly repeats the same three sounds, followed by my name-sound.

"Beh..." I pull her close and run the end of my nose over hers. Beh takes a long, deep breath before she settles her head right next to where her hand is splayed across my chest and closes her eyes.

I know the heart beating below Beh's palm belongs to her.

⸻ ❖ ⸻

I can't stop smiling.

Beh's eyes are closed, but her fingers are making gentle circles through the sparse hair on my chest. Our breathing is finally back to a normal level, and though I can still feel my heart beating underneath her touch, it is not as frantic as it was. My muscles are relaxed, and I feel euphoric.

I run my hand through Beh's hair, which is sweaty and tangled now, but makes her seem all the more beautiful because I'm the one who made her hair sweaty and tangled. I wonder if I should bring her the wood carving so she can pull the tangles out again.

Beh likes to have her hair smooth before she goes to sleep even though it's all messed up again by morning. I touch my nose to her temple and decide to get it for her. Turning us both to the side, I lay Beh gently against the fur and touch the backs of my knuckles over her cheek.

I want her to know I will care for her.

Always.

Just to make the point, I climb out of the furs, shivering a little in the cold air, and tend to some of the things I should have done before taking my mate. I rebuild and bank the fire, make sure all the drying meat is turned over, and check the outside of the cave to verify there is nothing about that might be dangerous to her.

Cold wind comes from the north, and I run my hands up and down my arms as I quickly relieve myself into the ravine. There is a bright half-moon and many twinkling stars to show my way in the cold night, and I can see the shimmer of the light off my skin. When I'm finished, I see a dark smear of dried blood on my penis.

There is no pain, and I know I'm not injured. I feel fantastic except for the sudden sinking feeling in my stomach as I realize the blood is definitely not mine, and there is only one other place it could have originated.

There isn't much blood, but I know immediately that I must have hurt Beh when I put my penis inside of her. I remember when she cried out at first, but she didn't tell me to stop. I thought she had felt like I had and had cried out from the intensity of our joining. It never occurred to me that she might have felt pain.

I was careful and gentle. It should not have hurt her.

Clearly, it did.

Panicked, I rush back into the cave, crying out for her. Beh sits up straight in the furs and looks at me with her eyes wide. She makes a lot of sounds, which get louder as I reach for her legs and pull them apart. She tries to shove my hands away at first, but I need to know how badly she is injured. In the dim firelight, I can't see any blood on her.

With a yell, Beh pushes my hands from her knees. When I look at her face, she stares at me with her brows knitted together and makes more noise. She doesn't appear to be hurt at all. Her mouth-noises are soft and don't include the *no* sound, and her face isn't angry-looking.

If I hurt her, wouldn't she be angry?

Grabbing my penis in my hand, I point to the blood on it. Beh sighs as she moves her head back and forth. She takes my hand and brings me over to the fire and the large pot she keeps near it. She dips one of the squares she made from her leggings into the water and uses it to clean both of us off. Her own calm demeanor seeps into me, and as she touches me, I feel my muscles surrender to her peace.

There really isn't very much blood on me—just the one, small streak. I watch Beh clean herself and see there is a little bit more, but nothing significant, and Beh seems just fine when I examine her again to be sure. She doesn't appear to be in pain or even discomfort. She smiles and touches my arm softly as she finishes washing and brings me back to our bed. She picks up the fur we were lying on and tosses it into the pile with the one I spilled semen on earlier.

Beh must not like the idea of sleeping on the furs when they get wet like that, and I wonder why. She does like to have everything a certain way, that is for sure, and I assume this is just one more thing she wants to keep clean.

She continues to make sounds as she plumps up the remaining furs and sits back down in the center of them. I crawl over her to lie down, and she lays her head on my shoulder and wraps her arm around my waist. After drawing a clean fur over the top of us, I hold her close to me and watch the entrance to the cave to make sure my mate is safe.

Beh quickly slips into slumber, but I do not. Though physically drained, my mind cannot seem to relax enough to doze off. I think about Beh and babies and if there will be enough food for three of us in the winter. I wonder when Beh will give birth to a baby if one just started growing inside of her.

I end up spending much of the night just watching my mate sleep.

My mate.

There are no more questions in my mind; she really is my mate now.

When I look down at her, I wonder if there is a baby growing inside of her belly and if it will look like me, and I feel myself smile at the idea. I know I will have to do better—try harder—if I am to properly care for her and her children, but I don't mind the idea at all.

I also know that sometimes you have to try to put a baby in your mate many times before one starts to grow. I'm not sure how many times, but I intend to try to put a baby in her as often as possible until I am positive there is one growing inside of her. Besides, it feels so good to put a baby in her. Just thinking about it makes me want to do it again, but Beh is asleep and I don't want to wake her up. I will definitely try to put a baby in her again in the morning.

I take a long, deep breath and lean my head back into the furs. As my eyes close, I wonder if I can put more than one baby at a time in her, or if she has a baby inside of her already, if I can put another one there. I think one at a time is probably enough since we don't have a tribe to help us with the baby. I think about the other mated couples in my tribe and remember clearly how they would come together even when the woman's belly was full of a child. I don't remember a time when two babies were born at once.

I feel Beh's steady breathing as she shifts a little in her sleep and mumbles some quiet sounds. They resemble the sound she made earlier, but most of her noises sound pretty similar. Only the *kiss* and *no* sound are different enough to notice. Most of the noises she makes just hurt my head, but I don't mind so much. She's my mate, she's unusual, and she is mine.

Finally, after reliving each moment of mating with Beh, I fall asleep with my mate in my arms.

CHAPTER THIRTEEN

Lying on my stomach, I peek out from under my lashes and watch my mate as she pokes around at the dishes near the fire. She adds some of the grains we've collected along with ground nuts and antelope meat. Once all the ingredients are to her liking, she stirs it with one of the flat rib bones of the antelope.

I'm still smiling.

I haven't stopped since last night.

Well, and early this morning.

As soon as Beh's eyes fluttered open, I rolled her over and found my way inside of her again. She had winced a little when I first entered her. Still concerned I had hurt her the first time, I pulled back out immediately and tried to find out what was wrong. Beh used our hands to show me what I had forgotten.

Using her fingers to guide mine, Beh rubbed at her sensitive spot and opening again, and I noticed she was not as wet and slippery as she had been the night before. My thumb rubbed at the spot above her folds while my fingers prepared her opening for me. When I felt her get wet inside, I replaced my fingers with the head of my penis at first, and then the rest of it followed gently. She had felt so good that I filled her with semen quickly. Then she took my hand and held it against her. She bucked her hips against it as she moaned and cried out for me again.

I really, really like it when she makes *that* sound—the one where she growls out my name-sound and hums at me. From now on, I will make sure she makes that noise *before* I put a baby in her. When I put my penis inside of her, it feels too good to slow down. Besides, once I finish, I'm really tired, and all I want to do is lie down. If I make sure she feels good first, then she might let me sleep afterwards.

Although I know there are many things we should both do today to continue to prepare for winter, I'm finding it hard not to watch her move around the cave. It has been so long since there was someone else with me, and just seeing movement in my cave still seems strange. When I had a tribe, there was always movement around. During the time I was alone, seeing something move was more likely a cause for concern than not. It's strange to adjust to seeing something move out of the corner of my eye without worrying what it might be.

Twisting my hips from side to side, I knock the fur away from my lower half, and I push myself onto my hand and knees. I jump up from the furs, yawn, stretch, and scratch my stomach. With light steps, I move over to the fire and capture Beh in my arms. I run my nose along her neck and then place my lips over the top of hers. Beh squeals and laughs as my fingers tickle up her sides but then pushes me away as I try to stick my fingers into whatever she is cooking.

I only want a taste.

I wait patiently until breakfast is cooked, and after we eat, Beh gathers up the bedding furs in a pile, along with the extra wrap I cut for her from the boar's hide, and stacks it all by the cave entrance. She slings the carrying basket over her shoulder and wraps her feet up with the funny foot coverings. Realizing she is ready to work for the day, I grab my spear in hopes of finding a large animal that is maybe docile or hurt enough for me to kill it. I should dig another pit trap, but I think gathering the easier foods might be better for my mate in the long run than spending days trying to catch a large animal.

We could use the extra fur, but we also have enough to get by for the winter. Some of it will need to be replaced by spring or at least moved to the bottom of the pile in the sleeping area. Between the foods we have already gathered, the boar and antelope meat as well as the fish, we should have enough dried meat for the winter. I'll just have to supplement it with some rabbits during the colder months.

While I fish at the lake, Beh washes the furs in the cold water. As I wait patiently for a fish to come close enough for me to spear it, I remember last night. I think about what it felt like to join with my mate. When I glance over at Beh, I see her kneeling by the edge of the water.

My mouth goes a little dry, and my penis immediately stands at attention. My spear and the fish forgotten, I am drawn to my mate. I loosen and remove my wrap as I near her, allowing it to fall to the ground as I keep going. Beh hears my approach and glances over her shoulder, and her smile quickly changes to wide, staring eyes that focus below my waist.

She makes some noises, but I do not hesitate. I drop to my knees behind her and pull her furs to the side. The little pink scrap of fabric is thankfully absent, and I barely register the same color out of the corner of my eye in a pile of things Beh has been washing, lying off to the side.

Trying to ignore the throbbing desire between my own legs, I remember my lesson from this morning and find her opening with my fingers first. I rub the spot she likes so much until she is gasping for breath, and I can feel moisture on my fingers. I slide one inside of her, move it in and out, and then add another. When she feels ready, I take my penis in my hand and position myself.

I hear Beh's gasp as I push slowly inside of her for the second time today. She rocks back as I enter her, easing my journey deep inside. I close my eyes, and I can feel the velvety texture of her channel as it covers me and engulfs me. I hold her hips firmly as I begin to move in and out, trying not to give into the desire to move rapidly. Moving too fast is bound to make me fill her quickly, and I want this to last a little while.

I remember my promise to myself from this morning, and I lean over her with my chest to her back, reach around and find the swollen little nub right above where I've entered her. Beh cries out as soon as I run my finger over it, and I feel her internal muscles clench down around my penis.

I am not expecting that.

"Hoh! Hoh!" I cry out as my hips rebel against my thoughts and thrust harder into her. A moment later, I empty myself deep inside her body.

With my forehead resting between her shoulder blades, I move slowly with shallow motions as I keep touching her spot. With my semen lubricating her inside, it is not difficult to keep thrusting inside of her, even though my penis isn't very stiff anymore. Beh groans as she reaches back to grab the wrist of the hand that still grasps her hip. She pulls it up to her chest and pushes it firmly against her covered breast.

I'm not sure what she wants me to do, so I grip and rub her breast with the same rhythm as my fingers near her entrance. I soon feel her nipple harden through the leather and try to pull at it. Beh's hand covers mine between her legs, and she pushes firmly against it as she pants my name-sound a few times before she hums and gasps.

Her legs shake as she cries out once more, and I release her breast so I can wrap my arm around her waist and keep her from falling to the ground. I want to do the same myself, really, but the rough sand near the lake isn't the most comfortable place for a nap. Besides, even though I have slept in the open in the past, I have Beh to protect now. No mate of mine will ever sleep outside of our cave. It isn't safe.

I help her stand on shaky legs and hold her tightly against me as she rests her head on my shoulder. My hands run over her back as her breathing slows. Once she has relaxed again, I help her gather up the wet furs, pick up my spear, and we head back to our cave.

As we walk across the field, still gathering the grains from the tall grasses and adding them to Beh's shoulder basket as we go, I notice Beh seems to not be walking quite right. She is walking slower than she normally does, and looks like she is in pain as she takes a step.

I stop her in the middle of the field and look into her eyes. She is not crying and doesn't appear upset at all. I drop the furs I am carrying and kneel down in front of her to pick up each of her feet. I can't tell if they are injured or not with the foot coverings over them, but I poke at them anyway and watch for her reaction. She does not cry out or act as though she is in pain, though she puts her hands on her hips and starts making a lot of mouth sounds at me.

Her feet do not appear to bother her, so I move up her legs—examining them closely, but I find no injury. As I reach their apex, Beh's noises become a little louder and she pushes my hand away. I look up to her eyes, and her head moves from side to side.

"No," she says.

I quickly move away.

Beh sighs and takes a step forward, holding out her hand. Tentative, I place mine in hers, and she pulls me close to her. With the side of her face placed against my chest, she makes soft sounds and hugs me against her. I don't understand but decide to watch her closely as I follow her back to the cave. I hang the furs outside so the wind will blow them dry and then fill one of Beh's cups with water so she has something to drink.

I'm still worried about her.

Beh tries to add some wood to the fire, but I take it away from her and push her back a little. I point to the grass mat and have her sit on it while I prepare food for her.

I make sure she rests for the remainder of the day. That night, I want to put a baby in her again, but Beh pushes my hands away from her. At first I think she is angry, and I try to figure out what I did to upset her, but she runs her hands over my beard and lets me hold her as she falls asleep.

She must not be *too* upset with me, but I am still confused.

And hard.

I consider using my hand to make my penis feel better, but I remember how Beh wanted the furs cleaned off when I spilled on them before, and I don't want to upset her either with messy furs or by waking her up. So I just close my eyes and try not to inhale through my nose because she smells so good. Eventually, I fall asleep beside her.

The next day, Beh's bleeding time starts. I'm pretty sure that means there isn't a baby inside of her yet, since I remember women in my tribe didn't have their bleeding times when their stomachs got bigger with a baby. I'm disappointed and want to try again, but Beh won't let me. As soon as I remove my furs and approach her, she pushes me back and uses her no sound.

She doesn't let me mate her at night when we go to bed either.

Or the next day.

In fact, she doesn't let me try to put a baby in her again until her bleeding stops several days later. By then, I feel so tense, I only manage to thrust inside of her a few times before my seed empties into her.

I'm glad I made sure she felt good beforehand. As soon as I'm done, I fall asleep.

Beh is in good spirits the next day, and she tugs at my hand when we approach the lake. I try to stay away from the water's edge because I have a sinking feeling she is not just planning on bathing herself, and the day is definitely a cold one. All I really want to do is take Beh back to the cave and try putting a baby in her again—I want to make it last longer this time—but she is intent on making a whole lot of noise with her mouth and washing every piece of clothing and fur she has touched in the last few days. When she is done with that, she lays the pieces out to dry and pulls my wrap from my shoulders.

I hold tight to it for a moment but then realize as long as she has my *wrap* in the cold water, she is not trying to wash *me*.

I should know better.

She lures me with her mouth and her hands to the water, and even though I know what she is doing, I can't help myself. I try to get behind her, but she turns and moves me to the water instead. As I plead with my eyes, she makes me immerse myself, just as she has. I shiver and wonder what she will demand when there is a layer of ice near the shore. Will she still want me to get in the water?

Not a chance.

Not even for the opportunity to put a…

Well…

Maybe.

She wraps a clean piece of fur around my shoulders and gathers up the rest of the bedding she brought with us. My mate is thorough in her washing, and I realize she is planning on washing everything we have been sleeping on or wearing, regardless of the cold of the day. With a groan, I lie down on my side and cover up with a dry fur to rest.

Beh makes constant mouth-noises as we head back to the cave.

I'm exhausted from being cold and wet. I don't know why, but resting near the water has made me more tired than I felt before. Beh, however, appears to be energized. I try to block out her sounds, but she doesn't stop.

The furs are still damp, and they are cold and heavy on my shoulder. Beh is carrying all the grain we collected as well as some cattail roots, nutgrass, and puffball mushrooms. She has a handful of reeds as well, and I wonder if she is going to try to make another basket with them.

She makes more sounds. The noise is constant. She even waves her hands around a bit when she makes all that noise.

I blow a long breath out my mouth and look at her sideways. She glances over to me with a bit of a smile and continues with the noise. I don't understand why she has to do that all the time. It's annoying, and even though I would do anything to protect and provide for my mate, I can't take any more of the noise.

I finally stop in my stride, drop the furs to the ground, and grab Beh by her arm. She halts in her tracks as I pull her beside me. I take my hand and place it over her mouth firmly as she looks at me with wide eyes. I growl low in my chest as I stare straight into her eyes. When I release her, her eyes narrow at me, and she huffs through her nose as she turns and starts back down the path to the cave. She is thankfully silent the remainder of the journey.

When we get to the cave, I drape all the furs that are still a little damp where they can dry before I tend to the fire. Once the fire is burning brightly, I sit in front of it to warm up and eat some of the grain and nut concoction Beh made for breakfast along with some of the dried antelope meat. I hold out some of the meat for Beh, but she doesn't take it from me or look at my hand.

Actually, she turns away from me a little, tightening the fur wrapped around her shoulders.

"Beh."

She doesn't look at me. In fact, she turns away a little more. I call out to her again, but she doesn't respond at all. I crawl over to her and hold the meat right in front of her face, and she shifts to the side again, nearly turning her back to the fire…and me.

Maybe she just isn't hungry.

I bring her water, but I get the same reaction from her. I bring her the wood carving for her hair, and she jerks away from me. Confused, I shift back on the dirt floor of the cave and away from her. I glance back up, and Beh opens her mouth briefly but then snaps it shut before she turns her back to me again without making any sounds at all.

I sit back on my heels and try to figure out just what is wrong, but I can't think of anything. I reach out with one finger and poke her arm, and her eyes finally meet mine. They are blazing with anger. I quickly look back down and sit on the dirt floor. I pull my knees up to my chest, wrap my arms around them, and duck my head a little behind my legs.

I watch my mate, but she doesn't move for a long time.

"Beh?"

Nothing.

My legs bounce up and down a little, and I try to hold them still, but it isn't really working. Why is she not acknowledging me? I don't understand what I have done wrong. I went in the cold water and washed off like she wanted me to, and I carried the wet furs back to the cave.

I didn't hunt today—was she upset all we had was dried meat to eat? I had not hunted or fished since before her bleeding time. Maybe she was tired of dried meat. I bring some of the grains to her; there is no meat in it at all, just some fat from the boar.

She still doesn't look at me, so I sit back down and hug my legs again.

Is she upset I haven't put a baby in her yet? Maybe if she put her mouth on mine, I can rub her with my fingers, and she will start getting wet. Once she is wet, I can make her feel good with my hands before I try to put a baby inside of her again.

"Beh, khhisz?" I look to her as her head swivels around, and I am met with another icy stare.

This one fades quickly as she looks me over, though. Her shoulders move up and down as she takes a deep breath and drops her face into her hands. Soft sounds come from her mouth as she rubs the heels of her hands into her eyes. Without looking up, she reaches one hand out toward me.

I look at it and then back to her, but her face is still covered with her other hand. Tentatively, I reach out and touch the ends of her fingers with mine. When she doesn't pull back, I move a little closer and take her hand. She pulls at it, bringing me to her side before she wraps her arm around my head.

I sigh in relief as I lay my forehead on her shoulder, glad that whatever it was that upset her has passed and hope she will now let me take her to our furs and hold her hips while my penis is inside of her. I am still feeling the tension of not mating with her for so many days, but Beh has made it obvious that she doesn't want to be touched there during her bleeding time.

For a while, I stay close to her, trying to gauge what she will do next, but we end up just sitting there. Thinking about putting a baby inside her has made my penis hard. Cautiously, I run my nose over the edge of her shoulder, not knowing how she will react. I glance quickly to her eyes, making sure she is still over her anger, and I see her softened expression. Her hand slips over my cheek and soft sounds come from her mouth.

"Khiz?"

"Kiss." She smiles and leans toward me, our mouths joining together and our tongues quickly following. She strokes her fingers down my arms, and I bring myself up onto my knees to get a better angle to taste her mouth. I cup her face with my hands, and her palms move to my chest and shoulders, pushing the fur wrap away from me so she can touch my bare skin. It makes my entire body shiver, but I'm no longer cold.

I can't wait any more.

I grab for Beh's wrist and pull her with me to the back of the cave where the furs lining the depression will be soft and comfortable when I take her. I coax her down into the furs with me and place my hand on her waist. My penis is throbbing, and I want to be inside of her so much it is actually starting to hurt a little. Beh smiles at me, and her face looks flush in the firelight. She comes down to kneel beside me and places her mouth on mine again.

The remaining furs we are wearing are quickly discarded along with the little pink scraps Beh wears. Her arms wrap around me, holding me against her body with my hard shaft pressing into her stomach. I grind my hips into her, and it feels wonderful.

It has only been a few days since the very first time I was inside of her, and now I feel like I have to be inside her as soon as possible, or something horrible is going to happen. I don't know what, but I know I want it—*need* it—right now. The idea of waiting another minute is not a welcome one.

Beh seems to have different ideas.

She guides my hands over her body, starting with her hips and moving up her sides. I alternate between looking into her eyes, which stare intently back at mine as her mouth makes quiet noises, and watching my hands touch her sides, her stomach, and her breasts. I watch and feel as she changes the pressure from tentative to more definite, especially around her breasts. She always moves slowly and usually with just a small amount of pressure—not too light or too hard.

She holds my hands against both of her breasts at once, and I run my thumbs over the nipples. The darkened areolas constrict, and the little buds in the centers stick out. My thumbs circle them each slowly, and Beh rewards me with a long groan.

She covers my mouth with hers, releasing my hands to do what they wish at the same time. She wraps her arms around the back of my shoulders, gripping me tightly and pulling me against her. I let out my own moan as my hips push into her stomach again, creating more friction along my shaft.

I need more.

Beh's mouth, now released from mine, moves quickly over my chin and neck, distracting me from all other thoughts—even about my penis. Her tongue flicks out over my flesh, and then her mouth covers the same spot, sucking slightly and bringing warmth quickly to my skin.

"Hoh!"

Beh's eyes meet mine as I look down at her. She moves back, placing her mouth on my shoulder and moving from one side to the other across my throat as I kneel in front of her, immobilized by the sensation. She moves back, places her closed lips at the center of my chest, and then moves back up to my mouth.

Unable to stand it anymore, I wrap both arms around her and push her back against the furs, covering her body with mine in the process. Our tongues find each other while my hand runs slowly down her side, trying to remember how much pressure she had used before. My fingers trace over her stomach, circle her navel, and then drop lower. They travel through her hair and down between her legs, finding her opening and that other little spot that makes her gasp and call out my name-sound.

Using soft and gentle touches, my fingers explore her folds while her tongue tastes my lips, and her fingernails scrape lightly on my back. It feels good when she does that, and reminds me that I still haven't managed to get inside of her yet. My fingers revolve around her opening, capturing the moisture there and using it to help their penetration into her body. Beh's hips buck, pushing my fingers deeper inside while she reaches down and holds the palm of my hand against her pubic bone.

"Oh...Ehd...Ehd..."

"Beh!"

Her hips buck again, rocking in time with my hand as I bring forth her cries of desire. I feel her body tighten on my fingers, and I remember what it felt like when her muscles constricted while I was inside of her. I wonder if I can make that happen again.

She moans my name-sound one more time as she falls back against the furs. I remove my fingers from her and run my nose up the inside of her arm then over her shoulder and along her neck. When I reach her ear, I take the lobe in my mouth and suck gently, just as she had done on my shoulder.

Beh hums and her fingers grip my back as I rise up and look down at her. She is so, so beautiful, especially when she is panting and her face is flushed. She is the most beautiful when her hair is tangled because I make her feel like *she* makes *me* feel when I am inside of her.

She reaches up and touches the side of my face again, then runs her hand down my chest and across my stomach. The heat from her fingers encircles the shaft of my penis, and for a moment, my eyes close as I revel in the sensation her fingers bring to me.

This isn't what I want though.

I want to be inside of her.

Moaning with the effort, I pull away from her and grip her sides firmly. I start to roll her to her hands and knees, but she makes noises and rolls herself back before I can get between her legs. I look up to her, afraid she is angry with me again, but she is smiling as she moves her head from side to side. She reaches up toward me, takes my hand with hers, and pulls me back over the top of her.

Rubbing against her stomach again feels wonderful as our mouths meet, and for the moment, I am lost again in her taste. Quickly though, I am reminded where I really want to be, and I try to flip Beh over again gently.

She doesn't let me, and I don't understand why not.

I wonder if she is not as wet as she wants to be, so my hand finds its way back between her legs, and I touch her warm folds. They are so slick from before that my fingers slip right inside of her, and she arches her body to meet my hand. I love the noise she makes when I do that, so I am again distracted as I begin to massage her spot with my thumb, and she moans along with my movements.

Beh's hand trails down my side and over my rear before she reaches around to touch me. Her fingertips run slowly from my scrotum to the head of my penis and I gasp. For a moment, I can't even bring in enough air, and my body stills. Beh's fingers stroke back, then wrap around me again. Her other hand pulls my mouth back to hers, and her tongue runs over my lips. I move my hands to her waist, knowing if I do not get inside of her soon, she'll be upset about the mess on the furs. I can't hold out much longer.

Her leg coils around my thigh, and she tightens her muscles, bringing me forward as her heel pushes against my backside. Her hand is still wrapped around the shaft of my penis, and she strokes it up and down once, causing me to moan. My hand grips her hip again, pulling at it in order to turn her to her stomach. Again, she resists, and instead, she pushes up with her hips as she pulls against me with her heel, and I feel my head graze her opening. Beh's hips shift again, and her hand strokes me forward.

My wide eyes stare up at my mate as I try to figure out just what she is trying to do. Her eyes sparkle as she smiles at me and slowly strokes her hand over my face. She makes whispering sounds as she moves her hips again, and the response of my body is automatic. As the tip of my penis feels the warmth of her body so close, I push.

Finally, though not in the right position at all, I am buried inside of her.

CHAPTER FOURTEEN

"Hoh!" I cry out as I am again encompassed by her body. The heat of her wrapped around me is incredible, just as it has been before, but it also feels very different. The angle of her body has allowed for deep penetration more easily, and I find myself not only completely surrounded by her, but the glans at the end of my shaft has hit a barrier deep inside her channel. I am as far inside of her as I can be.

Beh's neck arches and her head tilts back as she pushes up against me and gasps. Looking down to where we are connected, I am almost finished with just the sight of her underneath me.

I can clearly see where our bodies connect, and as I pull back and push forward, the visual of my penetration is beautiful, but there is more. With her knees bent and her legs spread wide, I can see all of her—not just where I enter. I can see where the short hair begins and ends and the soft, puffy outer lips that surround her intimate body. The inner lips wrap snugly around my shaft as I move, coating it in their slick wetness with every thrust.

From this angle, I can watch her hips rise from the furs as she meets my motions, bringing us closer together with every plunge. As my eyes move a little up her body, I am met with another wondrous sight: each time I enter her, her breasts move.

They shake and wobble and jiggle, and it's *fantastic*.

I lean forward a little, thinking maybe I will hold myself up on one elbow and try to catch one of her breasts with the other hand, but as I move against her, my pubic bone rubs over the top of Beh's mound, and she moans out my name-sound.

I pause and look at her face. She is beautifully flushed again, and her hands run along my shoulders and back, and then down to my waist. When Beh is on her hands and knees, she can't touch me while I'm inside of her, and I begin to note the advantages to taking her in this position. As I bear down again, her cries intensify and her fingers grip my backside, holding me deep inside of her as she shoves up against me frantically.

I glance down and realize I'm now firmly pressed against the spot at the top of her folds, where I usually rub my fingers. From this position, I don't need to use my hands.

Keeping myself inside of her, I rotate my hips once, and Beh's body shudders beneath me. Her fingers further dig into my backside. I pull back, press into her, and rotate again—trying to make my pubic bone use the same motions my fingers have before. This time, Beh cries out louder. A couple more times and I can feel her gripping my shaft as she arches her back and neck at the same time.

It's glorious.

Her arms drop to her sides and then rise as she rests them above her head. Her eyes open, and she looks up at me with a wondrous grin on her face. I smile back and then run my hands up her sides and over her breasts as I lean over her body completely, bringing my chest to hers. The backs of my fingers trail all the way up her arms over her head, and I grip her hands as I start moving again.

I move slowly at first, feeling the sensations over the whole front of my body as it rubs against hers. I feel her breasts against my chest and her warm breath on my neck. Our hands lock, the fingers threading through each other as I press her down against the furs and increase my pace.

Beh moans again, and I feel her legs come up around my waist, wrapping me up in her warmth as I thrust harder and deeper than I have before. I lay my forehead against her shoulder as the sensations tingle through my entire body before converging in my groin to explode and drown me in the feeling of releasing deep into her.

My shaking muscles cause me to collapse on top of her, completely drained. Beh's hands run down my arms and wrap around my shoulders, and I work my arms underneath her back to hold her close to my chest. We are both still breathing hard, and I can feel her heart thumping in her chest against my skin.

Thinking I might be crushing her, I roll us both to our sides, still holding onto her. The way her legs are still wrapped around me, I manage to stay inside of her as we move together. Beh's hand reaches up to push damp hair from my forehead before she leans in to press her lips lightly to mine. She speaks softly—the same sounds, over and over again—as her fingers explore my face.

Her eyes narrow slightly, and her brows push together. I poke my fingers in the place between her eyes and try to fix the wrinkled spot there, which makes her giggle. When she laughs, her body shakes and my penis drops out of her. I push back against her body, but I'm too soft to get back inside of her now.

Maybe soon, though.

Beh pushes her lips together as she tries to stop laughing and then places her mouth against my temple. Her lips are warm and soft on my skin, and I lean toward her to place my lips on her cheek and then on her forehead.

Her palm cups my jaw, and her eyes look intently into mine as she makes the same collection of sounds again. I place my mouth on top of hers, hoping she won't make noises all night. I lay my head back on the furs and hold her body close to mine. My hand runs over her skin, finding her breast and remembering how it moves when I am thrusting against her.

I start to wonder what other ways I could try to put a baby inside of her.

⋯•••◉•••⋯

The chill in the wind this morning is far colder than previous days. I wrap my outer fur tighter around my shoulders as I check over the landscape for any signs of danger. The fur is cut long and hangs down my back to keep the wind off of me. Seeing nothing of concern, but thinking of the impending cold, I collect some wood from the recess between the rocks above the cave entrance and bring it back inside. The stores are getting low.

Beh is asleep again, but I am not surprised. The sky is overcast, and the cave is still dark. I also woke her up twice during the night to put a baby inside of her. I tried to move really slowly the last time, hoping she wouldn't wake up, but she did.

I stack some of the wood neatly in a nice dry part of the cave, close to the fire but not too close. I need to gather more and think maybe I will do that today before it gets any colder. It takes a long time to gather a lot of wood since there aren't many trees near the cave, only the small grove near the ravine, but the wood from the trees there doesn't burn well. I have to go to the pine forest near the lake to collect better wood, and I can't carry very much at a time.

As I am stacking the wood, I notice there is a small piece of flattened bark up against the wall of the cave by Beh's clay dishes. There is also the small flint knife I gave to Beh when she was trying to cut up some of the boar meat. I pick up the bark to toss it into the fire when I notice there are a bunch of parallel lines carved into it, presumably with the piece of flint. I cock my head to one side and peer at it, but I can't fathom why Beh would put marks on a piece of wood. Though my first thought is to toss the piece of bark into the fire, I shrug my shoulders and lay the wood back where I found it instead. I may not know what it is for, but one broken dish is enough for me to learn not to mess with the things

176

Beh has put to use.

I look outside again and see that it is really quite late in the morning even though the overcast sky doesn't give much of a clue. I decide I need to wake Beh so there is still time to gather a decent amount of wood before dark.

I drop down next to her and reach out to touch her shoulder.

"Beh." There is no response from my mate, so I try a little louder. "Beh!"

Beh grumbles and rolls, taking the edge of the fur and pulling it most of the way over her head. I can't help but smile at the act. The little noise she makes is like a small animal's squeak. I pull at the edge of the fur, but her fingers grip hard. She holds tight to the edge of it, so I know she is really awake.

On impulse, I stick my feet underneath the fur and snuggle in beside her. I feel her body push back against mine as it seeks the warmth, and I wrap my arm around her waist. My nose slides across her shoulder blade and up to her neck as my fingers trace little light circles around her side and belly.

Beh squirms at my light touch, her grunts of protest escaping even as she giggles. I smile against the skin of her throat and run the backs of my fingers across her belly. She wriggles and laughs as she makes loud sounds and grabs my hand. I pull, bringing her to her back so I can look at her face.

Her eyes are bright, and her smile is glorious. Her hair is everywhere, creating a soft, fluffy brown cloud behind her. She gazes up at me and makes the collection of sounds she has been repeating often when we are together in the furs.

I smile back at her and then bring my mouth to her neck to suck on the skin. I'm growing hard quickly, and I know I need to stop. We have no time for mating this morning; we have to gather enough wood before nightfall. Our stores of food are growing, but we don't have quite enough to get us through the winter. The cold morning reminds me how soon winter will be here.

I pull away from her, and Beh scratches at my jaw with her

fingers, making more sounds. I start to turn from her to get up, but she grips my shoulders to hold me close to her. I tilt my head and smile back as she makes more noise. This time, she includes both of our name-sounds, which is strange.

But, that's my mate!

I nuzzle the tip of my nose against her and start to get up again. Again, she holds me back, saying our name-sounds together with another sound. I sigh and lay my head next to hers. I look over my shoulder to the cave's opening and wonder how late in the morning it really is.

"Ehd!"

My head moves back to look at her as she makes her name-sound, another sound, and then mine. My hand reaches up and touches her lips softly.

"Khzz?"

Beh sighs and places her lips quickly against mine. Smiling, my fingers tickle her sides again before I push myself out of the furs and pull Beh with me. We have too much to do to lie down any longer. As Beh eats, I gather up the tools we will need for the day. When she's ready, we head to the pine forest.

I use the large chunk of flint I have sharpened into a hand axe to break the logs into manageable chunks. Even though the day is bitter cold, and the sun is not shining, the work is hard and I soon discard my outer fur wrap, choosing to work wearing only the one that wraps around my waist. Beh watches me work and also busies herself stacking the pieces I have cut so we can carry them back.

We make two trips, but we still don't collect much wood, and the day is already late as we head back for the third load. Beh's noises have gone from quiet and occasional to a little louder and much more constant. I can see she's not happy, and I assume it's because of the cold weather and the hard work. Still, we need the wood, and we can only carry so much at a time.

Beh makes some more sounds and then stomps off toward a hollow log I had already discounted; it's too eaten out by termites to be worth hauling back. She sits by it anyway, knocking it around, then sitting back on her heels and just staring at the ground. When I glance up from my work a moment later, I can see her shoulders shaking.

I jump up, worried she may have hurt herself, and find my mate staring at a piece of broken, hollowed-out wood with tears running down her face.

"Beh?" I drop to my knees and reach out, and Beh comes into my arms.

The day is late, and even though I know we should bring a couple more loads of wood back, I also need to take care of Beh. She is upset, and though I don't know why, I know I have to care for her until she feels better.

There are only a few pieces of cut wood, so I lead Beh over to them and position her arms to carry them. Once she curls her arms up and around the logs, I bend down, put one hand behind her knees and the other behind her back, and lift her up.

Beh grips the wood a little tighter and lays her head against my shoulder, still crying, as I begin the journey back to the cave. I look down at her closely, making sure she is not actually hurt, and run my nose over hers so she knows I will care for her. I'm tired and my muscles are sore, but Beh comes first.

I carry my mate back home as dark clouds begin to form on the horizon. The wind picks up, and I hold Beh close to my chest as I pick up my pace. We barely get the wood into the crack in the rock before the clouds begin to pour rain from the sky.

Beh heats water in one of the clay pots, and her tears eventually dry. After we eat, I watch her stand at the entrance to the cave and watch the storm soak the fields outside. She stares without moving for a long time, but she relaxes back against me as I come up behind her and wrap my arms around her waist.

She turns her head back to face me, and I press my nose against her cheek, which earns me a smile.

We are stuck inside the cave for several days as the storm

continues on, accompanied by thunder and lightning, but we make good use of the time. I barely notice it as Beh's cries echo in my ears and throughout the cave.

I grunt with the force of filling her again and again as my mate's hands run up and down my body—gripping my shoulders and arms, then sliding quickly down to grab at my backside and encourage my relentless pace.

"Oh…Ehd…uh…uh…"

The sound of my name-sound on her lips encourages me, and I grind against her with every thrust. I move my hand from her hip up her side and grasp hold of one of her breasts. I watch her face as my thumb and finger pinch slightly at the nipple—just as she showed me to do—and her mouth opens into a scream as she shudders around me.

Her fingernails dig into the flesh of my rear, pulling me deeper into her and holding me steady as I fill her with semen and the possibility of new life growing in her belly. As often as I am inside of her, I think it must be soon that she will stop her monthly bleeds as her stomach becomes round and swollen.

I can't wait.

I slump against her, sweaty and worn out. Beh wraps her hands around my shoulders and drops her head back to the furs as she tries to relax her breathing.

The skies continue to pour upon us. My mouth presses against Beh's throat quickly before I pull out of her and get up to tend to the fire. There is plenty of wood for now, but I am worried we may have trouble collecting enough for winter. Rain has been constant and violent since the night I carried Beh back to the cave, and we have not been outside since.

Moving to the crack in the cave, I look out over the steppes. The ravine is flooded, and I am glad the cave is elevated enough that the rising water should not be able to reach here. It would have to rain for many, many more days for the water to rise that much. I hope it doesn't.

We need more wood.

As it is, the wood in the forest will be wet, and I won't be able to put it in the cache above the cave for fear it would rot before it could be used. We have also lost days of work at a crucial time. This means no more wood has been gathered, no more rabbits or fish have been caught, and no more plants have been added to our baskets.

At least we have worked on making a baby.

A lot.

I smile and walk back in to find my mate cooking, using her clay pots and making flowing, bird-like noises. There is rhythm to the sounds, and one sound flows into the next without pause. She just started doing this the prior day, and I find it much more agreeable than the noise she usually makes.

I go to her side and sit, resting my head on her shoulder and watching her mix things together, coming up with much more flavorful foods than I ever had on my own. I run my nose against her neck and sigh, content.

<hr />

Even with the work of chopping the soggy wood, it's too cold to remove my wrap.

The rain has finally stopped, but we have been left with temperatures that are enough to freeze the ground in the morning, and the afternoon sun does little to warm it up. Under the cover of the pine trees where the sun does not reach, the cold is bitter, but at least the wind is minimized.

Beh is near a small clearing of brush, working diligently.

I have no idea what she is trying to do and have already given up trying to get her to help me with the wood even though I made another flint axe the right size for her smaller hands. She is determined to do whatever it is she is doing instead. All I know for sure is that she hauled one of the old furs all the way down here even though it had been recently washed in the lake along with everything else.

Kneeling in front of a large log on the ground, I'm focused on my work and not paying close attention to her as she starts making a lot of loud noises. The sounds are not the alarming ones but the ones she seems to make when she is happy about something, and there is even some laughing accompanying them. I pay no attention because I'm almost done chopping through the large piece of wood on the ground in front of me, and I don't want to break the rhythm. I'm focusing hard, and I'm briefly startled when Beh steps right up in front of me to drop a pile of fur and sticks at my feet.

I glance up at her, somewhat annoyed by the interruption, and then down at the pile. Beh continues to make excited noises as she kneels down and spreads out the hide on the sides of which she has attached two long poles. When I look closer, I can see she has cut strips of leather, shoved them through holes in the hide, and then wrapped the straps around the poles to hold it all together. The thick branches are long, and the ends of the poles stick out farther than the hide itself.

I haven't the slightest idea what it is supposed to be.

I take a long breath, huff it out of my nose, and go back to chopping.

Beh makes more noises, which I try to ignore as I finish with the wood. The damp chips clinging to my arm are itchy, and I just want to get this done and return to the cave with at least a little bit of wood to try to dry by the fire. The cold is an indication of how little time we really have left, and now that I have a mate to protect, it would not do to have me freeze to death looking for wood in the snow instead of keeping her warm in our furs.

"Ehd!"

I keep chopping.

"Ehd!"

I wipe my forehead as I break through the piece I have been working on and go on to the next log.

"EHD!"

I finally glance up, and Beh's eyes blaze down at me. She makes a lot more noise and points down to the sticks and hide again.

She's covered it with the chopped wood.

The entire hide holds not just what I have cut up but also some of the branches that were lying around loose and work well for rekindling the morning coals. On the hide is far more wood than either of us can carry in many trips back to the cave. Beh reaches down and grasps the ends of the two sticks on one side of the hide and stands—raising the whole thing off the ground. The hide does not touch at all—just the other two ends of the branches. She takes a couple of steps backwards, and the whole pile moves with her.

Now I understand what she's been doing, and my eyes open wide at her discovery. I stand and approach her, reaching out to run my hand along one of the long poles. Beh smiles and makes more sounds as she drags it a little farther.

I catch up to her and take the ends of the poles in my own hands. I lift the whole thing up a little, and I can hardly believe how light it is. There has to be something wrong with the wood we've gathered. Maybe it's hollow.

I check over the pieces even though I know they weren't hollow when I chopped them up. They are solid and heavy. I bend down and try to pick up the hide full of logs, but I can barely move it! I go back to the ends of the sticks and grasp them tightly before pulling it all backwards.

It moves so easily!

Turning to my mate, I drop the sticks and wrap my arms around her shoulders in thanks.

With Beh's hide on a stick, we get all the wood we need hauled back to the cave that day. We even have enough time for me to reset the rabbit traps, collect water, reeds, and cattails by the lake, and still return to the warmth of the cave before nightfall.

I watch Beh with her clay pots and see her with different eyes than I saw her with the previous evening. How did she know to make such things as pots from clay and a way of carrying things I have never seen before or even considered? Now that I have seen it, it seems a natural and easy thing, but I don't think I ever would have thought of it on my own.

Rubbing at her shoulders and back and touching my nose to the side of her face and neck, I try to show her my gratitude. I use her wood carving to help her untangle her hair but pull back when she tries to do the same for me.

I want to do everything I can for her.

That night, I wait for her to call my name-sound over and over again in pleasure before I finally enter her. When I am done, I bring her food and water and then hold her tight to my chest as she sleeps. The next day, I take grasses from the field and weave them into a new mat for Beh, though it isn't a very nice one; at least it is not falling apart like the old one.

Beh watches me and sometime shakes her head back and forth with a little smile on her face. I think she is pleased. I hope she is. During the day, we use her hide on a stick for gathering. Every night, I touch her gently with my hands and my nose. She brings her lips to mine, and I feel her pleasure over and over before I place myself inside of her.

I would have done anything for her before simply because she was mine to protect and because I wanted to put a baby inside of her, but her hide on a stick has changed so much. I'm now in awe of her in a way that is far beyond her beauty and willingness to allow me to provide for her and take me inside of her. Previously when we walked to the lake, there was only time for one trip in a day. We would often leave some things behind simply because we could not carry them back. With the hide on a stick, I can catch many more fish to dry, and Beh can bring her clay back to the cave to finish. We work harder and faster at the water's edge to pull up cattails and even collect nutgrasses, mushrooms, and grain on the way back.

No matter what we load onto the hide on a stick, I can still pick it up and carry it—with far more than I ever could have carried in my arms. I don't understand it at all. It's not just a matter of balance. With Beh's hide on a stick, I can actually lift more weight than I can without it.

It's puzzling and wonderful.

Aside from that, we can place scraps of hide on the larger one and use it to hold the grain and other smaller plants as we gather them, instead of having to hold them while we gather. This has made collecting grain especially easy, and we can collect more grain in a single trip.

In just three days, we are almost completely prepared for winter.

After we eat our final meal of the night, I begin to pamper my mate again, starting with her hair. I am especially thankful because after she washed her hair in the lake, she decided it was too cold to get in the water, and I was spared a bath. Her hair is dry and doesn't have many tangles, but I work on it anyway. I enjoy touching it.

Soon, we move to our furs, and I take her into my arms. Our mouths meet, and I find her soft breasts and then the folds between her legs. Her knees fall away from each other, and her hips buck against my fingers as they slide in and out of her. She cries my name-sound, shudders, and drops into the furs.

My breath hurried, I roll over between her legs to position myself, but Beh's hand on my chest stops me. There is light in her eyes and a small grin on her face as she pushes me off of her and onto my back. I lay there confused as her fingers brush the hair from my forehead and cheeks, spreading it out on the furs behind me before her hands runs down my neck and over my shoulders.

My eyes drift closed, and I shiver as her fingers run over the length of my body, stopping at my waist and running back up again. She massages my shoulders and arms, and I look up at her, wanting her to know she did not need to do this—I was already so grateful to her and didn't need reciprocation. She gazes back down at me, her eyes soft as she gently strokes my cheek.

Her smile grows larger as she raises herself up and tosses one of her legs over my body, straddling my waist. I look up at her, confused for a moment, but then immediately distracted as she sits straight up and raises her arms over her head and up through her hair. The affect lifts her breasts high as her hair cascades over her arms and shoulders.

"Hoh!" I can barely breathe, and it has nothing to do with her sitting on my stomach.

Beh leans over a little, and her breasts hang in front of me like the most tempting of fruit. I reach for them, and I am rewarded with her groan of pleasure. She leans down farther to press her lips to mine, her tongue gaining entrance into my mouth as her hips slip lower. I can feel my hardened penis between her legs, and she moves back and forth, coating it in her slick wetness.

What other ways could I try to put a baby inside of her?

I feel her hand wrap around my shaft and hold it pointed up, away from my body. She raises herself higher on her knees, and all I can do is stare wide-eyed at her as she positions me at her entrance and slowly lowers herself onto me.

My chest seizes, and I cannot breathe. Along with my head against the furs, my eyes roll back. I would cry out if I could, but no sound escapes me. I feel her rise up, only to lower her body again, burying my length inside her channel.

When my eyes open, my breath escapes in a rush at the sight of her. Her hands rest on my chest as she raises and lowers herself over me. My hands, I realize, are motionless against her breasts, and I quickly rectify this with my caresses. She moans, tightens around me, and my hips respond in reflex—pushing up against her in an attempt to get deeper.

Beh begins to move faster, her motions quickening as her breasts bounce in my hands. I push up with my hips, arching my back and pushing up with my heels, but it isn't enough. My hands release her breasts and tightly grip her hips.

My muscles strain to lift and lower her as quickly as I can, the friction relieving me of all other sensation as I push into her repeatedly. She leans over me, her hot breath on my shoulder as she matches my movements, and the change in angle is too much. The pressure builds and quickly ignites fires within me, and I scream out for her as I fill her body.

Beh continues on, stroking slowly a few more times as I finish with a shudder, and then she lays her head against my shoulder.

Finally, I wrap my arms around her as my mind revels in how incredible she is, and my exhausted body falls into sleep.

CHAPTER FIFTEEN

I lay propped up on one elbow and look down at my mate, trying to understand.

Every time I touched her today, she pushed my hand away. Now she sleeps before I have been inside of her, my advances again refused. It is the first time we have not come together before sleep since the last time she was bleeding.

I don't understand, and my chest hurts.

She didn't seem angry with me or upset about anything. She had just gently taken my hand and moved it away when I tried to reach for her, making the *no* sound at the same time.

Now she's sleeping quietly, and I can at least wrap my arm around her waist and hold her against me. I consider putting myself inside of her while she sleeps, but every time I have tried that in the past, she has woken up. I'm afraid if I make another attempt, she won't be happy with me.

She rolls to her side, exposing her back to me. I move up against it to give her more warmth, pulling the fur around us at the same time. The fire is burning brightly still, and the cave is warm, but winter will be upon us very soon.

I lay my head down next to hers and inhale the scent of her hair. My nose touches her neck, and I close my eyes to begin a nearly sleepless night.

The next day is no different.

Neither is the next night.

I try everything to appease her. I make foot coverings out of rabbit fur to give to her, make her a new flint knife, and I give her all the very best pieces of meat from our dinner. When we are at the lake, I even immerse myself in the frigid water because I know it is her preference.

Nothing works.

On the following night, I hold her to me, press my lips to her neck, and look into her eyes as she touches me with her hand. Even though I want to hold out, she strokes me until I moan and spill on the ground. She won't let me touch her between her legs though she isn't bleeding.

I huff, angry with myself for not lasting longer when she gripped me. I look up to her and feel my chest clench. She smiles at me, but her eyes are sad. Whimpering softly, I pull her into my arms.

"Khiizz?"

She makes sounds with her mouth, and I try to silence her with my lips. Her hands grip my shoulders, pushing against me a little before I feel her relax and open her mouth. I move down her chin and throat—just as she has done to me before—but she stops me.

She takes my face between her palms and makes a lot of sounds. I can see tears forming at the corner of her eyes, and I still don't know why she is upset or why she is refusing me. Does she think we don't have enough stores for winter? Her hide on a stick has seen to it that we do. There is even extra, so we can be sure she gets enough to eat even if a baby starts growing inside of her.

With my thumb, I reach up to brush the tear from her eye, and her gaze drops with her hand. She touches her stomach for a moment and then waves her hands in the air as she makes more loud sounds. I cringe at the sound, and Beh sighs heavily before taking my face in her hands again.

Her mouth moves, and soft sounds come forth. I close my eyes and wish the sounds would stop, and she would just let me be inside of her.

She doesn't.

The next day, we go back to the lake, taking the hide on a stick with us. Though I still marvel at how well it works to carry things back to our cave, I can't concentrate on anything. I haven't slept well in three nights now, and I am tense and frustrated with my mate.

It is a little warmer, and Beh removes her wrap and the little pink bits of cloth to wash herself in the lake. Just looking at her body upsets me, knowing that for whatever reason, she will no longer let me touch her in that way.

Beh reaches down into the water with one of the little pieces of fabric she cut up and uses it to rub soaproot under her arms and around her neck.

I want her, and not being allowed to have her is really, really making me angry.

With a growl, I pick up the piece of flint I have been working on, turn, and stomp toward the edge of the forest. I hear Beh call to me, but I ignore her. I plop down in the grass away from her and turn my back, not even glancing in her direction as I continue to pretend to work.

The flint piece is too small, and the rock I use to knock pieces away from the core of the stone is too hard for any delicate work, even when I reduce it to a usable size. It ends up breaking, so I mostly tap away at the pieces, flicking bits of sharp flint all over the place and not really caring what I might end up with when I am done. Beh calls to me as she finishes her bathing, and I look up to see her walking toward me.

I glare at her out of the corner of my eye but don't move. She places her hands on her hips, and loud sounds come from her mouth. Raising my shoulder a little blocks my vision because of the thick wrap around me, and I can't see her glaring eyes. My head already aches from the lack of sleep and the glaring sun, so I turn away from her and begin to tap at the flint again.

Beh goes quiet, and a moment later I look up, just to see where she is. She is only barely visible at the edge of the water where she sits near the large, flat rock where she usually tries to shape clay. She smashes her fingers into the muck and smacks it around on the stone. I go back to my own work after a couple of deep breaths.

I don't know if I am angry about her rejection, sad about it, or afraid she will never let me touch her again. Memories of being alone through the last winter—the nights of howling winds, the cold chill as I huddled by the fire and stared at the embers, and the pain in my stomach that was not just from hunger—flood through my head. As I remember what it is like to be without anyone, I realize that if Beh never lets me put my penis inside of her again, having her with me is still be better than how it was. As long as she lets me hold her close to my chest, protect her, and keep her warm, everything will be all right.

With her, I feel complete and content.

I smile a little at the realization. Even though she does not let me inside of her, she still lets me put my mouth on hers, and she still stays in my cave. She keeps me company in our furs at night, and when she smiles at me, I feel warm inside.

I don't care about anything else.

I brush the flint chips from my lap and look up at my beautiful mate as she smashes clay against a rock. I stare at her as my smile brightens, and just as I am about to get up and go to her, movement near the edge of the forest closest to Beh captures my attention.

There is a man approaching her quietly from behind.

His hair is light in color and tied back against his neck with a piece of sinew, and his beard is thick. He wears fur wraps much like my own—from the simple cloak around his shoulders to the tied and wrapped fur piece around his midsection that hangs part way down his thighs. He has foot and leg coverings that nearly reach his knee. He is older and larger than I am, and he walks with purpose toward my mate.

Everything happens in the flash of time it takes me to get to my feet.

Without hesitation, he grabs Beh around her waist, and she lets out a startled cry as he pushes her to the ground. I can see the look on her face turn from annoyance to terror as she tilts her head to look over her shoulder and realizes the man behind her is not me. His hand comes between her shoulder blades as he pulls at the ties on his wrap and tries to place himself between Beh's legs.

I know exactly his intent.

He wants to put *his* baby inside *my* Beh.

With a roar, I rush toward the lake.

The other man turns to me, his eyes wide with shock. He hadn't seen me when he approached her since I was nearly hidden at the other edge of the pine forest. Now he turns toward me with Beh still in his grasp. She cries out, her arms and legs flailing against him as he tries to maintain his grasp around her body.

I run, my arms spread out wide and my throat becoming raw with my screams. He stands to full height and flings Beh to the side as he prepares for my onslaught. I do not care that he is larger. He is trying to take Beh from me, and I will *not* let that happen.

I can't.

I can't be without her.

We collide, and our bodies fall to the ground, half in and half out of the water. With a quick roll, he is on top of me. I feel the sting of his fist against my face as I struggle to right myself. He hits me twice more before I manage to punch back, sending him to the side. I follow him, trying to gain ground as I swing my arms wildly with the hopes of hurting him. We roll over each other, first with him on top, but I shove against him with all of my strength. As I pull back to hit his face, he kicks at my stomach and throws me off of him altogether.

I land on my backside near the water line but push myself to my feet quickly. He comes at me, ducking his head at the last moment and ramming into my stomach, knocking the air from my lungs. Falling to the rocks, I gasp and hit his back a few times but to no avail. I twist and turn as we grapple and manage to get my knee against his chest to shove him from me.

I can hear Beh yelling, but I can't look at her right now. My back is aching from where he knocked me to the ground, and I can still just barely draw breath. As the other man regains his footing, I pick up rocks and start hurling them toward him in hope of hitting him in the head, but my aim is off, and he comes at me again.

We circle each other, and I know that I can't beat him with just strength. He is far larger than I, and his strength much greater. My chest hurts, and I can feel bile burning the back of my throat at the thought, but in my mind I know I can't win. If I don't win, he is going to take Beh and put his baby in her instead of mine. He may even take her away from me completely.

I scream at the very thought and try to jump up and gain some advantage in height, but he is prepared for me and throws me easily to the ground. He jumps on top of me, and again I feel his fists. One strikes my temple, and for a moment everything goes dark.

When my senses return, he is no longer on me, and Beh is screaming my name-sound. I shake my head and push myself up on my elbow as I try to focus on the two of them not far from me. He has a firm grip on her arm and is pulling her to him as he backs away down the beach.

Crying out again, I jump up and rush over to them. The man is lifting my mate up off the ground, and she is screaming and kicking out with her legs. He looks up at my approach, growls, and throws Beh down to the rocks below him.

Just before I reach him, I see a short piece of driftwood on the ground in front of me, and I crouch to grab it with my hand before I leap at him again. He swings his arm and connects with my shoulder, but I grip the driftwood tightly and swing it at his head.

He screams in pain and wraps his arms around his head. I hit him again, this time across his back. He waves an arm at me, but I duck out of the way, and his swing is ineffective. The next time I swing, I connect with his jaw, and he flies backwards against the rocks.

Rolling unsteadily to his hands and knees, he scampers on the ground for a moment before he gains his footing and runs for the trees. With a scream of victory, I run for Beh, who is lying motionless near the water. Dropping to my knees beside her, I lift her head from the ground and push her hair out of her face.

"Beh!"

Her eyes are closed, and she doesn't stir when I call out her name-sound. There are visible bruises forming on her cheek and arms, but I don't think those would cause her to sleep. I wrap my other arm around her shoulders to lift her further from the rocks.

There's blood all over the rocks where her head landed. Beh's hair is red and matted, and her blood is all over my hands and her face. I pull her into my lap and hold her tightly, trying to push the blood away from her skin, but it keeps coming out of a gash near her temple. She must have hit her head on the rocks when he threw her to the ground.

I keep trying to push the blood away with my fingers, but it just doesn't stop. It drips and pools on the ground as I cry out her name-sound, but she doesn't open her eyes. My chest feels like it's trying to crush itself, and my throat is tight and sore as I cry out for her but receive no answer. My hands shake as I hold her head against my shoulder and rock back and forth. I feel warm tears leaking from my eyes.

I don't bother to push them away.

My forehead hurts when I squeeze my eyes shut and tuck my face against her tangled hair.

"Beh?" I shake her shoulders a little, but she does not move. I shudder as tears stain my cheeks again, and I turn my face to the sky and scream.

<hr/>

I don't know how long I sit on the rocks, holding my mate against my chest—I only know that as the wind blows colder, it finally gets my attention, and I look up to see the sky turning red with the sunset.

Beh has not moved.

I gasp and cough, trying to clear my throat so I can breathe properly and then decide I just don't care. My stomach roils, and I have to turn my head over my shoulder as I retch. I swallow hard through bile and mucus in my throat and cough again.

"Beh?" I whisper. I run my thumb over her cheek, and her skin is cold. I'm gripped by another sob as I lay my ear against her chest, barely able to keep my grip on her as I listen closely…

…and hear the shallow but steady beat of her heart.

I need to get her back to the cave to warm her.

Stumbling to my feet, I lift her in my arms. Part of me wants to just run as fast as I can to get her to safety, but her furs are still lying on the ground near the edge of the lake, and I don't want to risk falling and dropping her. I refuse to put her down though, and I hold her with one arm as I bend at the knees to reach her furs and place them over her body. I gather everything I can in this way and tuck her close against my body as I begin to walk.

It's good I know the paths as well as I do because I can't focus on where my feet are going, only on the woman in my arms and the blood on her face. Another cry rips through my chest as I keep up my slow but steady pace, trying to make sure I don't jostle her too much.

The sun sets behind my back just as I reach the steppes on the other side of the pine forest. I can see the cliff that holds our cave, but it still takes some time to get there. Making my way up the slight incline and then through the tight crack while carrying Beh isn't easy, but I hold her tighter and manage to get inside.

It's dark, and the fire is nothing but embers.

As carefully as I can, I lay Beh in our furs at the back of the cave. I place the side of my face against her chest once more. She still hasn't moved at all, but I can hear her heart beating. Taking a deep breath, I stumble to the fire and quickly rekindle the flames, add logs, and rush back to Beh's side.

She is still, and her skin remains chilled.

I rub my hands up and down her arms in an effort to warm her and then grab all of the spare furs from around the cave to pile them in the depression where we sleep. I lie beside her, wrap her in the furs, and push her hair from her forehead again.

The gash no longer seeps blood, but it is nasty looking even in the firelight.

"Beh?"

Nothing.

I feel tears in my eyes again, and I sniff loudly. It's hard to breathe through my nose. I touch Beh's cheek and then the edge of her lip. I press my mouth to hers, but I get no response.

I can feel her breath coming from between her parted lips.

I wrap my arm around her waist, and I bring her against me. I lay my head on the furs beside hers and watch her face, waiting for her to open her eyes or mouth and make a sound. How many times have I been annoyed with her strange noises, wishing her to be silent like she is now?

My chest clenches again.

Finally, I realize I would give anything to hear my mate's sounds again.

CHAPTER SIXTEEN

I sleep very little, waking often to see if Beh's eyes have opened. I wonder if she just needs to rest and will wake up when the sun rises in the morning, just like she does every morning, but she doesn't. I try shaking her and yelling, but it doesn't help. I hold her head up and attempt to get some water down her throat, but it mostly spills out around her mouth. I think she swallowed a little, but it is hard to tell.

I can't make her eat though.

Dipping a scrap of cloth from Beh's old leggings into water I warmed by the fire, I slowly wash the blood off of Beh's face. Beh doesn't like being dirty at all, and I hope cleaning her off will help wake her up. I try to get the blood out of her hair as well, but that's not very easy because her hair is so tangled. I try a little water first, rubbing the strands between my fingers to loosen the dried mess, but it doesn't work well. I pull her up against my chest and try to use the wood carving to get the snarls out, but holding her limp body and using the wood carving at the same time isn't easy. It takes a long time to make it smooth.

I take the time—Beh likes her hair clean and without tangles.

What does it matter if she's asleep?

My own head is throbbing, and my cheek is sore and swollen from where the other man hit me. As long as I don't touch it, it's not too bad. If I forget and bump it with my hand, it hurts, but it is nothing like how Beh is hurt.

I sniff and feel my sore eyes begin to tear up again.

"Beh?" I push some of her hair off her forehead and look at the cut. It doesn't bleed anymore, but it's bright red around the edges, and her skin is bruised all around her temple and down around her eye. I touch my nose to the spot below the black and purple marks and close my eyes.

I wonder what I will do if she doesn't wake up, and I don't have an answer. As I lie back down next to her and pull her into my arms, my stomach growls, and suddenly I know exactly what I will do. If she doesn't wake up, then I will just lie here with her until I don't wake up, either.

———————⟫•••❖•••⟪———————

I don't bother to move from the furs when I wake. I hold Beh against me, checking to make sure I can still feel her heartbeat in her chest and her breath on her lips. I run the tip of my nose over hers and whisper her name-sound, but there is no response from my mate.

Remembering how she woke up every time I tried to put a baby in her while she slept, I wonder if I can wake her up that way. The air in the cave is chilly as I remove my wrap and try to enter her body, but I can't stop the ache in my chest, and my penis doesn't get hard, so I lie back down and pull her close to me again.

"Beh."

I rock her body as I had back at the lake, whispering her name-sound over and over again and wishing I could hear her say mine. Choking sobs escape from my mouth as I tighten my grip on her and wonder if there is anything else I can do.

When the sun goes down, the cave is pitch black.

———————⟫•••❖•••⟪———————

It's dark.

The wind howls outside, and I wrap the furs tightly around Beh, making sure she doesn't get cold. I have to hold her close to me because I can't see her in the dark and cold of our tiny home.

⟶ ••◦◐◖◗◑◦•• ⟵

"Ehd?"

"Beh…"

"Ehd…"

I feel the soft touch of fingers against my cheek and squeeze my eyes shut. I don't want to wake from this dream. I might be a little colder than I prefer to be in my dreams, but I can hear the funny sounds my mate likes to make, so I will take the cold without complaint.

"Ehd!"

My eyelids part, and I see Beh's beautiful face turned toward mine. Her lips are dry and cracked, and she is pale in the subdued light coming from outside the cave. I feel as if my body is covered by giant rocks as I look at her and realize I must still be dreaming. When I wake up, she will have her eyes closed and won't say my name-sound again.

But she does. She does say my name-sound, and her eyes are still open.

"Beh?" My eyes open wider as I realize I am not dreaming this time, and her eyes are really open. She is really awake and making sounds again. "Beh!"

I cradle her against me and hold on as tightly as I can without hurting her. I sob her name-sound over and over again as I hold her, and my chest feels lighter as she raises her hand to grasp my upper arm. Pulling back a little, I look over her face—just to be sure she really is awake—and run my hands softly over her skin. As my fingers touch her parched lips, I quickly jump up to bring her some water.

Moving is difficult because I am weak from lack of food and

drink. I force myself to haul the water skin over along with one of Beh's clay cups. With my arm around her shoulders, I help her sit up a little to drink. She ends up taking too much and coughs but only for a moment. She quickly takes another drink after the coughing subsides.

I place the cup down and touch the side of her face gently. Her eyes move slowly to mine.

"Beh…" I stroke over her cheek with the pad of my thumb, and I am rewarded with her smile and strange sounds.

I love them and press my lips off to the side of her mouth so she can keep making noises.

Carefully, I lay her back against the furs and go to warm up something for her to eat. I move over to the circle of stones next to the clay dishes and the dried meat and use a short stick to poke into the fire pit to find coals.

I am met with nothing more than cold air and ashes. I drop down to my rear in front of the cold ashes as the reality of it sinks into me.

The fire is out.

There is a pounding ache all around the back of my head, which makes it hard to think, but I know exactly what I have done. I didn't think Beh was going to wake up, and I had let the fire go out.

I glance over my shoulder at Beh, still lying on the furs but at least with open eyes. I can see her fairly well from the light coming in the cave's entrance, and she smiles at me when our eyes meet. She must not realize what's happened.

Taking the risk, I move my hands through the ash, trying to find any bit of heat in the pile, but there is none. It is only cold and dusty. Some of the ash billows into the air and makes me sneeze.

When the fire burned my home and tribe, I had taken part of it with me and kept at least a spark of it alive through the first season I was alone. As the days grew colder, I forgot to bank it one night and woke to a cold campsite. Though I had made fire before, it had always been with the help of others to keep pressure on the stick and blow at the tinder if enough heat was created to light a bit of wool or hair to get the fire started.

I had no one to help me, and it had been three days of trying before I managed to get another fire started. Beh can't wait that long. She is awake now, but she is still injured. I need to be able to care for her, and to do so, I will need fire. I don't think Beh is well enough to help me.

I take a deep breath, fighting the desire to go lie back in the bed and succumb to the weakness I feel and the leftover despair of thinking Beh would not wake up. I can't let myself give up now, though, just because I feel weak and tired. I have to help Beh, even if it will be hard to get another fire started. I also can't take three days to make it happen. The cave is cold, and my mate needs warmth and food to get better.

Lining up some of the kindling Beh collected with the hide on a stick, I find a long, straight branch that should work well to make fire. I stumble outside to the cache of firewood and find a dry piece of outer bark that is fairly flat. I also strip off strands of inner bark from one of the logs. Running my fingers through my hair, I pull out several strands and bunch them up with the shavings from the log. Together, they should make good tinder if I do manage to produce a spark.

When, not *if*.

I failed my mate when I let the fire die, and I have to make it right, now. I have to make a fire for Beh. I won't fail her again.

I get everything I need together and go check on Beh. I bring her water and dried meat along with one of her cups full of acorns. I quickly break them open with a stone and place my lips against her forehead before I go back to my fire-building materials. I can hear Beh making her sounds, and I look back over my shoulder at her, listening closely.

I love her sounds.

Placing the shavings to one side of the flat piece of bark, I use my flint knife to carve out a small depression in the center of it. Once it is the right size to firmly hold the straight stick, I place the end of it in the hole and raise myself up on my knees. I hold the stick between my palms and take a deep breath. My hands begin to rub back and forth rapidly, setting a quick rhythm as I push down on the stick to create more pressure along with the friction.

Beh continues to make sounds, and I feel my heart quicken just to know she is there behind me in the furs, awake and okay again. She still needs care –I know that. I also know I will never, ever fail her again. I will not leave her alone for even a moment, and I definitely will not allow our fire to go out again.

As if to remind me of the reason, a cold wind blows through the mouth of the cave.

When my hands reach the bottom of the stick, I quickly move them back to the top again, trying to keep the pressure on the end of the stick against the bark. The stick rotates as fast as my palms can move, and I try not to let myself slow down as my knees begin to ache against the stone cave floor and the muscles in my arms fatigue. I'm weakened by lack of nourishment and a little dizzy, but I keep going.

I glance toward the fur and see Beh's eyes are closed. In a panic, I drop the fire-starting stick and rush to her side. Groggily, her eyes open, and I hold her tightly against my chest for a moment as I feel my cheeks moisten with tears of relief. I feel her hand against my face, and the tips of her fingers rub the tears from my cheek.

I feel a strange combination of both light and heavy in my chest. I am grateful that Beh is still all right, but I also know I will have to start all over again on the fire. My arms and knees already ache, but I can't afford to rest. I can't take days to get another fire going.

I eat a few of the acorns and chew on dried meat to give myself some strength. Beh tries to sit up but looks so tired. She runs her hand through my hair as I place my forehead against her shoulder for a minute. With a long sigh, I move back to the fire-making tools to begin again. I use an old fur on the ground as a little padding for my knees.

Before long, my shoulders burn with the pain of overuse; sweat drips from my forehead, and I still do not have a fire. Beh moves up slowly, making soft noises as she approaches me, but I try not to look or allow myself to get distracted again.

I need this fire. Beh needs it. I have to provide for her.

The thoughts keep me focused through the pain in my muscles. My palms push the stick toward the bark over and over again, continuing the friction to increase the heat. My eyes twinge as sweat runs into them, but I keep going—never slowing down, never stopping. After what feels like days, I can see the tiniest bit of smoke right at the edge of the little hole where the stick meets the bark.

It is then Beh makes a loud, sharp sound, and the stick flies out of my hand.

With a cry, I grab for the bit of hair and bark, but it is too late —the pressure lost, the heat diffused. I feel my shoulders slump forward as the exhaustion comes over me, and my eyes slowly turn to my mate, whose sounds startled me.

"Beh!" I cry as I look into her smiling face and wonder if her head doesn't work right anymore. She has to understand the importance of fire, and she has to know I will have to start over again now.

She holds out her hand and makes more noise, smiling and waving her other hand toward the back of the cave. When I look to her palm, I see the little round thing that came off of the funny leggings she was wearing when I first found her. It's not very shiny anymore because it's covered in dust. It must have been lost in the dirt on the floor of the cave.

I narrow my eyes in confusion. She is excited because she found the little round thing, and this excitement is enough to warrant startling me? Does she not realize our fire is out? I want to grab her and shake her in frustration, but I realize she might still be sick.

She makes more noise and then laughs.

My mate is very, very strange, and sometimes it's extremely frustrating.

I slump to the floor, tired and sore with a blister on my palm. I grip my hair with my hands and pull at it a bit. I bring my knees up to my chest to drop my head down on them. Beh continues with her noises, and though I want to be annoyed by them, I am not. She's still making noises, which means she is awake and all right.

But for how long?

As if in answer, a gust of wind finds its way from the entrance to blow against my sweat-covered skin, chilling me quickly. I need to get a fur to cover the entrance, which would help with warmth in the small cave. Still, we need fire more than anything to provide us with heat, a place to cook, and also a way of warding off any predators that may seek shelter for winter in our cave.

"Ehd!"

I open my eyes to look up at her. She points to me, then to the round thing, and then to the fire-stick, bark, and tinder. She is making noises faster now, holding the little round thing up and pointing at my waist. I tilt my head and lay it on top of my knees as I watch her animated display. When she points at my lower body again, I wonder if she wants me to put a baby in her now.

It might keep us warm, so she does have a point.

I get up and move closer to her, placing my hand on the side of her face and running my nose over hers. I run my hand over her shoulder and down her arm, stopping at her wrist. I wrap my fingers around it and start pulling her back toward the furs.

"No, Ehd."

Beh's sound doesn't seem angry, but I still cringe and take a step back from her. When I look to her, she is holding up the round thing and reaching for my waist. In the fold of my wrap is my flint knife, which she takes out and holds up next to the round thing. She makes more noise and moves closer to the fire-starting materials.

I start to sit back down, but she grabs my hand and brings me next to her. The noises continue as she points at the fire-starting things, the flint knife, and the round thing over and over again. She makes eye contact with me and says my name-sound.

"Beh," I respond.

She sighs and shakes her head rapidly. With another deep breath, she positions her hands—one holding the round thing and the other my knife—right over the top of the flat piece of bark and the tinder lying on top of it. She rubs the little round thing over my knife, and a small dark scratch appears over the surface.

I grunt and grab it away from her. She makes a lot more noise, but when she reaches for it, I will not give it back. I need that knife; it's my best one. I don't want it marked up or broken by the little round thing. With a huff, she gets up and goes to the back of the cave, picks up another piece of flint—the axe I use for chopping wood—and returns to the fire area. Her eyes meet mine with a glare, and her jaw is tense. She raises her eyebrows when I narrow my eyes, but I make no move to stop her this time.

She rubs the flint with the round thing again and makes a dark mark on the surface of the axe. She does it again and again. Her eyes narrow and the muscles in her arm tense. She lets out a little growling sound, which I find very, very enticing.

In my distraction, I almost miss what she does next.

Her frustration growing, she slams the little round thing against the flint hard, and a tiny spark of light flies into the air before it is quickly extinguished.

Beh lets out a whoop much like the one she made earlier, startling me again. My eyes grow wide as she hits the round thing against the piece of flint again, producing another spark that lands on the bark below with a tiny wisp of smoke.

"Hoh!"

Beh's eyes turn to mine, and she smiles broadly as I look from her to the things in her hands to the tinder below. I move my face down closer as she strikes the flint again, and when the spark drops to the bark, I blow softly…and the spark goes out.

I look quickly to Beh's eyes, and the sounds from her mouth are quiet. Her eyes narrow and focus in concentration as she leans over. She moves to strike the flint again, and a spark flies into the air and hits my nose.

"Ahh!"

I jump back in pain and surprise, rubbing at the burned spot.

Beh's sounds are louder as she drops the flint and round thing and then brushes at my nose. It doesn't really hurt but does surprise me. I look up at my mate through my lashes as she looks over my face and then runs her thumb over my cheek.

It's distracting, but as she picks up the flint and round thing again, I remember more pressing issues, and we go back to trying to start a fire. Beh strikes the flint, and after a couple more times the spark hits the tinder directly, and when I blow, a tiny flame arises. Only a few minutes later, I add a few thin sticks and move the burning bark to the stone circle. A few minutes after that, there is a roaring fire blazing.

Leaning back on my heels, I look at the fire. Now that the task is complete, I have no idea what to think of how it was accomplished. I have never seen a fire started so quickly except in a lightning storm like the one that burned the forest and killed my tribe.

Like the hide on a stick, I have no idea how Beh would ever think to do such a thing to make a fire. How can fire come from the little round thing? Is that what her tribe uses to make a fire? Is that why it is part of her leggings?

There are too many questions in my head and no way to get any answers. I drop down to my backside and feel the tension begin to flow out of my body as I breathe deeply. We have fire again, and my mate is awake.

I glance at my mate who is sitting on the grass mat and smiling broadly. Her eyes turn to mine, and they seem to glow in the firelight. I crawl over to her and wrap my arms tightly around her middle, placing my head in her lap and my face against her stomach. I hug her tightly in gratitude and awe as she strokes my hair and makes soft, whispering sounds.

Finally, I know we will be all right.

CHAPTER SEVENTEEN

As the first flakes of snow begin to fall from the sky, I look out across the cold steppes with more comfort than I would usually feel at this time of year. When I work my way around the hide that partially covers the entrance to our cave, I see the reason why and smile.

Beh makes quiet, rhythmic sounds as she stirs cooked grains, cattail roots, and rabbit meat together in one of her clay pots. She has made another one, a larger one, and it lies in the coals of the fire just outside the cave. With the hide on a stick, we dragged back the large pot from the lake, and Beh bathed me, using warm water heated in a clay pot over a fire. That way, Beh can wash both of us off without freezing me half to death in the process. With Beh's firemaker, it is easy to have a fire anywhere we go, even down by the lake.

I have no idea why my mate likes washing so much or why she pushes me to do it as well, but it seems to make her happy. When my mate is happy, she smiles and lies down in our furs at night with her legs spread as I take her slowly, filling her with my seed to start a child.

Beh calls out to me, and I turn from the darkening sky and move back inside. She holds one of her clay bowls up to show me our food is ready to be eaten. I look around the cave and marvel at how much we have gathered over recent days using the fires by the lake to quickly dry fish and rabbit as well as using the hide on a stick to return far more than we could carry on our own. There are clay containers and wrapped hides full of food, enough to take us through the winter even if we already had a handful of children. There almost isn't even enough room for it all. The stacks of grains, dried meat, and hides are encroaching on the cave's living space.

Beh calls me again, bringing me from my thoughts.

My heart beats faster just looking at her.

I go to her and kneel beside her for a moment before I lay down on my side and place my head in her lap. Sometimes I prefer just having her scent all around me to the meals she makes. I roll to look up at her and am graced with her smile and her fingers on my cheek. I also notice that she has discarded the leather ties around her waist and between her legs that catch her blood and again wears the little pink cloth instead.

I hope she has no more bleeding times. I tell myself the reason for my thoughts is because I want her to get round with a baby growing in her, but I also don't like it when she pushes me away when she has her bleeding time. My mate likes everything to be clean and dry, and putting my penis in her while she is bleeding is clearly not an option.

There are other times, though, even when she is not bleeding, that she still refuses to let me put a baby in her. I think maybe she is tired on those days since we have gotten so much of the work done for winter, but there are other days where the hard work doesn't seem to bother her. There was also a day when she didn't let me touch her, and I just kept her inside with me all day and brought her everything she needed.

She still would not let me try to put a baby inside of her. Not even a little bit.

I reach up and run the backs of my fingers over her cheek. I can feel my own heart starting to beat faster in my chest as I wonder if she will receive me tonight—if this would be the time a baby starts growing inside of her. I turn my head to kiss her thigh, eliciting a giggle from my mate.

"Kiss?" Beh smiles down at me.

"Khizz!" I sit up so I can reach her better and place my lips over hers. Placing my hands on either side of her head, I warm her lips with mine. She has definitely been sampling our meal, and I can taste it on her tongue.

Beh's hands trail up my back and grip my shoulders. I continue to run my lips over hers as my hand slides down her neck and over her breast. When I seek out the opening to her fur, she pushes my hand away and makes some sounds. Reaching around me, she brings back a bowl full of food and places it in my hands.

I sigh and take the bowl with a pout. I am hungry, if I am to admit it to myself, but I would rather hold Beh in my arms and maybe choose to return to the furs early this night—just to avoid the cold, of course. As I tip the bowl into my mouth, I feel Beh's soft fingers pushing a strand of my hair off my face and around my ear.

It tickles.

I reach over and do the same to her, winding a long strand of her soft hair around the curve of her ear. I follow the strand all the way down her shoulder and back with my fingers until I reach the end. Beh smiles and I can see her cheeks turn red in the firelight as she glances away. I scoot a little closer to her, abandoning the bowl to the side as I reach up and push more of her hair away from her face and off her shoulder.

She reaches out and does the same to me again.

I feel my lips turning up into a smile as we go back and forth, moving closer and closer together each time we reach for one another. Finally, I am close enough that I run my nose over her cheek as she tucks more of my hair off my forehead and behind my ear. My hand moves from its loose position on her waist to a more firm position on her thigh, pushing her fur open so I can touch her skin.

She shivers under my touch, and I pull her closer to me as I open my own wrap—determined to warm her with my skin. I'm hard, and when her leg brushes against me, I gasp.

Beh's lips cover mine again, and I reach between her legs with my thumb to rub against the hard little nub I find there. She groans into my mouth as her hands twist in my hair, and her hips push against my hand—looking for more friction. She doesn't let me touch her there for very long, though.

My mate knows exactly what she wants, and I am grateful.

Beh raises herself up on her knees and shifts so that my thighs are between hers. I feel the tip of my penis graze her opening. I can feel her moisture gather around me before she grips my shaft and positions me at her entrance. Like she does when she climbs on top of me, Beh slowly lowers her body over mine, encompassing me in warmth, her scent, and a feeling of peace and oneness.

My hands grip her hips, and I slowly raise and lower her body over mine, bringing us together slowly as I watch her eyes. Beh hums and wraps her arms around my neck as she moves up and down with me, her eyes partially closed and her mouth turned up in a beautiful smile.

When I feel the pressure collecting in my body focus and explode into hers, my skin is covered in the warmth of her breath, her skin, and her smile. I don't cry out as I sometimes do but lay my head against her shoulder and moan softly into her skin as Beh utters short, sharp gasps and shudders around me.

My chest rises and falls as I look up at her, mesmerized by her in too many ways to consider. Despite her oddities, she is without a doubt perfect in every way that matters to me. Her hands run over my face, scratching at the short scruffy beard on my jaw before she leans in to capture my mouth with hers. When she leans back again, she is still smiling.

Lifting her body a little, Beh climbs off of me, and I start to turn back to the bowl of food, wondering if it's still warm at all. Before I get the chance to determine the warmth of the food, Beh grabs my hand and tugs at it. I look over to her and tilt my head to one side. Her smile and blush are back, and she tugs at my hand again until I move toward her. Beh turns immediately and heads for our furs.

Beh is still hungry...but not for food.

⤐ ∙∙●◐◗◉◖◑●∙∙ ⤏

The wind outside is loud and cold, but in the firelight of the cave, wrapped up in warm furs and the arms of my mate, everything is warm and comfortable. My arms and legs feel heavy, and I find it difficult to keep my eyes open as I curl my body against Beh's. I can feel her fingers on my shoulders and in my hair, and it makes me smile.

Beh makes soft sounds as her fingers run along my cheek and jaw. One finger stops at my lips and runs back and forth over the bottom one. I can hear her making the same sounds over and over again, and I take a deep breath and settle against her shoulder. My eyes fall closed again, and it is warm and peaceful here.

Beh's finger runs across my lips again then over to my ear and back to my nose. It tickles and I suddenly sneeze. Beh begins to laugh as I rub at my nose to get rid of the tickly feeling. Beh covers her mouth with her hand, but I can still hear her snickering and see the sparkle of laughter in her eyes.

She's so beautiful.

Fully awake now, I roll over on top of Beh and capture her laughing mouth with my lips. We roll to the edge of the furs and back again as Beh's giggles turn to groans. I can feel her hips pushing up against mine, and I am very glad she no longer bothers to wear the little pink things at night.

Beh's hands push on my chest, and we roll again—this time with her ending up on top, straddling me. She reaches for my hands and places them over her breasts as she rises up on her knees just far enough to position me at her entrance and drop down with a gasp. Her hips roll as I thrust up into her, both of us quickly panting and sweating despite the chill of the cave. Our furs fall around us, but I barely notice.

She is enough to warm me—inside and out.

Grabbing her hips, I roll us again and end up with her pinned below me as I slowly move on top of her, using deep, hard thrusts until she is crying out for me as I fill her again. I run my nose along the warm blood vessel on the side of her neck and then to her ear before I lay my head against her shoulder. I press my body against hers for a moment before moving to lie beside her.

I look up at her and smile as she looks down with shining eyes and brushes hair away from my face. Beh's lips move and noises come out—the same sounds repeated again and again. Her eyes look at me intently, and I can see them tighten slightly as the sounds come out softly. Her hand is on the side of my face, and I can feel slight pressure against my skin where she touches me.

Then she makes our name-sounds sounds with another sound in between them. She leans forward a little when she does, and she puts her fingers on my lips. I watch her, not sure what she is going to do next as she takes my hand in hers and places my fingers over her mouth. She usually gets angry when I cover her mouth with my hand, and now she is doing it herself.

My mate is strange.

She makes the sounds again, and I can feel her lips move under my fingertips. She says her own name-sound, then another noise, and then my name-sound, all with my fingers touching her lips.

"Beh," I whisper. I feel her mouth turn into a smile.

"Ehd." She makes more noises, pauses, and then takes a deep breath. She makes the one sound again, and I feel the way her lips and tongue move as the sound comes out. At first, her tongue touches the back of her upper front teeth. Her mouth drops open a little more, but finally closes again with her top teeth barely touching her bottom lip as air rushes out, completing the noise.

So much effort for one sound!

She does it again.

"Llll…" I place my tongue behind my teeth like she does, and her eyes widen. Her head bobs up and down rapidly as she makes the sound again. I open my mouth and round my lips.

"Aww…" Finally, I watch her teeth tap her lip.

"Ffff…"

She makes the sound again, and she gives me a glorious smile as well.

"Llll…ooaawwffff…" The noise doesn't sound the same at all. I try again. "Luh…awwfff."

"Love." Her sound is quiet and succinct. It takes me longer to repeat it.

"Luhhff."

Beh's eyes become large and round as she quite literally squeals and grabs a hold of my head, laughing and crying as she makes the sound over and over again. Her lips cover one side of my face and then the other and then finally come to rest on mine. I feel her tongue against my mouth and I open to her. When we break apart, I hear her make the sounds again.

"Beh loves Ehd."

"Luhffs!" It kind of sounds like the noise an old wolf makes when trying to clear snow from its nose. I have no idea why Beh is so excited, but I wrap my arms around her anyway—enjoying her heat and the comfort her body brings as it lies next to mine. Outside, the cold wind continues to howl, and the snow continues to fall, but in here, we are safe, warm, and together.

The noise itself doesn't matter as long as Beh is happy.

———————⟫•••◗◖•••⟪———————

The snowstorm has lasted a long, long time. Outside, the sun hasn't been visible, and the passage of days is impossible to determine. I sleep with winter's heaviness, enticing me to the depth of the covers and my mate's warmth, but Beh does not. When I do stir, she is sometimes tending the fire or cooking. Often she is just lying beside me and slowly stroking her fingers over my hair in the dim light of the cave.

This time when I wake, Beh is nestled beside me and breathing slowly. My shoulders are chilled, and I see the furs have fallen from us. I quickly pull them back up and wrap my arms tightly around Beh. The skin of her back is cold, too, but quickly warms when I wrap her back up again.

The cold has stirred me from my deeper sleep, and my eyes stay open as I watch Beh slumber. Remembering other winters in this same place on my own is enough to cause my heart to hurt. Then, when I opened my eyes, there was nothing to see aside from the burning embers of the fire.

Being careful not to dislodge the fur from her again, I get out of the sleeping area and lay logs across the coals. The flames spring immediately to life again. In their light, I can see a round bowl with traces of grain inside as well as a fur lying next to the rocks, wrapped around something.

I unwrap the fur, and inside is the large, deep pot Beh made with a lid over it. When I remove the lid, there is a layer of something at the bottom. I'm not exactly sure what it is, other than it looks like it has some of the acorns and pine nuts on tops of it.

I stick my finger in and poke at the concoction. My finger goes easily through to the bottom of the pot. I curl it around to bring some out, but it doesn't really stick to my finger at all as I expected. I stick in a couple more fingers and dig some of it out. The consistency is soft and just a little moist, but not wet. It's just a little bit crumbly, but mostly it feels…fluffy.

I sniff at it, and it smells of cooked grains and nuts. Putting some in my mouth confirms it, but the texture is completely different from anything I have eaten before. I like it though, and it quickly fills my stomach.

I hear Beh's noises and look over toward the furs. She's lying on her side, propped up on one elbow. She smiles at me, and I quickly bring the whole pot over near the bed so I can crawl back into the furs with her. We eat; I put my penis inside of her for a while, and then I fall back to sleep.

⋙•≫≫●≪≪•⋘

The warmth and comfort of Beh's presence have become commonplace but not taken for granted. When I wake, Beh's heat is the very first thing I notice. I nuzzle against her skin and revel in the feelings that course through my body when I touch her.

I'm wrapped around her with my head on her shoulder, and when I tilt my head, I look up at my mate. She lies on her back with her head tilted toward me and her eyes closed. I snuggle closer to her, and my hand runs slowly up and down her side.

I accidentally brush against her breast.

It's warm, too.

And soft.

I trace one fingertip around the nipple, but I can't really see in the dim light of the fire. Her breast is mostly covered with one of our sleeping furs anyway. I can still feel it though, so I do. Beh shifts a little in sleep, and I pause for a moment.

Though I would like to try to put a baby in her again, I don't want to wake her. I'm not completely sure how long we have been asleep, and I already tried earlier in the night, hoping it would make her feel better.

Beh's eyes kept tearing earlier in the day, and I don't know why she is sad. There had been several days after the snowstorm finally passed that she was upset—she had even gotten angry at one point and thrown the little stick into the fire. I recognized it as the one she had been marking with her flint knife. I am sure she has been marking it every day, but after she burned it, she didn't mark a new stick. It has been many days since she had done that, and she hasn't cried since.

Not until this evening.

My arms wrap around her, and I move my body up so I can pull her against my chest. She rolls easily, and even in her sleep, her arms find my shoulders. I reach down and pull the furs back over us—all the way up to the back of her neck. We had discarded our clothing into a pile and just used the furs in the sleeping area. It is more comfortable this way, especially since more time is spent in the furs than out of them.

I hug Beh to me once more, but then I remember how soft her breast is and reach between us to touch it again. It's still warm, and her skin is smooth. Her breast is full and round, and she groans a little when I palm it, so I stop.

I really don't want to disturb her even though I'm getting hard just lying beside her.

I look toward the cave's entrance and wonder if the day will bring sunlight or just more clouds. If it is warm enough, I might try to find some fresh meat—it has been some time since we have had any. We haven't gone hungry at all though, which makes me smile and hold Beh closer. Even on my own, I would not have been able to eat as much during the winter days and still expect to have anything left come spring.

Beh keeps taking our food and doing strange things with it. She smashes up the grain using a rock and one of her clay bowls, then mixes it with fat and nuts and leaves it in the coals for most of the day. She then cuts it with a flint knife into little squares and gives me some with a bowl full of stew.

It tastes good, but I've never seen anyone make so many different things to eat. No one in my tribe ever made such things. There are other foods I think she tries to make, but they don't turn out as well. She made hard, flat things from the grain, but they burned in the fire. She wouldn't let me try to eat them afterwards.

I hold Beh through the remainder of the night, thinking of how different winter is with her here. Just as light begins to be visible through the hide over the cave entrance, Beh stirs and looks at me.

Her brilliant smile lights my day more than the sun lights the sky.

Beh reaches up and touches my cheek.

"Love," she whispers.

"Luffs!" I respond, and her smile brightens even more.

Without a doubt, I will do anything for her.

The wind on the steppes bites at the exposed skin of my cheeks and neck. I tense my shoulders and try to bring my head down into my fur, but the wind seems determined to get up underneath my coverings and chill me as much as possible. I quicken my pace back to the cave and my mate.

Near the entrance to the cave, some of the wind is blocked by the cliff, and it isn't quite as cold there. I tuck the two rabbits I caught in my traps under my arm and grab some of the wood out of the cache above the cave. Once I'm inside, my body gives forth an involuntary shudder as the temperature change hits my skin.

Beh looks up from the fire, smiles, and begins her noises. I drop the rabbits and go to her quickly.

"Khizz luffs?"

Beh snickers and presses her warm lips to my cold ones. She makes more sounds –a little louder this time—and rubs at my frigid cheeks with her hands. My skin warms quickly with her touch, and I go to the side of the cave to skin the rabbits for our dinner.

Beh has a lot of the other food already cooked, so when I give her the thin pieces of meat, it doesn't take very long before we can eat. Beh makes a lot of noise between bites, touching various things around her as she does. She used to do that a lot—holding up one of the clay dishes to me, or maybe a stick or a fur—but she would often get upset after a while, so she didn't do it very much anymore. She switches to the rhythmic sounds, which I like better, until I finally cover her mouth with mine and take her to our furs.

Early the next morning, my eyes blink open, and I'm a little disoriented from waking so early. Winter is for deeper, longer sleep, but something has pulled me from slumber early.

It's my mate.

Beh is next to me in the furs, positioned up on her hands and knees and completely motionless. I look up at her just in time for her to cover her mouth, jump up, and bolt toward the cave entrance. Rolling out of the furs, I run after her and find her leaning over the edge of the ravine, vomiting. She is trying to keep her hair away from her face at the same time, and I can see she is struggling.

I move to her side quickly and wrap her hair behind her neck —holding it with one hand and steadying her with the other. After a couple more times, she sits back on her heels and starts to shiver. I pick her up, and she turns her face away from me. Once we are back inside the cave, I bring her the water bag, some dried mint, and a fur to wrap around her shoulders. She chews the mint, rinses her mouth, spits into the coals of the fire, making them hiss, and leans against my chest as I hold her tightly. I rock her gently in my arms, but my mate is unusually quiet the entire day.

Beh makes very little noise all day and falls asleep as soon as she lies down on the furs at night. I hold her close to me, and when I fall asleep, I remember one of my brothers who vomited for days and days until he died. Two more of the children in our tribe died the same way during that winter.

The next morning, the same thing happens.

On the following day, I haven't slept at all, and I am terrified. I hold Beh and rock her in my arms. She makes a few noises, but her eyes are dull, and she looks so tired. Later in the day, she drinks some of the meat broth I make for her over the fire and eats some of the leftover grains she cooked the previous night.

She seems fine, but then again, she seemed fine later yesterday as well. I refuse to let her go, even for a moment. When she goes outside to relieve herself, I stay right at her side. She yells and tries to push me away, but I won't budge. She finally goes, and then I pick her up and carry her back inside despite her feeble struggles.

Beh growls at me but ends up putting her head against my chest as we sit back in front of the fire. I place my chin on the top of her head and close my eyes.

"Ehd." I perk up at the sound of my name-sound, realizing only then that I was starting to doze off. I look at Beh, and she looks up at me. She makes a lot more sounds and touches my cheek.

"Luffs." When I make that sound, Beh always smiles. She usually says it back, too, but this time her smile doesn't touch her eyes, and she says nothing in return. Instead, she takes my hand and puts it on her stomach.

"Ehd," she says softly. I feel her hand press mine against her stomach, and memories flood through my brain. Women in my tribe who would be sick like Beh has been—often when they first woke up in the morning—would sometime later begin to show the child growing inside of them.

My fingers twitch, and understanding rises from the skin of my fingers, where they touch the warm belly of my mate, all the way up my arm and into my brain. My insides feel warm and gooey as my head is filled with thoughts of Beh's stomach growing big and round. The pictures in my head continue, and I think of a tiny little person suckling at her breasts while I hold both mother and child to keep them safe.

"Beh?" I look at her, and my cheeks begin to ache due to the size of my smile, but I can't help it. I lift Beh from my lap and put her down gently on the grass mat by the fire. I then lean down and brush my nose against the center of her stomach, right below her navel.

Finally, I have put a baby inside my mate.

CHAPTER EIGHTEEN

Taking a long, deep breath, I inhale the scent of spring. It's not really here just yet, but it is close enough that the air feels and tastes different. I can hear the chirp of birds as they begin to fly around in the shrubs near the ravine, and I wonder if Beh would like to eat their eggs.

I wonder if the baby will like them, too.

Beh comes up behind me, her eyes still blurry from sleep with one of the bed-furs wrapped around her shoulders. I drop to my knees and press the side of my face to the little swell between her hips just like I do every morning. I haven't felt the baby move inside of her yet, but I remember when my mother was carrying my little brothers and sisters how her stomach would move when they kicked and rolled.

I can't wait to feel the baby I put inside of Beh move.

Beh uses the fingers of one hand to thread through my tangled hair as I look up into her face. The sun shines down and hits her hair from behind, making her look as if she is glowing. Wrapping my arms around her waist, I hold her tightly for a moment before I stand again. She holds my hand with hers and uses the other hand to keep the fur clasped at her neck. It is still quite chilly outside even with the sun shining and spring weather obviously on the way.

"Khizz?"

Beh leans toward me and places her mouth against mine as I touch her cheek with the backs of my fingers. I take a long, deep breath again before leading her back into the cave where she can stay warm.

My mate's stomach grows as the days grow longer and warmer. As winter ends, we have plenty of stored grain and dry meat to last us a while, but it's good to find something fresh and green to eat.

There is clover blooming all over the steppes, and I alternate between just eating it where I sit and watching Beh as she walks around collecting the flowers. When she bends over to pick them, I feel myself grow hard as I think about the previous night and how much wider her hips seem to be as I thrust inside of her. Beh is growing along with our baby, and I am sure she has never been as beautiful as she is now.

I scratch at my chin and jaw. The beard I have grown over the winter is fuller than it has been in previous years, and it's itchy now that the day has grown warm. I rub at the back of my neck, too, and realize how long my hair has gotten. Beh's hair is really long, and I watch as she reaches behind her head and wraps her hair around itself, twisting and turning it into a long cord down her back.

Intrigued, I move over to her and run my fingers down it. It doesn't hang down as low as it usually does, but I'm sure she didn't cut it. Beh turns and looks at me over her shoulder, making sounds the whole time with her mouth. I look to her and then to her hair in my hand. I give it a little tug and Beh swats at my fingers.

"No, Ehd!"

Worried she will continue to be mad, I drop down and nuzzle against her belly. I glance up at her and then quickly look down again. I run my nose over the fur wrap around her until I feel her hand on my head, and I know I am forgiven.

Beh picks more flowers, some mushrooms, and the buds and tender young leaves from many of the plants as we go by on our way to the lake. I grip my spear tighter as we approach, making Beh stay in the shadows of the evergreens as I scan the area first. I am not going to take any chances at all—not when Beh has a baby inside of her.

Every time we come to the lake, I'm reminded of the man who tried to take Beh from me.

Once I am certain there is no one else around, I pull the little round firestarter from a fold in my fur wrap and use it and a piece of flint to get a small blaze going. Beh goes to the water and fills one of the water bags. She lays it on the hide on a stick and then fills a clay pot with water. She takes my hand, and I don't bother to fight about it. I quickly immerse myself and let Beh scrub at my hair and face. Once she has deemed me clean enough, I sit next to the fire and try to warm up a bit while I watch Beh bathe.

She drops her furs to the ground, and I see she is still wearing the little pink things even though they seem a little stretched over the top half of her, and the bottom half kind of folds and rolls over itself underneath the bulge of her stomach. I feel my smile broaden as she turns to one side, and I can see the silhouette of the bulge where the baby is growing.

I keep my eye on her as I go to the edge of the water where flint can usually be found. I find a good-sized piece and a stone to knock against it. I need some sharper knives as many of mine have become dull with use. I get a few long, sharp slivers and then go back to the water near Beh and sit down to wait for her.

The ends of my hair are still wet, and they feel chilly against the back of my neck. I reach behind my head and grab a chunk of hair and then use one of the new flint blades to saw through it.

"Ehd!" I hear Beh call out my name-sound and I look up at her. Her eyes hold shock and confusion, and I immediately drop my flint and pick up my spear again. I look all around us but see nothing out of the ordinary. When I look back to Beh, she is walking toward me.

She stops and lays her hand against my head, making a bunch of noises as she runs her fingers over my hair. She reaches up with her other hand and grabs hold of the end of my hair on one side—the side I have already cut shorter—and shakes her head.

Running her hand down my arm, she pulls me down to sit on the stones as she takes up my last bit of flint and goes to work on my hair. It doesn't take her long, but when she is done, she takes me back to the lake and washes me off again. I run my fingers through the shorter strands, and I am surprised at how even it feels. I usually end up with long bits in random places around my head.

Beh makes more mouth sounds, takes my hand, and sits me down near the fire. I wait as she grabs one of the cloths she uses to wash and dunks it in the pot of warm water. She looks over my face very carefully, and I stay still under her gaze. Beh reaches up and rubs the hair on my face. Then she presses the warm, wet cloth to one side of my face and holds it there.

I'm not sure why she's doing this—she's already washed my face—but I don't move to stop her. The warmth feels good as she washes my cheeks and neck.

My mate picks up one of the flint blades in her hand and removes the cloth from my skin. With a slow, smooth motion, she runs the edge of the blade across my jaw. I widen my eyes as I watch her smile come across her face.

"Luffs?" I don't know what she's doing, but she seems very happy about it, so I stay still as she runs the edge of the sharp rock over my neck and cheeks. When she's done with one side, she does the other. She puts down the flint and holds the warm cloth to my face again—first one side and then the other.

Beh sits back on her heels and give me another smile as she makes noises. She takes my hand and presses it against my cheek.

My beard is gone!

The skin of my face is smooth just like Beh's. I run my

fingers all over, but there is no hair anywhere. It feels strange but nice as well. My face isn't itchy anymore and feels soft when I touch it.

I look at Beh, who is still smiling and making mouth sounds. I rise up on my knees, take her face in my hands, and look into her eyes. They flicker around my face and head as I lean close and first run my nose over one cheekbone and then the other. Her hands cup my face, too, and she rubs her thumbs over my cheeks before her lips press to mine.

I place my hands on her shoulders and then run them down her arms and wrists. I move them to the front of her and lay them over her rounded stomach. Beh looks down, her eyes becoming wet as she looks at my hands on her belly.

"Beh, luffs?" I hope it will bring back her smile, and it seems to for a moment. I can feel how worried she is, and I am not sure if she is worried for the baby, our food supplies, or for something else entirely. I only know I want her to be sure of me and know that I will provide for her and protect her and the baby. I will never let anything happen to them, and I will make sure they both have enough for next winter. I will always take care of them first, making sure there is plenty for both of them in the coming seasons.

My hands push the tears from her cheeks, and Beh tries to smile at me.

"Loves," she whispers.

I wrap my arms around her to show her everything will be all right. Beh's tears finally dry, and we gather up everything to bring back to the cave.

As the days pass from warm to hot, Beh's belly gets bigger, and she doesn't seem to be as sad as she was early on. Sometimes, she still gets upset for no apparent reason, but she always does that. It's just a part of her.

My mate is unusual, and I couldn't be happier about it.

Fresh foods and meats are plentiful in the spring and summer days though most of the game is in the form of birds, rabbits, and fish. We need another large animal for its hide—the baby will need to be kept warm—so I dig another pit trap along the steppes far from our cave home.

Beh tries to help at first, taking a large, flat rock and scraping the dirt away from the area I've selected on the trail where many large aurochs have passed to get from their feeding and living areas to the lake. If I could get one of the large oxen to fall and injure itself in a hole, I would be able to finish it off quickly. They are so large, a single one would provide not only plenty of meat but also sinew for tying, hide for clothing, and bones for tools. Its horns and organs can be useful for many other things as well.

Once Beh sits back and grimaces with her hand around her stomach, I make her stop trying to dig with me. I know it will take days to make the pit trap even if she does help, and I don't want her in pain. She backs off with a sigh and goes to the hide on a stick to pull out the reeds she had collected at the lake. She begins to weave them together, and I have to smile at how quickly she makes something useful.

The things she makes are far from pretty, but they can usually hold something.

I continue to dig, getting into a rhythm that doesn't allow for much thought. The steppes are hot today, and the sun burns down on my bare skin as I work, creating what must be a river of sweat running between my shoulders and down my back. Beh startles me a little when she brings over the water skin and makes me drink. She makes a lot of sounds and runs her hand over the side of my face as she smiles at me.

I think she likes it when I don't have a beard, so I let her cut it off when we go to the lake to bathe. It always makes her smile, and then she runs her hands all over my face. Usually after she's done touching it, she grabs my shoulders and places her mouth on mine. Soon after that, she grabs my penis and puts it inside of her.

I'm glad she still wants to do that even though she already has a baby in her. I still wonder if another one will start growing, too, and if they will both come out at the same time. That never happened to the women in my tribe, though, and I have seen plenty of babies being born.

The day grows late, and I'm not even halfway done. I would stay until nearly dark if I were on my own, but I want Beh back in our cave and safe before nightfall. We make a quick trip to the lake where Beh takes my hand and starts making a lot of noises as we approach the far side. She takes me to where the best clay can be found, points at it, and then points at the hide on a stick.

She goes to wash in the lake, and I sigh as I start to dig. After several handfuls of clay are sitting on a grass mat on the hide, I lean back and stretch out. My eyes move over to Beh for a moment, and then I slowly and automatically scan the line of trees for any signs of danger.

In the woods off to one side, something catches my eye. I stare for a moment, trying to figure out what it is, but I'm not sure. It looks like a large, round rock, but it is bright white. Intrigued, I get up from my place by the little inlet to the lake, check Beh once more, and walk a little ways into the trees.

As I approach the white rock-like thing, I realize there is more white stuff on the ground there, not just the round part. I don't have to get very close before I realize exactly what it is—the white, round skull of a person. The other pieces consist of a handful of ribs, part of the spine, and hip bones. There are a few other random bones scattered about as well.

I recall the man who had attacked Beh in the autumn and know this was the way he ran after I hit him with the log. I lean over and see that the surface of the skull has a long crack in it. The crack is in the same area where the log struck him.

I have to swallow as bile rises to my throat, and a shudder runs through my body. I take several steps away from him, not wanting to feel sorry for the man who had tried to take Beh from me but unable to feel happy to know he could not threaten us again because of what I had done.

I had never hurt someone before.

Never.

I hear Beh calling my name-sound and swallow hard again before turning back to the clay and the hide. When I walk out of the woods, Beh makes many noises and runs her hand over my face. Her eyes narrow with concern as her sounds become soft, and she looks over my shoulder into the forest. As she touches my arm, I realize I am shaking.

I quickly take her hand and lift up the end of the hide on a stick, intending to head straight back to the cave. Beh has other ideas, though, and drags me over to the water to wash me off. The cool water over my hot skin calms me, and for once, I am grateful for her insistence on cleanliness.

The sun has nearly set by the time we reach the cave, and we are both exhausted from the day. As soon as we have eaten, we go to our furs. As I place kisses over her huge belly, I wonder how long it will be before the baby decides to come out and if the baby will look like me. Beh's hands run over my face and shoulders, and my fingers tease at her nipples and between her legs until she cries out for me.

That night, I dream.

I am holding Beh's hand as she balances on the balls of her feet over a pile of soft furs. Her eyes are squeezed shut as she makes a groaning sound while I reach down and catch the baby that falls out from between her legs. The tiny thing lets out a long, healthy wail, and I hold it up for Beh to see. Beh's eyes go wide, and she collapses to one side—unmoving. I shake her and scream her name-sound, but she doesn't respond. Her face transforms into that of a woman from my tribe...one who died while giving birth to her daughter...

When I wake, I'm covered in cold sweat and shaking. I swallow hard to stop myself from crying out loud and reach my arms around Beh to bring her close to me. She mumbles in her sleep and fidgets—it seems hard for her to find a comfortable position now—but then settles back down.

I had forgotten about the woman in my tribe who had been trying to give birth for so long in the middle of the winter, only to fall just after the child was born. Though the baby was healthy and survived off the breast of another woman, the mother never even opened her eyes long enough to see the child.

My mother had given birth with ease to so many children, I haven't even thought about how it was sometimes difficult for others. What if Beh can't get the baby out for a long time, and it hurts her? What if the baby doesn't come out on time or comes out too late? What if she needs help, and I don't know what to do?

What if something happens to Beh—how will I take care of the baby? I don't have another mother to nurse it, and I've never seen a man use his nipples that way. I'm pretty sure they don't work. How will the baby survive?

How will *I* survive?

I have lived on my own for a long, long time, and just the last few seasons with Beh make me realize there is no way I ever want to be alone again. I would never be able to survive without Beh with me. I wouldn't even want to live if she were no longer here.

I reach over and rub Beh's round belly, hoping the contact with her skin will calm me. It works to a degree, especially when the baby begins to move around, and I feel little knees and elbows —at least, I think that's what they are—poking against the inside of Beh's stomach. It doesn't seem to move quite as much as it used to, and I think maybe it's too big to move around so much.

What if the baby is too big to come out?

I can feel the panic rise inside of me as I pull Beh closer to my chest. She groans and rolls over, her blurry eyes taking in my face before she lays her hand against my cheek.

"Ehd?" Beh makes a lot of sounds with her mouth, and I can see the worry in her eyes. As I look at her face, my mind conjures images of her with glassy eyes and pale, cold skin. I shudder, and I feel tears at the corners of my eyes.

Without further sounds, Beh wraps her arms around my head and pulls me down to her chest. Her body moves back and forth slowly within the furs, rocking me and running her fingers through the hair on the back of my head. I try to calm my thoughts, but the only thing that brings me any peace is staring into her eyes.

<hr />

Beh spends days digging a small, baby-sized depression at the back of the cave behind our sleeping furs. She places the softest of the furs around soft, dried grasses. She uses the leather from the auroch caught in the pit trap to make a pile of little triangle shapes though I can't understand what she intends to do with them. All I know for sure is to stay out of her way. I tried to help many times, but Beh shoves me away, not accepting any assistance.

She acts as though her head is hot with sickness, but it isn't.

Her mouth noises are almost constant, but so is her desire to pull me down into the furs and put me inside of her, and she has been like that for days and days. At first, I was thrilled. Now, I am completely worn out.

I watch as my mate takes handfuls of cooked grains and meats from the pot near the fire and licks them off her fingers. She moans in the pleasure of the taste, and the sound that might have made me hard earlier in the day only makes my penis twitch a little as she looks up at me and smiles through her breakfast. I feel my cheeks ache at the smile I give to her as she struggles to stand.

I reach down and take my mate by her forearms to help her up. She stumbles slightly, but I keep her upright. Beh gasps, and she grips my arm even tighter. When I glance down, I can see her knuckles pale with her tight grasp. She releases me with one hand and uses it to rub around and underneath her belly as her breath escapes in quick little gulps. We stare into each other's eyes, and understanding passes through them.

Finally, the baby is coming.

CHAPTER NINETEEN

The sound of my mate's breathing and the slight crackling of the fire are the only sounds in the cave. The echo of Beh's last round of screams has faded away though it seems the sounds may forever be lodged in my brain.

I don't remember the women of my tribe taking so long to have a baby.

Beh takes a long, deep breath, and I watch her face closely for a moment before tentatively offering her one of the clay cups with water in it. She closes her eyes and squeezes my hand but doesn't take the drink. At least she doesn't throw it back at me this time.

The sun has set outside, and Beh is exhausted. My dream comes back to me, and I try to hold her close and give her comfort, but she sometimes pushes me away. I try not to think about something terrible happening to her or the baby, but I can't help it. My chest hurts and my throat tightens up. I had wanted to put a baby inside of her since I first brought her back to the cave, but now that the baby is really coming out, I'm frightened.

I know Beh is too. I can see it in her eyes.

Her breathing becomes more rapid, and her fingers clench my hand as she cries out again. I wrap my arm around her to steady her. Her current hands-and-knees position seems to be as good as any of the others she has tried, but the baby still doesn't come. Beh's fingers grip around my hand and into the old, worn fur on the ground below her. I tried to put the softer ones below her at the beginning of the day, but Beh moved all of them to the little divot she carved out for the baby.

After the pain seems to have passed, Beh drops to her side on the floor. I reach out and stroke her face, but she doesn't look to me.

"Beh?"

I see her eyes tighten a little and her chest rise and fall with a deep sigh, but she still won't look at me. I touch her cheek and then her shoulder. Beh just closes her eyes. She holds her breath and doesn't make a sound, but I can tell by the tension in her body that another pain has hit her. After a while, she lets out a gasp and starts breathing again.

"Luffs," I whisper as I touch her cheek again.

Another sigh, but now she looks at me. Her lips twitch into the slightest of smiles before another pain hits her, and she cries out again. Her mouth makes a multitude of strange sounds as she reaches out, pulls me to her, and then pushes me away again.

Then she cries out and pulls me back. I can't keep up with where she wants me to be, and my own lack of knowledge makes me angry at myself. I don't know enough about how to help a woman deliver a baby, and Beh needs more help than I can provide for her.

Beh brings her knees up a little, but the way she is lying on her side doesn't work very well. She's so tired though; I don't know how she can keep going. I wonder if she could take a little nap for a while and then try again. Several more pains hit her, but Beh doesn't get up from her side. It seems the pains are worse when she lies that way, but she is hardly able to move any longer.

I don't know what to do.

Abruptly, Beh's eyes go wide as she tries to roll over but can't. I rise quickly to help her, and a moment later she is back on her hands and knees again, rocking slowly back and forth as she moans.

Beh grabs my arm and uses it for leverage as she gets up on her feet and bends her knees, balancing on the balls of her feet. I move to kneel in front of her, and she wraps her arms around my neck and holds tightly to my shoulders. She cries out again and again as tears pour from her eyes. I want to push the wetness away, but I'm afraid she'll fall if I let go of her.

As Beh strains with clenched teeth, I glance down and see the crown of a little head with dark hair peeking out from between her legs.

"Hoh!" I reach down with my hand, and I can feel the baby's hair, wet and warm.

Beh grunts and grips me, then seems to relax for a moment, and the baby's head disappears back inside of her again. A moment later, Beh leans her head against my shoulder and pushes. Again, a little head can be seen when she does.

Over and over again—each time I reach down, thinking this will be when the baby comes out, but it doesn't. Finally, as the light from the morning sun begins to trickle into the cave and Beh is nearly unable to keep her footing any longer, it happens.

With a final wail, Beh digs her fingernails into my shoulders and pushes. A wet, slopping sound accompanies a tiny, wriggling figure as it drops from between my mate's legs and into my hands. I gather it in one arm, and with the other, I slowly helps Beh to lie on her side. She's still panting, crying, and laughing all at the same time. Beh reaches out toward my hands as a delicate cry escapes the lips of our new child.

I look down into my arms at the tiny little girl that lies in them.

I am a father.

With the only possible exception being her mother, I have never seen anything so beautiful as our daughter. She's so small lying in my hands that I'm afraid I will break her. Her tiny fingers grasp at nothing, and her little legs kick at my wrists as she cries.

I look to my mate. Her hair is damp and hanging in her eyes, but her smile is bright as I take the baby and lay it in her arms. Tears fall from Beh's eyes as she looks at the child. The baby's eyes squeeze shut, and she lets out another, tiny wail. As Beh brings the child to her breast, I look to the cord that still connects them. Remembering what the women of my tribe did, I take out a long strand of sinew and tie it around the umbilical cord near the baby's stomach. I take a second piece and tie it a little lower.

Beh suddenly gasps and looks up at me as another pain slices through her body. I place my hand on her stomach and feel the tenseness of the muscles below her skin. I reach out and take the baby to wrap her in the soft fur Beh had set aside, and her cries diminish a little. I hold her in one hand and quickly cut through the cord with my flint knife, right between the bits of sinew. Now that she's wrapped tight, I can lay the baby in our sleeping furs long enough to help Beh deliver the placenta.

By the time the task is done, my mate and child are both worn out—Beh from the labor and the baby from her crying. I get them situated in the furs and bring Beh water and cold cooked grains. Beh makes mouth noises and points a finger toward the fire. I add some logs to it to make it blaze again, and Beh sighs and moves her head from side to side. She takes the cup of water I brought her and dips the edge of one of the leather pieces into it, then proceeds to wipe the streaks of blood and mucus from the baby's face.

I find one of the little squares of cloth near the fire and notice the water-filled clay pot Beh set out earlier when she first started feeling pains. I bring it over along with the cloth. Beh smiles as I help her wipe down the baby with the warm water and then use the cloth to wash Beh's legs and face.

Wanting to be sure Beh has everything she needs, I take meat from the fire and a cup full of nuts over to the sleeping furs and feed them to her as she tries to get the baby to suckle at her breast.

It takes several tries, but eventually the baby's tiny lips wrap around her mother's nipple, and reflex takes over.

Beh winces as the baby latches on and then relaxes her head into the furs. I grab one of the extra furs and roll it into a little ball to place under her head since she likes lying that way. She looks up at me, and her eyes shine.

"Loves," she whispers.

"Luffs!"

Beh and our daughter settle deeper into the sleeping area while I gather up the old fur that is now covered in blood, wrap the placenta up in it, and head outside the cave. I don't go far—I would never leave my new family alone for long—but only far enough to find the hole I had dug some time ago and dump the fur-wrapped placenta in it. I cover it with dirt and leaves to keep predators away and then head back to the cave.

The baby is still busy suckling though she seems to be asleep at the same time. Beh's eyes are open but glassy, and I think she is only partially awake. I try to get her to eat some more food, and she drinks some meat broth before waving me away.

Though the sun is high in the sky, I crawl over my mate and baby to lie down with them in the warm furs. I watch in awe at the pair of them and wonder if there is any possible way for me to be happier than at this very moment.

I reach over to push the hair from Beh's forehead, and I realize the baby's hair—now that it has dried a bit more—is not the same color as Beh's. It has a golden-red tinge to it, which I know is more like mine. This prompts me to look at her face more closely, but she is too interested in her mother's breast to show her whole face to me, and her eyes are still closed. I wonder what color they are and if they will be large and blue like her mother's. Her fingers are tiny but long, compared to the rest of her little hands, and her cheeks are full and round with red splotches all over them from crying.

Beh's fingers curl into my hair, and she brings my face close to hers to press her mouth to mine.

"Khzz," I whisper when she releases me, and I'm rewarded with her lips against mine once again. She makes many soft sounds as her eyes stare at my face. I watch her mouth move as the noises come out from between her lips, and I'm grateful they are quiet noises. I reach out and wrap my arm around both the baby and Beh before I lay my head down on the furs.

I look up at Beh for a moment, but just the act of lying down has done me in, and I find myself drifting off quickly. With the warmth of my mate and my child to comfort me, I take a long, slow breath and smile.

As I doze off, I wonder if I can put another baby in her now.

⇒ ••◦●◖●◗●◦•• ⇐

The first few days are hard.

Beh is so tired, and the baby doesn't sleep very long at a time. It's been a while since I have been around a baby. My youngest sibling was already several seasons old when the fire took my tribe, and I forgot how messy they can be. Beh uses the little triangles of leather with some of her squares of cloth inside to wrap around the baby's backside, and I end up washing the stinky things outside of the cave along with the straps of leather Beh wears to absorb the blood from after giving birth.

We make a lot of trips to the lake using the hide on a stick to carry not only the supplies we gather but also our baby. She lies in the middle, surrounded by furs, and looks around her with wide, blue eyes that are exactly like Beh's. She wriggles and moves around a lot when she's placed on her back, and her skin is wonderfully soft. I like to touch the corner of her mouth and watch her turn toward my finger, looking for milk.

She's so pretty, just like Beh.

Even with little continuous sleep, we have to prepare for winter. I fish at the lake as Beh holds the baby close to her breast and digs for cattail roots. Once she has many of them loaded on the hide, she sits to feed the baby for a while. I go back to my work until I hear her call out my name-sound.

"Ehd!"

Quickly, I look up and around the area, but there does not appear to be any danger, and Beh's sounds don't seem alarmed. Picking up the three small fish I have caught, I go to her and crouch down to make sure the baby is all right. She sucks at her mother's breast greedily and makes little grunting sounds as she does.

I smile.

"Ehd." Beh reaches out and touches my chest. Then she places her hand on her own chest, right above her breasts. "Beh."

I narrow my eyes at her as she places her hand on the baby and makes more sounds. I tilt my head to one side and try to listen closely to her sounds, but they're just noise. She keeps going for a while, and I get bored. Just as I am about to stand and go back to fishing, she grabs my hand and holds tight.

"Ehd...Beh..." she repeats, and then touches the baby again.

Slowly, understanding comes to me. Beh wants a name-sound for the baby. I don't know why she is asking me since mothers always make up the name-sounds for their babies. I wonder if the sounds she has been making are supposed to be a name-sound, but I don't think that's possible. There are too many strange sounds all together for that.

Maybe she doesn't know what to call her.

"Beh," I say as I touch her shoulder. I place my hand on top of the baby's head then reach over and place my hand on Beh's lips. I pull back and look at her expectantly, waiting for her to tell me the baby's name-sound.

Her eyes stay on mine for several minutes before she looks back to the babe suckling her and runs her hand over her soft head. Then she makes a combination of sounds that remind me of the noises she sometimes makes when she cooks—the ones that all run together. She looks up at me and smiles, repeating the sounds more slowly.

It's still a ridiculously complicated amount of noise for a name-sound, so I'm not sure what she is doing. She makes the sounds again and again, and I watch her lips and tongue move together.

"Sheee…lah…"

At the last part, her tongue flicks over the back of her teeth in a somewhat familiar sound.

"Luffs?" I question.

"Laaaah," Beh says. "Sheee-lah."

"Luuhh…" Why does she make all her sounds so complex?

"Shee-lah."

"Luh."

"Ssss-lah…"

"Llllah…"

We go back and forth for some time before Beh sighs and shakes her head at me. She makes a long, loud trail of sounds, and I look around to make sure she hasn't attracted any unwanted attention as she sighs again.

"Lah?" she says quietly.

Much better.

"Lah," I repeat with a smile.

Lah chooses that moment to release Beh's nipple and turn to the sound of my voice. My smile grows larger as I run my finger over her tiny, soft cheek, and she blinks at me before turning back to her meal. Beh laughs and reaches out to pull me close and put her mouth on mine.

"Lah," she says softly.

"Lah."

Our daughter has a name-sound.

⟶ ⬦⬥⬦⬥ ⟵

Winter comes early in the form of heavy snows.

The weather changes quickly and without warning, but we

have plenty of food and should have enough if the winter isn't overly long. As Lah takes her nourishment from her mother, Beh is hungry more often than she used to be. Still, I think there should be enough.

I hope there is.

Snowflakes fall from the overcast sky as I wrap my outer fur closer around me and survey the snow-covered field. I also hope that Beh will let me try to put another baby in her soon, but she pushes me away every time I try. It has been a long time since I have had myself inside of her, and I miss it. I've tried to just touch her, but she is still bleeding from the birth, and she won't let me do that either.

Once Lah is sleeping, Beh will put her hand on me until my seed spills on the furs. It feels good but isn't what I want. I want to hold her to me while I move, taste her lips and hear her cry out my name-sound as she shudders around me.

Pushing the fur that covers the cave entrance to one side, I slip through the crack and into the warmth of the cave. I shake my head rapidly to send the snow flying in all directions. I hear some laughter from the other side of the cave and smile to myself. After I use the thick fur to cover up the crack leading to the outside and to keep the winds from us, I move to the other side of the cave where my family is.

I drop the two rabbits I caught in traps to the side of the fire— I will skin and cook them later—and turn to my mate. Beh hums and makes her fluid sounds as she sits with Lah near the fire. Whenever Beh makes noises with her mouth, Lah watches her face intently. I come up behind them both and sit, wrapping my legs around Beh's hips and my arms around them both as we keep ourselves warm by the fire. Outside, the wind howls and the snow blows, but inside we are content.

Beh turns her head toward me and leans into my chest as I place my chin on her shoulder. Lah's eyes meet mine, and I think I see the corners of her mouth turn up a little. My heart beats faster at the sight of the little girl who seems to recognize me now. Before too long, I think she will actually smile at me.

Beh's sounds are soft, and she cradles our child in one arm as she reaches around my head to grip the hair at the back of my neck and bring my mouth to hers. I press against her, and my tongue traces the outline of her lips.

As we part, we open our eyes and look closely at one another. For a long moment, we just stare. It is not at all threatening or uncomfortable; it's just the two of us, together, and my skin warms at the thought of being with her.

With a sharp cry from our daughter, we are both brought back to the moment. My chest shakes a little as I try not to laugh, but Beh does not even try. Lah's eyes go wide as she looks up to us both, startled into silence by the strange sounds we make. Then her eyes squeeze shut, and she lets out a long, shrill cry.

———————— ••••◗◗••••———————

My head hurts.

As she grows, Lah makes almost as much noise as her mother.

There is a part of me that likes watching the two of them as they look at each other and make sounds, but the constant noise inside the cave makes the temples on the side of my head throb. Our home has begun to feel a little cramped with three people in it. There is barely room for me, Beh, and Lah, the size she is now. She is all wriggly and squirmy when you hold onto her, but she cannot move anywhere on her own. Once she is more people-sized, this cave will not be big enough for us. Besides, by the time Lah is grown, Beh should have had several children. We could have a whole tribe by then, and a tribe would definitely not fit in our cave.

At some point, before Lah gets too big or before I put another baby in Beh, we will have to look for a new place to live. This is not the only thought that concerns me. I'm also worried about Beh because she still doesn't seem to want to have me put another baby in her at all.

Lah sits on her plump backside with her mother holding out her arms for balance. The baby rocks back and forth a bit and squeals. Beh makes a lot of noises at her and then turns to make noises at me. Lah looks to me, too, and lets out another squeal as she bounces up and down.

I have to laugh because she looks so funny when she does that, but at the same time, I can't wait until spring when I can get out of the cave and away from all of the racket. The solitude of hunting on my own seems more appealing all the time.

I go to the entrance to the cave and pull aside the fur to look outside. The sky is overcast, but the air is slightly warmer than the day before, and the thick snows are finally starting to melt. Just as an excuse, I get one of the clay bowls and take it outside, fill it full of packed snow, and stare up at the sky for a few minutes until the wind chills my ears. When I go back in, Beh has placed a suddenly sleeping Lah on a pile of furs for her nap.

I place the bowl near the fire to melt the snow and come to Beh's side. She strokes our daughter's cheek, and Lah makes little sucking motions in her sleep before letting out a long yawn.

Beh yawns, too, and I lead her over to the sleeping furs near the baby and coax her down. She needs more sleep—we both do —but she rarely seems to fall asleep when Lah does. She spends all that time just watching her.

Hoping to help her rest, I get into the furs with Beh and wrap my arms around her middle. She turns her back to me and presses it against my chest so she can look at the baby. I tuck my head against Beh's shoulder and inhale. Her hair always smells so good. I grip her tighter and push my hips against her. Beh stiffens slightly, and I know she can feel me hard on her back.

I didn't mean to; I just can't help it.

I feel her chest rise and fall with a long breath before she rolls to face me. Beh places one hand on my chest and reaches up with the other to cup my face.

"Luffs, khizz?"

Beh's smile lights up her face, and she reaches around my head to bring me close to her. Her lips touch mine gently and then with more need and an open mouth. Lying back against the furs, I let her do as she wants. I don't want to push; it has been so long since she has done more than just a quick touch of lips to mine before gently discouraging me from more. I don't want to ruin this, whatever it may become.

Her tongue touches mine, and her hand runs down my neck and over my shoulder where she grips it tightly. I press my hand to her back and bring our bodies closer together, moaning slightly into her mouth as my penis is pressed between us in the most wonderful way.

Beh moans, too, and she moves her hand down my chest and wraps it around my shaft. I take a long, deep breath and try to keep myself together as she strokes me.

I like it when she does that.

I want more.

My hand finds her breast underneath her furs, and my thumb rubs at her nipples softly. At least they don't appear to be so sore anymore like they were when Lah was first learning how to get milk from her mother. Beh would wince every time Lah would latch on, and when I tried to touch her breasts, she made that *no* sound.

Beh's hips rock against my body even with her hand trapped between us. I'm so close to her entrance, and I know if I just moved her hand away, I could be inside of her very quickly. She doesn't want this, though, and I will never understand why there are times she does not.

She is panting softly as I continue to touch her breast and press my lips to the side of her neck. Her skin is salty there, and I lick over it with the flat of my tongue, making her groan loud enough that she presses her face to my shoulder to keep from waking Lah.

Then she pushes me away, and I end up on my back, sweating and with a heaving chest.

She sits up and wraps her arms around her legs for a moment, resting her forehead on her knees. She makes some noises, including my name-sound and the luffs sound.

"Beh Luffs." I repeat, and I reach for her.

She turns and smiles at me before she reaches out and places her hand on my chest.

"Beh Luffs Ehd."

Her fingers move down, and I think she is going to just move away at first, but then she lets them stay against my skin—trailing down the center of my body to my stomach and then lower. Her fingers run along my length, causing it to jump up and down with excitement.

I try to steady my rapid breaths as she strokes it with one finger from tip to base and then back up again. She adds another finger, and then wraps her hand around it. She moves up and down a couple of times, and then holds my penis so it is standing straight out from my body—pointing to the ceiling of the cave.

Then she leans over and takes my penis in her mouth.

"Hoh!"

I sit up quickly, the shock of my mate's actions causing my body to react almost violently.

Beh has my penis in her mouth.

In her *mouth*!

I can't put a baby in there!

Beh's hands rest on my stomach and thigh as she leans over me, and her mouth engulfs half of my length before she moves back up. Her tongue runs over the tip, and then she goes back down again. At first, I want to push her away, but the confusion over why she would do such a thing halts my movements just long enough to *feel*.

Her mouth is warm and wet, and her tongue strokes down the sensitive line on the underside of my penis.

"Beh…"

Her eyes look to mine as she hears her name-sound, and I see them sparkle with playfulness as well as desire. My hand reaches out and touches the side of her head, pushing strands of her hair out of the way as I watch her move back down again.

I am caught in the sight and the sensations. Even though my mind cannot understand why she would consider doing this to me, I am not going to stop her.

Definitely not.

Her mouth moves up again, and her lips caress my hard flesh as she wraps them around me. As I watch, her cheeks hollow, and I suddenly feel more of my length being pulled into her mouth by the suction.

"Hoh! *Hoh!*" My breath comes out in short gasps as my legs tense, throb, and shudder. My hips buck upwards—pushing my penis farther into Beh's mouth as I feel my seed follow the sensations of my climax.

Beh's eyes widen slightly and then close as her throat bobs. She pulls back, releasing me and sits back on her knees.

With my own eyes wide, I reach over and bring her face close to me, my eyes dancing between hers to try to understand what would have caused her to do such a thing—and how I could get her to do it again. I examine her smirking face and realize she seems…*proud.*

Closing my eyes, I lean forward and drag the end of my nose from the tip of her nose all the way up to her forehead and then back down. When I look at Beh again, she is still smiling, and it makes me feel warm inside despite the chill inside the cave.

"Khizz," I whisper, and she brings her mouth to meet mine. She tastes strange, and at first I pull away, confused. I quickly realize it is my seed I taste on her and press my lips to hers again. My tongue reaches into her mouth, and I consider the strange saltiness. It makes me wonder: *What would she taste like?*

I reach for Beh's hips and quickly lift and turn her to lie her down on the furs. She lets out a short squeal of surprise but quiets herself with a glance toward our sleeping Lah. I place my lips on her once more and then slide my hands down the sides of her body as I move myself downwards as well.

I take her legs in my hands and push them up and to the sides. I can see her opening there though my penis isn't ready to respond just yet. That's not my plan, anyway. I lay down between her legs, propping myself up on my elbows as I glance up at Beh's face.

It's flushed and beautiful.

Moving closer to her core, I first touch the tip with the end of my nose, inhaling her scent before I reach out with my tongue to find that place that is so sensitive. Beh's body reacts immediately, and her hips buck. I can't keep up with her movements, so I wrap my arms around her thighs and hips and hold her to the furs.

My tongue finds her again, swirling first around the little bud at the top of her folds and then lower to explore the folds themselves. The taste is not unlike the taste of her mouth had just been but somewhat more subtle. Her flesh is incredibly smooth on my tongue, and I can't help but taste inside of her as well.

This also causes her to jump, and I have to hold her down some more, which makes her moan too loudly. I still as I hear Lah stir in her own furs not so far from us. I glance at Beh, who now has one hand over her mouth. She uses the other to push me from her hips, and she rolls over to reach for Lah.

After stroking the child's cheek a few times, Lah has settled back into sleep.

I sigh in relief.

A moment later, Beh is on her knees in front of me, pushing me to my back. I want to protest, but I am also hoping maybe she will either put my penis back in her mouth or even inside of her to try to make another baby, so I allow her to maneuver me to a supine position.

The next thing I know, she is straddling my chest backwards. She leans over, and I feel her warm breath near my groin again. At the same time, she shifts closer to me, and I realize what she wants.

My hands grab for her backside and thighs and I bring her folds to my mouth again. She moans, but this time the sound is stifled as she wraps her lips around my semi-erect penis. I groan against her flesh, humming into her, and I can feel her legs tense around my head. She moans as well, which sends vibrations through my length and into the rest of my body and further hardens my penis.

My tongue works up and down her, trying to follow similar motions my fingers have used in the past to bring her pleasure. Beh hums and moans around my penis at the same time, and I can hardly cope with the dual sensations. When she begins to suck, I know I can't last much longer.

My tongue works furiously against her little nub—stroking and circling—and Beh pushes her hips into my face as she rocks back and forth over me. The tip of my penis hits the back of her throat as I feel her body shudder around me. I can *feel* more than I can *hear* her cries, which brings me over the edge as well as my penis empties into her mouth again.

Beh rolls to her side in a heap next to my legs.

I force myself to pull my knees up, swing around, and wrap her in my arms. Her breath comes in short pants, and I can feel the beat of her heart against my chest. She makes a few soft noises as she strokes my cheek with her fingers, and I stroke her neck with my nose.

Finally, I recognize the positives of versatility.

CHAPTER TWENTY

Lah grows so quickly.

By the time winter is upon us, she holds her head up and looks around the room without assistance. She is fascinated with watching the fire and with her mother's breasts, which are constantly large and round with milk. I can understand Lah's interest, as I am quite fascinated with them myself. Aside from being much bigger, they are now more sensitive when I touch them, and since Beh finally allows me to put my penis in her again, I try to touch them all the time. It seems to make Beh think of making more babies or at least be willing to try to make another one.

After the first blizzard, the winter is mild with little snow, which makes it easier to get to the lake for water. Sometimes I go on my own, which worries me, but I want Lah to be kept warm, and it is still cold even without snow and ice coming from the sky.

Lah has not yet learned how to crawl around the cave, but as soon as she learned how to roll from her back to her front, she began to roll herself to get anywhere she wanted to be. I am afraid she will roll herself right into the fire, so I line the outside of the fire pit—far from the heat—with extra wood to keep her away from the flames.

Our daughter usually sleeps, wrapped in the furs with Beh and me in the night though she often naps in her own little pile of furs. I like those times, since Beh will usually let me touch her and try to put another baby in her then. Sometimes when I try to sleep, Lah will reach over and grab at my nose and make strange sounds, which causes Beh to laugh.

Beh always makes whatever sound Lah makes right after Lah makes the noise. I never considered before that Beh's children would have some of her oddities, but I don't mind. Well, except when it makes my head ache.

I head to the lake for fresh water, and Beh stays in the cave with Lah. There is only a dusting of snow left on the ground, and though there are no buds on the trees, I can feel the approach of spring in the air, and I'm glad for it. We have enough food for many more days, but our grains are gone and there are only nuts and tubers left to supplement the rabbits I find.

When I return from my lake trip, Beh is holding and rocking Lah in her arms with a worried look on her face. She immediately starts making loud and frightened noises, and I rush over to her and place the water skins on the ground by the fire. She says Lah's name-sound many times, and her sounds are fast. Finally, she takes hold of my hand and places it over the baby's head.

Lah is very warm to the touch, much warmer than she usually is, and she's not even wrapped up in a fur. I help Beh wipe her down with cool water and then wrap her securely in rabbit fur. Lah begins to shiver, and I take her and her mother to the sleeping furs and secure them both in my embrace. The next morning, Lah's lips are dry and cracked, and she has trouble latching onto Beh's breast to feed.

Lah is sick.

We use the water from the skins to bathe our daughter to try to cool her skin, but it doesn't work and quickly uses all our fresh water. Every day I must run back to the lake for more. I don't want to leave Beh and Lah, but the snow is gone and there isn't enough to melt. I run the entire way, and though my legs and chest hurt from the exertion, I don't pause to rest. I just push forward all the way back to the cave.

Inside, Lah stays at her mother's breast though she is too weak to suck. Her tiny face and body have been hot for days, and even using the cold water from the lake does not seem to help for long. Beh makes more and more noise and even seems somewhat frantic at times—like she is waiting for me to do something.

I don't know what to do.

After building up the fire, I take both of them back to the sleeping furs and cover us all together. Beh hasn't slept much, and she needs her strength. I take Lah from her and coax her into lying down and stroke Beh's hair as she tries to sleep. Lah lies in my arms, silent and still. Her hot skin warms me, and it would feel pleasant in the cool air of the early morning if I didn't understand that her fever had lasted too long. She isn't getting better.

I understand as memories from the past consume me.

There were times when my mother had spent entire days just holding my baby sister, who had developed a fever only a season after her birth. Mother held her and rocked her, and father brought cold water, but it didn't help—just like it isn't helping with Lah. Mother pushed me away when I tried to get near, just as she did with my other brothers and sisters. In the end, when my baby sister stopped moving and breathing, father just held mother as she cried.

Lah stirs and lets out a tiny, weak cry. I pull her closer to my chest and run my nose over her cheek until she stills again. At least Beh remains asleep. I think she will need her strength even more soon. I glance at Beh's face and picture her in my mind as my mother had been. I recall my father in his own grief as he tried to comfort her. My mind replaces my parents with me and Beh, and I think of myself holding Beh after…after…

I will have to put her in a deep hole and cover her up, so animals don't get to her body.

I shudder, and my throat becomes tight and dry. I hold Lah closer to my chest and move slowly back and forth—rocking in time with my quiet sobs as the sun sets outside the cave. I lie beside my mate, keeping our daughter close to my chest and succumb to sleep.

It's cool and dark in the middle of the night, and I am awakened suddenly.

Lah's cries are weak, and I sit up immediately to reach for her, but Beh already has her in her arms. She holds her to her breast, but Lah will not take hold of her nipple. I try to help, but I don't know how to get her to nurse. Tears run down Beh's face as Lah's cries grow quiet. She no longer has the strength to make sounds.

Crossing my legs on the furs, I pull Beh into my lap against my chest—wrapping my arms around them both. I reach for one of the furs and wrap us up together, and I desperately want to give comfort to my mate, but there is no comfort to be given. I rock slowly back and forth, but I find I am growing numb inside. Thinking about what I know is going to happen brings a pain to my chest that I cannot bear.

Soon, our daughter is going to die.

Through the day and night, I hold them both close to me as I watch the coals from the fire grow dim. It's chilly in the cave, but knowing I can start a fire quickly with the little round thing keeps me from moving away from my family. I don't want to let go of them, not even for a moment.

My eyes are burning as day begins to break, and warm light shines into the crack of the cave.

It is then I hear the strangest sound.

It almost sounds like a horde of insects right next to my face, but it's far too loud. It's so loud, it actually hurts my ears, and I tuck my head down into the space between Beh's shoulder and neck, trying to cover up my ears. Beh is wriggling in my arms, and when I tighten my grip on both her and Lah, I feel Beh's hand push against my chest as she tries to turn in my grasp.

The noise begins to wane, and I find myself with Lah's warm body in my hands as Beh pushes out of my arms and gives the baby to me. I watch, dumbfounded, as Beh leaves the furs and runs toward the crack in the cave. A moment later I stand, wrap Lah in one of the furs, and follow my mate outside into the dim morning light.

In the field outside the cave is the strangest thing I have ever seen.

The source of the whirring sound seems to be giant, concentric circles—transparent and spinning in grey and blue streaks around and around. They are huge, towering at least three times my height, and the noise outside the cave is deafening. Inside of the sphere are flashes of red and gold that look like sparks from the fire, bright enough to hurt my eyes.

As I stand with my mouth open, the circles begin to spin slower and slower, and the red and gold flashes become more frequent and start to take shape. As the flashes take form, I can see the image of a man begin to appear in the center. He is tall and dressed in a long, completely white garment from his shoulders to part way down his legs. Beneath the white wrap, I see leggings that are the same design as those Beh was wearing when I first found her though the color is like the color of pine needles in spring.

When the filmy circles stop spinning, they simply disappear like the smoke from a fire, but there is no warmth. The only thing left in the field is the man, standing perfectly still with his arms extended slightly in front of his body. He is holding a strange, black, rectangular object in his hands.

Nothing less than sheer terror grips me.

Beh screams out and starts to run forward, but I am torn and don't know how to react. Whatever is happening, it can't be safe, and I want to keep her from going near the man, but Lah is in my arms, and I need to keep her safe as well. By the time I can shift Lah into one arm to try to grab for Beh, she is out of my reach, and

I'm too stunned to chase after my mate.

She runs straight to the man and throws her arms around his body. I watch him as his arms encircle my mate, and he holds her close to him with the black rectangle held in one hand at her back. My breath catches in my chest and won't come out. Immobilized by fear, I hold Lah closer to me and watch Beh as she takes a small step back, still holding the man's hands, and begins to make sounds at him.

His mouth opens, and he makes more noises back at her.

Beh makes more sounds, and he makes more noise. They go back and forth until I feel like the pressure in my chest is going to cause my body to come apart. I realize I'm not breathing and force myself to take a breath, which comes out as a sob.

Beh looks over her shoulder at me and makes more sounds. I can hear the fear and pain in the noises she makes and force myself to take a few steps forward, unsure and still terrified. I have no idea what's going on, but it is obvious this man knows my Beh.

His hands move up and cup her face, and I see tears begin to pour from her eyes. I need to go to her, but my feet don't want to take me closer to the strange man, his bizarre clothes, or to the spot where the giant circle-thing has just been. I shift forward then retreat again before I force myself to take a step toward my mate. I want nothing more than to bring her back into the cave and defend my family from the stranger.

I move closer, and the man turns his head to look at me. He has lots of fluffy hair underneath his nose but no beard around his face, which makes him look very odd. His hair is dark—the same color as Beh's, and when I step closer, I can see his eyes are also the same color as Beh's, and his face is similar as well. He is also very old, and there are patches of grey in his hair. Still, the resemblance is unmistakable.

This man must be Beh's father.

I swallow hard and hold Lah closer to me. She's stirring in her sleep, and when I look down, her eyes flutter open then close again. It grips my heart, but I am so confused I don't even know what to think: not about Lah, or Beh, the strange man who has suddenly appeared in the field outside our cave, or the intense noise that has so recently encompassed the whole area.

The man—Beh's father, without a doubt—looks into my eyes while Beh continues to make noises. He glances over to her, and I take the opportunity to crouch down a little and try to come up behind her without him noticing. Father or not, I don't trust him. I don't know what he is doing here or how he appeared in the field near our cave. I want Beh with me—close to me, like Lah is. I want her arms around our daughter while I hold her.

I know Lah doesn't have much time left.

I want us together.

We should be together when it happens.

Slowly, I approach Beh's back and reach out to grab at her hand. Beh makes more sounds, and the man holds up a single finger, pointing it toward the sky as he shakes his head rapidly. I try to pull her back to me gently, but she resists.

"Beh!"

Her head swivels toward me, and her father makes more sounds.

I hate, hate, *HATE* the sounds!

With a growl, I pull harshly at her arm, bringing her to my side as I start to back away. Even knowing this man has to be her father doesn't matter; she is mine, and I don't understand what is happening. I need her. Lah needs her.

The stranger begins to make his sounds much louder, and I roar back to silence him. Beh touches my cheek, and she makes soft, relaxing noises at me, but it does nothing to calm me. My heart is pounding, and my breath is quick. I want to pick her up and run back to the cave with her. I want to find my sharpest spear and guard the entrance, forcing this unknown away from my family.

I need to protect Beh and Lah.

"Ehd," Beh whispers softly as her hand runs over the side of my face. She leans close and touches my nose with hers. Another tear runs down her face. "Luffs."

"Luffs," I repeat.

"Luffs Lah," Beh says, and her sounds are choked by her tears. She makes more sounds, and I hear Lah's name-sound among them. Beh's eyes look into mine, and her sadness cuts through my heart.

"Lah..." I look down at the child in my arms. Her eyes are open again, but they are dull, and where they should be white, they are yellow. She stares up at me as her little chest hops up and down with labored breaths.

Beh removes her hand from my face and drops it to Lah. She slowly pulls the girl from my arms and looks into my eyes as she backs away from me. I stand there in the field, stunned. My body chills from my shoulders all the way down my torso and out my limbs. I don't understand, but the feeling of dread is unmistakable.

Beh turns around and holds Lah in her outstretched arms. Her father reaches out and takes the baby carefully and gently in his arms. His eyes dart from the baby to his daughter and then to me.

More sounds.

I take a step forward, and a growl from my chest escapes. Beh holds her hand out toward me with her palm up.

"No!"

I stop moving, but the growl continues.

More noises.

First from him, then from her.

His eyes grow sad, and his head bobs up and down.

A choking sob comes from my mate as she backs away from the man and grabs a hold of my upper arm tightly. Her shoulder pushes against my chest, trying to propel me backwards. I stand still, bracing myself against her as my eyes harden at the sight of this man with my daughter in his arms. She is sick—dying—and I don't want her anywhere but with her mother and me.

He cradles Lah gently and uses his other hand to poke at the black rectangle thing he holds. A moment later, the humming, whirring sound begins again. Beh pushes hard against my chest again.

"Ehd!"

I look into her eyes, and the pain and hurt are too much. I can no longer hold back the sob that has been caught in my throat. Beh wraps her arms tightly around my neck as she pushes me with her whole body, forcing me backwards. I look out over her shoulder as the blue-grey sphere forms and spins around Beh's father and Lah. It moves faster and faster, the noise becoming painful to my ears again. I squeeze my eyes shut and cringe from it.

My mate grabs a hold of my shoulder and pushes me away roughly from the spinning thing. I feel as if my head is spinning just as fast, and through the noise and the confusion, I realize she has left Lah there, inside of the thing with her father.

"Beh...Lah!" I look from her to the field where the flashes of red and gold now surround my daughter. I try to move toward it, but Beh holds tight to my arm, and an odd, prickly feeling covers my skin as I get closer. It makes the hairs on my arm stand up, and my head begins to pound. I hesitate, staring ahead as the image of the man holding my baby changes from outline to formless shape and then is gone.

The whirring sound doesn't fade this time but simply stops.

"Lah?" My eyes search Beh's, and she moves her head back and forth as tears flow freely. I look from Beh to the bleak, empty field and back again.

Her body goes limp and weak, and I have to catch her in my arms to keep her from falling. Crouching slightly, I pull Beh up into my embrace and hold her to my chest, just as I had been holding our Lah only moments ago.

"Lah!" I cry out louder. Beh tightens her arms around my neck, and she tucks her head against my shoulder and sobs.

Her cries drown out my own screams.

"LAH!"

Finally, I realize our baby is gone.

CHAPTER TWENTY-ONE

I sit, staring.

The snows have melted. The trees have new leaves, and the field outside the cave is empty.

Completely empty.

In my hands is one of the leather triangles Beh would wrap around Lah to keep her from getting too messy when she relieved herself. In my mind are all my memories of her—how she smelled after her mother cleaned the dust and dirt off of her face, the way she would roll right off of the furs to try to get wherever it was she wanted to go, and how she felt lying securely in my arms.

I should be hunting and gathering food, but I can't do anything except sit on the ground and watch for some sign of my daughter.

There is none.

"Ehd?"

I glance up toward the cave at my mate. She called to me before, but I didn't move to go back inside. She walks over and holds out her hand to me. Our fingers wrap together, and I move up to my knees, glancing out over the empty field again as I do.

Empty.

Completely empty.

"Lah?" I turn my eyes to Beh's and see the dark blue color that had lived in our daughter's eyes as well as the eyes of the man who took her away.

Beh makes soft sounds and runs her fingers though my hair. It's getting long again, and I wonder if she will make me sit still long enough for her to cut it shorter. I nuzzle my head against her stomach with my eyes closed, just inhaling the scent of her skin for a while.

When I open my eyes again, I focus on the three small lines that grace Beh's skin along her abdomen. They are marks left over from when she had Lah inside of her. I reach out with a single finger and stroke them slowly one at a time. When I look up again, Beh's cheeks are wet.

I haven't tried to put another baby in Beh since Lah disappeared from the field in front of me. I also haven't eaten or slept much. Beh did drag me down to the lake once, but I refused to get into the water, and I didn't try to catch any fish. I only sat on the rocks and waited for her to be ready to return to the cave.

As I continue to look at Beh, the feeling of sorrow and dread which have overwhelmed me since Lah disappeared seem to twist inside of me until they are replaced with shame. In my own grief, I haven't been a good mate to Beh.

My nose runs over each of the little lines as thoughts of her stomach getting round fill my head. It is spring, and I should be hunting to provide for my mate. I should be collecting wood and replenishing the cache above the cave. I should be making a trap for large animals so I can replace the leather and furs that have become worn with age.

Looking up at Beh, I can see her sadness for Lah but also her worry for me—for us. I should be providing for Beh. I should be protecting her. I should be trying to give her another baby to help ease her pain of losing our first.

Lah is gone, but Beh is young and strong. I will put another baby in her, and I will have to make sure when I do that there is enough food and other supplies to keep Beh healthy while she carries and then nurses another child.

I stand and pick Beh up in my arms. She lets out a little squeal of surprise, which makes me smile. I remember when she has done that before and wait to see if she will make the *no* sound.

She doesn't.

I carry her inside the cave and set her down. My hands cup her face, and I lean in to drag my nose across her jaw.

"Khizz?"

Beh wraps her arms around my neck as our mouths touch. My penis hardens at her touch, and I would very much like to be inside her right away, but I remember how I refused to get in the water at the lake and how much Beh likes me to be clean. I break away, smiling at her and wiping the wetness from below her eyes.

Gathering the hide on a stick and some of the collection baskets, Beh and I go to the lake. She collects cattails, reeds, and mushrooms while I set traps for rabbits and fish. Before we leave, I immerse myself in the cool water and let her use soaproot to wash my hair. When she is done with her own hair, I sit behind her and use the wood carving to help her get rid of the snarls.

Beh keeps turning to look at me, and though my thoughts continue to return to Lah, I focus on my mate. I hope she will forgive me for not taking care of her as I should and will let me try again.

We return before the sun sets, and I lay my mate in our snug furs. Our mouths and noses meet, and I hold her tightly against me as I fill her. She calls out to me and refuses to let go even when we are both too tired to move any longer. Eventually, Beh rolls to her side, and I move up behind her, holding her back to my chest as she sleeps.

Beh is still sad, too, but she cooks the remaining grains at the back of the cave and gathers fresh buds to eat. She still tends the fire and makes sure we have water to drink. She is so beautiful, and I have been neglecting her.

I can't do that any longer.

She is everything to me, and I have to be a good mate to her.

My heart still aches for Lah, and I know another child will not be the same, but as I look at Beh, I realize there are many possibilities ahead of us. As I stroke her cheek, I know that every child that comes from her will be a part of us both, and each one will fill my heart again in a new way even if the hole left by Lah's absence never completely fills.

Beh turns again, and she reaches up with her hand to stroke over the short hairs on my face. I nuzzle against her with my nose, press my lips to her skin, and turn my attention to the front of the cave.

I have to make sure she is safe.

⸺⸺⸺•••◦◖◗◦•••⸺⸺⸺

I stand, stretch my arms above my head, and look down at the fire, which is now built up again. The clay pots are empty, none of the cooked grains remain from breakfast. Beh's appetite of late is amazing. I finish my stretch and move over to the other side of the fire.

Everything has been easier this time—from the moment Beh took my hand and placed it over her abdomen to tell me there was a baby inside her until the day our son was born. I can only hope the next one is easier, too, though I don't think there is another one growing inside of Beh yet. Hopefully the next one will be born in the spring, not the middle of winter like Lee was.

Lee's eyes are lighter than Lah's—and I think they might be the same color as mine. A few days after he was born, Beh pointed to my eyes and to his over and over again. They look like the color of the evergreens when the sun hits the needles. I don't know what color hair he will have because he is still almost completely without.

As soon as I sit, Beh drops a piece of leather over my lap and lays Lee in the middle of it. I hold him as he wriggles and squirms, and his mother uses bits of cloth and warm water to wash him completely like she does every day. She does not want him dirty at all and washes him much more frequently than she ever did Lah. I don't understand, but when it comes to my mate, I rarely do.

I am content again, though. My nightmares stopped not long after we realized another baby was coming though Beh still sometimes cries out for Lah in her sleep. She did last night, but when I held her close, she settled down. I remember how scared she seemed, and I look up to her face.

"Luffs!"

Beh looks up at me and smiles, which is what I want. She takes the end of the cloth and wipes my cheek with it. There is probably soot on my face from when I was cooking breakfast. The water feels good and cools me off.

Lee doesn't seem to like it, though, and cries and squirms, trying to get out of my arms and crawl away. He's been crawling all over the cave for several days now and even managed to find his way to the outside the previous morning. Now he heads for the crack of the cave every time he's let loose.

Beh laughs as I hold Lee up, and she finishes his cleaning. When she is done, I lay him down, hoping he will sleep a while so I can put another baby in Beh, but Lee doesn't cooperate. With a giggle, Beh pushes us both outside, and I take Lee to the field to let him crawl naked through the grass while I use a piece of flint to sharpen up a new spear. I need to hunt antelope for their skins though the variety of meat would also be welcome.

Lee rolls over to his side and peers at me with squinted eyes. He pushes his chubby body to a sitting position and pulls at the grass around him. Then he looks back to me.

"Da da da da da da da!"

He makes as much noise as his mother. I worry he will never be quiet enough to become a hunter and provide for his mate. Of course, I also wonder where he will find a mate. Siblings are not good mates, and that is all we can give him. Someday, we are going to have to go looking for other people. I can only hope to find a tribe who will be friendly. For the time being, I have been searching for a larger cave, but I haven't found any bigger or better than where we live now.

"Ma ma ma ma!" Lee raises his arms in the air and bounces up and down on his bottom. I hear Beh coming out of the cave behind me, and I turn to watch her, naked and glorious in the summer sunshine. She goes immediately to our child and picks him up in her arms, nuzzling his cheek with her nose. He grabs at her breast, which makes her laugh. She carries him over and sits beside me to feed him.

I put down the flint and spear and turn to face her, reaching out and picking them both up to place them in my lap. I wrap my arms around Beh's middle, giving Lee my forearms to lie upon while he nurses. He seems to be the most comfortable that way. Anytime I can, I hold Beh when she nurses the baby. When we are all close together like that, I can run my nose over Beh's neck, smell her hair, and watch Lee, too.

Beh makes quiet sounds as Lee stares at her face and sucks. His little hand rests possessively right above her nipple, and he grasps at it repeatedly as if he needs the reassurance that it is still there and still full of milk. I lay my head on Beh's shoulder, and we both look out over the field toward the pine trees and watch the birds soar across the sky.

The day is not too hot, but sun is warm. I close my eyes to its warmth and tilt my head up a little. After a few minutes, Beh lifts Lee and turns him to her other breast so he can complete his meal.

It's making me hungry, too.

Beh turns her head so she can see me better, and the smile on her face encompasses my heart. She reaches up and lays the palm of her hand against my cheek.

"Beh loves Ehd. Beh loves Lee."

"Luffs Beh!" I make the sounds and watch her eyes light up

and her smile grow. "Lee luffs!"

Beh's smile turns into a laugh, which startles Lee enough that the nipple slips from his mouth. He begins to cry, and I reach up with one finger to stroke his cheek until he quiets down and goes back to suckling. Beh leans her back against my chest and sighs.

I think she is content, just as I am.

I close my eyes again and listen to the sounds around me. Beh's quiet breathing, Lee's noisy suckling, the birds in the trees, and the insects in the field all fill my ears. The bugs are particularly loud, and seem to be getting louder.

And louder.

Beh gasps, and I feel the tension move from her body into mine.

I know the sound is not insects, and my body begins to shake as the sound increases to the point where my ears are aching. Silver-blue streaks appear in the field in front of us, circling with increasing speed. The sense of dread I felt when Lah was taken from us returns with tight pressure in my chest. For several moments, I am frozen and unable to react to what I am seeing.

Again, as it was long ago when Lah disappeared, red and gold speckles flash inside the sphere, sparking like embers from the fire in the dark cave at night, and I remember what happened the last time those sparks appeared in the field. Without waiting another moment, I cry out and jump to my feet, carrying Beh and Lee with me. Beh's feet hit the ground, and she starts to pull away from me —toward the sparking, spinning thing that is appearing in the field.

"Beh!" I scream at her and grab her arm. Glaring at the sparkling shape that is beginning to take form, I grab my spear from the ground and pull Beh and Lee behind me. I am completely resolved, and I will not allow Beh to stop me as I push at her side —forcing her back toward the cave despite her noises and struggles.

I will *not* let *anyone* take Lee from me!

Turning quickly, I use one arm to encircle Beh's waist and the other to hold my spear out toward the spinning thing. It is beginning to slow, and I recognize the image of a person in the middle of the sphere. I pull sharply at Beh, whose loud sounds are increasing, and drag both my mate and my son to the safety of the cave.

Pushing them through the entrance of the cave, I turn and crouch with my spear ready. I block the opening with my body and ignore Beh's hand pushing against my shoulder and her sharp noises. Lee is crying angry cries at being separated from his mother's breast, but I refuse to acknowledge either of them.

I have to protect my family.

"Ehd...Ehd..." Beh's hand strokes my shoulder, and her sounds become softer as the man's form takes shape in the center of the whirling circles.

I will not let him take our son.

I won't.

I won't!

My chest heaves with labored breaths as I grip my spear. My hands are shaking, and I want to steady them, but it is as if the thoughts of Lah disappearing so long ago are dropping from my head and down into my chest, crushing me underneath their weight. I remember the man I hit to protect Beh all those seasons ago. I remember what happened to him, and I steady myself in case I have to fight. I have done it before, and I can do it again.

The whirring sound stops, and I can see the more distinct shape of the man as the circles fade away. The man and whatever is in his arms is all that is left. It is definitely the man from before. His dark eyes and furry upper lip are the same.

I tighten my grip on my spear and raise it with menace.

"Ehd, no!" Beh grabs hold of the top part of my arm and shakes me, yelling.

Standing firmly at the entrance, I growl and pull my arm from her grasp. I step forward, though I don't allow enough room for her to slip around me. The man is walking slowly toward us, and I scream out a warning to him. I hold out my spear and stamp my foot as Beh pushes against my back, but my feet are planted firmly, and she can't move me out of the way.

I don't know why she is trying.

"Ehd!" she cries out again, and once more she grabs hold of my spear-arm. "Lah!"

I have to close my eyes for a moment, drenched in the memories of the little girl who was the first child I put inside of Beh. The crushing feeling I haven't felt in a long time is back, holding me down and making my grip on the spear falter.

I will not let him have Lee!

Again I scream at the approaching figure of the man, who slows and stops. His eyes dart between my face and Beh's. She keeps saying my name-sound and even reaches around to grab hold of my face. I glance at Beh, and the expression on her face is frightening.

She is obviously as scared as I am.

Her hand presses against the side of my face, and a single tear drops from her eye.

"Lah," she says softly, and points toward the man.

I look back to him and focus on what is in his arms. I see a bundle, wrapped in strange material tucked into one arm while the other hand grips a big, black, square...*thing*. I don't care about the thing, though. My attention is captured by the bundle that suddenly squirms and then cries out.

I recognize the cry.

It has haunted me since the day he took Lah.

The man takes another step closer, and I can see a tiny face encircled by the white cloth in his arm. The whole bundle moves, and the little mouth opens up again in a long cry. It's not the weakened cry I remember from the last days she was with us, but the strong, healthy cry that filled my ears on many nights when Lah would wake hungry or cold.

The man is holding my daughter.

"Lah." Her name-sound drops out of my mouth and falls into the air. My stomach feels like it does if I eat something that has been sitting in the back of the cave too long, and I can feel it rolling around inside of me, threatening to expel breakfast. Beh is pushing against my shoulder with warm, damp hands, trying to get around me. I don't know what to think.

It has been more than an entire set of seasons since the stranger took Lah away, but she looks exactly the same. She's the same size, and she makes the same cry. I know it's her—I can feel it in my heart. I don't think Lah is still sick either. She had been so weak when he took her, and now her cry is much stronger. I look at the man holding my daughter, and I narrow my eyes at him.

He took her. She was sick, and he took her away from us.

A low growl comes from my chest as I grip the spear a little tighter. If I step away from the cave, Beh will get out from behind me, and he might take her, like he did Lah. He could take Lee, too. My stomach roils again. I can't move away without putting the rest of my family in danger, but the man isn't close enough to use the spear on him. I glance around at the ground near the cave, looking for rocks to hurl at him instead.

I feel Beh's breath on the side of my neck, and she grips the top of my arm tightly as her chest presses against my back. The man in front of me makes sounds, and Beh makes sounds at him in return. His eyes stay on mine, and I do not look away from him. His sounds get louder as do my growls.

Beh grips my shoulders, and she yells out more sounds. The man's eyes narrow and his head bobs up and down once. He takes a few steps toward us, and I crouch lower, readying my spear. His arms reach forward, and he lays Lah down just a short distance from my feet before backing away entirely.

I look to Beh, then to the man, and then down to Lah. The bundled child squirms on the ground and cries out again. Her sounds compel me forward, but I'm scared for Beh and Lee. As Lah's cries increase, I hold my spear behind me to block Beh and watch the man closely as I take a step forward. Both the man and Beh stand motionless as I take another step. When I am close enough to bend down and touch Lah, the tightness in my stomach and chest disappears.

It *is* her.

My daughter.

My Lah.

My fingers grace over her tiny cheek, no longer burning with fever. She looks exactly the same as she had, only her lips are a little fuller, no longer chapped and dry. When I pull back on the covering swaddling her, I can see her arms are chubby, and her skin is soft. I reach out and pull her from the ground, holding her tightly to my chest.

I close my eyes, and I can feel the burning behind them as her warm skin meets mine. With my cheek pressed to hers, our warm tears mingle, and I revel in the sound of her loud, angry, healthy cry. I can feel the beat of her heart against my skin, and I take a deep breath to inhale her scent—like her mother's but slightly sweeter.

Another loud sound invades the moment.

"No!"

Beh's *no* sound startles me, and I glance over my right shoulder to look at her. Her eyes are wide and full of fear, and her hands reach out toward me. I hear the thump of rapid footsteps to my left, but I cannot react in time without dropping Lah.

Suddenly, there is a sharp pain in my arm, and everything goes black.

⟶ ⬤⬤⬤◗◆◖⬤⬤⬤ ⟵

I awake with my head pounding.

I'm surrounded by the familiar scents of the cave, the furs in which we sleep, and Beh's body near mine. I reach for her warmth automatically and feel another smaller body curled between us. My ears pick up the rhythmic sounds of a suckling baby, but at the same time, I can hear the cries of another.

The sun still shines into the crack from the outside of the cave, and the fire burns brightly, but the light inside the cave is dim. Even so, my head throbs more, and my eyes ache as I open them.

Between us, wrapped in strange, soft cloth and suckling at her mother's breast is Lah. For a moment, I think I have awakened from a bizarre dream—that maybe she was never taken from us and was never even sick—but the sounds of another remind me that is not so.

Lee pounds his little fists on the fur wrapped around his mother's lower half as he tries to crawl between us to determine just what this other child is doing with his milk. Through my hazy vision, I watch him try to push his sister away. Beh picks him up with her free hand, smiles, and makes soft noises. She places him against her other breast, which he immediately grabs and shoves into his mouth. His green eyes narrow and glare at the little girl who feeds beside him, and he sucks harder.

I try to move my head a little closer to them, but I become dizzy immediately. I close my eyes again, but it only makes it worse, and I groan. I feel Beh's hand against my jaw and hear her soft sounds.

"Shh, Ehd."

I look at her face, and I can see her eyes are red and swollen, but she is smiling. I drop my eyes back to Lah. Her eyes have closed and her mouth has stilled. Lee is still scowling at her but seems content enough with milk in his mouth. Looking back and forth between them, it is obvious Lee is a whole season older than Lah in size. Lah was born late in the summer and became sick at the beginning of the previous winter. She looks to be the same size as she was then, just fatter and healthier than when I last saw her. Lee had been born in the winter, and it is now midsummer again.

Lah should be much larger than Lee, but she isn't.

My head swims again.

I hear more sounds coming from the other side of the cave.

The sounds are deeper in tenor than the ones Beh and Lee make, but I remember hearing the same tone before. The sound was coming from the man.

I raise my head, ignoring the throbbing in my temples and the nausea in my stomach. Across from the fire on the ledge where Beh had lined up her various collection baskets, sits the man— Beh's father. He wears the same strange, white wrap that hangs down to his thighs, and his legs are covered in leggings like the ones Beh used to wear. They are a lighter color blue, though, and don't seem to be as form-fitting or thick. The material looks thin as it flows with his legs when he moves around.

He sits with his back curved and his elbows down at his knees. There is something on the ground near his feet, but I can't tell what it is. My eyes are still having trouble focusing through the pounding ache in my head.

His mouth opens, and sounds similar to the ones Beh makes flow rapidly from between his lips. Beh's noises follow, and Lee's eyes open wide as he looks between them both, distracted enough to release Beh's nipple for a moment.

"Da-da-da-da!" Lee turns back to the nipple after making his noise and closes his eyes as he latches on and returns to eating.

Still dizzy, I try to push myself up, but Beh's hand against my chest sends me back into the furs. When I try to move my legs, they do not want to cooperate. I feel as if I have been running for an entire morning or that I haven't slept all night. I might be able to push Beh away and make myself stand, but her soft hands on my skin and whispers of my name-sound calm me, and I lay back down.

I glance at Beh's father and watch him warily as Beh takes both sleeping children from her breast and lays them together in a pile of furs next to me. I grab for her hand as she moves to stand, and she grips my fingers briefly before moving to the side of the cave where her father is seated, pulling her leather wrap up around her shoulders as she goes.

For a moment, I want to follow and take her farther away from him, but I realize I may have been asleep for some time, and if he had wanted to take them all away, he would have already done so. Also, as her father, he wouldn't want to harm her, I believe.

So I do not move when she goes to his side, but I watch closely as she curls her legs underneath her body to sit near his feet. I try harder to focus on the object there and realize it is much like the thing he was carrying in his hand when he first appeared, but it looks different now. He reaches inside of the thing—the *container*—and pulls out a small, cylindrical object. It makes a strange noise when he shakes it, and he makes sounds with his mouth. Beh's head bobs up and down, and he places the object back in the container.

Beh's father repeats his actions with many strange-looking things, but my mind is still fuzzy, and I am having trouble keeping my eyes open. I roll slightly to look at the forms of my two sleeping children. Lee's hand has reached out and grasped his sister's arm, pulling her fingers to his mouth where he sucks at them in slumber. I reach over and lay my arm across them both protectively.

Finally, my entire family is together, and I smile.

CHAPTER TWENTY-TWO

Beh and her father sit at the fire and make constant noise. It hurts my head, but it makes Beh smile and laugh.

Leaning down, I scoop up a rapidly crawling Lee under one arm and bring him near the fire. Beh has finished preparing our breakfast, and Lah seems to have finished hers already. Beh lays her down on the strange, soft material Lah was wrapped in when Beh's father brought her back and gently checks the other, smaller cloth that is wrapped around Lah's bottom to see if it is wet. Lee has one as well, attached in the front with a small, shiny stick that is so sharp at the end it goes right through the covering. Beh's deft fingers are able to attach and remove the little shiny stick quickly, but I end up with a bleeding finger when I try it.

There are many strange things Beh's father has in his bizarre container.

I sit next to Lah and hand Lee over to Beh. He has already eaten but seems more demanding of Beh's time now that Lah is with us again. Even though it is only the second morning his sister has been back with us, he notices that his time is now shared.

Beh and her father continue to make noise while I eat and rub Lah's feet until she falls asleep.

"Ehd?"

I look up to Beh when I hear her call my name-sound. She reaches over Lah and places her hand on my chest.

"Ehd." Beh taps my chest with her fingers.

"Lah." She touches the top of Lah's head.

I narrow my eyes a little as her hand moves to her father's white-clad torso.

"Dad."

My eyes meet his, and I scowl.

I don't really know how I feel about the man. He took Lah from us in a way I can't really fathom, and even though he has returned her, the method of return is too odd, and I don't understand what has happened to my little girl. Part of me is grateful she is back and seems healthy again, but another part of me is mistrusting; I don't know why he has returned or what he will do next. I have been ignoring his presence for the most part, hoping he will just disappear again.

Beh repeats the sound she made again and again, and I realize she must be saying his name-sound. I look from her to him again, and his blue, Beh-like eyes flicker between mine. I don't want to acknowledge him because all I really want is for him to leave quickly and never return.

Lee chooses that moment to begin to make his own noises.

"Da da da da da!"

Beh beams at him as she repeats the sounds he makes. Lah's feet kick out in her sleep, and I turn my attention back to her, rubbing her toes until she slumbers more deeply. Beh reaches over and she places her hand on top of mine.

"Dad," she says again.

I meet her eyes before briefly glancing back at her father. My eyes drop to my meal, but I am no longer hungry. Instead of eating more, I reach over and take Lee from Beh, pick Lah up in my other arm, and walk outside of the cave with both of them.

The sunshine is warm, and I know summer will be upon us

soon. I take both of the babies near the ravine and not near the field where Beh's father keeps appearing and disappearing. I don't want them too close to the area at all. Lee is squirmy and wants to move about on his own. I place him on the ground, watching him carefully as I rock Lah in my arms.

I'm tired and confused, and I hope a little time away from *Dad* will clear my head. At least I am provided with a distraction in the form of my son, who tries to put most everything he can grab off the ground into his mouth. While balancing Lah on my knee, I take things away from his little hands despite his protests.

I hear my mate's sounds behind me and look over my shoulder at her and Dad coming out of the cave. He holds a small black rectangle in his hand—one I have seen him carry before. My heart begins to pound, and I quickly grab Lee and pull him back into my arms. Beh and Dad walk toward me, and I walk a few steps backwards.

I will not let him take them away.

As they approach, I continue moving away, slowly circling to one side. If I get the children to the cave, they will be easier to protect, but Beh and Dad are between me and the entrance.

"Ehd," Beh says softly as she reaches toward me. At the same time, she uses her other arm to reach out and press against her father's chest. He stops moving forward, and only Beh approaches. I eye her father as she comes closer, watching him intently until I feel Beh's hand against my cheek.

I look at her, and I see sadness in her eyes.

She's been crying, and I instinctively move closer to her, wanting to offer her comfort. Her eyes meet mine, and she sniffs a little. She tries to smile, but it doesn't remove the sorrow from her eyes. She moves her fingers from my face to the tops of each of the children's heads before she places her hand against my back and guides me toward the cave. I follow, unable to take my eyes from her as we move around her father in an arc, keeping a good distance between us.

He makes sounds, and Beh responds with more noises from her mouth.

My eyes dance to his and narrow as an instinctive growl emanates from my chest. Dad walks in an opposite arc away from us, heading to the middle of the field outside our home. Beh whispers my name-sound and leads me in silence the rest of the way to the mouth of the cave.

I stay near the entrance, holding both children tightly as Beh moves away from me. I feel the tightness and panic in my chest as she walks away from the cave. I have no idea what she is going to do as she heads to the middle of the field, steps close to her father, and wraps her arms around his waist. She leans the side of her face into his chest, and he returns her embrace.

For a moment, the nightmarish vision of Lah in the man's arms as they vanished from my sight returns. My breath rushes out of me in a gasp as I think of Beh in Lah's place…of losing her.

Before panic can overwhelm me, Beh releases Dad's waist and walks backwards away from him. She raises her hand up with her palm facing him as she moves back to the cave. I can see her shoulders shaking in quiet sobs, and I don't know what I should do. I want to hold her, comfort her, but the babies are taking up both of my arms, and I'm afraid to let them go.

I place myself as close to her as I can and lean my body into hers. Beh turns quickly and lifts up her arms to wrap them tightly around my head, making me lean over to her. She holds me so tight it hurts, but I don't mind. Her face rests on my shoulder, just above Lah's sleeping head, and she turns to watch the center of the field where the bizarre, insect-like noise grows quickly.

I try to shift Lee up on my shoulder a little better so I can at least touch Beh's hair with my fingers as I look from her red eyes to the field. The swirling circles encompass Dad, making me dizzy as I try to follow the motion with my eyes. Beh's tears stain her cheeks as she raises her hand to him a final time.

Then he disappears.

I hope he never returns.

With the babies still in my arms, I move around Beh and push against her gently to encourage her back to the cave. With one last look toward the field, she turns and I follow her.

Later, when the babies are settled in for the night, I wrap my arms around Beh. As soon as I do, she begins to cry again. She turns around and buries her face against my shoulder as she wraps her arms around my neck. I hold her as her quiet sobs shake both of us.

With one arm around her shoulders, I use the other to run my hand up and down her arm. I brush over a small spot on her shoulder and tilt my head a little to examine it in the firelight. It's very small—just about the size of the tip of my smallest finger—right at the top of her arm. Just a little, rigid bump under her skin. I run my finger over it.

Beh sits back in my arms and glances at her shoulder and then to me. I see a red tinge cover her cheeks for a moment before she lays the side of her face against my chest.

"Beh loves Ehd," she whispers softly.

"Luffs!" I call out, and look to her face for her smile.

She doesn't have one.

"Luffs." I repeat, and her eyes turn to me. "Beh luffs."

She reaches up with her fingers and strokes my cheek. She makes more rapid sounds, which I can't follow and don't recognize, but at least she finally smiles at me.

"Khizz?"

Her smile broadens, and she leans up to place her lips upon mine as I brush the tears from her face.

<hr>

Lah grows so quickly, I begin to wonder if she will catch up with Lee.

Beh laughs as Lee tries to run away from her, his tiny feet carrying him much faster than I would expect from someone so small. Lah laughs, too, and tries to keep up with her brother with her rapid crawling. Beh quickly catches first one, then the other, and brings them back to the cave for the night.

As she does most nights since Dad disappeared, Beh brings out the rectangular flat thing that opens up over and over again from the container. Each time she opens it, there is something different to be seen. Yesterday, it looked like seeds inside. Tonight, the flat part appears to be flowers, but when I try to touch them, they are just smooth and a little warm—not like flowers at all. My fingers grace over it and my eyes narrow. I shake my head a little, not understanding her fascination with a flower you can't eat.

My mate is weird.

"Khizz?"

Beh places her mouth on mine for a moment before turning back to the flat thing. I return to ushering Lee and Lah toward the sleeping furs. There are many strange things in the container left by Beh's father, and I try not to touch them if I can help it. Beh usually pushes my hand away when I do try.

The children are a little more difficult to get to sleep now. They want to play with each other instead of lying down and closing their eyes. It takes some foot rubbing and some time, but once Lah is asleep, Lee gets bored and follows his sister's lead. Beh puts the flat thing back in the container and closes it before lying on the furs beside me.

I roll over on top of Beh, who covers her mouth to stop her giggle. I touch her bare sides with the backs of my fingers, and I run my nose across her shoulder, over her collarbone, and down to her breast. I continue down, and Beh fists her hands in my hair as I take her sex in my mouth. When I look up through my lashes, she is biting down on her lower lip, trying not to cry out, which makes me smile and work harder.

I feel her shudder around me, her thighs practically smashing my head before I rise up on my knees and guide myself inside of her. She's so warm and slick inside…it is not long before I have to stifle my own cries against her shoulder to keep from waking our children.

I think she already has another baby in her; she hasn't had her bleeding time for quite a while, but I want to make sure.

<hr />

As the seasons pass, our children grow.

I awake to Lah and Beh making soft sounds by the fire.

Lee is stretched out beside me, and I am amazed at how long he is. I'm sure he will be a tall, strong hunter when he is fully grown. Someday, he will make a good mate.

Of course, I still need to find another tribe.

It is a thought that comes to my mind often now with both of the children growing so fast and learning so many things. Beh has been teaching Lah how to boil water, using rocks heated by the fire, as well as showing both children the inside of the flat thing and pointing to different flowers and trees outside. Lee has been trying to help me make tools from flint, though so far, he has only ended up with broken pieces of stone. He's learned to set traps for rabbits and caught his first one just a few days ago.

Beh makes noise at both of them all the time, and they make noises right back at her. I don't mind though. The constant sounds remind me that they are all here with me. They can make as much noise as they like as long as we all stay together.

Though we haven't seen anyone since the man who attacked Beh, I still wonder what others will think of their sounds. I'm concerned it will make it hard to join another group if we do find one. I know we need to search, and with spring near, it will be a good time to travel to find other people. If we don't find anyone before summer, we can make our way back and start saving for winter again.

Though the cave seems smaller now that Lee and Lah are bigger, the work goes much faster with them helping. Of course, now that they no longer drink their mother's milk, much more food needs to be gathered, too.

Another reason to find a tribe.

I stretch my arms above my head and yawn. I scratch at my stomach for a moment as I watch Beh and Lah by the fire, making breakfast. Lah's hair is lighter than Beh's—almost like mine—and it is long enough to cover her shoulder blades now. I would like to watch them all morning, but I need to go outside to relieve myself.

I urinate into the ravine and think about how lucky I am to have Beh, Lee, and Lah. Even though I have tried over and over again, I have not managed to put another baby inside of Beh. I wonder now if we will be able to make any more. She does not have bleeding times, which is nice because she never makes me wait, but it doesn't seem right for a woman as young as she is.

Still, both of our children have lived past toddler age, which doesn't always happen. Neither of them has fallen sick, and they are both strong.

I yawn again, scratch the stubble on my chin, and wrap my fur back around me to ward off the morning chill. I walk slowly back to the front of the cave, inhaling the clear, fresh air and listening to the sounds of birds. They remind me that we will be able to hunt for eggs not too long from now, and Lee loves to climb the trees.

"Lee!"

My son beams at me as I enter the cave, makes sounds at his mother, and then grabs the small spear I made for him. He is still young for hunting larger animals, but I know he wants to try, and we need the meat. The spring plants are still hard to find, and I'm tired of rabbit.

Lah makes gruff noises at her brother and Beh, but Beh responds loudly, and Lah grumbles as she sits next to the fire and begins to fiddle with fresh grasses. She's been weaving new mats and has already surpassed her mother's skills. Lee follows me out of the cave, his sounds diminishing quickly.

He doesn't make noises when his mother and sister are not

near us, which I like.

We travel up the cliff to the high steppes. The wind blows much harder here, and I wrap my fur a little tighter around my shoulders as we walk toward the area where I spotted the antelope herd the day before. Lee walks silently behind me as we move through the grass to the far side. It takes some time to reach the area since the herd has moved to fresher ground.

We find a group of rocks and crouch behind them to watch the herd. There are a few pregnant females but no young for us to hunt yet. Lee begins to fidget as I watch the movements of the animals, and I place my hand on his leg to still him. I point across the field toward a single female who has walked away from the herd. As we watch her, she approaches a large puddle of melted snow to drink.

I think it will be a good place to dig a pit trap, but we will have to wait until the herd moves away. I know Lee will be disappointed, but we won't be able to start until nightfall. I decide to head back home to eat. We will return later.

Before I manage to stand up to go back to the cave, the herd begins to move toward us. I glance across the field just as several of the antelope begin to run away from the large puddle and the lone female. She raises her head, but before she has a chance to run, men appear with spears in their hands and surround her.

Lee makes a sound, and I quickly place my hand over his mouth to silence him.

I narrow my eyes to focus across the field and watch as the men close the gap around the animal. She panics and runs to try to get between them, but they stab at her with their spears, and she falls to the ground. A large man with dark, curly hair moves closer and plunges his spear into the animal's neck.

I look to my son and wish he had stayed back at the cave. I don't know how safe it is for him to be around unknown people. I would rather approach them alone to determine if they are friendly, but with the amount of time it would take me to return Lee to the cave, they could be gone.

Other men join the one who killed the antelope. There is a younger, light-haired man and another with dark hair like the first. All of them drop down to the ground near the beast and begin to strip the animal of its flesh.

I startle as my son grabs my arm. He points across the field, and I follow the direction with my eyes. Coming from the opposite end of the steppes is a group of women and children. One of the women is very tall—almost as tall as the men—with bright yellow hair, while another is small and dark. An older man and woman, also with light-colored hair, trail behind. Finally, a young, brown-haired woman brings up the rear of the group. Each of the women holds a small child in her arms.

My family needs a tribe.

Taking a deep breath, I stand and begin to move toward them. Lee steps up beside me, but when I glance back at him and narrow my eyes in warning, he moves to a safe distance behind me. I turn my attention back to the group as they congregate around the animal.

I walk slowly with my spear lowered but visible. As we close the distance, the older man in the back of the group turns toward me. I see him tilt his head to one side, and his expression is friendly. He takes a step to the side and smacks the large man's shoulder with the back of his hand.

The group stops their work, and they all look toward us. The large, curly-haired man grins, and his eyes light up in greeting.

Finally, we find other people, and they are friendly.

CHAPTER TWENTY-THREE

I had forgotten how much easier it is to prepare for winter with the help of a group.

It takes some time to find a cave large enough to hold all of us, but we do. Our new tribe had a home in the forest, much like where I grew up, but the spring rains destroyed it, and they needed a new place. The cave we find is on the opposite side of the lake near the cave Beh and I shared with Lah and Lee, and it is set up high in the rocks away from many dangers.

It's not large, but it's perfect for our small group. Peh is the oldest male. He and his mate, Met, live in the area farthest away from the entrance and drafts. Their son, Ehm, has children who are nearly grown, but no mate. I don't know what happened to her. All of the children have the same, light brown eyes as Peh and Ehm and dark, curly hair.

Ehm and Peh are very impressed with Beh's hide on a stick, and they use more hides and sticks to make additional carriers. With more people, we can bring down larger animals and carry them easily back to everyone else to skin the animals and prepare the meat in the safety of the cave.

My mate's ideas are impressive though nothing impressed

them more than the little round fire-maker.

When we first found our new home, we had no coals with us to start a new fire. Peh and Ehm began to get sticks and tinder together to start the long, difficult process of making a fire when Beh came over with a shy smile and started one with the round thing and a piece of flint. They were so impressed, they had her make another one and then show them how as well. Beh also taught the women how to make dishes from clay, and Met showed Beh how to dig a tunnel behind the fire, which makes it burn hotter. When they use the hotter fire to dry out the clay, it ends up stronger and less likely to break.

Though our tribe narrows their eyes at my mate and children when they start making a lot of bizarre noises, they have still accepted us. I think Beh's valuable ideas helped with that a lot.

I walk around the large community fire to the section of the cave where my family lies down to sleep. It is not as warm and cozy as our little home was, and the mouth of the cave is almost as large as the entire cave. It is more of a deep depression in the side of a mountain than a proper cave, but it is just the right size for our growing tribe. We hang furs from long poles, wedged between rocks to keep the drafts away, and it's easy to light a fire without having to worry about the smoke not being able to escape.

Peh and Beh seem to get along very well, especially after Beh notices he walks with a limp, and she finds a good, strong stick and shows him a way to use it to help him walk more easily.

I am very happy that there are more children for Lee and Lah to get to know. There are both girls and boys close to the same size, so they will be able to have mates when they are old enough.

Jeh and Feh have many children though the small baby Feh had been carrying when we first met was stillborn. She is pregnant again now, and that child should be born later in the fall. Beh and I only have two, but they have both lived long enough that I don't worry too much. I still try to put another one in Beh every chance I get.

Lah races up to me and throws her arms around my waist. I hug her back and smile down at her as she makes incomprehensible sounds at me.

"Lah luffs!"

Her smile is so much like Beh's, it makes me warm inside, even when the days are cold. She looks up at me, and the sunlight makes her eyes sparkle before she presses her cheek against my chest. I am amazed at how tall she has grown already. It seems every time I hug her she has grown more.

I shudder a little, thinking of how long we were without her, and I am glad we are now on the other side of the lake—away from the field where Dad came to steal her away. We still travel back to our little cave sometimes, usually to spend a little time away from the rest of the group or to dig for the mushrooms that grow near the ravine. Beh keeps her strange, black container full of even stranger things there, up on the shelf in the back. Though she carries the little rectangular flat thing full of images around with her, the other objects remain in the little cave we called home for so long.

Lah releases me and runs back to the community fire to help prepare the evening meal. Beh is rubbing the dirt off of some plants she dug out of the ground near the edge of the forest. There are large, bulbous tubers at the ends of them, which look a little like the wild onions she likes, but they are bigger and purple. She was excited when she found them and pointed out an image of the leaves from her flat thing to Lah and Lee. The three of them made a lot of noise back and forth before digging them up.

Beh cooks them in hot water for a long time, and when I taste them, they have a strange, sweet flavor. The rest of the tribe enjoys them as well. It's good to have new things to eat, and no one gets sick from them.

I sit with my arm around my mate after we eat and watch the sun go down outside the cave. The nights are still quite warm, but I pull her back against me and relish the heat from her body. Lah and Lee sit with the other children by the firelight, trying to make sharp spears from long sticks and flint.

Tomorrow, Lee will go with me and the other men to kill a large animal. It will be the first time he has tried. I am both excited and wary because large animals can be dangerous, but if we can bring down two of the large aurochs that have been drinking at the lake over the past few days, we will have enough of both meat and hides for the winter.

My son will be a man.

I inhale the scent of Beh's hair and nuzzle my nose against her neck. She takes the cue, and we slowly make our way to our furs, covering up with a large hide to give us a little privacy. I try not to moan too loudly as I enter her slowly. Beh arches her back, pushing her hips up against me as I grind into her. Her hands tangle in my hair as I tuck my head between her neck and shoulder. Her skin is salty and warm, and my heart beats faster to feel her so close to me again.

My Beh, my mate.

My fingers brush over her nipples softly, and I feel her tensing, trying to quiet her own cries as she comes undone around me. I press my mouth to her neck, nipping at her playfully as I increase my tempo and quickly fill her.

Rolling to my side, I hold her against me as our rapid breathing calms. Beh runs her hands through my hair, and I know what she is thinking; she will cut some of it off again soon. I smile against her skin.

She always takes care of me.

Running my nose up to her ear, I blow warm air against her skin until she wriggles against me and pushes me away a little. I raise myself up on one elbow to gaze down at her beautiful face. She is smiling up at me, and her cheeks turn red as I stare into her eyes.

So beautiful.

"Ehd?" she whispers softly, and I touch the end of her nose

with mine.

Beh reaches to my hand on her hip and slowly brings it to her belly. Her eyes twinkle as she pushes my palm into her abdomen. I glance down and feel my smile grow.

I know I have finally succeeded in putting another baby in her.

⸻ ➤➤➤◆◗◆◆➤➤ ⸻

My heart pounds in my chest, warming my insides as the fire warms my skin. Beh clutches at my hand—her nervousness obvious—as Lee walks around the fire and reaches out to take the hands of Jeh and Feh's daughter, Ney. I see a tear form in my mate's eye as Lee makes soft sounds in Nay's ear just before he touches the end of his nose to hers. He runs the tip up the bridge of her nose to her forehead, and Nay smiles broadly as her cheeks tinge pink. She looks at him sideways as he makes another sound, her eyes narrowing a little, looking at his mouth.

I know how she feels about Lee's sounds. Beh's noises were so strange to me when I first met her. Still, Ney accepts Lee as he is, and I know he will provide for her and give her children.

Beh turns her face to my shoulder, trying to hide her tears. I don't understand why she cries, but my mate cries at a lot of things that make no sense to me. Lah takes her mother's other hand and squeezes it, too. I wonder how Beh will respond when Lah moves from our sleeping area to her own. I cannot decide yet which of the young men she favors—Mik or Ty—though I know Ehm would like our families to be joined. Of course, if Lah does not choose Ty, Ehm's son, then we will still be tied together at some point in the future, when my youngest daughter, Kay, will be old enough to mate. There are only two boys of suitable age, and both are Ehm's children.

Lee and Ney disappear into the darkest part of the back of the cave, and Ehm helps an aging Peh over to where Beh and I stand. Peh's smile is reserved. He still grieves for Met, his mate who died in the winter, but he shows life in his eyes again. Watching him try to continue without Met makes me think it will not be long before he also lies down and doesn't get up again.

I know if Beh dies before I do, I will not survive. At the same time, I hope that her eyes close forever before mine. Though I would join her directly afterwards, I know when I look at her what kind of pain she would feel if something were to happen to me. I do not want her to feel that pain—the pain of losing her mate.

As hard as it would be, I would rather feel it for her.

Jeh embraces me roughly, then lifts Beh into the air and spins her around. I reach out to steady Peh, who rolls his eyes at his son but still chuckles a little. Feh marches over and smacks Jeh's arm until he puts Beh back down again, red faced and laughing.

I shift Fil, our youngest son, to my other arm. He's really far too big to still be carrying, but I have allowed him to play the baby far beyond what I should. He is our last though. I knew we wouldn't have any more soon after he was born…

Beh had fitted Fil in the sling she wore around her shoulders so he could nurse while we walked. Lee and Lah had decided to stay behind and hunt, but Kay was with us—running back and forth on the small trail that led from the tribe's cave to the little cave we had lived in before.

It had been late spring, and Fil had been born the previous fall. We had not been to the little cave all winter, and Beh seemed anxious to get there. Once we arrived, I built us a fire—in case she wanted to stay the night—and had Kay help me air out the furs that were still there.

Beh had gone to the funny black container and pulled something out. It was not something I had seen before—a long tube with a bit of red at one end and black stripes down the side. Beh took it out and held it in her hands for a while, and once I had Kay settled on the furs for a bit, I went over to find Beh with tears in her eyes.

I knelt before her and took her face in my hands, not understanding, but knowing she still needed me. I wrapped my arms around her and held her close to my chest, encompassing her and Fil together. She put the thing aside and wrapped her arms around my head, holding me tightly for a short while before pushing me away a little to pick up the long object again.

Then, Beh had taken a deep breath and looked into my eyes. I didn't understand what she was trying to communicate other than...regret. Sadness. Decisiveness.

She took the object and held it against her arm. One more deep breath and she pushed part of it with her thumb. She winced, and I grabbed the thing away from her. There was blood on her arm—just a little bit, but I threw the thing out of the mouth of the cave while I fussed over her arm for a while.

We went back to the tribal cave soon after, and that night Beh began to bleed. She bled for days—many more than she normally did—even more than after she had given birth. Her stomach cramped painfully, and she had me make her hot water, boiled and mixed with leaves from a plant she found, which seemed to help. I had been terrified, but eventually the bleeding slowed and stopped, and Beh was no longer in pain.

I had known then that we would have no more children, and I spoil Fil because of it. I keep him with me almost all the time, afraid to miss a single second of his life. It has been easy since he is silent like me and doesn't make all the strange noises his mother and other siblings like to make. His eyes are the same color as his mother's, large and expressive. He is perfectly capable of walking back to our area of the cave, but I carry him anyway.

Beh just grins and moves her head back and forth. She still makes sounds at Fil, and he will watch her mouth move and has repeated a few of her sounds. When he does, Beh is ecstatic, and Fil is just confused. I hold him close to me and touch his cheek with my nose.

I'm familiar with his frustration at his mother's constant sounds.

We lie in our furs, Beh still teary-eyed and Lah sitting on the furs and staring at her hands. Sometimes she looks over toward the section of the cave that will be for Lee and Nay and sighs. Kay moves close to Lah and makes sounds, and Lah responds. Beh's noises come out sharp and biting, and both girls quiet and lie down.

I lay in the center, with Beh and Fil on one side and Lah and Kay on the other. If I lay on my back, I can reach them all. Lah lies the farthest away now—like Lee had before. She rolls to look to the mouth of the cave and away from me. She will choose her mate soon; I am sure. She and Lee will still be close, but everything will also be different now.

My family is growing up.

⸺ ••••◉•••⸺

My bare feet are cold. I didn't realize how cold it would be away from the cave with the wind whipping around off the lake. I probably did know, but I forgot. I seem to forget a lot of things lately, like the name-sound Kay and Gar gave their latest child. I just can't seem to commit it to memory.

Beh's coughing makes me forget about my feet as I pull her closer to my chest, holding her as steadily as my old arms still can. She weighs almost nothing, which is good for my arms but also the reason I carry her. She is too weak to walk by herself.

Lee knew we wouldn't be returning—I could see it in his eyes.

Holding Beh up a little higher on one side quiets her cough, at least for now. It never quiets completely, and it has grown steadily worse as winter approaches. Her arm around my neck barely grips at my skin, a testament to her weakness. She has hardly eaten and has only taken a few drinks of water in the past day. All the plants she has used to help me or someone else in the tribe feel better have made no difference.

"Hoh!" I stumble on a tree branch lying across the trail and have to catch my balance to keep from dropping Beh. She giggles —the sound reminding me of the beautiful young girl I found so long ago—as she touches the side of my mouth with her finger.

The laughter brings back the coughing, and I hold her close as I pick up the pace. I don't want to arrive too late. I want to be in our cave when the time comes.

I don't know why, but I feel it is important to be there. It is where we learned about each other—where we truly became mates. It is where I put Lah and Lee inside of her and where they were both born. It is the place Beh always wants to return to at least once every summer, just to look around and go through the strange things inside the black container.

Maybe she thinks of Dad when she does that.

I stumble once more as I climb the slight ledge from the ravine to the mouth of our cave. I'm glad there is still daylight outside as I take a quick peek to make sure no animals have taken up residence since we were last here.

The cave is empty.

I turn sideways to carry Beh inside, but I can't get the angle right for us both to fit through the narrow opening at the same time. I have to place her down on her feet and hold her up from behind as we both make our way through the crack. There are many older furs lying in the back of the cave where we used to sleep, and I lay Beh on top of them while I use her little shiny round thing to quickly make a fire.

My back aches as I straighten up, tossing a few more pieces of wood at the blaze as I rub at my spine. I hear Beh calling out my name-sound and quickly move to her side, my own pains forgotten. I lie down beside her and pull one of the furs up around us. I cradle her frail body in my arms, holding her up a little as another coughing spell takes her breath from her.

Once it has subsided, I lay her back down and curl up alongside her. She shivers, and I pull another fur over us. It seems hard for her to stay warm these days even though it's not too cold yet. I shift as close to her as I can, letting my body heat soak into her. I hold her as the sun goes down, and the warmth of the fire fills the small cave.

I think of the first day I saw her, sitting at the bottom of my hunting pit. I remember how obstinate she was at first, though when I think back on it now, I realize she was only confused and frightened. I remember when she first untangled my hair for me and the little wooden carving I had made to help with the task.

I made another and gave it to Lah when she mated with Ty. Kay also received one when she mated with Gar. Many of the other men began to carve similar gifts for their own mates and daughters.

I remember the first time I was inside of Beh, touching the soft skin of her back as waves of pleasure moved over me. I remember when I placed my hand on her belly and felt Lah kick. I remember when Kay was born and how Lee helped me cut the cord and place his new sister on his mother's stomach.

I remember it all.

Beh's hand trembles as she reaches up and touches my jaw. Her fingers are soft and cool, and I lean into her touch as she strokes my skin.

"Beh...loves...Ehd," she whispers, and her eyes sparkle at me just like they did the first time I tried to put a baby inside of her. It seems so long ago, but also so recent, as if time isn't really relevant to the feelings inside of us both.

But time still moves, and there is nothing I can do to stop it.

"Luffs Beh," my mouth utters, and I am rewarded with her quiet smile and the touch of her thin fingers on my cheek. "Ehd luffs Beh."

For a long time, I just look at her eyes. They are different with her age but still the same. They still hold me captive, wanting to spend every moment of every day looking into them. She looks into mine as well, and a small smile stays on her lips. Her fingers touch my mouth, and her throat bobs as she swallows and takes another labored breath.

"Khizz?" I reach up and push her silver hair away from her

forehead.

Beh's smile broadens, and I move closer to press my mouth to hers. Her lips are soft and warm, just like they always have been.

Slowly, she pulls away and lays her head against my shoulder. I settle down into the furs and look down at her face. I can feel her struggling breaths against my skin as I hold her close. She turns her face to me and gives me a final smile.

Again, she turns into my chest, and I feel her lips press against my skin. Another labored breath. Another.

No more.

My eyes burn, and my chest tightens. I pull her to me, tucking my head against her shoulder and inhaling the scent of her hair. My nose trails over the textured skin of her neck, and I place my lips lightly against her jaw.

I can't stop the tears. I don't want to cry. I'm too *tired* to cry. My life with Beh was beautiful, transcending everything that set us apart from each other and bringing us together with our family and tribe.

I shouldn't cry.

I rub my cheek against her shoulder and tighten my grip. I wrap my arms around her and twist our legs together as well, just for good measure. I want to make sure nothing can separate us. I want to be positive we will remain together forever.

I settle myself against Beh's body, sniff her hair again, and let out a long, deep breath.

Finally, I close my eyes for the last time.

CHAPTER TWENTY-FOUR | EPILOGUE

Many millennia later...

"Elizabeth! Isn't that your mom's find?"

I sigh, shrug my backpack further up my shoulder, and turn to see Teresa and Sheila coming up behind me. They both grab an arm to link through their own before dragging me to the next museum exhibit.

The Prehistoric Lovers.

"Is her group still being investigated for fraud?" Teresa asks.

"Yeah, I guess," I reply. "No one's admitting anything, and they haven't found any kind of real evidence it was planted on purpose."

"What was planted?" Sheila asks. Her parents totally forbid any television watching or internet use, so she never has the slightest idea what's going on in the world. I can't imagine not having a television, or an iPad, or my phone. Just...no.

I really don't want to go into it all with them, so instead of answering, I lean over and push the little button near the edge of the exhibit that holds the skeletal remains of two prehistoric people, wrapped in a tight embrace.

"*The Prehistoric Lovers,*" a soft, feminine voice begins.

Mom's voice always reminds me of when she would read to me before bedtime, and I smile as it chimes through the museum's speakers. *"The dig, located near Pecs, Hungary, was discovered..."*

Several other patrons join the group—some from my senior class and some just the usual museum visitors. The find received a lot of national attention from the get-go, but when its validity was questioned because of one of the items found at the site, the media went berserk. I don't understand their fascination with the whole thing, really. I mean, it has to be a mistake, right?

"...carbon dating establishing them far earlier than any other Homo sapiens' remains discovered..."

I look over the various objects found at the site. Most of it is the usual stuff. Aside from the actual, fossilized skeletons wrapped in an everlasting embrace, there is evidence of a cooking fire, including some bits of broken pottery that were found in a nearby lake that were thought to be the same age. The pieces aren't really fired, like I learned to do at the YMCA last summer, just rough clay pieces. The break is strange, making a unique zigzag pattern down the center.

"...controversy around the site began when a small, round button was discovered amongst the remains..."

A spotlight comes on, and I have to roll my eyes. I can't believe they are actually highlighting the thing that has made everyone question the entire find. The light reflects off a small, silver button with letters spelling out "JORDACHE" in a semi-circle around it.

"...though no real explanation has been determined..."

"Oh my God!" Teresa exclaims as she reaches down and grabs at the metal button of my jeans, which also happens to have "JORDACHE" stamped on it. "I always knew you had the fashion sense of a Neanderthal!"

Teresa goes into a fit of hysterical laughter, and Sheila giggles into her hand. I'm sure she'll try to use this as a way to get me to reconsider a shopping expedition to Atlanta this weekend. I have way too much homework, and between Mom's find and Dad's experiments, I'm the only one doing any housework these days, too. The dirty laundry is going to form its own system of government if I don't get it washed soon.

"...through the use of modern testing methods, the age of the button shows it to be of the same time frame as the rest of the finds at the site. Many religious groups are now using it as evidence that such dating methods are unreliable, and that creationism should be..."

I tune out my mother's voice and look over the rest of the display. There is more pottery, which is the part that excited Mom as much as anything. Apparently, no one was making pots back then. I would have thought it was obvious, kind of like the wheel. I mean, even *I* can make clay dishes, for goodness' sake. There are also little crisscross patterns in one of the rocks, which Mom thinks were left by a woven basket of some kind.

Seriously—how hard can it be to weave some reeds together?

Despite my lack of interest in the archaeological field, I do have to admit the people intrigue me. They are wrapped together in a tight embrace, legs intertwined and arms encompassing one another. You can almost feel the emotion coming from the slate of limestone in which they are embedded. They lie facing each other with their heads so close, giving the impression they have just shared their final kiss.

"Do you think they did it doggy-style?" Sheila giggles again.

I swear, I may be just as virginal as she is, but with her upbringing, she's never even seen a soap opera love scene. She just found out last week that there are positions other than missionary. Regardless, she's totally ruined the imagery for me, so I turn away.

"Is it too early to head to the food court?" I ask. Between Mom's digs and Dad's lab, I've spent half my life in this museum. The rest of the displays are ones I've already seen.

"We're supposed to get through this exhibit," Sheila looks down at the folded schedule in her hands, "as well as the two after it, then break for lunch."

Two of the people behind me start talking about how my mother must be a fraud or at least employing the most unscrupulous of assistants in order to get herself better known in the archaeological world. I look over and vaguely recognize the guy as one of the other professors in her department. I scowl as he takes the lady he is with by the hand and leads her over to the life-sized model of a giant sloth. Sheila and Teresa start to head in the same direction.

"I'll meet you guys at lunch, mkay?" I call over my shoulder as I make my way to the back of the exhibit and my father's office, not giving them a chance to reply.

Dad's not an archaeologist, like Mom, but he's still in the science world—physics and the property of matter and all that crap. I would think of him like another Bill Nye the Science Guy, but Dad has no personality for TV. He'd bore the poor kids to death with his long-drawn-out explanations of Einstein's Theory of Relativity, Higgs boson particles, wormholes, or whatever. Anyway, he's always trying to prove his theories. Something about Mom's prehistoric find has him convinced that his theories regarding time travel are right and that string theory is a joke. I have no idea what he's talking about, but I'm just now taking my first semester of physics. Most of what I've learned so far is the same stuff I've learned from old episodes of the *Big Bang Theory*.

Dad's not in his office, so I make my way around the desk and to the door behind it. I open it and call out for him, but he's not in his lab, either. I hope I can at least interrupt him long enough to see if he wants to have lunch with me or something, but he is nowhere to be found.

I give up, deciding I will have to face the masses again through the rest of the exhibit hall before I can eat. Being the energy conscious chick that I am, I flip off the light switch as I start to leave.

There is something glowing green in the very back of the lab. Curious, I flip the light back on.

The green glow is too dim to be noticeable with the lights on, but I move over to it anyway, feeling somewhat drawn. Ever since I was a kid, I liked poking around at the stuff in Dad's lab, so I don't really think much of it when I go to investigate a bit more. Besides, I really don't want to join the rest of my class until it's time to eat, and I have time to kill.

Back behind a bit of a divider, kind of like the cube walls you see in office buildings, there is a long lab table in the corner of the room. Right in the center of it is a tall, cylindrical object, which is from where the light originates. There's something rather blob-like in the center. The substance looks like it's floating in a gooey liquid and reminds me of those old lava lamps.

Along with one of those large car batteries and a couple of books, there is a stack of paper on the table next to the green thing, covered with my Dad's scrawl. It's Dad's notes to himself, and I have to smile to see there isn't a single bit that makes any sense on the whole page. Only Dad can tell what Dad is talking about most of the time, as Mom always says. This is just a bunch more of his chicken scratch.

DNA subject 1(M) –unable to categorize -not H. sapiens. Brain differentiation. Broca's area?

DNA subject 2 (F)—H. sapiens - related to me?? (retest- use different control)

Button– steel not aluminum—4.23 meters from the remains

Pottery dates match—164,230-164,235

After that, there are a whole lot of—as far as I'm concerned— nonsensical equations. I look back to the green stuff, which seems to be sloshing around inside the cylinder a little faster but is otherwise pretty boring.

I turn around to go. I figure I've probably screwed around in here long enough, and I need to get back to my group. Whatever

Dad is doing, he obviously isn't around for lunch. I hope he'll be home in time to eat dinner with us tonight at least.

As I turn to walk away, I stub my toe on the lab table, and the whole thing rocks for a second as my toe throbs in my shoe. I try not to fall on my face as I hop on one foot and rub at my toe. I quickly look over the contents of the lab table to make sure I haven't screwed anything up.

The green glow fades in and out, which it wasn't doing before. I peer around it and see a slender wire in the back, which seems to be at least partially disconnected from its source. I reach behind and grasp the end and then shove it back into place.

In an instant, my whole arm feels like it is vibrating, and I am nearly blinded by green light. The room seems to twist and turn itself inside out, transforming both the green cylinder and the rest of the table into a swirling cascade of color and light. Nausea and dizziness overwhelm me. My vision blurs as streaks of bright lights in red and gold flood my eyes until I have to close them. Blood pounds in my ears, and for a moment, I am sure I am being pulled to pieces.

Then it all stops.

With a shudder, I open my eyes.

I see dirt.

And some roots.

For several minutes, I just sit there as my mind tries to make sense of what's going on. It fails miserably, and I just stare in disbelief at the rough dirt walls around me and the clear sky, visible when I peer overhead.

I'm in a hole.

Still disoriented, I look around and try to get my bearings. It's obvious I am no longer in Dad's lab, but where am I? I glance down beside me, and I notice a large, dark patch of ground just a few inches away from my hip. I reach out to touch the dark stain, and my fingers come back sticky and red. There is blood on the ground next to me.

Holy crap!

My stomach roils, and for a moment, I think I am going to be sick. Somehow, I manage to keep from throwing up, but I make sure to breathe through my mouth and not look to the ground beside me again. I wipe my hand on the dirt wall, trying to clean off my fingers without really watching what I'm doing. It doesn't work well.

I have to get out of here.

I stand, but I can barely reach the edge of the hole, and I can't get enough leverage to pull myself up. When I try, the dirt crumbles in my fingers and rains down on my head. I run my fingers through my hair, and dirt flies all over the place. I shake my head again before slumping back to the bottom of the hole. I try to remember all the crap Dad tried to teach me about survival in the wilderness, but not much is coming to mind.

Don't panic.

I make myself take slow, deep breaths and try to figure out what I should do. From down here, I don't even know if I *am* in the wilderness! When I listen, I don't hear anything except the sound of the wind, but that doesn't necessarily mean there is no one within earshot.

"Hey!" I cry out. I stand and cup my hands around my mouth. "Hey! Is there anybody out there? I'm stuck! Help!"

When that doesn't work, I let out a long, continuous scream as I jump up and down. By the time my throat is feeling raw, I try one last time to pull myself up, but the dirt gives way and I drop back to my rear end, leaning on my hands for support. I close my eyes for a moment, trying to get those deep breathing exercises to calm me, but they don't. I shake my head, let out a long, slow breath, and look up again.

I am met with a wild shock of long, reddish-brown hair that sticks out all over the head of a young man. His hair is long enough to hang past his shoulders, and his face is covered in a short, rough beard of the same color. Where he isn't covered in hair, he's covered in dirt. From the middle of the dirt and hair, he peers at me with the most beautiful, bright green eyes I have ever seen.

I stare at him for a long, long time as he stares back at me, and images from Dad's lab fly around helter-skelter in my head. The plan was to just stop and say hi and maybe grab some lunch with Dad. I was there only moments ago, but now…now, I definitely am not.

Where am I?

The man at the top of the hole has clear, intelligent eyes, but he's wearing nothing except a scrap of leather around his waist, and he's carrying an ancient-style, stabbing-type spear. Whoever he is, he's not from twenty-first century Georgia.

When am I?

Finally, regardless of my current confusion, I realize my life is about to change in a very drastic way.

THE END

Or the beginning...

OTHER TITLES BY SHAY SAVAGE

THE EVAN ARDEN TRILOGY

  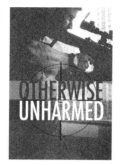

OTHERWISE ALONE - EVAN ARDEN #1
OTHERWISE OCCUPIED - EVAN ARDEN #2
OTHERWISE UNHARMED - EVAN ARDEN #3

SURVIVING RAINE SERIES

SURVIVING RAINE - #1

ABOUT THE AUTHOR

Always looking for a storyline and characters who fall outside the norm, Shay Savage's tales have a habit of evoking some extreme emotions from fans. She prides herself on plots that are unpredictable and loves to hear it when a story doesn't take the path assumed by her readers. With a strong interest in psychology, Shay loves to delve into the dark recesses of her character's brains–and there is definitely some darkness to be found! Though the journey is often bumpy, if you can hang on long enough you won't regret the ride. You may not always like the characters or the things they do, but you'll certainly understand them.

Shay Savage lives in Ohio with her husband and two children. She's an avid soccer fan, loves vacationing near the ocean, enjoys science fiction in all forms, and absolutely adores all of the encouragement she has received from those who have enjoyed her work.

Made in the USA
Monee, IL
02 August 2023

40346260R00174